The Tour

Andrew Mackie is a film distributor and producer. His company Transmission Films acquired and released such indie hits as *The King's Speech* and *Lion*. His executive producer credits include *Ride Like a Girl, Tracks, Candy, Sweet Country, Holding the Man* and *On Chesil Beach*. In 2012 and 2013 *The Australian* named him one of the twenty-five most influential people in the Australian arts. Andrew has always been fascinated by all things royal and has long felt that the Queen's tour of Australia in 1954 was ripe with dramatic potential. *The Tour* is his first novel.

Dear David,
Hope you enjoy!
Cheers
Andrew

The
Tour

ANDREW MACKIE

MICHAEL JOSEPH
an imprint of
PENGUIN BOOKS

MICHAEL JOSEPH

UK | USA | Canada | Ireland | Australia
India | New Zealand | South Africa | China

Michael Joseph is part of the Penguin Random House group of companies
whose addresses can be found at global.penguinrandomhouse.com.

Penguin
Random House
Australia

First published by Michael Joseph, 2021

Copyright © Andrew Mackie, 2021

The moral right of the author has been asserted.

Cover design by Louisa Maggio © Penguin Random House Australia Pty Ltd
Cover images: woman © Ilina Simeonova/Trevillion Images; landscape by lovelah/
Getty Images; tiara by SergValen/Getty Images; bunting by James Weston/Shutterstock;
border by Vasya Kobelev/Shutterstock
Typeset in Sabon by Midland Typesetters, Australia

Printed and bound in Australia by Griffin Press, part of Ovato, an accredited
ISO AS/NZS 14001 Environmental Management Systems printer

A catalogue record for this
book is available from the
National Library of Australia

ISBN 978 1 76089 023 0

penguin.com.au

For Amy

Only some of this story is based on fact.
Very little of it, actually.

To be clear, what follows is a work of complete fiction.

Prologue

November, 1953

After more than two weeks at sea to simmer the tension between them, Violet and Daisie Chettle couldn't stand each other, let alone stand *next* to each other. Not even to meet the Queen.

On the main deck under the hot afternoon sun, the eighty-strong crew of the *SS Gothic* waited silently for Her Majesty and the Duke to board. Over twenty minutes had passed as the men sweated in their heavy pressed uniforms and the women felt the sting of the Jamaican sunlight on their impeccably made-up skin.

Violet stood halfway along the third row, wringing her hands against her stomach as a seagull gloated on the port-side railing, its mouth cocked open in the repressive heat. She was about to meet her idol, Her Majesty Queen Elizabeth II. She'd long adored the monarchy, and this sudden proximity to it was a greater accomplishment than she had ever imagined.

'The pomp and aggrandisement of this woman! She was only crowned five months ago,' Daisie had lectured Violet earlier that day. 'It's all a pantomime. Fool the people. Distract them from the machinations of politics and entitlement.'

Violet had shushed her. 'Smite the Lord's name if you must, but stay away from the Crown,' she'd whispered angrily, fearful they might be overheard.

She observed the seagull on the railing. It danced sideways, closer to the rows of freshly shaved men in clean naval regalia.

Daisie stood in front of her. 'Your uniform would be an enticing target to a bored seagull,' she heard Daisie remark to the towering officer standing to attention at her right. His gaze remained unwavering.

'To attention! Her Majesty Queen Elizabeth II of England, and the Duke of Edinburgh,' the steward announced loudly, and within seconds the Queen and Prince Philip appeared from the starboard doorway, escorted towards the waiting group by the po-faced Private Secretary Ratcliffe.

Violet's heartbeat accelerated. She'd been instructed to avoid eye contact but couldn't help stealing a glance. Poised, youthful, feminine, perhaps slightly withdrawn, the Queen might have been any young woman on a great occasion. Her skin was flawlessly fragile, paler than the impression gained from paintings and photographs. She wore a blue pleated dress, a single string of pearls and a pillbox hat that sat just so on her judiciously waved hair. She smiled patiently as she walked along the front row.

Prince Philip shone just as brilliantly. He was tall and imposing, but even his blinding naval wear, a vivid white suit with matching cap, couldn't subdue the humour that radiated from him. He paused to chat jovially to a chief engineer, as if they were old friends, then glanced down the line at Daisie, who stood out among the uniformed men like a wildflower in the desert. She blushed at the attention, a gentle smirk following in its wake. Violet scrunched her nose nervously, willing Daisie to stop being herself.

The Queen's official lady-in-waiting, Lady Caroline Althorp, hovered. Lady Althorp was a refined, well-bred woman with a slender neck and pale girlish skin despite her thirty-one years. As they approached Daisie's place in the line she discreetly whispered near the Queen's shoulder.

'You're with Lady Althorp?' the Queen asked Daisie, her eyes round with genuine curiosity. The sharp timbre of her voice made the routine enquiry sound personal and authentic. Violet couldn't help but watch and listen.

'Why yes,' Daisie replied, unintimidated, adding, 'Your Majesty,' as an afterthought.

'Thank you for your service,' the Queen responded seamlessly before she glided on.

Violet breathed out. 'Never look at Her Majesty directly,' she'd been told by Lady Althorp, 'unless you are invited to do so.'

Violet's chest tightened again, her heart leaping at the thought of her turn. She parted her lips slightly to take in more oxygen. She stared straight ahead, her hands clasped in front of her as instructed as she resisted her instinct to fidget. 'Still. Perfectly still,' her inner voice repeated.

The shape of the Queen approaching edged into her peripheral vision. Violet's breathing became heightened again, and she focused on the foreground as the Queen passed mere inches before her.

Then she was gone.

Violet's shoulders dropped as her heart sank.

Her Majesty stopped to chat with the chef two places along. The seagulls cawed and trilled. They weren't laughing at Violet, but that's the way it sounded. Once again Daisie was the chosen one and Violet simply didn't exist.

And then the vomit rose in Violet's throat.

PART 1

1

On the hottest day of the summer of 1947, twelve-year-old Daisie Chettle watched a bead of sweat gather on her twin sister's forehead as they waited in the living room for their parents to stop arguing. The drop collected on Violet's brow as their parents exchanged tense whispers in the kitchen.

'Another desperate promise. How many *slices* have you had since *her*?' Daisie heard her mother exclaim in a hushed voice.

Edith Chettle then appeared through the kitchen doorway, her face flushed from heat and anger. It was the first time Daisie had seen her mother's calm façade broken. Red-faced, perhaps partially from shame, her father, Edward, also entered, pacing the living room carpet like a threatened dog, uneasy and stung. Guilt was written all over his stalking frame.

'Sit,' said Edith. Daisie hoisted herself onto the couch beside her sister as their mother gingerly lowered herself into Edward's arm-chair. He lingered anxiously behind.

'One of you will live with your father for a while.' Daisie knew it was serious because she'd called him 'your father'. She always called him Ted, so this felt solemn and strange.

'Daisie,' he said, unable to look her in the eye, 'you'll live with me. It'll be me and you for a bit.'

Daisie saw her sister's face fall, and that sadness washed over her. She didn't want to be separated from her sister or her mother, but she didn't have the courage to do anything but nod. Daisie was accustomed to getting her way over Violet, yet the quiet delight she usually took in her sister's jealousy couldn't extend to this.

A month later, on their thirteenth birthday, Father brought home a white rabbit in a hessian bag. Daisie was delighted, naming it Nicholas after *The Life and Adventures of Nicholas Nickleby*, which they'd seen that past weekend. At first the creamy white creature slept in her bedroom inside a milk crate, but as Nicholas grew, Father's cramped flat in Worcester Park proved to be no place for pets.

'The hay and pellets attract cockroaches and mice,' he complained. 'And vermin beget more bloody vermin.'

Six months later the trial separation ended, and Edward and Daisie moved back into the family home in Kingston upon Thames. Nicholas and his hutch took up residence in the cramped courtyard. The Chettle family settled back into their old patterns, but in the space between words something had changed forever.

Father continued to choose Daisie over Violet, whether it was taking her for tandem rides on his beloved motorbike, a fire-engine red Norton 20 that had taken him longer to restore than the war had run, or bringing her to work for the day at the brickworks.

On her and Violet's sixteenth birthday Father gave Daisie a packet of Gold Flake and took great pleasure in teaching her the right way to hold, light and inhale a cigarette. She vomited most of the afternoon. But in time she took to it, giving them another shared interest that excluded Violet. She'd worked out that deep down Father had wanted a boy, at least one, and having twin girls had likely put paid to that.

In late November 1952, a few months after the girls turned eighteen, Nicholas contracted myxomatosis. The rabbit lost sight in his left eye and a large tumour started to form near his spine. Daisie knew that her beloved pet's days were numbered, and her father agitated for its end to be hastened.

On the first Friday in December a smog as thick as tar descended, choking London and darkening its already grey skies. The charcoal mist penetrated their freshly washed clothes, giving everything the odour of rotting eggs. As Daisie brought the pungent washing in she noticed that the hutch door was open and Nicholas was gone. Despite her father's protestations, she convinced her mother to go out looking, dragging her from front garden to parked car along Grove Lane and Alfred Road. Neighbours were recruited to join the search. Although it was only three o'clock in the afternoon, the light dwindled under the blanket of mist. She relied on the headlights of passing cars to search the wild privet shrubs that lined Hogsmill Lane in Kingston Cemetery.

'I can't see a thing. Perhaps we should return in the morning,' suggested Edith gently, her breath steaming in the cold, still air. 'He'll be fine overnight. Having the time of his life, I'd imagine.'

But Daisie ignored her, squinting in the faint light for any hint of the rabbit's snowy coat. Her back started to ache as she dashed from tree root to shrub, crouching under branches and driven by thoughts of the dogs and wild foxes that roamed the park at night.

'It's late. We have to go,' her mother insisted.

Edith sighed as Daisie pushed on, searching diligently in the murky stillness until she reached the intersection of Villiers Road, where a row of juniper shrubs offered an enticing haven for a frightened rabbit.

'He's here, I know it—'

Before the condensation from Daisie's breath had evaporated, Edith's foot caught on a spiky low branch. She stumbled forward through the shrub onto the roadway. The front wheel guard of a red double-decker rushed unseen from the mist, clipping her head and shoulders. Edith's body was flung with unnatural force against the granite cobblestones, where she stopped hard against the stone gutter.

It took an eternal moment for Daisie to accept what she had witnessed. The cracking sound of bone against rock found its home deep inside her.

The pastor told her not to blame herself, his intended gentle words of consolation shocking. Nobody else had mentioned fault, not even Father, for whom the rabbit was the sole culprit.

Except Violet. Resentment bristled in the silences she served in her daily routine to remind Daisie where the blame rested. Their relationship shifted into the darkness. Daisie didn't have the fortitude to push back, so the guilt lodged, numbing her sense of self and virtue to a new normal.

The House of Commons later reported that more than six thousand Londoners lost their lives to the respiratory effects of the six-day Great Smog of December 1952. Edith was the only victim of the smog who did not pass to hypoxia.

2

Violet blamed Daisie for what had happened, an accusation made subtly yet insidiously via impatient glances and trivial acts, such as leaving dried rabbit droppings in her shoes.

The three remaining Chettles endured the funeral. For Violet, everybody else's grief was the immediate burden. Daisie seemed to exist in a dulled state. Their father remained silent and withdrawn, too focused on withholding emotion to give a eulogy. It was left to Violet to take charge and greet the hundred-odd mourners who turned out to show their respects on a drizzly morning at St John's Church.

Despite the hushed mass of distant cousins, neighbours, friends and colleagues that crowded the small cathedral, only one member of Edith's immediate family attended. Aunt Maisel looked barely anything like their mother. She had the ruddy complexion of somebody who drank too much, and clomped across the church floorboards in orthopaedic shoes. She pushed by the pastor to grasp a handful of sandwiches from the table behind Violet and Daisie. It had been six years since Violet had seen her, yet she was wearing the same tired mink stole that smelled of unfinished taxidermy. Maisel cocked her head towards Violet, blinking in recognition as a slice of cucumber flopped across her grip.

'You've grown up,' she gushed. 'I missed your mother, but I missed you two the most. Such a shame what happened. All of it.'

Violet recalled her mother being dismayed when Maisel had stopped replying to her letters after the separation, even though she'd initially taken her side over Father's. As the church emptied and the mourners circled the Chettles to nod their condolences, Violet watched Father navigate desperately away from Maisel through the crowd. But Maisel's hulking frame easily cornered the three of them in the vestibule.

'A great loss, Ted. For all of us. I was hoping Hazel would make it,' Maisel said as she craned her thick neck to peer across the crowd. Father visibly blanched.

'Hazel?' asked Violet, her eyebrows flicking with curiosity.

'You made your speech years ago, leave it, for Christ's sake,' her father told Maisel, his bony elbows steering the girls towards the exit.

Violet's eyes questioned her auntie as the musty smell of the flaccid mink filled her nostrils.

'Who's Hazel?' Violet said, while Father pushed her towards the mourners squeezing by, his hand against her lower back.

'Have I put my cursed foot in it again, Ted?' Auntie Maisel worried.

'About what? What *it*?' Violet persisted.

'She's in Australia, banished to the colonies,' Maisel said dismissively, as though it were the equivalent of being deceased.

Father grasped Violet's sleeve and pulled her out into the drizzle with her sister.

The three of them walked to the cemetery further along the way, her father staying apart from the line of mourners.

'Hazel?' Violet asked him again.

'Not now, Violet,' he said angrily as they rounded the stone fence into the overgrown garden.

Soon enough the casket was brought and lowered a mere three hundred feet from where Mother had died. Father left the graveside before the pastor had finished the sermon and headed in the direction of the Spring Grove pub, leaving Violet with Daisie. Violet's eyes stung from restrained tears, but she took deep breaths and kept herself composed. Daisie was still in a trance of sorts. As soon as the final 'Amen' was uttered, she turned towards home, leaving Violet to deal with the wake alone.

An hour later, as the drizzle settled, Violet returned to Grove Lane, exhausted of soul and mind. She carried a plate of left-over cucumber and cream cheese sandwiches that a neighbour, Mrs Bulvers, had kindly made. She'd meticulously crafted them into round, bite-sized portions with tufts of dill dabbed into the cheese at the edges. It seemed a shame to waste them, particularly given the square edges of the bread had already been wasted to achieve the effect.

The living room was the place that felt the emptiest since her mother died. Violet glimpsed her reflection in the mirror above the fireplace and gasped; for a moment she had seen her mother staring back. She walked into the kitchen and slumped in a chair. Daisie had kicked off her wet shoes on the kitchen floor, as usual, knowing Violet would deal with them.

For the first time in as long as she could remember, the house was still. The absence of her mother, her new reality, started to sink in.

Then a soft murmur broke the overbearing silence. *'Safe and sound at home again, let the waters roar, Jack.'* Violet could hear Daisie's low, scratchy singing voice. She carefully climbed the stairs, avoiding the creak of the fifth and eighth steps, to stop in the hall near the doorway of their shared bedroom. Daisie was inside, singing a sea shanty their mother would often croon while bathing. Violet closed her eyes and lost herself to sadness.

One more time with glad refrain, let the chorus soar, Jack.
Long we've tossed on the rolling main, now we're safe ashore,
    Jack.
Don't forget yer old shipmate, faldee raldee raldee raldee
    rye-eye-doe.

Daisie stopped singing and the silence rushed back in. Despair landed heavily in the pit of Violet's stomach. She emitted an involuntary cry, giving her presence away and coughing to cover it up. Daisie closed the bedroom door, two feet from where Violet stood in the hallway.

Violet stopped at her parents' bedroom door, sniffling back the last of the tears and wiping her eyes with a damp sleeve. She pushed open the door to the small double bedroom that could barely house the bed, a wooden cupboard and a mirrored dressing table. The small window overlooked Mrs Bulvers' muddy courtyard and cast a square of light on the unmade bed. The far side, Father's side, was pushed up against the wall. He'd always climbed over their mother to go to the toilet in the middle of the night, but no more.

Violet walked slowly over to the bureau and pulled the top drawer open. She lifted her mother's porcelain-backed brush and held it close to her face, observing the dark brown strands of hair still caught in its bristles. Violet had encouraged her mother to buy the brush for herself last Christmas at Wickham's Department Store on Mile End Road. She pushed her finger into the jewellery box, nudging through the collection of brooches and necklaces that were now tangled and abandoned.

In the next drawer down rested Edith's prized mauve cashmere pullover, wrapped delicately in tissue in anticipation of her next evening outing. Violet leaned in to smell it. Her mother's perfume still lingered in its fine strands.

Hidden behind was the lid of a worn shoebox. The pullover had been folded to approximate the height of the box, obscuring it at the back of the drawer. She reached in, lifted the heavy box onto the rumpled bedsheets and opened the torn lid. It was a mess of photographs, her mother's box of memories.

Violet shuffled through the images, some of which she'd never seen. Of the twins as toddlers, of her father and mother holidaying in Brighton before she and Daisie were born. Of relatives and grandparents she barely knew. Of Father beaming with his forced-grin photo face, over and over.

There was even a photo of Mother on the steps of the University of London in Hull before she graduated and war took precedence. Standing alongside four girlfriends, all beaming brightly in patterned skirts and low socks with curled hair tight around their cheerful faces, her mother looked the happiest Violet had ever seen her.

At the bottom of the box she found a sealed envelope. In her mother's rounded handwriting, the intended recipient of the long unsent letter had been written:

To: Hazel Lawson
Address:

The rest was blank. Violet turned to check the hallway and held her breath.

Nothing but the silence of emptiness.

She exhaled, curiously turning the packet over in her hands. She slid her finger along the brittle glue of the lip, breaking the seal.

Six monochrome photographs slid into her palm. The images were of Edith and a woman identical to her. Both were aged nineteen or twenty and stood beside bicycles on a bushy country lane.

An identical twin sister. Violet cupped her hand to her mouth as the truth landed like a lie.

She flicked through the pile, then examined the photos closely, holding the ghostly faces up to her eye. Her mother had a small mole on her left cheek. The woman on the left had that tiny speck whereas the other woman didn't. She wore a bright red carnation in her coat buttonhole, perhaps a convenient way for others to differentiate the women.

She shuffled to another image, of two identical girls no more than five years old. Both clutched matching knitted rabbit dolls that hung from their hands. At the bottom of the photo were two handwritten words: *Rosie & Poppy*. Violet stuffed the photographs back in the envelope, then into her blouse pocket. She placed the box back behind the sweater and padded downstairs.

Standing in front of the fireplace, she extracted the photo of the girls with the bikes. She delicately rested it on the mantelpiece, carefully positioning it like the first offering of a shrine. Violet took a step back and stared at the image that stood between her mother's glass vases.

Father returned an hour or so later, his pain anaesthetised with heavy doses of stout. He stopped in front of the mantel, confused by the photograph, which he stared at as though it had appeared from beyond the grave.

From the kitchen, Violet watched him sway before the photo as she tipped diced carrots into the pot. 'Cooking a hotpot for tomorrow,' she said. He continued to stare at the photo in a daze. 'Mrs Bulvers left us sandwiches if you want them.'

Father said nothing and stumbled upstairs. Violet ate two sandwiches, threw the rest out lest they attract cockroaches, and headed up to her room, where Daisie lay in bed. Her eyes were closed but Violet could tell she was awake. She rested the envelope on the bedside table.

Daisie opened her eyes as Violet crawled into bed. 'What's that?' she asked, her eyes level with the packet.

Violet pulled the blanket up to her neck. 'Did you know about her? Auntie Hazel?'

Daisie opened the envelope and shuffled the photographs in her hands. She paused at the image of her mother and the doppelganger clutching their rabbits. 'Rosie and Poppy?'

Violet just shrugged. She reached up to turn the light out.

'Why didn't she say anything?' Daisie asked. But Violet had no answer to give.

Later that night she was woken by Father rattling around downstairs. When he bumped into something – the kitchen table, most likely – with a numbed groan, Daisie stirred but did not wake.

The next morning the photograph was gone.

3

It wasn't until a few months after the funeral that Violet realised her stinging sense of grief had made itself at home, rather than fading as she'd expected. Christmas, what little there had been of it, hadn't helped. Despite Violet's fascination for royal pageantry, the impending Coronation did little to enliven her mood.

Her father's drinking increased. Each evening he'd start at the Duke of Buckingham, arriving home after the ten o'clock close to drink whisky, ignoring Violet's complaints that his dinner had gone cold. Later, as the money ran thin, large bottles of ruby port replaced whisky as the late-night digestif of choice. Violet understood the need to dull one's anguish. She even considered it herself as a means to soothe her grief. But although she was eighteen, Father wouldn't have stood for it.

The only time he became talkative again was in his most drunken state, and it was usually for the worse. 'The rabbit. It all started with the damn rabbit,' he muttered to himself as he fumbled with the kettle late one night. 'Diseased thing infected us all.' Violet knew Daisie could hear the accusations as she lay in bed upstairs. He spoke loud enough to ensure she did.

The sisters had finished their secondary education the year prior and planned to go to college. But it transpired that only Violet received a letter of acceptance from the London School of Printing and Graphic Arts. After the brickworks stipend ran out – they had 'most regrettably' let him go – Father convinced the bank manager of their mother's death and started drawing on her savings account. Just over two thousand pounds had been set aside for the girls' education, earned from their mother's job teaching English at Tiffin Girls'.

The savings account was soon depleted, and the meagre NHS and unemployment benefit payments could do little to keep the rent paid. While other families in Grove Lane were buying television sets, planning Coronation parties and watching Patrick Troughton as *Robin Hood* over dinner, the Chettles were barely scraping together enough money to buy potatoes.

Edith had always encouraged the twins to get an education. The only consolation in Daisie's college rejections was that their mother wasn't there to hear the bad news. In any event, Father didn't have the money for *any* education. It didn't seem to cause him much anxiety – the girls knew he thought a woman's place was at home – but he had tolerated the notion until the money ran out.

'I'm sorry,' he said to Violet as she poured his cup of tea. 'Not enough money.'

'For what? Food?'

Daisie looked up from her magazine.

'College.'

'Mum's savings?'

'There isn't enough.' Father's teaspoon scraped in the cup.

Violet's teeth perceptibly gritted. 'How much is left?'

'Three hundred pounds. Give or take.'

Violet sighed as he quietly sipped his tea. The silence was broken by one of his coughs, loose and wheezing, like a damp engine trying to ignite.

Daisie stood and pulled on her coat, seemingly desperate to escape. 'I'm going out,' she muttered, charging towards the front door like it was a fire escape during a fire.

'We're to start working then, Daise,' Violet said. 'I'll be delaying college another year.'

It wasn't a question, and neither Father nor Daisie answered it.

Father coughed again as he reached for the cigarette packet. His wheezing intensified. He stood, hands on his knees to try to alleviate the chest pain, snatching the dishcloth to shield his mouth.

'You're bleeding!' exclaimed Violet.

His face went red as he choked and slumped against the table.

Daisie ran next door, where Mrs Bulvers called an ambulance. By the time it pulled up outside the house Father was unconscious. The doctor wasn't sure whether it was the cigarettes or the fog that had done the most damage.

On Friday morning Daisie was the only one in the ward with Father. She held his hand gently, his forefingers stained by cigarettes, as his breathing became thinner and raspier. The doctor administered morphine but her hope faded with Father's consciousness. As he choked his final breath, Daisie felt a numbness subsume her, as though she'd swallowed the opiate herself.

Violet arrived to see Daisie sitting by the empty bed, her eyes red. Father's watch and toiletry bag rested on the bedside table. It was the only evidence he'd been in the tiny hospital room at all.

'Where is he?'

'It's just us now.' Daisie stared at his pillow as though she were still conversing with him.

Violet slumped into the nearest chair.

'I was at a job interview. In Ditton,' Violet confessed.

Daisie slid open the bedside drawer to collect her father's things. She froze.

'What's wrong?' asked Violet. She rose to her feet and went to her sister, leaning over the drawer to see what had caused Daisie's reaction.

Wedged in the fold of his fading brown leather wallet was the photo from the mantelpiece. It had been torn in half.

'It's Mum,' uttered Daisie.

Violet removed the image reverently and held it close to her eyes. The woman in the photo had the large red carnation in her lapel button. Violet's eyes widened.

'What?' Daisie said, reaching for the photo.

'It's nothing.'

'Well?'

'It's Auntie Hazel.'

'That's Mum.'

'It isn't.'

'Stop trying to—'

'I'm not!'

'He just passed, Violet!' Her words were amplified by the room's austerity. 'He's gone and you're suggesting—' In frustration at having to utter the words, Daisie snatched the photo from Violet's hands and ferociously crumpled it into a ball.

'Give it to me!' Violet hissed, grasping at Daisie's fist. As Violet pursued her, Daisie screamed, determined to protect her father from another accusation.

A young nurse appeared at the door, breathless and obviously expecting a medical emergency, not a family dispute. In the second of distraction, Daisie popped the photo into her mouth like a pill, rabidly chewing it into a ball.

Violet's backbone wilted in defeat.

'Always you,' she said with a sigh. 'Always about you two.'

Daisie stormed past the stunned nurse into the hospital corridor, the echo of her receding heels broken by her single choking cough.

Violet sat on the unmade hospital bed with a resigned slump, in the awkward presence of the nurse and the space left by Father, as grief's familiar grip tightened.

4

The *West London Observer*, June 24, 1953
Wanted: Housemaid. Housekeeping, commode, tub and tile wall cleaning, dusting, washing painted woodwork, polishing silver-ware plus other tasks under direct supervision. Physical req'ts: Stands, walks and kneels constantly. Educational req'ts: Read and write. Sex: Female. Age: 17–25. Must be without encum-brance. References preferred but not essential. Surroundings pleasant. Contact: Mrs Turner, Elmbridge End, Surrey

Violet was successful in securing the job. Her fervent resolve greatly impressed the house manager at Elmbridge End. While menial, the work would place her in an environment a cut above her own station, with a highly regarded family that held royal connections, and she had been preparing for this her entire life. When she was five she'd role-play with Daisie.

'I'm the lady-in-waiting,' she'd announce, poised at the top of the stairs with one of her mother's dresses draped across her like a toga.

'I'm Queen Victoria,' Daisie would then declare. Violet would happily lapse into being her elegant slave. Eventually Queen Victoria would abuse her power, but for short bursts Violet was the lady she dreamt of being.

She commenced work at Elmbridge End the following week. Violet had rehearsed the journey to work the Sunday prior. She took a twenty-minute stroll from Guildford station down Portsmouth Road along the River Wey, passing the Ship Inn before turning into the lengthy grand driveway. Door-to-door it could be completed in twenty-five minutes.

The gravel entry to Elmbridge End was lined by two rows of magnificent wych elms and led to a turning circle outside a vast three-storey brick and flint mansion. The house was surrounded by acres of wooded gardens and verdant lawns. Violet would've gladly transfused blue blood via a blunt needle to live there. She imagined the wild game that roamed the forests behind, in hopeful wait for the privilege of being hunted by handsome aristocrats.

A black Daimler turned off the main road and crunched through the gravel towards her.

'Lady Althorp,' Violet whispered to herself as the car passed. Fourth daughter of Lady Rose and Lord William. Her sisters had married conscientiously, leaving Lady Althorp to run the house alone. *Fine breeding*, Violet thought, like it was the solution to everything.

On the first day Violet dropped a teacup on an antique carpet in the master guestroom. Fortunately, the florid pattern obscured the stain and nobody was the wiser.

On the fifth day she referred to the house manager, Mrs Turner, as Miss Turner.

'Mrs! Mrs Turner!' the woman scolded in a Dickensian manner. Violet struggled not to stare at the untrimmed patch of mole hairs on Mrs Turner's right cheek while she berated Violet for the indiscretion. 'Imagine if I were Lady Althorp? You'd be fired on the spot!'

By the fifteenth day Violet had settled into a routine. She was able to change the linen in four bedrooms as well as dust, air, sweep, polish, replant, arrange, scrub and fluff the entire wing before noon, plus attend to any houseguest tea or service requests.

By the thirtieth day Mrs Turner hadn't found further cause to criticise her performance. Violet glimpsed Lady Althorp only when she occasionally arrived or departed. She was a model of pale elegance, aloof in the best of ways and always accompanied by her tan Airedale Terrier. The slender strands of dog hair Violet found on the guest duvet covers suggested the animal roamed his domain after dark.

'Mr Humboldt came by today. Seemed pretty angry,' Daisie announced from the couch as Violet returned home. The children across the road played noisily in the street outside, enjoying the late summer sun.

'What did you tell him?' Violet asked as she eased her shoes off by the door.

'Told him to talk to you.'

Violet sighed. 'We're running out of money. I'll ask him for more time.'

'Can you ask for a raise?'

'I've only been there a month. How's your job hunting going?'

'It's more work than full-time employment, without the pay packet,' Daisie complained as she flopped back against the cushions.

'We're broke, Daisie. In one week we will default on the rent and they will throw us out. There's no more time to ponder your glorious career path,' Violet complained as she put on the kettle. 'One of the cooks mentioned that Mrs Turner has placed an advertisement in the *Surrey Herald* for an additional maid. That odd girl from the weekend shift, Gertrude Sparrow – she told him she'd seen it. Said her sister was going to apply.'

'A flock of sparrows nesting at Elmbridge End.' Daisie smirked as she pulled a cushion over her face.

'I'm putting you up for it.'

'Ha! I'd be a terrible maid. I can't even cook,' Daisie's muffled voice protested.

'It's just cleaning. You know, the reverse of all that mess you make here.' Violet glanced towards the kitchen where dirty plates and cups cluttered the table.

Daisie sighed from under the cushion, cornered.

'There's no shame in it. Mother did it while she was studying.'

Daisie huffed and headed upstairs.

'We're running out of money,' Violet yelled after her. 'Next week it will be a decision between food and rent!'

Daisie slammed the bedroom door shut.

Violet stepped out into the courtyard with her tea. 'Happy nineteenth birthday,' she muttered to herself.

Violet shed displeasure as it took to her, whereas Daisie bottled up anxiety until it released itself in a disproportionate scene. No display of anger would pay the rent, and by the time Daisie came down for breakfast in the morning, Violet could tell she was slowly resigning herself to the inevitable.

'I'll do it,' Daisie said. 'Poorly, but I'll do it.' She slammed the door shut so hard Violet thought the three flying ducks mounted above the couch would shatter on the floor.

Violet convinced Mrs Turner to employ Daisie sight unseen, on the basis that they were twins and 'utter facsimiles'. Mrs Turner sat in the far corner of the staff room in a grotto under the stairs. Neatly arranged on the little desk were a single pen, a lamp and a diary that lay open at the current date. Mrs Turner had no real need for a desk; it was her way of showing that she was engaged in more than the drudgery of domestic chores, elevating her superiority when mortals came to beg.

'We're exactly the same – you can even call us both Violet,' Violet promised Mrs Turner. She was trying to charm the woman as Daisie might have, but she knew she was coming across as irritatingly desperate. Mrs Turner had no interest in pleading from a mere maid. However, she seemed drawn to the idea of not having to interview a dozen uneducated girls from south-west London. And after all, Violet had proven herself an efficient and reliable staff member.

'Very well. Your fate is your word. She slips up, you're as good as last Sunday's ham,' Mrs Turner said, her eyebrows raised halfway up her forehead as she marked the single sheet of paper on her desk decisively.

'My reputation is at stake,' Violet lectured Daisie that evening. 'You'll be obedient and efficient. You'll be exact and tidy – the opposite of how you treat our home. You'll do whatever I say. And if they refer to you as "Violet", you'll respond as if you're me. You're a servant now, Daisie. This is what we must do to survive.'

A particularly unpleasant August morning welcomed Daisie's first day of work. The rain had poured all evening – not a run-of-the-mill Dorset drizzle but a heaving Judgement Day downpour.

'Rain's no excuse to be late,' said Mrs Turner, who stood in the staff hallway. She raised an eyebrow as they closed the door behind them. Violet made a deferential nod.

'Which one's the other one? Not Violet, the new one.'

'I'm Daisie Chettle,' Daisie replied nervously, glancing up at Mrs Turner's facial hair as a single raindrop crawled down her own forehead and onto her nose.

Mrs Turner evaluated Daisie with squinted eyes, the way she might a suspected art forgery.

'Right. Daisie. The better-looking one,' she said casually, as though establishing her method to tell them apart. 'I suspect we'll need to come up with a collective noun for you two.'

Violet's face reddened in anger at Mrs Turner's insensitive comment, and she bit her lip until it nearly bled. Mrs Turner glanced down with a tart disdain at the growing puddle of rainwater on the patterned Axminster carpet.

'Atishoo!' shouted Daisie involuntarily and so unexpectedly she didn't have time to cover her face. The sound echoed through the house and caused Mrs Turner to physically recoil.

Violet clenched her jaw, willing the soggy carpet beneath her feet to swallow her up.

'Well, don't stand there flooding the place. Clean yourselves up before we all catch whatever *it* is.'

'Yes, Mrs Turner,' the twins said in unison. They rushed to the locker area, leaving an incriminating trail of dripped water behind them.

'A disaster. You are a disaster. Why did I think this was a good idea?' Violet said under her breath.

'I'll leave,' Daisie replied hopefully.

'Oh no, you're not getting off that easily.'

'*Mrs* Turner. Why's an unmarried woman called a "Mrs" here?' Daisie asked with genuine curiosity.

Violet pressed her forefinger to her lips. 'You never know who's listening,' she whispered cautiously. 'The walls have ears.'

'Well, shut up and stop talking to the walls then!' Daisie rolled her eyes and slammed her locker door shut.

'So, remember, we're to clean and dust, swap linen, ensure fires are lit, fetch hot water, plus any other tasks the house manager directs you to do,' Violet lectured again as they brushed their hair and tied their identical aprons. 'Stay out of the way of anybody above you – that means pretty much everybody except for the stablehands and the grounds staff, who are best avoided, regardless. Be wary of the laundry and scullery maids, too.'

'How do I tell who is better than whom?' asked Daisie without sarcasm.

'Fingernails,' Violet whispered.

Daisie looked down at her hands.

5

October, 1953

'*Noose for a Lady* is playing at the Odeon?' Violet suggested with hopefulness in her voice. 'We could wait out the storm inside. It'll be warm. It might even be fun, for a change?'

A downpour had trapped Daisie and Violet at Kingston station on their way home from work. Daisie had forgotten her umbrella again and Violet had stepped in a puddle on Fife Road, ruining her saddle shoes and blotching dark mud on her pale stockings.

'I'm exhausted,' Daisie complained.

'That's called *working*,' Violet replied. 'Mind, I spend more time fixing your slapdash efforts than doing my own tasks.'

There was a time when they had gone to the cinema every Saturday afternoon. Mum would accompany them and they'd sit towards the front and watch whatever was screening that week. If it was an 'H' or 'A' category film, denoting Horror or Adult, then all the better.

'I'd prefer you learned here, rather than out there,' Mum once said, pointing towards the nearby pub strip on Old London Road as she purchased three adult tickets to *The Browning Version*.

'It's been so long since we've been,' Violet urged Daisie. She watched the frown form above Daisie's eyes. Seemingly, Daisie could think of nothing worse than spending more time with her sister, but the wind and rain were biting and the main feature *did* star Dennis Price.

'Very well,' Daisie relented. 'But only if we can get some Spangles.'

Being midweek, the cinema was mostly empty. The lobby decor was 'fading grandeur', its opulence twenty years out of date. The polished brass fixtures and ceiling-to-floor velvet curtains, tied with sashes as thick as wine bottles, were like the adornments of a museum whose artefacts were light and shadow.

Their wet heels clicked across the chessboard marble floor. Daisie checked their damp coats and Violet purchased two packets of mixed Spangles sweets with the tickets.

The twins had no trouble finding seats towards the front of the empty auditorium. On the two seats between them they rested their damp handbags.

'When was the last time we came here?' pondered Daisie aloud.

'Ages. That Brando film, *Viva Zapata!*'

'We should come more often,' Daisie replied, as thunder rumbled outside. It was a rare olive branch.

Violet offered her the sweets. They sat and waited for the lights to dim, crunching the brittle Spangles between their teeth like cubes of ice. Daisie giggled, their chewing in sync, crunching like footsteps on gravel.

Before the room darkened, a man in his early twenties sat directly in front of them, blocking their view even though the auditorium was otherwise deserted. He wore a perfect suit that fit like he'd been tailored since birth. His deep red hair was slicked sideways with a heavy gob of Brylcreem.

'What a rake,' Violet whispered to Daisie.

'It's Ginger Brando,' Daisie joked under her breath. They sniggered together, their identical laughter resonating loudly enough for the man to hear.

He craned his neck and frowned at the sight of them, perplexed as to which one of them had made the remark.

'If it isn't the Dolly Sisters, reunited at last. Unless I'm seeing double. It *was* a long lunch,' he remarked in a refined clip. Looking smug, he turned back to face the screen.

'Dare we provoke the ginger outlaw?' Daisie whispered.

Violet nodded apprehensively. Daisie reached over and prodded the man's bony shoulder. His slight physique would not have withstood even a half-hearted game of rugby. 'Would you mind moving? There are plenty of seats in the mezzanine.'

He chortled to himself, then turned back to eyeball Daisie. She held his gaze. Rather than bite, he lazily got up and sauntered to the end of the row.

'So rude,' Violet commented victoriously as she popped an orange Spangle into her mouth.

'Yes, and how rude of him to leave,' Daisie replied with a cheeky grin. 'I do like the red ones,' she said, shaking the box of coloured sweets. They burst into laughter.

Rather than sitting down, the man turned into their row and walked back towards Violet, smiling devilishly the entire time.

'Oh, here he comes,' Violet whispered nervously. She crossed her hands on her lap and held her chin high, front and centre.

'The view from here is much better,' he said in a conspiratorial tone as he squeezed passed Violet and sat beside Daisie on the far end. 'I do hope nobody sits in front of us.'

'Do you m-mind?' Violet stammered.

'Y-yes, I actually do,' he said, mocking her. 'Guess it's not hard to confuse you two, despite appearances,' he confided to Daisie. 'Hate seeing movies by myself.'

Violet glared. 'If you wouldn't mind, my-my s-sister and I want to watch the f-film.'

'We could move to the seats in front of her?' he proposed to Daisie, leaning to talk into her ear and causing a blush.

'Don't encourage him, Daisie,' Violet hissed.

'Oh, nice to meet you, *Daisie*,' he said, further maddening Violet.

The lights dimmed and the Pathé newsreel fanfare sounded but Violet gathered her coat, gesturing to Daisie that they should move or leave. Daisie frowned her eyebrows and shook her head. Ginger Brando smirked, cognisant of the coded dialogue going on between the sisters. With a sigh Violet slumped back into her seat.

'It's a busy month for Her Majesty,' the narrator exclaimed with jaunty excitement, over new film of the youthful Queen Elizabeth smiling regally. 'Preparations are underway for the six-month tour of the Commonwealth, where the royals will stop at Bermuda, Jamaica, Fiji, Tonga, New Zealand, Australia and the Cocos Islands. This will be the first visit to the Commonwealth by a royal sovereign since the Coronation five months ago.'

'Sounds like a dreadful holiday to me,' their unwanted companion joked. Daisie smiled coyly. Violet slumped deeper in her chair.

As the main feature began, Violet could see Daisie discreetly examining the well-spoken stranger, so she did the same. He wore unblemished, medium-brown leather shoes and seemed a viable alternative to the usual applicants for Daisie's attention. She knew Daisie would be somewhat disappointed when he kept his hands to himself during the film.

Violet stood to leave the moment 'The End' appeared, but Ginger Brando wasn't to be deterred, and neither was Daisie. They strolled together out of the cinema talking animatedly, while Violet grumped and lingered, irked by jealousy.

Outside, the rain had passed, and the evening dark was settling in.

'Walk you to . . .?' he proposed.

'Along Wood Street,' Daisie willingly replied. Violet's eyes sunk, the sting of rejection familiar. This wasn't likely to be another momentary humiliation, but a rejection in favour of Daisie that promised to linger like the smell of mothballs.

Violet followed, eavesdropping from a short distance and almost clipping the man's leather heels as he slowed near the turnstile.

'I'm having a small gathering on the weekend – I'll have the house to myself.'

He let the suggestion hang in the air as Daisie raised her eyebrows.

'Too many men, though. Perhaps you'd like to be the centre of attention?'

Violet coughed in disapproval, though Daisie made certain to ignore her.

'Galsworthy House on Kingston Hill.'

'Galsworthy House?' Daisie echoed.

'That's the one. Can't miss it. Name's William Dunclark, by the way. Or you can call me Bill. Take your pick.'

'Why, thank you, Bill.' Daisie did not play her cards, although she shifted her weight to one foot and twirled slightly.

Violet coughed again, more loudly.

'Bring your shadow, if you must,' Bill said, nodding in Violet's direction. 'I have to beat feet. Nice to meet you, Daisie.' He smiled charmingly. 'You too,' he said towards Violet, before strolling lankily towards the high street.

Daisie beamed. Violet, her arms knotted, glared cynically at her.

'I'm nineteen – I can do what I want,' Daisie said in retort to the unasked question, lagging behind her. 'He's the bee's knees, don't you think?'

'Over my dead body.'

Daisie rolled her eyes. 'If only!'

'I think we've had enough dead bodies for the time being,' Violet muttered under her breath.

Daisie stopped, stunned by the remark's callousness. Violet tightened her jaw with a glimmer of regret in her eyes.

'He could be a cad,' Violet argued. '*Or* a Tory.'

'Good!' said Daisie as she began walking again.

The following day they cased his address on the way home from work. Galsworthy House was a vast estate on Kingston Hill, opposite Richmond Park. The neo-Georgian mansion featured two wings that extended either side of a semicircular lawn.

'I always wondered who lived here,' Violet said, her interest piqued.

'So, is he still a rake?' Daisie teased. It was reassuringly clear that William Dunclark was derived from upright stock and more than reasonable means.

'I suppose we'll find out,' Violet said. It was as close to an apology as she could manage.

The front door opened. 'Scurry!' Violet hissed. The girls scattered, as a smartly dressed older couple emerged and walked towards the cream Bentley parked in the driveway. Violet and Daisie ran alongside the fence with their heads down, giggling as though they'd been caught by the headmaster.

6

On Saturday afternoon Daisie strolled through the imposing sandstone gates of Galsworthy House. Violet shuffled behind, fussing with her outfit like her life depended on it. Even though she was only the chaperone, Violet had found herself anxious about the party all week. While they'd attended a mixed school, Violet had never been on a date, even as a third wheel. Daisie had dated the occasional boy, and put far more effort into her appearance than Violet cared to. Yet, even when they wore the same outfit, it was Daisie's confidence that drew the glances of men on the street. Violet knew Daisie preferred it that way, and Violet had no interest in competing for it. She couldn't care less whom Daisie had kissed under the horse chestnut trees by the Kingston Bridge tow path.

But this time, Daisie's enthusiasm for Bill, and his for her, gnawed at Violet. It was Bill's apparent status that prickled her. For the first time she felt a sting of competitiveness. He reminded her of the loutish Hampton School rugby boys she disliked so much, with their bunched socks, sweaty hair and spiked boots that wreaked havoc on the Wick's soft grass.

'I've underdressed, I know it,' Violet said, irritated with Daisie. 'I look like I should be handing out hors d'oeuvres.'

Daisie wore the bow dress that their mother had sewn for herself and worn to the 1949 Grove Lane New Year's Eve gathering. Its purple floral pattern and thin matching leather belt highlighted the mauve blush Daisie had applied to her cheeks, its cut revealing a hint of curvature.

Violet had wanted to wear it but Daisie got to the dress first.

'You're tearing it!' Violet exclaimed as they tussled the garment between them that afternoon.

'I'll make my bed every day for a month,' Daisie offered.

'You should be doing that anyway!'

'He's *my* boyfriend.'

Violet was so shocked by the admission she let go of the fabric, sending Daisie backwards onto the floorboards crowded with discarded outfits. 'Boyfriend?' Violet exclaimed incredulously as she stood over Daisie. 'If that fish stick is your boyfriend, then I'm the Duke of Edinburgh's occasional paramour.'

Now, as they walked along the driveway to Galsworthy House, Violet sighed with her arms crossed tightly across her chest. Under her coat, she wore a plain black knee-length shift dress that hung as it would on a coat hanger and wouldn't have looked out of place on waitstaff. 'I look like bloody Augusta Grumbole from the kitchens,' she complained. 'Even the groundsmen make themselves busy when she loiters with intent.'

Daisie knocked twice on the handsome double front doors as Violet lingered, chaperoning from six feet behind. Bill swung open the heavy doors with a theatrical flourish, his face flushed and smelling of alcohol.

'The twins are here! Brilliant. Trevor, you have to see this!' he shouted to somebody inside.

The gathering consisted of thirty or so twenty-somethings – predominantly men with polo shirts and no shoes who sprawled throughout the luxurious household. For the first few seconds every eye in the house turned to them, surveying the twins like curious lions evaluating the meat proportions of wildebeest. Within seconds their attention pivoted back to drinking, smoking and talking about Very Important Things.

'Lovely house,' Daisie said, gazing up at the room-sized chandelier. The foyer was all marble and oak with two long hall-ways that stretched in either direction. Its outhouse would've been bigger than their own house.

'Two dozen bedrooms,' Bill quipped, a single eyebrow arched at the possibilities. Violet seethed. 'Fireplace that could garage a Volkswagen Beetle,' he continued. 'That's the crest up there.' He gestured towards a coat of arms hanging above the mantel.

'You have a family crest?' Daisie gushed, gazing up at the fleur-de-lis insignia.

'No, the family we bought it from did. Fell on hard times, poor sods, so Dad picked it up for a steal. End of the line for them, I suppose,' he said, chuckling at his unintentional pun. 'Should've invested in steel.'

He led them by a row of empty bookshelves towards a ballroom with six leather couches that had been haphazardly arranged into a living space. A lad, no more than eighteen years of age, dribbled a football across the polished wood.

'John Galsworthy used to live here. *The Forsyte Saga*? Must try to read it sometime,' Bill said as he toiled at a mirrored bar cart.

'I *did*. All three parts and both interludes,' Violet interjected.

'No, I meant *I* must try to read it. So frightfully busy with training and whatnot. Exams, that sort of thing.'

'Are your parents home?' asked Violet in the tone of a disapproving parent.

'God, no. They're holidaying in Switzerland, hence the bash.'
Bill brandished two tumblers of clear liquid and ice. 'Be rude not to
take advantage,' he added with a wink. 'Gin with a dash of tonic?'

'Not for me, I—'

'Thank you,' Daisie replied, cutting off her sister and bringing the
glass to her lips. Her restrained wince hinted at the drink's toxicity.

'Right. Make yourself at home. There's food through there,
I think. Or somewhere, I don't know. Daisie, why don't I show you
around the house?'

He steered her away, leaving Violet marooned in the cavernous
ballroom. Each drop kick and punt of the ball echoed off the walls.
She imagined all the dukes, marquesses, earls, viscounts and barons
that would have commanded this grand space, and what it had now
been reduced to.

'You the burlesque girl?' the boy enquired as he edged the ball
towards the fireplace at the far end of the room. It bumped the tool
rack, sending the irons crashing to the floor.

Violet turned and walked away without answering, pacing out
onto the grass to explore the grounds, despite the cold. From a
tidy garden grotto by the bay windows, she spied her sister. As the
guests became drunker and noisier, Daisie became more popular.
Violet, Daisie had once told her, had never had the ability to 'scale
up', as Daisie would call encounters with those of greater means.
Violet knew she was right: Daisie craved attention, but Violet's
shyness always won in the end.

The carp in the pond nibbled and thrashed at the blades of grass
Violet sprinkled onto the water's surface. She checked her watch.
It was now late afternoon, and ordinarily she would be preparing
dinner at this time. Her stomach was complaining, but she didn't
want to go inside to see if there was any food and be faced with the

popularity of her sister. Eventually the tightness in her bladder out-
weighed her reluctance and Violet ventured inside to find a toilet. She
poked her head through doors here and there, wandering the majestic deserted corridors to the sound of Eartha Kitt's '*C'est si bon*',
imagining she were a prospective buyer. She poked her head into an
empty corner suite deep in the east wing, with arched windows overlooking the rear lawn. She dragged her fingertips across the cream
walls and went into an adjoining private bathroom that boasted
polished marble floors and enough space to host a dinner party.

'I'll take it,' she said, nodding to herself. 'Have my things
brought here.'

Violet relieved herself and checked her hair before tracing the
sound of Patti Page's 'How Much Is That Doggie in the Window?'
back to the party with some reluctance.

Somewhere along the main hallway, an arm gripped her right
elbow and pulled her into an empty study like a hooked fish. It was
Bill with a gin glass balanced in the other hand. He steered Violet
against the wall as his arm snaked behind her back with wilful
insistence.

Choked by fear and conflicting thoughts, Violet froze. Bill
emptied the glass, rested it on a dresser and kicked the door shut
with his right foot.

'You found me,' he said as the space closed between them, his
aroma thick with the pungence of alcohol. He smirked to himself,
emboldened by gin and privilege as he lowered his lips towards hers.

'I mustn't,' Violet whispered.

But the kiss was well underway before she could protest further.
It quickly occurred to her that the kiss itself was surprisingly pleasant. It was the first time anybody had shown any interest in her. The
physical contact lasted only thirty seconds, but to Violet it felt like

minutes. Bill detached himself from her now eager grip to regain his breath. Violet, short of hers, stared into his eyes.

'Daisie, you are a red fox,' he said, pleasantly satisfied, before frowning at her flinch. He glanced downwards to her clothes, and then nervously back. His face crinkled in realisation.

'Terribly sorry, I thought you were the other one.' Embarrassed, Bill took a further step back.

Violet kept her eyes fixed on him, trying to hide the strange feeling of rejection burning in her chest.

'Shall I continue?' he asked, a satisfied leer growing on his lips. Violet wondered what Daisie would do. She would do the wrong thing, she thought. Just once, why shouldn't Violet know how that felt?

In the moment she spent considering it, Bill acted. He shifted closer to her again with renewed confidence, his body pressing firmly against Violet's after her silent acquiescence.

'*Our secret,*' he whispered before he mashed his lips against hers, pushing her head back until it thudded against the wall. His hungry, insistent hands clawed at her dress as if she were a wrapped gift. He poked his unshaven chin into her neck, licking as though it were desirable. His sweaty right hand crawled over her neck, his left hand hoisting her dress hem. Then he pawed at her breasts like a trapped dog as Violet gasped for air and nudged his hand away.

'Please,' he asked quietly, almost desperately.

Surrendering to the freedom Daisie always seemed to feel, she nodded, urging him towards her, offering him the encouragement to kiss her again. He pushed his lips onto hers, extinguishing any further words. Violet let the man who'd sought her sister clumsily do what he wished with her body. She fixed her dulled stare on a deer head mounted on the opposite wall, its vacant eyes set oddly out of alignment. The indiscretion lasted only a few minutes, but the guilt would last a lifetime.

Violet huffed in anger as Bill let her go. Mostly anger at herself. Soiled with regret, she felt neither the aura of womanhood nor the sense of satiated jealousy she had expected.

Bill took a self-conscious step backwards, glancing at her uncertainly as though re-evaluating his conquest.

'Don't tell Daisie,' he sheepishly uttered as he tucked his shirt back in. He swiped his fringe and stepped into the hallway, slamming the door behind him.

'We're going,' Violet told Daisie when she reappeared thirty minutes later. She stood behind the couch on which Daisie was regaling six boys with a ribald joke about two secretaries. Bill lingered off to the side, mixing a drink. Violet was determined not to cry until she got home.

'*You're* going,' Daisie retorted. 'I'm just getting going.'

The boys laughed and some drank as though it were a toast.

'One secretary had a strict two-drink limit,' Daisie continued, 'because after one drink she starts to feel it and after two anybody can feel it!'

'We have to go, now,' Violet urged her.

'Go, then! Don't wait up for me.'

With her handbag clutched to her stomach, Violet closed the door behind her.

Her mind cursed with self-blame. How would she ever explain her momentary lapse of reason to Daisie? She pledged to keep it to herself and trusted Bill would do the same.

Violet held herself together until she reached Hogsmill Lane, where flowers that she had left to mark her mother's accident now hung dead from the fence post. Violet sobbed deeply into her sleeve, crossing Grove Lane to avoid a neighbour before disappearing inside the cottage.

7

It had been three days since the party and Daisie still hadn't heard from Bill. She'd thought about him quite a bit since then and was slightly affronted, verging on offended, by his lack of engagement. After all, they had kissed briefly late in the evening, away from the eyes of his friends. It was pleasing enough. She'd kissed tradesmen at the Spring Grove pub and he was in no greater class in that regard. But this time, in Bill's bedroom, Daisie had withheld herself so as not to bounce the cheque.

'Stay away from him, he cannot be trusted,' Violet had stammered the next evening over spam and peas, when Daisie mentioned the party. Daisie, reading it as rabid jealousy, was delighted, and encouraged to pursue the relationship. She couldn't bring herself to tell the entire truth.

'Oh, he did not kiss you, you're just making it up. To make me hate him! You are quite pathetic,' Daisie said dismissively.

She had been seduced by the promise and grandeur of Galsworthy House. The bedroom walls of the poky Grove Lane cottage started to lean in, seemingly intent on suffocating her. More than once she'd fallen asleep and dreamt of spending her days strolling the corridors of Galsworthy House, making the staff enact her most ridiculous whims.

After a dreary week of middling rain, and much discouragement from Violet, Daisie made the spontaneous decision to drop in to Galsworthy House unannounced.

'Violet!' Bill said as he stood, confused, at the front door.

'Violet?' Daisie frowned.

Bill took a breath in panic, as though his head had been thrust underwater.

'Oh, of course I'm joking,' he stammered unconvincingly. 'I imagine you get that joke often.'

Daisie drank three glasses of his parents' prized Dom Pérignon champagne and then challenged him to a drunken game of croquet on the back lawn in the drizzling rain. Daisie insisted he teach her how to drive, turning each stop shot into an opportunity to push her body into his. She delighted in catching him peeking at her damp blouse.

'How's your sister?' he asked with a tremor in his voice, refilling his glass after her ball roqueted.

'Thinks you seduced her. Did you seduce her?'

Bubbles surged over the rim of Bill's glass. 'Of course not! She's an ogre.'

'She looks exactly like me!'

'I mean she's a bore. And a liar. Anything she tells you is desperate fabrication. Happens relentlessly. Those chasing a marriage of convenience.'

'Have you told your parents?' Daisie asked as Bill fussed about mopping up the spilt champagne.

'God, no!'

'About us.'

'About what?'

'Us?'

He let out a sigh as though relieved. 'They're old-fashioned, want to set me up with a friend's daughter. Plastics money. Some equine monster.' His finger gently touched the tiny mole at the base of Daisie's neck, examining it with squinted eyes like he'd made a discovery.

The sound of a car engine and tyres crunching gravel seized Bill's attention. 'Oh Christ, that's the car. They're bloody early again!' He shoved Daisie towards the back garden gate. 'You've got to go, I told them I was alone.'

'What does it matter?' Daisie complained as he urged her towards the path.

Bill distracted his parents in the main hall as Daisie stumbled through a spider's web behind the tennis court. She traced the stone fence to an overgrown gardener's gate that bordered Richmond Park. As she pulled at the gate, which was entangled in creepers, she heard the sound.

Thunk.

It was the same sound she'd heard when her mother died, the heavy thud of flesh, bone and stone. Daisie glanced around desperately to see a garden worker moving a pile of fence stones behind a shrub. *Thunk.*

She pulled at the gate until the vines gave way and the gate swung open with a rusty creak. By the time she left the grounds, Daisie's scowl had set deep. She didn't appreciate being ejected like some Spring Grove tart. Her frustration was compounded by having to walk a mile across sodden grass with her bag in one hand and her brand-new heeled shoes in the other. It wasn't until she reached Broomfield Hill Lane that Daisie realised she'd left her favourite cardigan behind.

To make matters worse, by the time she got home, her esteem and stockings sullied, the tickle of a cold had developed in her throat.

8

'Daisie!' Violet barked through the doorway.

Daisie leaned against the doorjamb under the awning of the staff entryway, holding a cigarette and watching the rain spatter puddles.

'Lady Althorp has called. For *you*.'

'What have I done now?' Daisie sniffled. Her sore throat had developed into a head cold.

'Something you *didn't* do, most likely. Hurry up!'

Daisie exhaled smoke and tossed the cigarette into a puddle, where a sea of discarded butts were bounced and buffeted by the rain like tiny life rafts.

The twins entered the laundry room, where the permanent frown of estate steward Mr Fullsome glowered. He stood beside Mrs Turner, drumming his fingers impatiently on his crossed arms.

'About time. Follow me,' he said wearily.

Violet fussed nervously with the buttons on her apron as Daisie followed them out. She anticipated the worst: Daisie would be fired and she'd go back to paying the rent and feeding two mouths with her salary.

The wood-panelled walls of the Elmbridge grand foyer space framed two oval staircases. Matching pink Derby lidded vases topped the rosettes. Between the staircases, above the enormous fireplace, hung a large portrait of Lady Rose Althorp, a haughty nineeenth-century courtier and deceased mother of Lady Caroline.

They walked in a miserable conga line through the main foyer, Mr Fullsome leading with Mrs Turner behind him and Daisie out of step at the rear.

''Scuse us, sir,' a maintenance man muttered, dipping his balding head as the group passed. An unwrapped portrait of Lady Caroline rested against the wall behind him.

Daisie glanced between the two portraits. The resemblance of mother and daughter was uncanny.

'Alert me when you've taken it down,' Mrs Turner ordered, flicking her hand at the portrait of Lady Rose.

'Yes, ma'am,' the maintenance man said.

One of the scullery maids peered around the corner of the southern passageway, the bags under her eyes heavy. Daisie glared, sending the girl scampering back to the kitchen like a frightened crab. She enjoyed intimidating the scullery maids.

They circled their way up the eastern staircase, then walked along the wide main hallway until they reached the door of Lady Althorp's corner salon.

Mr Fullsome knocked twice. Inside could be heard the high-pitched bark of Lady Althorp's dog. Daisie had heard the animal's bark from the west wing but had never sighted it.

'Come in,' came a refined female voice from within.

Mr Fullsome swung both doors open. The meticulously groomed tan terrier playfully bailed them up at the threshold, its ungainly legs bounding like a newborn lamb's, its tongue dangling out of its mouth like a bookmark. Mrs Turner could barely disguise her distaste for the beast, pulling her ankle-length dress in close to avoid its fur.

The salon was an impressively large drawing room with a black concert piano at one end and large rain-flecked windows overlooking the gardens. Mess covered the floor, the pattern of the carpet barely visible under all the paperwork, racks of clothes, crates and suitcases.

Lady Althorp, perfectly poised, sat at a delicate antique desk. Her porcelain complexion and long, slender neck suggested a physical vulnerability that was contradicted by the focused strength in her eyes. Her tightly pulled back brunette hair framed an intelligent face. She wasn't typically beautiful and didn't appear to be the type who concerned herself with it. Lady Althorp wrote in a ledger, the pen gracefully poised in her delicate right hand like a conducting baton.

'Daisie Chettle,' announced Mr Fullsome ominously. He backed out of the room to join Mrs Turner and closed the doors to leave Daisie to her fate.

Lady Althorp continued writing.

The dog sniffed the air, checking for danger. Daisie rubbed the fingers of her left hand gently together, coaxing the animal towards her. He padded over to prod at the folds of Daisie's uniform with his wet nose. The beast's eager snout nuzzled her fingers.

Lady Althorp continued to work while the clock listened, its *tock-tock* filling the room. Daisie took an impatient breath. The terrier returned to a worn spot by the window, satisfied the threat posed was minimal.

Lady Althorp finally finished a notation and rested her pen on the desk. She blankly contemplated Daisie in the manner of a vendeuse evaluating an overweight debutante. Daisie met her gaze. Why was this creature considered to be of so-called finer standing than her?

'So to it then,' began Lady Althorp. 'Are you married?'

'Not yet,' Daisie responded quickly.

'Good for you,' Lady Althorp said with a kind smile. 'No children to speak of, then?'

'Certainly not.'

Lady Althorp smiled to herself. 'Who needs them? Men. At your age,' she added, as she affectionately scratched the dog's neck. 'What can be better than the company of animals? This is Max. Come closer, Daisie. Neither of us bite. We only bark.' She directed Daisie towards a baroque chair.

Daisie sat on the priceless furniture, flattening her dress as Max studied her movements with his beady eyes. Lady Althorp didn't speak. It was like a test. Violet would have blabbed something incomprehensible by now to fill the silence. But Daisie sat and waited, unblinking like a gunslinger, until it became nearly unbearable.

'So, to the point. On occasion I act as a consort for the Palace. More often since my sister Meg gave up the game. You may be aware that Her Majesty and the Duke are about to tour the Commonwealth for six months, three of them to be spent in Australia, to renew love for the Empire and all that. Fifty thousand miles of it, apparently.' Caroline read from a thick leather-bound document. 'Sydney, Bondi Beach, Katoomba, Dubbo, Broken Hill, Bundaberg, Yarra Ranges . . .' She looked up with a wry smile. 'It is as though these places were named by Edward Lear. I'm exhausted just pronouncing them.' She tossed the tome onto the desk. 'Mrs Grimsdyke and Miss Seacole were to be my help on this tour. But, alas, neither recovered from the inoculations, and the risk of taking them to sea for weeks on end is too great. The *Gothic* departs in five days, so I'm in a spot of bother. And God knows I don't want the Palace assigning me any of their spies.' She leaned forward and whispered with a smile, 'The way they gossip amongst themselves is something frightening. I need somebody I can stand to be around.'

Lady Althorp paused and started writing in her ledger again. 'I've seen you. That oval window in the corner? Looks directly down at your little smoking spot,' she said nonchalantly as she wrote.

Daisie glanced towards an alcove where, indeed, a round window provided a direct overview of her hiding spot by the staff entrance.

'I'm partial to Viceroys too. Don't worry, I won't tell. Other staff stand and puff with a vacant look, as you'd expect. But there's something on your mind.'

Daisie gave nothing away, not even a blink. But inside she felt the easing of a claustrophobia, its smother so familiar she'd forgotten it was there. The promise of escape made her shoulders lighten and her heart tingle.

'Your main responsibility will be to serve me and me only. Otherwise, be neither seen nor heard. The reputation of the Crown, and the Althorp name, will rely on your and Miss Sparrow's discretion and professionalism.'

'Miss Sparrow?' asked Daisie softly. Her sense of freedom diminished with the mere mention of a travelling companion, and the ceiling of the suite felt like it suddenly had dropped towards her, boxing her back in. She'd tasted freedom and now knew what she was missing.

'Yes, do you know her? She's a weekend maid. Quiet little thing, but I have a feeling you'll work well together. So that's the short version. The question that remains is whether you are available, or even interested in the opportunity.'

'Do I need a passport? I'm lucky to visit Tolworth, let alone—'

'No matter, they will sort that out at the Palace.' Lady Althorp looked up at her curiously. 'I was sorry to hear about your parents. To lose both within such a short space of time – from experience, I know how devastating it is.'

Daisie looked to the floor.

After a beat Lady Althorp changed the subject. 'Of course, it's a big decision for a girl your age. But I'll need to know today. You'd need to visit the Hospital for Tropical Diseases in Fitzrovia for immunisations and ensure there are no reactions. It's the colonies, so you'll feel like a pincushion once the day is through. Only thing they won't protect you from is picking up a shocking accent. I'll have Mr Sinden drive you and Miss Sparrow there this afternoon.'

'Can I think about it?'

'Of course, though to be honest I thought you'd jump at the chance. Don't let me down, or I'll be in a right spot.'

During her lunchbreak, as Daisie tried to light a cigarette in the cool breeze, she glanced up at the oval window. There was no sign of Lady Althorp.

'They want *you* to go on the royal tour of the Commonwealth?' Violet exclaimed as she paced around Daisie. 'For six months? In *five days' time*?' Violet's eyes were wide with disbelief. 'Is this an elaborate prank?'

Daisie finally succeeded in getting the cigarette lit.

'Travelling with the royal family! You don't even have a passport!'

'They'll get me one from the Palace,' Daisie said casually in an exhalation of smoke.

'Oh! The *Palace* will get you one!'

'Doesn't matter anyway, I'm not going.'

'No,' Violet whispered incredulously. 'You can't be serious.'

'Trapped on a boat for six months with that lot, treated like a serf round the clock? Going to the middle of the desert or God knows where? I mean, the idea of getting away from you is very appealing, but at least here I go home at five.'

'But the Queen!' Violet cried. 'You'd be travelling with Her Majesty! Royalty by association.'

'Do you know a Miss Sparrow? Weekend shift?'

'Why?'

'She's going too,' Daisie said in a desultory tone.

'Gertrude Sparrow? *Her?*' Violet stood speechless as the gravity of the rejection settled. Then she perked up. 'I could take your place! They could swap us out. Oh, please, Daisie.'

'Pull yourself together,' Daisie said dismissively. She could feel the hallway walls leaning in, and the chandelier hanging above them dropping towards her face, as though its crystals were about to touch her scalp.

'You could say I'm you. We could swap names!'

'You know, maybe I *do* want to do it,' Daisie pondered aloud, sensing Violet's growing desperation and comforting herself by taking the opportunity to rile her. 'Bill can wait.'

Violet seemed to flinch at the mention of his name. 'You'll be working for people like Mrs Turner the whole time. Worse – they'll have real titles! And superiority complexes to go with them.'

'Maybe I'll meet a nice prince. Or a commander. Even a divorced earl.'

'This is *my* dream. It's wasted on you,' Violet hissed as she paced.

'Miss Chettle?' Mrs Turner's voice beckoned from inside. 'It's past break and you're needed!'

Violet sighed, then returned to her chores without another utterance.

Daisie flicked her cigarette into the garden and cast her eye again to the window above. Lady Althorp was watching, one elbow propped on the other wrist, her cigarette poised by her cheek. Their eyes held for the longest moment before Lady Althorp turned away. Daisie smiled to herself and returned to work.

9

The rear seat of Lady Althorp's Daimler smelled of elegance, whereas Gertrude Sparrow smelled like death. Both of the maids' right sleeves were rolled up, revealing tied white bandages at the elbow. Five injections – from disagreeably large needles – had been administered. Daisie felt perfectly fine, whereas Gertrude hadn't responded well to the inoculations.

'It's throbbing, my brain is throbbing,' Gertrude said, clutching her sweaty head like it was going to explode. '*Please* don't tell Mrs Turner. I don't want to—' She clasped her hand to her mouth. 'I think I'm going to be sick.'

Daisie held her breath until whatever was in Gertrude's guts passed as indigestion.

'You need to see a doctor,' Daisie insisted.

'We just saw a doctor!'

'*Another* one.' Daisie glanced in the mirror to see if Mr Sinden was listening.

'I'm fine,' Gertrude declared loudly for Mr Sinden's benefit. 'Never been in finer health after those five big lovely hypo-doomic needles.' She put her hand to her chest and gagged, like a cat trying to cough up a Christmas decoration. 'If they reject me, someone else'll take my place,' Sparrow hissed desperately.

Daisie imagined her sister throwing herself at the opportunity, her throat tightening. 'You can do it, it's not far now,' whispered Daisie encouragingly, coaching Gertrude like a prize-fighter's trainer. 'Think of the Commonwealth!'

'The Commonwealth,' Gertrude echoed unconvincingly. She tapped her chest with her fist, trying to expunge her lungs.

The car paused at a Belgravia stop sign.

Gertrude lowered her voice to a conspiratorial tone and whispered. 'I may be hallucinating, but Adolf Hitler is driving this car.'

'Beg your pardon!' Mr Sinden declared in offence.

'You'll be all right,' urged Daisie as she clasped the girl's clammy hand.

'I really think I'm going to vomit,' Gertrude blubbered, on the verge of tears. 'On this nice leather.'

'Deep breaths. Let's open the window, Gertrude. If you don't keep it together, you'll be back doing the weekend shift for the rest of your life. Until you die. Alone.'

'Promise me you'll tell Connor I love him.'

'Who's Connor?'

'A fella I met at the Slaughtered Lamb last week.' Gertrude urgently wrapped her hand over her lips.

'You can hold it in,' urged Daisie. 'You can do it, Gertrude!'

But she couldn't.

Mrs Turner was furious. Her hirsute mole too, which turned a lighter shade of puce in her fury. It would take a professional cleaner two days to expunge the smell of Miss Sparrow's mess from the Daimler, which was much less than the time it would take for Gertrude Sparrow to recover.

*

Violet was secretly delighted at the news of Miss Sparrow's reaction to the inoculations. Like Cinderella being sent for to try the glass slipper, Violet felt her heart swell when Mrs Turner came to fetch her for an audience with Lady Althorp the next morning. She held her breath for almost the entire walk to the suite, passing through the grand foyer and up the stairs as Daisie had done.

She was terrified to be in the salon, let alone taking the journey that lay ahead. Max sensed her fear, sitting at guard like a sphinx before her. A busy Lady Althorp was being shown a range of gowns by an emissary from Buckingham Palace, so the meeting was short and to the point.

Violet was offered and accepted Gertrude Sparrow's position on the tour. 'I won't l-let you down,' she nervously promised Lady Althorp.

Violet went to Bloomsbury for the injections, by taxi rather than chauffeured car. She clenched her teeth as the needles slid into her, but got through them without ill reaction.

'Seacole told me,' Daisie blurted out as they stepped onto the driveway towards home. 'Didn't have the guts to tell me yourself?' She scowled.

'I don't expect you to be happy about it,' Violet said, 'but we need the money.'

'That's a lie! We're making enough.'

It was a lie, but Violet held her line. 'I would never lie to you, Daisie. I'm your sister.'

'Is there *nothing* I have which you don't have designs to take? You'll suffocate me, Violet. Unless I get to you first,' Daisie threatened, hastening her step forward along the gravel path. In the final three days before their departure, the girls were outfitted with grey and white tour uniforms finished with gleaming ivory buttons, tailored by the renowned Palace designer Norman Hartnell. For Violet it may as well have been a silk ballgown.

'Why is my photo worse than yours?' Violet complained as she examined her passport. Her face looked dour and despondent. In contrast, Daisie's photo looked as though it had been lifted from the social pages of *Tatler*, her smile seductive with a hint of malevolence.

'I think he's captured our essence quite well,' Daisie said, admiring the booklet.

On Sunday they were given a full-day briefing on protocol in the east drawing room of Elmbridge End by 'Mr Clumpton from the Palace'. Mr Clumpton was an impatient sort, throttling the Chettles with information, then stamping his foot if they queried any of it.

'I said the left side, dearie, the left!' he shouted as Daisie placed a fork too close to the dessert spoon on a makeshift dining table. His balding head turned as pink as his pockmarked, bulbous nose each time there was a mistake. Mrs Turner watched nervously from the sidelines, keeping her mouth shut should she incur any of his wrath.

'You must concentrate,' he bellowed as Daisie faltered on the range of Commonwealth nomenclatures, with Violet faring only slightly better.

'You're just going too fast!' Daisie countered bravely, as Violet tried to calm her with a hand to the shoulder.

'I have to teach two tearaways who don't know their baronets from their margraves basic propriety within a matter of two days,' he said, stamping his right foot and causing the rehearsal Royal Doulton to rattle.

'Focus, ladies, focus!' Mrs Turner offered unhelpfully.

'Deep breath, Daise,' Violet muttered. 'I'll make pea and ham soup for tea.'

Daisie inhaled and articulated her fingers to expunge the frustration. It reminded Violet of how she would coach Daisie down from anger when they were teased in the schoolyard by Lottie Lewis, who would goad them, knowing Daisie would always be the first to bite.

'Lazy Daisie Chettles, you got nits in your armpits!' she yelled once during a head-lice inspection, trying to rally a laugh from the other girls. Daisie clocked Lottie in the eye socket, and Lottie reacted by landing her knee in Daisie's groin. Violet pulled them apart, suffering some scratches to her arms as the schoolyard chanted and they shredded each other like cats. After all three had been lashed by the vice-principal, they became fast friends, bonded by their own little war story while the real war was ending. Turned out all three had nits.

That evening Violet caught the train to Morden to pick up the suitcases from Lottie Lewis's mother, which Daisie had forgotten.

'Can't believe our suitcases are going on the royal tour!' Lottie's mother squealed as she lined up five suitcases on the front step. They were all heavily dented, and plastered with stickers of nearby holiday destinations. 'What do you think it's going to be like, ey?' she asked. 'You nervous?'

The questions caught Violet off guard. 'It's an honour to serve the Empire,' she said in stock response. But it wasn't until the words were spoken that she realised she meant it.

'Perhaps you'll end up meeting the Queen, ey? That'd be loverly, wouldn't it?'

Violet smiled affirmatively. She spent the trip home trying to scratch the Brighton Pier stickers off the luggage before dragging it along the uneven pavement and into the house.

The day before departure she gave Mrs Bulvers the care-taking instructions; she was agreeable – excited, even. It was her way of being able to tell the neighbourhood she'd 'assisted' Buckingham Palace.

'Oh, I missed Mr Smithson this morning. Can you please cancel the milk delivery?' Violet asked as the bandy-legged woman nosily poked around the kitchen.

'Yes, yes, Daisie,' Mrs Bulvers reassured her. Violet didn't bother correcting her, as Mrs Bulvers was already busy peering through their rear window into the courtyard. 'So, you *can* see my house from here!'

Before she could get Mrs Bulvers out of the house, Violet had to patiently answer her questions. The queries of friends and neighbours had started to show a consistency, most falling into four categories: *Have you met* her *yet? Have you met the Duke yet? Isn't he dashing?* and *Do they speak British in Australia?*

Violet spent the rest of Monday afternoon shopping on Penrhyn Road for clothes. 'Hot and sunny' was the estimate provided for the Australian climate. Unfortunately, in November the high street stores had very little in the way of summer wear.

Violet made certain she was in bed before Bill dropped Daisie home, so she didn't risk having to see him. Despite her warning Daisie had persisted with the relationship. Violet suspected Daisie persisted out of spite for Violet rather than affection for Bill.

She heard a car slow outside and the front door close. The bedroom floor had been taken up by the ugly suitcases. Daisie climbed over them to reach her bed. Within seconds she started murmuring gently in her sleep.

'Daisie?' Violet whispered, but Daisie was already out like a light.

Violet tiptoed into their parents' room. At Violet's insistence it had been left untouched, the stripped mattress with its dark blood spots a reminder of their father's painful end. She slid open the second drawer and took the unsent envelope of photos. Violet licked the flap and resealed it, then slid the envelope into her bag inside the folds of a lime cardigan.

Violet stepped over a suitcase like a crane, trying not to wake Daisie, and crawled gently into bed. She turned the light off and drifted into a light slumber. She dreamt that Queen Elizabeth became her new best friend, that the dashing Prince Philip was conflicted about his strong feelings for each of them, and that she found Aunt Hazel and delivered the letter personally.

10

Newsreel audio
November, 1953

The Royal Tour Begins!
At London airport the giant BOAC Stratocruiser Canopus
is ready for a royal mission to fly Her Majesty the Queen to
the most distant corners of her Commonwealth. The royal
car arrives after a drive through London from the Palace. Arc
lights blaze down on the scene as cameras record this historic
moment. A solemn moment as the Queen walks to the shining
silver and white aircraft that is to take her to Bermuda, the first
stage of her fifty-thousand-mile tour.

Meanwhile, ten thousand miles away, Commonwealth
nations prepare for the arrival of Her Majesty Queen Elizabeth
and the Duke. Excitement mounts and preparations are
underway, as a Queen they have never seen is coming.

Back home, a final wave before Her Majesty returns home in
May. The great aircraft taxis out to the runway. With Canopus
go the wishes of all in Britain.

Good luck and godspeed.

*

Before dawn, Violet heard a car and peered out the window. Bill halted his silver convertible Jaguar with a skid outside the Chettles' cottage on Grove Lane.

'This isn't Sinden,' Violet hissed at Daisie. 'You told me Sinden was coming.'

'I thought this might be more fun.'

The twins emerged from the house into the darkness, shuffling with their heavy suitcases as though they'd just arrived at Ellis Island. Violet locked and double-checked the door, sliding the key under the potted lavender.

It was the first time Violet had seen Bill since the party. He extended his hand with a smile, acting as though nothing had happened.

She found the Jaguar's compact rear seat impractical even before the five suitcases were rammed in on top of her. Daisie slid into the roomy front passenger seat as she tied her hair down with a silk scarf for the drive.

'It's only ninety minutes to Southampton.' Bill glanced in the rear-view mirror. Violet caught his gaze from behind a boxy valise that rested on her lap. His eyes flicked nervously, before she turned away, furious.

Bill revved the engine and accelerated away with a showy rumble. The tyres yelped as the Jaguar overtook a milk truck and skidded onto Surbiton Road. In the back seat each veer and slew pushed the luggage into Violet's body, the manic dishevelling of her hair in the wind the only sign she was even there.

They made good time through Alton and Winchester and approached Southampton Port at five to eight, just as the sun rose over the dark-green tree line of the vast common. The Royal Liner *SS Gothic* crept into view, towering over the adjacent warehouses.

The morning sunlight touched the tips of its vast smokestacks, which leaked steam in anticipation of departure. A string of colourful Commonwealth flags danced between the masts, presiding over a sparkling white hull that glowed in the murky water of the Solent.

Violet, legs numb from the weight of their luggage, spied the ship through a crack between two suitcases. A twinge of nerves trembled in her stomach, a welcome change from the sickness of being in Bill's presence.

A gatehouse attendant directed the car towards a loading apron beside the *Gothic*'s gangway. Two porters in crisp navy jackets bearing gold braid and epaulets circled around the car, opening the doors on either side. 'Palace staff, sir?' one porter asked Bill as another pulled the bags off Violet. Her relief at the dead weight being lifted was surpassed by the exhilaration of hearing the words 'Palace staff'.

'Yes, we're with the Palace,' Daisie replied with a tone of calm entitlement as she was escorted from the vehicle. Violet hobbled behind Daisie and Bill towards the *Gothic*. A third porter stamped their passports and placed their luggage onto a trolley. Their suitcases contrasted with a matching crimson set of Lady Baltimore suitcases like backwoods cousins.

'Welcome, ladies. The steward on deck will show you to your cabins,' said the chief porter sporting a knee-length overcoat with silver trim.

'Excuse me, is there a ladies' room?' Violet asked.

'On board, ma'am, yes, the *Gothic* has many lavatories,' he replied patiently.

'Perhaps you could come visit me in Australia,' Daisie proposed to Bill.

Bill rolled his eyes with disdain. 'There's a reason convicts got shipped down there, you know,' he muttered. 'Harold Penrose did a school year in Victoria, said it was nothing but heat, dirt and isolation. You couldn't drag me. Give me the Côte D'Azur any day.'

Violet saw him recoil slightly as Daisie leaned towards him for a kiss. He then cleared his throat as though to make a speech. 'Daisie, it's been something of a pleasure. However, at this juncture, it would make sense for us to sail our separate seas, as it were,' he said in an oratorial tone, as though reading from palm cards.

Daisie scrunched her nose in confusion and mounted her hands on her hips.

'Therefore, I wish you well,' he persisted, flustered and perhaps a little intimidated by her. 'All the best for your travels and your future existence.'

'Thank goodness,' Violet hissed under her breath. 'Daisie, let's go.'

'Are you trying to break up with me?' Daisie asked pithily, while the porter kept his head down tending to the bags.

'Well, a-actually, umm . . .' Bill stuttered, edging backwards to his car.

'Well, are you?' Daisie insisted, following him.

'Of course not, just saying farewell!' he said in desperation.

'Good.'

He steered his lips towards hers. The passionless kiss endured long enough for everybody to notice, momentarily stealing the attention of a few dock workers who had lingered to admire the Jaguar.

'Watch your footing, ma'am,' a porter warned as he assisted Daisie onto the narrow walkway bridging the dock and the *Gothic*'s bow. Violet stepped onto the rise.

'Palace staff only beyond this point, I'm afraid, sir,' interrupted the porter, as Bill made to follow.

He stopped short. 'So long, Violet,' said Bill. 'All the best to you.'

Violet turned to face him, the uncertainty of her own affection for him heavy in her eyes.

'This is where the *Titanic* cast off, you know,' he quipped, making light of the moment.

'Farewell, William,' she replied quietly, before turning to step onto the narrow gangway. Twenty yards below, the dark water churned menacingly between the *Gothic*'s hull and the dock wall. Her view of the agitating sea water triggered a sense of nausea to go with her tight bladder. Violet raised her chin and took in the salty air, taking long strides across the planks and towards a future of serving the monarchy.

PART 2

PART 2

11

Day 1: Southampton, 70 miles south-west of London
Population: 169,510
Weather: 42 degrees Fahrenheit, considered balmy for the
season
Fact: Between 1807 and 1809 the novelist Jane Austen lived
in Southampton, when it was regarded as the most unsanitary
town in England.

'First day at school, ladies,' said the cheery young steward at the top of the gangway. He wore a short-sleeved white shirt and black and gold epaulettes that sloped earthwards from his slight shoulders. He extended a hand to assist Daisie onto the polished deck. 'I'm Steward Spencer. Joseph.'

'Violet and Daisie Chettle,' Violet announced from behind.

'A fine day for it. Shame the Royal Highnesses are missing out. As you probably know, they're joining us from the Caribbean. Please allow me to show you to your quarters, ladies.'

Violet's face dropped a little at this news. Even the grand *Gothic* seemed a little less impressive without the royals on it. Joseph led the twins across the starboard deck, their matching presence catching sideways glances from the busy deck crew.

He held open a door that led to a carpeted interior hall-way. Finished in polished chrome and lacquered wood that offset a thick crimson carpet, the corridor stretched as far as Violet could see.

'Oh my,' she couldn't help saying aloud as Joseph waved a hand.

'Used to be a cargo liner. Much more resplendent now, I'm sure you'll agree.'

'Lovely!' Violet twittered, breathing the rarefied air deeply as she gawked through every open door.

'I can't believe this!' Violet whispered excitedly into Daisie's ear.

'Don't make a puddle,' Daisie whispered back coolly. 'You're behaving like an excitable school girl on an excursion to Windsor Castle.'

'This is my life now,' Violet said in a hushed tone, ignoring her full bladder.

Joseph ushered them through a majestic club room with huge leather couches and wooden racks stocked to the roof with fine wine and brandy. Picture windows along one wall gave a magnificent view across the deck to the docks beyond. Violet noticed that the napkins had the royal coat of arms embossed in navy blue. She so badly wanted to touch them. 'This way to your accommodation,' Joseph said, heading behind a narrow staircase to a tight cast-iron door. 'Just a short walk.'

He spun the wheel lock and pushed the heavy door open. 'Down we go!' he said. 'Watch your step, bit dark in here.' Daisie reached out to steady herself against the walls as her eyes adjusted to the pitch-black.

They arrived at an iron corridor that stretched off to each side. The walls and floor were unpolished industrial metal, every surface and panel heavily bolted.

'This way, I think,' Joseph said as he turned one way. Then he paused. 'Actually, this way,' he said, striding off to the other. The girls followed dutifully, their heels clunking rhythmically as they traversed the rusty corridor, each step echoing through the hull. Every ten feet or so a bulkhead light cast a dull glow into the dimness.

'Bit tight down here, I'm afraid,' he warned as they descended another dark staircase.

'Coming through!' said a chipper male voice from the darkness ahead.

The girls pressed against the wall to allow a deckhand to squeeze by. The rhythmic clunk and whir of an engine echoed from somewhere nearby.

After two more flights they'd truly passed beyond the realm of natural light, and the still air smelled of dank sulphur. They passed a bank of blinking utility consoles and turned into another inadequately lit passageway. Violet could barely see her own feet.

'Watch the puddle!' Joseph said.

Violet started to breathe faster as though short of air. 'Is there a lavatory?' she asked.

'Yes, there is! Down here somewhere.'

'Oh God, may I—'

'Pace yourself,' Joseph cut in. 'The air down here is really thin,' he said, as though this were a good thing.

'Welcome to the bottom!' he announced, raising his hand in a flourish. 'We call it the "bottom" because it *really is*.'

Daisie propped a hand on her hip, taking a moment to catch her breath as Violet clutched her bladder. 'We must be close to Australia by now, surely?' Daisie asked. 'We'll need a guide to find our way back to daylight.'

'Sorry, I forgot your cabin was in the sub-floor section. Lower than the bottom we go!' he said, and they stepped into a small stairwell lit by a flickering bulb.

The group arrived at a nondescript cast-steel door. 'Home sweet home!' Joseph turned the rusty locking wheel with both hands and prised the door open. The heavy hinges yawned and scraped.

Beyond was a tiny room, about ten feet by twelve feet. It was little more than a steel box with two narrow bunks and some raised stowage. A single alarm clock sat between the beds on a fixed bench.

'This is it? Our accommodation? Our *royal* accommodation?' Daisie exclaimed.

'By order of HM!' Joseph said, oblivious to Daisie's disdain.

Violet pushed past Daisie into the room, still somehow elated to be there despite the large dead cockroach lying on the floor with its legs raised.

'Don't worry, they tend not to last long down here. The rats love them,' Joseph said without a hint of sarcasm.

'It's cosy,' said Violet for the sake of pleasantry.

'Cold, too. Make sure you rug up. We call it the "iron lung". Privy's there.' Joseph pointed towards an identical door opposite theirs. 'Flush twice, unless it's blocked, in which case don't flush at all. Otherwise you might drown.'

'Oh, thank goodness,' said Violet, pushing her way past them to get to the door.

'Wait!' he said, holding up a hand. 'I just remembered – it's blocked. Use the one two floors up.'

Violet winced. Joseph smiled and flicked the light switch to no effect.

'Light's stuck on. Thought they'd fixed that. Anyway, your bags will be delivered shortly. Now, if you'll follow me, I'll continue the tour!'

Daisie sighed. They followed him to the other end of the shadowy corridor, where he paused by a small room that was roughly the size of their cabin. It was equally industrial, housing a small table and six metal chairs. A gaunt laundry maid, no younger than sixty-five, sat at the table holding a cigarette. The exhaled smoke hung thick in the air with nowhere to go.

'Staff stewards' hall. Morning, Edna,' Joseph said to the uninterested woman.

'She looks like she hasn't seen daylight in months,' whispered Violet to Daisie.

'I haven't,' Edna said glumly, hearing every word.

'Nice to meet you. Lovely day,' Violet volunteered.

'Is it?' Edna asked genuinely. Joseph plunged further into the vessel down a side passage, as Edna returned to contemplating nothing.

'Laundry room in there,' he said, pointing at another poorly lit chamber. 'Fastest way to A deck is up here.' He turned up a flight of stairs and led them through another tight corridor where the group dodged a greasy engineer.

After they'd ascended four flights of stairs, the air started to feel as though it was circulating again. The group emerged onto the upper deck short of breath. The bright, clean corridor with its mauve carpet and brass fixtures was no comparison to the world below.

Violet leaned on her knees, trying to resist the pressure on her bladder as her eyes adjusted to the natural light. 'Are there any lavatories on this floor?' she asked.

'Or spare bedrooms?' Daisie added.

'I'm sorry, these rooms are for our guests,' Joseph replied.

'I'm a guest,' Daisie countered.

'You're a maid. These are for the Sovereign executive. This isn't a hotel, I'm afraid, and if it were, you'd still be a maid!' he said with a chuckle.

Joseph stopped at a lacquered wooden door, one of many that lined the grand hallway. 'Let's get this over with. Stand at attention, ladies,' he said tapping twice.

'Enter,' a gruff voice declared. Joseph pushed open the door to reveal a small cabin fashioned into an office. Filing cabinets lined one wall, an upholstered leather couch sat against another and a silver drinks cart was crammed behind a small desk. Cigarette smoke lingered here too, drifting into the corridor as Joseph crossed the threshold. He indicated for the girls to enter.

Behind the desk a stern, greying man in a pinstriped suit scrutinised a newspaper with his flinty glare.

'Major Ratcliffe, I'd like to introduce you to Lady Althorp's housekeepers,' Joseph said.

The man sighed heavily as though the maids were a chore before he'd even sighted them.

'Right. The matching set,' he said, before glancing up to ensure they were indeed matching. He returned his attention to the newspaper. 'Know your place, do your job,' he said as he flicked the page, 'and I won't have any need to speak to you ever again.'

'Yes, Major Ratcliffe,' Joseph responded militarily before ushering them out of the room.

'Th-thank you, sir,' Violet replied to the Major before Joseph pulled the door shut. She started fanning herself like a baroque spinster. 'Sir Michael!' she whispered breathlessly as a red tint filled her face.

'Major Michael Ratcliffe. Her Majesty's private secretary,' corrected Joseph. 'Believe it or not, even Her Majesty has a supervisor.'

'He looks exactly like he does in *Tatler*,' fawned Violet.

Daisie rolled her eyes.

Joseph pressed on, reaching an archway in the corridor that partitioned five doorways from the rest of the floor. Joseph pointed to an invisible line on the carpet. 'The Royal Wing,' he said in a hushed tone. 'Day cabin. Night cabin. But you never pass through this archway unless directed by a higher power.'

Violet nodded attentively, as if she were taking part in a study tour of the British Museum.

'Obvious how much power we have,' Daisie muttered loudly enough for Joseph to hear. 'We're literally at the bottom.'

'Daisie! Quiet!' Violet hissed. 'Joseph, is there a—'

But Joseph was already leading them away from the Royal Wing towards another doorway at the far end of the corridor. 'Last stop of the tour,' he said, tapping twice.

'Who is it?' a female voice responded from inside.

Joseph swung the door open. Lady Althorp's suite featured a double bed made up with cream-and-navy patterned linen and an upholstered armchair couch. On a silver tray by the bedside rested Lady Althorp's usual water jug laced with snipped parsley. A book entitled *The Village* rested on the narrow night table, brushed by a chiffon curtain that lifted inwards with the breeze flowing through the porthole window. The gulls of Southampton could be heard cheering outside.

'The Chettles have arrived, ma'am,' Joseph announced, gesturing at the twins. He bowed his head slightly, then left the room.

Lady Althorp looked up from her desk. 'You made it,' she said. 'Welcome aboard the *Gothic*.'

'Thank you, Lady Althorp,' they replied in unison.

'Your accommodation? Is it acceptable?'

'Well, actually, Lady Althorp, it's—'

'Yes, ma'am, perfectly acceptable,' Violet hastily replied, cutting off her sister.

'Right. My daily routine remains the same: seven o'clock cup of tea, medium-strength, thoroughly strained. It's best you make it yourself as they tend to underdo everything on board. My wardrobe is in the hold somewhere. I'll need you to fetch outfits from the dresser, clean this suite, change linen, take meal and drink orders to the galley and ensure they get them here. The water jug must stay full at all times. Plus dusting, running messages, liaison with the crew, lodging messages with radio control and generally assisting as required. That's the easy part. Their Royal Highnesses board in Jamaica, then once we dock in Australia the real work begins. You'll come to despise the sight of bouquets soon enough. I'm hoping you don't suffer hay fever or have an aversion to bee stings – a little known risk of the profession. You'll need some time to orientate yourself, understand the boat layout and get your sea legs, so to speak. Try to avoid associating too much with the crew – it's not a good look. Hopefully the seasickness doesn't get to you. Though you survived the immunisations, so you're halfway there. Any questions?'

'No, Lady Althorp.'

'Lady Caroline is fine.' She smiled to defy the awkwardness of the moment.

Violet followed Daisie's eyes as they wandered around the room. Two unpacked crates were stacked by the bed. A dozen long-playing records lay on a turntable; the album on top was *Dean Martin Sings*.

'I better get on with these,' Lady Caroline said, referring to the pile of folders on her desk. 'A letter for every occasion. There's less waiting in this role than the title suggests, unfortunately.

It's mostly fan mail and dressing up. Speaking of which, have you met Bobo yet?'

'Bobo?'

'Mrs Margaret MacDonald, the dresser? You can't miss her, she's all mouth. Practically raised Elizabeth. As a rule, if Bobo is upset, *she*'s upset.' Lady Caroline's attention returned to her desk and the mountain of papers. 'That will be all for now, ladies.'

Violet turned to leave.

'You like Dino, Lady Caroline?' Daisie asked.

'You've heard of him?'

'Our father used to play that record at two in the morning. Drunk. Dad, that is. Was.'

Lady Caroline smiled gently. Violet loitered at the door, quietly devastated, willing Daisie to shut up so she could go to the toilet.

'Though "Just One More Chance" is best listened to after midnight,' added Daisie.

'That it is,' Lady Caroline conceded, her eyebrows raised in pleasant surprise. With nowhere else to take the conversation, she turned back to her work.

In the corridor outside, Violet said, 'You can't talk about alcoholism in front of nobility. Her personal life is none of your business.' She winced as she wrapped her knees together.

'I think she likes me. Maybe I'll make it my business.' Daisie smiled.

Violet gasped as Daisie glanced impatiently in both directions. Joseph was nowhere to be seen. 'Which way back to the cabin?' asked Violet.

'*Down*,' Daisie sighed.

Violet spied a door marked 'WC' further along the corridor. She ran over, bumping into a tall crewman in a white navy suit as he exited.

'Pardon, hull breaching,' she exclaimed through clenched teeth, barely making it in time before groaning in satisfaction, louder than intended.

It was almost midnight when the *Gothic* finally swayed away from the dock, the pull against the tide gently rocking the untethered vessel. The *Gothic*'s horn boomed like cannon fire. The sound echoed throughout the ship, even to the lower-most decks.

The throb and grind of the ship's propulsion system whirred up. Unfortunately for the Chettle sisters, the source of the relentless noise seemed to be only a few feet from the iron lung. Daisie and Violet lay awake in their nightgowns on mattresses barely three blanket layers thick. Daisie had flicked the switch over one hundred times but the bulkhead lamp remained on. Violet was restless, and a growling sensation in her stomach didn't help.

'It's freezing,' Daisie complained.

'I'm boiling hot. I'm not feeling well . . . I hope I'm not seasick!' moaned Violet.

'You can't be yet – we're barely at sea! I can't sleep with that thing on,' Daisie complained from under a flimsy pillow. 'I feel like I'm being interrogated. Or incarcerated.'

'Maybe it switches off at a certain time?'

'Yes, once we've confessed!'

Violet resorted to tying a scarf over her eyes. Around one in the morning, just as she had started drifting off, a scratching sound came from somewhere inside the room. She sat up anxiously and pulled off the blindfold. 'Is that a rat?'

The scratching sound continued. Violet nervously peeked under the bunk.

'It's either a large cockroach or a small rat,' Daisie said as she pulled the pillow over her head.

Violet wrapped herself in the blanket, covering her eyes and ears as she suffered a percolating stomach. 'I don't know how I'm going to last two months down here,' she said weakly.

12

Day 4: *North Atlantic Ocean, 42°25´19.3″N 34°56´56.0″W*
Population: *0 (excluding transient vessels)*
Weather: *51 degrees Fahrenheit, light winds, cloudless skies*
Fact: *The Atlantic Ocean has a volume of 74,471,500 cubic miles, which equates to 1,309,933,998,467,992,489,578 cups of tea.*

By day four the *Gothic* had reached the halfway point of the vast North Atlantic Ocean, rarely sighting other signs of life during its gradual progress over the endless roiling deep. Daisie knew Violet's queasiness had subsided due to the decrease in her complaints.

Daisie had settled into a regular routine, more or less. It started at six in the morning and ran until around eight-thirty in the evening. Their assigned tasks barely occupied a single maid, so a truce was made to split her shift with Violet.

Lady Caroline spent most of her time reading in her suite. She made few demands, treating Daisie and her sister with respect and patience. Unlike most, she had also mastered the ability to discern which twin was which – a courtesy few others took the time to bother with. It was a most refreshing change from Mrs Turner.

Daisie enjoyed her time near Lady Caroline. Her warm, refined manner was seductive. Daisie would blush in her presence. Lady Caroline seemed to notice this, flattered perhaps, which made Daisie's small crush grow.

Occasionally Lady Caroline wandered to the rear deck to contemplate the ocean in the daytime sun. After a couple of weeks, Daisie took to waiting in a small nook on the outside rear aft deck, in a gap between the main lifeboat and the starboard railing, where she could inhale the fresh ocean breeze and a cigarette.

'The view doesn't change, yet for some reason I never tire of it,' interrupted a cultured female voice. Lady Caroline had found Daisie, appearing at the rail beside her. 'I hide here too,' she said as she gazed at the horizon. 'It's quite a different proposition, seeing the ocean *from* the ocean.'

'Up until now I've only seen it from Blackpool pier.'

Lady Caroline laughed out loud, causing Daisie to smile and easing the awkwardness. 'Mind if have one?' She raised her eyebrows towards Daisie's cigarette.

Cigarettes were hard to come by on the boat. The supplies steward who controlled the stock had grudgingly sold Daisie this one packet after she'd sufficiently charmed him. She paused before reluctantly offering the packet to Lady Caroline.

'Do you have a light?'

Daisie dug in her left pocket and offered a matchbox.

Lady Caroline's delicate hands fumbled with the matches, the flame refusing to spark in the breeze. 'I need my brass lighter,' she said out of the corner of her mouth as her lips clasped the cigarette. 'Works in a hurricane. I've tried.'

Daisie cupped her hands around Lady Caroline's to shield the match from the wind. Lady Caroline blushed the moment she felt the confident touch of Daisie's hands. As the tip of the cigarette lit, small puffs of smoke trailed into the wind. Daisie dropped her hands back to the rail, but Lady Caroline's held for a moment, as though still relishing the spark of contact.

'You're my saviour,' Lady Caroline said as she dropped the match over the side. They both watched it spin and fall until it disappeared into the rolling swell above the unseen propellers. 'So this must be a welcome change to hiding from Mrs Turner. I assume it's your first time to Australia?'

'Perhaps I've been many times,' Daisie said cheekily.

'Perhaps you have. Though you holiday in Blackpool, so I tend to think perhaps not.'

Daisie observed the smear of Lady Caroline's lipstick left behind on her cigarette. Lady Caroline seemed to sense her maid's eyes evaluating her. She glanced sideways to catch her stare.

'I have an auntie in Australia,' Daisie said.

'Yes, we all have one of those, I suspect. The one we don't talk about. Are you visiting her?'

'It's a long story. My mother passed before she'd decided to mention her.'

'Family's like that, isn't it? Even this one,' Lady Caroline said after a pause, nodding towards a British flag that flailed in the wind. 'She's lost a parent too. Like us.'

'I've decided it's easier not to remember. Anyway, I'm sure she's struggling enormously.' Daisie's remark, intended to be flippant, bore a greater callousness than she'd meant.

Lady Caroline pressed her lips together momentarily, but she inhaled and changed course.

'And your auntie? Are you close?'

'No. And it's still a long story.'

'My auntie told me everything about my parents. Usually after two of Uncle Harold's spritzers. I barely thought they were human until she told me what they used to get up to. Funny thing is, the worse the things she told me, the less I hated them. Then again, if I ever have children – Lord help me – I'd probably pretend I was something I wasn't too, lest they turn out like this. In which case, Lord help them.' Lady Caroline went to say something then stopped herself. 'Perhaps,' she concluded, 'the best we can do for our children is to limit the number of them.'

'She's my mother's twin sister,' Daisie confessed.

'She would know answers to questions you probably don't want to ask. I imagine it would be surreal to meet her. Like some type of reincarnation.'

Daisie didn't blink. Her eyes shifted out of focus, mesmerised by the notion.

Lady Caroline flicked her spent cigarette into the churning froth below. 'I'm showing too many cards. And you should get back to work, before your superior thinks you're hiding somewhere and smoking.'

Daisie blinked out of her reverie and straightened herself to leave. 'I hear she's horrible,' she deadpanned with a smirk.

'A razor blade, the gossips say. I cut both ways,' Lady Caroline replied, playing along. Daisie held her breath for a moment as the words sunk in. Lady Caroline put her hands on her waist, turning her gaze back to the sea, unfazed by the effect her words had had on Daisie.

'When we arrive in Kingston Harbour,' Caroline said, her voice back to business. Daisie lifted her head. 'I'll need Bobo to pull the blue Dior dress from storage. And one of you will need to fetch the tiara from the safe. Must scrub up for you-know-who.'

'Of course, Lady Caroline,' Daisie replied demurely as the wind dashed her hair. She crossed the deck out of Lady Caroline's sight, the encounter's strange electricity still coursing through her veins, the confusion of it rising at the possibility of betraying Bill.

13

Day 18: North Atlantic Ocean, 40°50′33.4″N 45°32′10.1″W
Population: 1,435,233,890 (including fish)
Weather: 52.5 degrees Fahrenheit, light chop
Fact: Unbeknownst to those on board the SS Gothic, *the wreck of the* Titanic *is only a couple of hundred miles north-west of this position.*

Violet's soft knuckles barely produced a sound on the heavy iron door.

On the third level below the waterline, port side, behind the engineer's station and near the flickering corridor light, was the door to Bobo's workshop. It was a windowless, featureless room filled with a head-spinning array of glamorous formal clothing, swathes of rich silk chiffon, velvet and satin. In addition to the rows of designer garments, the messy room was crowded with two ironing tables, three sewing machines and spools of thread, a steamer and four mannequin torsos, the last secured to the ceiling by ropes to prevent them tipping during rough seas.

'Mrs MacDonald?' Violet gently enquired.

'The Queen calls me Bobo, so ye'll as well – whoever ye are,' a booming voice announced from behind a rack of formal suits.

'Violet,' she replied. 'Violet Chettle, Lady Althorp's maid.'

'Oh, you two. Which one are ye? Oh, it doesn't matter – what does she want *now*?' Out of the shadows and into the glare of an overhead bulb stepped Margaret 'Bobo' MacDonald. Approximately fifty years of age with a flushed face marked by stress lines, she boasted generous hips and an unforgiving Scottish accent.

'She's requested the blue Dior dress. And the tiara.'

Mrs MacDonald exhaled at length before disappearing behind another rack, shuffling between hanging outfits that danced back and forth on their rail as she handled them. 'Aye, she's the Queen of England, is she? Takes precedence over the Crown? Everybody's through that door demanding something but I answer to a wee higher power, missy. Perhaps your lady-in-waiting can awa and do just that – wait.'

'My sincere apologies, Mrs MacDonald.'

Bobo creased her forehead, weighing up the sincerity of Violet's apology. With a grunt she crouched over a small safe under a sewing table, glancing suspiciously at Violet as she administered the code. 'Next time will ye come between ten and eleven, or yer lady will have to wear the clothes on her back, do ye hear me, lassie?'

'Yes, Mrs MacDonald.'

'Bobo!'

'Yes, Bobo,' Violet replied quietly, crossing her hands across her apron and staring at the iron floor.

The royal dresser slammed the door of the safe shut, spun the combination dial then heaved herself upright one leg at a time. Violet glanced up. Clutched in Bobo's meaty hand was a small mauve velvet pouch. With the other hand she unhooked a wrapped silk gown and laid both on an ironing trestle. 'Worth one hundred thousand pounds, that trinket. Not yer average party hat. Lose it and you'll be paying for it for the rest of your life, or longer!'

Violet hesitated, uncertain how one handled a piece of jewellery worth as much as an estate in Surrey.

'What are ye waiting for? A royal decree? Awa or I'll tell Lilibet yer a waste a time and space.'

Violet took the garment hanger with one hand and delicately collected the pouch.

'I want them returned immediately after use.' Bobo's voice echoed as Violet backed out slowly through the doorway, holding the pouch in her upturned hand like she was balancing a house of cards. 'For each pulled thread I pull one of yer wee fingernails. Be the closest to a manicure they've seen yet, I reckon.'

Violet dodged a sweaty engineer, his eyes white and blinking in the darkness. She dodged and danced to ensure the wrapped dress didn't touch the leaky walls. On level four the brittle shape of the tiara under velvet started to get the better of Violet. She paused momentarily under a lone bulb to stare at the pouch, her finger stroking its soft fabric. She glanced over her shoulder before pulling the latch on the WC. A light flickered to life as she hung the dress on the coat hook and, with both hands, gently placed the pouch on the heavily stained sink.

Violet took a deep breath and slowly unfolded the velvet pocket. Her heart rose in her chest. The tiara dazzled, illuminating the dingy locker-sized room with a star field that was not unlike the Long Ditton reproduction hall mirror ball back home. It was studded with a thick collection of diamonds, pearl highlights and an intense emerald the size of a fingernail at the tip, its magnificence matched only by the brilliant glow in her eyes.

Violet was hypnotised, turning the exquisite object over in her trembling fingers. 'Dare I?' she whispered to herself. She gulped. The delicate tiara was worth more than her life, but the allure of seeing herself as royalty was irresistible. Again, a voice inside urged her to experience what Daisie would choose to do.

She raised it as though her hands were those of the Archbishop of Canterbury, reverently watching herself in the small mirror as the tiara slowly descended, her coronation imminent.

'Anyone in the shitter?' a Glaswegian accent boomed. A fist thumped sharply against the door.

Violet, startled, fumbled the tiara. In a slow nightmare the crown bounced off the sink towards the floor. Her right hand instinctively lunged to snatch it from thin air, but her clumsy swipe batted it with an even greater velocity to the ground. It landed with a sickening high-pitched scrape, tumbling out of sight somewhere behind the toilet plumbing. A second small object rattled around the tiles, the sound pinging like a silver dragee on a tile kitchen floor.

Violet froze in panic. Slowly she crouched, her breathing starting again as she lowered herself to the floor.

'I've got to go, matey,' the voice outside boomed with urgency.

'Cross your knees!' Violet pleaded, her voice cracking with fear. She squinted into the shadows and padded her fingers on the dank floor, trying to locate the tiara by touch.

There! She lightly prodded the brittle thing in the dark, grasping it carefully before standing. As the tiara rose into the light, an empty circular saddle stared back like a curse. The emerald stone at its point was gone.

'Oh heck, Lord and saviour,' cursed Violet. She crouched again, fumbling desperately for the lost jewel. Among the grit and damp, behind the toilet brush, her right hand located a small rock. Pinching it firmly between her forefingers and thumbs, she brought it close to her eye under the dim light.

It was the emerald, duller without the adornment to showcase its grandeur.

'Phooey bugger bloody damn sod it,' she hissed between heightening breaths, and pushed the stone into the tiara. *Ping!* It fell to the ground again, rattling dangerously against the bars of a grate. Violet hissed, clenching her teeth as she hovered her fingers like pincers above the tiny stone. Slowly, nervously, she picked it up with a shaky hand.

A discarded wad of chewing gum had been pushed against the left underside corner of the mirror. Violet bit her lower lip in disgust and peeled a wedge of the sticky residue away from the wall. She jammed it into the tiara socket and forced the emerald into place with her thumb and forefinger. The disgusting adhesive worked, and the rock held in place, albeit at a slightly irregular angle.

'Curry night!'

The door shook again as the man outside beat it impatiently. Violet swallowed her nerves, wrapped the precious object back in the pouch, unhooked the gown and unlatched the door.

'About time.' The clammy engineer, leaning against the doorframe, scowled at her.

Violet didn't reply. She walked away from the scene of the crime with all the grace she could muster, which wasn't a great deal, and nervously deposited the outfit and the tiara in Lady Caroline's cabin. Then she scampered away as fast as she could.

14

Day 18: *Port Royal, Jamaica*
Population: *1,496,629*
Weather: *77 degrees Fahrenheit, incidental clouds*
Fact: *Port Royal, probably the most uninteresting region of Jamaica, is beset by natural disasters.*

Violet's nausea had returned. The damaged tiara had made her sick with worry, but seasickness, bought on by the ebb of the *Gothic*, was worse. When the ship stilled in Jamaica's Port Royal her queasiness eased, replaced again by the tiara guilt alone.

From the deck, Jamaica appeared to be little more than a thin archipelago. The rectangular port was stamped out of a green bluff and dotted with brilliant red poinciana trees.

'You cover for me while I go ashore,' Daisie said as they gazed over the railings.

'And risk *my* reputation? No.'

Teased by the warm breeze, the twins took in as much as they could from the vantage point of the deck. Off the starboard side stood the British Royal Navy administration offices, a Spanish-influenced two-storey barracks built of hardship and stone, one of the few structures that had withstood the earthquake of 1692, the fires of 1703, flooding in 1722, another fire in 1750, a major hurricane in 1784, an 1815 fire, then another earthquake in 1907. To add to that, Errol Flynn arrived in 1934 to film *Captain Blood*. Despite the mistreatment, a single tower poked above the trees, whose branches rustled and swayed as the squawks of seagulls punctuated the onshore breeze.

On the dock landing below, Violet spotted the odd uniformed naval officer among the muscular ship workers. A couple of the *Gothic*'s laundry girls pressed against the lower deck railing were gamely waving and tittering, shrieking every time their attention was reciprocated.

The imminent boarding of the Queen and Duke meant the tour was beginning in earnest. After more than two weeks at sea the *Gothic* crew had a renewed spring in their step as they prepared the ship for the final leg to Fiji, Tonga, New Zealand and then Australia. On the final day in Jamaica a written notice was posted to all cabins advising that Her Majesty and Prince Philip would be performing a staff inspection on the main deck at 4 p.m. All personnel were required to attend in full livery.

Violet fussed over her uniform for hours, using the laundry room press to ensure her blouse was as wrinkle-free as the tablecloths. She put particular effort into her hair. 'First impressions'—Violet repeated like a mantra as Daisie lay on the bed—'make a royal impression.'

At three forty-five they made their way up to the deck, joining the other staff. Major Ratcliffe ordered a formation in ten rows of eight, with high-ranking staff at the fore. Violet was taken aback to see Daisie standing in the first row.

Under the hot afternoon sun Violet waited, staring silently out at the harbour to pass the time. The occasional curious seagull landed on the railing, hopping along it to peer at the unusual gathering.

A whistle pierced the air.

Ratcliffe appeared first, his eyes flicking like a skittish body-guard's. Then the Queen and Duke emerged, walking side by side three steps behind him with an effortless confidence. Their sudden casual presence, devoid of fanfare, sucked the air out of Violet's lungs. She was *in the presence of royalty*.

Violet had never seen a royal person in the flesh. The only person of note Violet had encountered was the actor Terry-Thomas, who'd sat across the aisle from her one day on the 214 bus to Chertsey. She'd stared in unbridled fascination until he moved upstairs.

The Queen wore a blue pleated dress, a single string of pearls and a pillbox hat that hugged her perfectly styled hair. A small handbag hung over her forearm. Her complexion was flawless, and paler than the impression Violet had gained from paintings and newsreels. Philip, tall and dashing with a cheeky grin that seemed eager to jest, was radiant in full white naval regalia.

The Queen was businesslike, silently taking in each passing individual but rarely chatting. The Duke, on the other hand, seemed at ease, pausing here and there to converse with crew of all stripes.

The Queen slowed near Daisie and the air rushed back into Violet's lungs. Her nausea returned. Her Majesty spoke to Daisie, asking her a question and then thanking her with a gracious but subtle smile. Violet's mind muddled while her skin flushed red with jealousy. Then the nauseous sensation in the pit of her stomach came alive. In her peripheral vision Violet could see the Queen getting closer. She continued to inspect the serried troops with Lady Caroline and Ratcliffe, while the Duke dawdled behind. But the nausea inside Violet was sentient now. She convulsed to swallow some determined indigestion.

Lady Caroline clocked Violet with a look of recognition and

gave a subtle nod. Then the Queen passed by. She began to chat to a chef two places further along the line.

Violet gulped noisily on an urgent hiccup. The Queen glanced towards the sound. Violet clasped her eyes shut, willing her body to obey.

And then vomit rushed out of Violet's mouth. She clutched her hand over her mouth but the vomit sprayed through her fingers like a bursting dam.

Her Majesty froze.

'Oh my goodness,' she heard Ratcliffe exclaim.

Violet took a cautious step backwards, before the dam wall broke entirely and vomit splashed onto the deck. The spatter struck the Queen's cerulean silk shoes.

Violet aimed her mouth away from Her Majesty as another stream of putrid bile rushed forth, escaping with vengeance from the rotten pit of her stomach. The smell hung in the air as the russet fluid dripped off Violet's clothes and the uniforms of those standing in front. Lady Caroline rushed forward, stepping around the puddles, to put herself between Her Majesty and the mess, as those nearby gasped and recoiled in revulsion.

The Queen, porcelain perfection with an elegant veneer of makeup, stared at Violet as though she were an assassin. A small speck of brownish food, carrot perhaps, rested on Elizabeth's left cheekbone, spoiling her otherwise unblemished regal visage.

Daisie gasped as though verging on laughter.

Violet's urge was to run as far away as possible from the nightmare. But she stayed as the Queen was quickly escorted away by the Duke and Ratcliffe. Those left behind stared dumbfounded.

'You need to sit down, drink some water,' said Lady Caroline's reassuring voice. 'Take your sister downstairs,' she urged Daisie.

The rest was a blur as Daisie lead her delirious sister to the cabin. The image of her bile splashing off the Queen's perfect shoes replayed over and over in Violet's mind, the mix of horror and disdain writ large on her face.

'That was fabulous,' said Daisie, smiling as she wrenched open the door of the iron lung.

'I'm finished.'

'Not yet,' said Steward Joseph grimly as he arrived in the doorway. 'Clean yourself up and report to Major Ratcliffe's cabin immediately.'

As the *Gothic*'s horn boomed and the vessel steamed out of the harbour towards the open sea, Daisie helped Violet clean herself and change into a fresh uniform.

'I'm so stupid, I don't know what came over me.'

'I know what came over the Queen. Your breakfast,' replied Daisie.

But Violet was in no mood. She turned to the door for the walk to the top deck for her execution, carrying a mop bucket should the sickness return, and sobbing quietly to herself.

'Do you realise this was an assault on a head of state and I could have you charged and jailed? Lock you up below deck?' Ratcliffe raged, his face flushed the colour of merlot. 'I'd like to lock you as deep in the hold as possible. Though the lock-up is probably more luxurious than your current quarters.'

'I'm so deeply sorry, sir, it won't happen again—' begged Violet.

'Shut *up*,' he yelled, causing her to jump. 'Won't happen again? How does something like this happen even *once*?' He fumbled a cigarette from the packet, his fingers clumsy with rage.

'My deepest apologies to Her Majesty,' she offered as a final admission, her lip quivering as she held back her tears. 'I've been seasick since we left home.'

'You are to be confined to your cabin until we reach Sydney or – at best – New Zealand. We'll decide what to do with you when we get there. You're just lucky that finding replacement staff on the other side of the world is a right pain in the neck.'

'Thank you, Major Ratcliffe. Sir.'

'Don't thank me. She's your problem now,' he instructed Lady Caroline, who'd been standing at the door. 'Either of them cock it up and they'll be the first to be banished *from* the colonies.'

'I'm sorry, Michael,' Lady Caroline replied. 'How is *she*?'

'Indefatigable. As always. Needless to say, that was *not* the welcome party we'd planned.'

Violet felt a surging nausea again, the sickness returning with a vengeance as the *Gothic* ploughed through a thick swell. She raised her finger in an effort to get his attention.

'I don't care what you have to say,' he barked.

Violet grimaced and flexed her finger again. 'Sir, I—'

'Shut. Up.'

Violet seized the tin bucket and vomited.

Ratcliffe's face spoiled as though he'd been forced to drink sour milk. 'Go to your cabin. Get out of my sight and stay there. Now!'

Violet rushed through the door, scuttling towards the stairwell with the bucket clutched to her chest.

'Violet,' Lady Caroline called from behind. Violet stopped and turned back to her, wiping some coloured drool from her chin.

'Yes, Lady Althorp?' Her voice lightly echoed in the bucket.

Lady Caroline didn't seem to know quite what to say. She managed a half-smile, cast her eyes downwards and turned towards her suite, leaving Violet to her descent.

'No mail,' Daisie announced as Violet slumped onto her bed and squeezed her eyes tightly shut. She'd ruined her big opportunity when it had barely begun. For the first time she felt homesick. Though with her parents gone she wasn't certain what home meant any more. Violet cried herself to sleep.

In the morning the pillow was heavy and damp. Daisie had to take Violet's shift for the remainder of the voyage while Violet remained in the cabin, hiding from the world outside the iron lung. Her eyes grew conditioned to the dim light and her lungs gradually acclimatised to the thin air.

Then her regular cycle was late. A week passed and it still refused to visit. As the days went by, its absence was maintained and a strange new flavour of dread crept into her daily routine. By the second week the possible became likely. By the third, the likely became a certainty.

The seasickness and the sudden nausea she'd felt when she met the Queen now made sense. And she had only slept with one man in her entire life. The royal vomiting incident on board the *Gothic* became a secondary concern. Violet figured she had two months – maybe only six weeks – before any whispers of gossip would become irrefutable.

15

Day 86: *Sydney Harbour, New South Wales, Australia*
Population: 1,886,417
Weather: *84 degrees Fahrenheit, mild to rather warm*
Fact: *Known to the original Indigenous inhabitants, the Cadigal,
as Woccanmagully, Farm Cove was used as an initiation ground
where boys were 'made men' by having their upper right tooth
knocked out, giving them the right to kill kangaroos.*

Daisie peered through Lady Caroline's porthole window as
the *Gothic* slowed through a collar of bushy headlands under a
cloudless azure sky. A sailor's greeting of ships' horns and water
cannons heralded their arrival, filling the blustery warm air with
festive noise. A varied flotilla of sea craft, all bearing the Union
Jack, waited at the mouth of Sydney Harbour to escort the ship to
its final destination.

As the *Gothic* sailed proudly, a green and yellow ferry churned
through the turbulent water alongside it. Its bow proclaimed *South
Steyne Sydney*. It was loaded to the gills with so many rubber-
necking passengers that it tilted perilously to its starboard side.

The ferry's wake nudged a tiny rowboat into the churning sluice
between the vessels. Its occupants, a well-dressed man and his

terrified wife out to see the Queen, frantically paddled with the oars to avoid being subsumed by either vessel.

Commemorative cannons boomed from the adjacent shore as Daisie slid white elbow-length gloves over Lady Caroline's slender forearms. For the first official engagement, the landing and a welcome by the Governor-General and the Prime Minister, Bobo had chosen for her a subtle blue short-sleeved silk dress with a bust ruffle, a matching hat with a veil, cream Vivier shoes with stiletto heels, and a double string of pearls that sat perfectly around the gentle undulation in Lady Caroline's neck.

'Fifteen minutes,' Joseph instructed urgently through the door of Lady Caroline's suite before rushing to the next.

'Pour a shot of gin, would you, Daisie? Make it two.' Lady Caroline applied the finishing touches to her makeup with a blush brush.

Daisie lifted a bottle of Bosford Dry from the liquor trolley and poured two measures. Lady Caroline took one glass in her gloved hand as Daisie lifted the other.

'This bloody boat,' they said in practised unison. Lady Caroline tipped the clear liquid down her throat, wincing at its bitter after-taste. Daisie followed, barely flinching.

'Tell your sister she's cleared to return to duty. Poor thing has spent enough time below, regardless of what Ratcliffe says.'

'Chunder Loo won't know herself. I fear the sun might burn her skin like a vampire's.'

Violet's heaving antics had earned her the nickname of 'Chunder Loo', a moniker the Australian-born navigator said was a colloquial-ism in his country. Unfortunately for the oblivious Violet, it had stuck.

Lady Caroline slid a white Hermès handbag onto her gloved forearm and turned her hips to see her reflection in the mirror behind the cabin door. 'God, I look like my bloody mother,' she said, fidgeting with her belt.

Daisie met her eyes in the mirror's reflection and chuckled softly at the absurdity of Lady Caroline's remark. Despite her comment, Lady Caroline glowed with sophistication and elegance.

'Twenty-five per cent, Meg used to say.' Lady Caroline swiftly changed the subject. 'Be twenty-five per cent less glamorous, regal, impressive – whatever the mode – than Her Majesty. Any less than that and you risk a lashing from both press and private secretary.'

Daisie raised her eyebrows, struggling to imagine how anybody would believe she looked anything less than perfect.

Lady Caroline brushed a piece of thread from her skirt and nodded at her reflection. 'Right. Call the steward. You can walk me to the club room. Then you'd better fetch your sister, before we need to drive a stake through her heart.'

Daisie pushed a button near the door. The steward arrived a minute later to lead them towards the club deck. Walking behind, Daisie saw the hem of Lady Caroline's dress dancing along the carpet with a swishing sound, its sheer brocade hugging her legs like liquid.

They entered the upper deck club room where a dozen crew in full regalia stood to attention along the walls including Major Ratcliffe and Private Secretary Commander Jock Carville. A chorus of ship's horns, aircraft engines and the occasional enraptured cheer spilled in through the windows. Canapés and sparkling water were offered by a waiter, who instinctively ducked as the sound of jet craft exploded overhead.

'Vampire flyover,' Ratcliffe said to nobody in particular as he plucked a smoked salmon mousse off the tray. 'Six, by my estimation.'

The *Gothic* tilted sideways with a dramatic yaw. Everybody steadied themselves as the crystal glasses behind the bar clinked.

Daisie braced herself against the wall with a hand as the *Gothic* righted itself.

'They're letting too many civilian craft near the damn hull,' Ratcliffe complained. 'It's too choppy. Tell command there's no embarkation until the traffic is cleared,' he ordered an equerry, who nodded and marched urgently out of the room. 'There were men on surfboards three miles offshore, for goodness sake.'

The room hushed again. Queen Elizabeth and Prince Philip had made their entrance. The Queen glowed in an elegant cream organza dress that was perfectly twenty-five per cent more attention-getting than Lady Caroline's outfit.

Ratcliffe hovered, briefing the Queen and Duke on the landing details. The Queen, used to such routine, listened with no hint of anxiety while reviewing her speech notes.

Daisie couldn't help but stare at Prince Philip. He towered, exuding a relaxed confidence despite the rigid cut of his uniform. She barely blinked, his presence was so profoundly hypnotic. Once during the Atlantic voyage Daisie had glimpsed him playing deck hockey in his shorts. She had remained, unseen behind the dorade box, watching for as long as he played.

'Try not to salivate,' Lady Caroline remarked under her breath, her words tinged with sarcasm. 'I'm starving,' she said louder, changing the subject to the tray of canapés.

'So eat,' Daisie replied.

'White gloves. Can't be risked,' she sighed.

Daisie lifted a salmon canapé from a passing tray. She held it out for Lady Caroline between thumb and forefinger, poised like a zoo-keeper feeding a seal. Lady Caroline blanched, aware of the eyes of those around her. Then she smirked, enlivened by the subtle impropriety of it, and took the food on her tongue.

'Quick, another one.'

Daisie placed a second morsel into Lady Caroline's mouth, careful not to smear her lipstick. She chewed quickly, swallowed and walked over to engage the Duke.

The ship's momentum slowed. An equerry returned to the room and whispered over Ratcliffe's shoulder.

'The Governor-General, the Prime Minister and the reception party have boarded,' announced Ratcliffe. 'Your Majesty?'

The Queen, the Duke, Lady Caroline and the rest of the official contingent made their way into the hallway in single file. Lady Caroline turned to Daisie and raised her eyebrows. 'See you on the other side.'

16

The *Gothic*'s propulsion engine decelerated suddenly, the grinding wind-down of the engines loud enough to wake Violet from a deep sleep. She rubbed her eyes and sat up. They must have reached Australia at last.

Violet had spent two months exiled in the iron lung, missing stops in Fiji, Tonga and New Zealand entirely. At one point she thought that perhaps they'd forgotten about her altogether. But it was a lesser shame than what had transpired, and one in which she could hide. The bottom deck's labyrinthine maze was the perfect habitat for her misery to ferment. Like a hermit crab she emerged for meals and bathroom visits, scuttling back before eyes found her. By the time the *Gothic* had sailed into Sydney her skin was pallid and her hair was stringy, lending her the appearance of a subterranean Tolkien creation.

'Get dressed, Dracula, you're officially back on duty,' declared Daisie through the gap in the iron door. 'Time for metamorphosis.'

Violet smoothed her shaggy hair. She tried to imagine herself as a butterfly, but with the weight she'd gained she felt stuck at pupal stage. Slowly she ascended the stairs behind Daisie, dressed for duty.

'What's that sound?' Violet asked as they stepped into the top deck hall. She squinted at the brilliant sunlight.

'Australians. A million of them.'

Violet stepped onto the main deck behind Daisie. Staff lined the railings to watch the unfolding spectacle. She shielded her eyes from the vivid glare of the sun, and her mouth dropped.

Thick crowds lined every vantage point of a harbour whose waterline roamed and wandered into seemingly endless inlets and coves. In every open window and bunched along every foreshore a million tiny dots – Australians – cheered and waved wildly as bunting cascaded like sheets of rain.

'It's Tyne Bridge!' Violet exclaimed, pointing out the curved arch bridge that straddled the waterway as though it were levitating off the exhilaration. 'They copied it!'

The water's rippled surface glistened. It teemed with motorboats, speedboats, surfboats, sailing boats, ferries, board riders and waterskiers skirting the *Gothic*, which stood majestically in the main middle harbour.

Violet felt like she had arrived at the centre of the world rather than on the other side of it. She leaned over the railing where the royal barge ferried the Queen and Duke through the multitude of vessels forming a welcome corridor across the water. At least fifty boats were positioned in the guard of honour, the transport ferrying down the middle with a small police boat trailing behind.

About five hundred feet away on a floating platform, a dais emblazoned with the royal crest waited under the hot sun with ministers, prime and sub-prime, for the Queen's step onto Australian soil.

'The speech! The radio room will have the broadcast,' Violet exclaimed, pulling at Daisie to follow. The fresh oxygen invigorated her lungs after weeks of the stale, still air that sat heavy and thick throughout the the lower decks.

'That sounds dull!' Daisie replied unenthusiastically. 'I just want to get off this bucket.'

'Hurry!' urged Violet. Daisie grudgingly followed her up the outside stairwell towards the communications room perched at the front of the top deck. They stopped at the open doorway where a dozen male engineers and deckhands had gathered to listen. A mess of wires snaked up the wall and out to a *News Chronicle* reporter visible on deck outside the window. The twins slid beside a filing cabinet at the rear where they wouldn't be seen.

A radio feed was patched in with a whine, crackle and spit as the signal came to life.

'*A pull of wind caught the Queen's hat, but as she stepped from the barge she quickly adjusted it. Now she's advancing to be received by the Governor-General, Field Marshal Sir William Slim,*' the announcer narrated with breathless awe. After a welcome by the Sydney Lord Mayor (his accent a vowels-in-the-mouth drawl), the Queen spoke.

'*Standing at last on Australian soil, on this spot which is the birthplace of the nation, I want to tell you all how happy I am to be amongst you and how much I look forward to my journey throughout Australia.*'

Those in the radio room burst into applause. Violet joined in, beaming with pride.

The sweltering sun of the late Australian summer had almost faded over Sydney's western horizon, but the celebrations continued well into the night.

'From tomorrow we go ashore with Lady Caroline,' Daisie informed Violet as they ate meatloaf and boiled potatoes in the lower-deck staffroom.

The sisters retreated to their cabin down the lonely dank corridor. With the engine off their steps echoed in the darkness. Their airless cabin was insulated deep in the harbour like a submarine, a world away from the exhilaration of Sydney above. In the excitement Violet had almost forgotten her misery, but returning to the iron lung brought the reality of things crashing back.

'Thank you for doing my shifts,' she offered as they stared at the rusty ceiling from their beds. 'Is Lady Althorp still upset?'

'She hates being called that.'

'"Lady Caroline" sounds so *familiar*.'

'Well, the Queen wore your bile. That's pretty familiar.'

Violet's teeth pinched the tip of her tongue.

Daisie relented. 'She's other things on her mind than you. She tells me things.'

'Well, make sure you know your place. You're not friends.'

'What would you know?'

'It's . . . it's not our place.'

Violet's words hung in the air for a moment before she took in a deep breath.

'Nonetheless, thank you,' Violet muttered before turning to face the wall.

Around nine thirty that evening Steward Joseph, smelling of red wine, appeared at their door. 'Airmail for Daishie,' he slurred, handing her an envelope.

'Bill!' she shrieked. Violet's face flushed with anger. Daisie snatched the letter, pulled on her dressing gown and hurried out of the cabin to head upstairs where there was fresh air and privacy.

Alone, Violet pulled the sheets over her head, sleep the only respite from the hopelessness.

<h1 style="text-align:center">*17*</h1>

The *Gothic* felt deserted. After two lonely months, mostly at sea, the majority of the crew had taken the opportunity to sample the carnival atmosphere of Sydney. The warm breeze ruffled Daisie's hair as she strode the stern-side deck. Points of lights scattered across the crowded harbour, almost as rich as the southern sky.

A commuter ferry marked *Kanangra* drifted into view about two hundred feet from the *Gothic*. Its deck, illuminated by festive tea lanterns, was crowded with passengers pressed along the rails to stare at the lone figure on the royal yacht. A group of children waved energetically. A few enthusiastic voices started singing in unison, the rest following in a what soon revealed itself to be a broadly Australian-accented chorus of 'God Save the Queen'. To her ears 'noble Queen' sounded like 'no bull kween'.

Other voices carried by the wind drifted up from a smaller craft that edged around the exclusion zone below. 'Is that her?' a woman's voice asked. The four inhabitants of the small rowboat bobbed in the crowded water hoping for a glimpse of royalty. 'Nah, just some girl,' the man rowing replied. 'A Pom, I reckon.'

Daisie smiled to herself. Under the deck light she turned the envelope over in her tiny hands, then tore it open to devour Bill's words as the fireworks popped in the sky above.

Dearest Daisie,

I'm writing this the morning after dropping you and your sister off at Southampton Port. On the drive home it rained. I'd neglected to pack the soft top in the boot due to all the luggage, so by the time I got back to Kingston the interior was rather soggy, as was I.

I've been thinking this past day or so, the fruit of that contemplation now settled in my stomach. I'm not yet prepared to accept monogamy. I'm simply too young. There are so many wonderful girls such as you. Where does one stop?

To the point – and for the sake of absoluteness – I must end our relationship.

I've also been intimate with your sister Violet. I know this may cause consternation, but in my experience honesty is best. While a cruel pill for you to swallow, it's best swallowed while you are far away.

I will always remember you and your family fondly, and request and insist that from this point forward you regard our relationship rescinded. One would understand should you wish to cease communication. It would be easiest for us both, really.

I'm hoping your travels haven't been too demanding and that you have arrived in Australia healthy and hale.

Yours,

William Dunclark

18

Violet was barely awake when Daisie strode angrily into the cabin.

'Violet!' Daisie hissed. She held her clenched fists beside her thighs like a boxer facing up to Freddie Mills.

Violet sat bolt upright in bed. She watched in alarm as Daisie yanked one of the suitcases from the overhead stowage, wielding it like a baseball bat over her shoulder.

'I knew you were jealous,' Daisie seethed. 'The desperation in your lies – I could tell!'

'What time is it? Is there a—'

With Donald Bradman precision, Daisie swung the suitcase into her face.

THOCK. The broad side of the case made contact, the hollow sound resonating through the iron bowel. Daisie dropped the suitcase to the floor like the bloody knife of an impulsive murder.

Violet hung in the air a moment, dangling like a cartoon boxer, her eyes dimmed, before collapsing like a ragdoll onto her pillow.

Daisie's bed was empty when Violet came to the next morning. Her head pounded like a heart. She gingerly prodded her left cheek, recoiling in pain at the gentlest touch. Violet involuntarily moaned as she righted herself. A ball of paper fell off her chest onto the floor. She winced and picked it up. As she read the crucial words on the crumpled sheet – *I've also been intimate with your sister* – she sucked in air as though she were about to dive.

The words shook Violet all the way down to where the baby grew inside and her stomach clenched like it had been pricked by a needle. She gripped the edge of the bedside shelf and eased herself up, swallowing the pain of her gyrating head. She glanced at the clock. She had two hours to pack her bags and report on deck for the transfer to land.

She stood before the bathroom mirror and assessed the damage. The bruise on her cheekbone was the size of a shilling and the same colour as the Blue Tit plums they used to steal off the overhanging tree at the end of Sheppard Close. She looked like she'd been unsuccessful in a street fight, which, to be fair, was partially true. Pulling her pristine uniform over her head, she flinched as the fabric brushed her cheek. She layered makeup over the bruise like a bricklayer, but to little end.

'Try to be more careful when opening doors,' the young medical officer suggested, his tone alternating between sarcastic and mildly sympathetic. He administered two plaster strips to the bruise. His breath was heavy with cigarette smoke and scotch from the night before.

'Thank you, Dr Somerset. I'll be more careful.' Violet winced slightly as she stood and swallowed heavily before making her way towards the deck to confront Daisie and the rest of the world.

*

Above the water level an assortment of exotic bird calls rang out from the shore, their strident sounds reminiscent of the local inflection.

The cicadas started cheering the warm dawn air as Violet sheepishly emerged. The white plasters strapped across her cheek stung.

'Picking fights, Violet?' one of the maids asked.

'Ran into a door,' Violet responded, resigned to the lie.

As she waited on deck with eight other maids for the 6 a.m. transport to Government House, Violet glimpsed Daisie leaning against the railing, away from the others, with her face scrunched in rage.

'It's not what you think,' Violet whispered from behind her. 'It's not the whole truth,' she pleaded.

'So it's a lie? Is it?'

'No, but—'

'*No, but* is a glad-ragged *definitely*. You've been *willing* it since the day we saw *Noose for a Lady*.'

'As willing as the fox for a hunt! I—'

'Don't speak to me any more,' Daisie interrupted, growling through her teeth. She fixed her eyes on a Navy patrol boat delicately intercepting two school boys hysterically paddling a kayak inside the *Gothic*'s exclusion zone.

'Morning, ma'am,' said an Australian male voice. Violet looked up to a sweaty-faced, bald Australian customs official in a heavy suit and tie. He was delighted to be there, dutifully checking their passports with a reverent smile as the crew loaded their bags down to the barge below.

Violet flinched as one of the suitcases was passed overhead. It was Daisie's, a deep Violet-sized face indentation prominent on the side.

*

The bloodshot morning sun rose in the east as the luxury transport boat cut through the harbour chop, navigating around the vessels that rubbernecked the *Gothic*. Violet had studiously avoided her sister, sitting on the other side of the boat beside Eunice Lackbottom.

'Or'right?' Eunice asked.

'I walked into a door.'

'Ay, I've done that too. Boyfriend back in Kent slammed my nose into it, that bastard.'

The barge slowed as it reached the crowded ferry terminal, pushing a wake that splashed against the wooden pier and doused a primped cluster of private school girls holding the dock post. A coterie of uniformed attendants wearing white caps emblazoned with the Australian coat of arms assisted the human cargo off the step and onto a red carpet.

'Excuse us all, coming through,' said a policeman as the crowd surged forward to see if anybody of importance was alighting.

The girls were ushered through a ten-deep throng, jostled on either side by the beat police who protected them with interlocking arms.

'I feel like Perry Como,' yelled the Duke's valet over the din.

The entourage was elegantly hustled towards four black government cars that idled on the nearby promenade. Violet glanced up at the vast buildings surrounding the quay, some seven or eight storeys tall and of a modernity unlike anything she'd seen back home. It was how she imagined New York. The tallest building, marked *AWA* at the scalp, was a breathtaking fifteen storeys tall. Its spire, stark against the profoundly blue sky, towered over everything around it.

Violet held back in the line to ensure she was placed in a different car to her sister, jockeying position to share a vehicle with one of the footmen, Mr Walton, and the Duke's valet.

'It's like home, but newfangled,' said Mr Walton, peering through the car window as they made the two-minute drive to Government House, ferrying through streets thick with tourists and families out for the royal occasion. A policeman manning a security point peered in the window as the car slowed at a yellow traffic barricade. His deep navy uniform was topped with a badged flat cap, lending him a more military-style compared to the bobby domes back home, which in light of the recent war had a German *Pickelhaube* odour to them. The Australian cap reminded her of those worn by the female police officers she'd seen very occasionally around Piccadilly Circus.

Large sandstone posts stood on either side of the wrought-iron gates of Government House. Officials and police checked their passports in a perfunctory fashion. The sandstone Gothic Revival building was of a style commonly seen near Kingston upon Thames. It was certainly a step down for Lady Althorp, let alone Queen Elizabeth. Yet the gardens beyond were immense. Palm trees spiked above the abundant flora, the tropical parklands stretching all the way to the next harbour inlet. And, as always, there was a cacophony of bird calls that sounded like the tuning of a tone-deaf orchestra.

'This way, ladies and gentlemen,' said a man in a deep blue suit, a native flower on his lapel, as they stepped into the foyer of Government House.

Violet moved into the crowded lobby, where the entire ensemble had converged. The foyer was dominated by two life-size portraits: King George VI and a maritime traveller, possibly Captain Cook, who stood stoutly in repose. At the far end, a portrait of Queen Elizabeth II hung above the stairs between two coats of arms.

'Paint's likely still wet on that one,' said a young Australian gentleman aged no more than twenty-three. He smiled, blinking twice as though he was trying to break her trance. 'Can I show you to your room, ma'am?'

'Miss Chettle,' Violet replied, composing herself.

'Of course, Miss Chettle. I'm Jack. I'll be showing you to your quarters. Follow me.' His Australian accent was thick and inflected skywards at the end of each sentence.

Jack led her down a lengthy wood-panelled corridor. The floorboards creaked underfoot as they passed a parade of nineteenth-century Australian portraits. 'Get in a fight?' he asked as they turned down a narrower side hallway.

'Pardon?'

'Your face.' He nodded towards her bruised cheekbone.

'Oh. I walked into a door.' She'd repeated the lie enough by now for it to be reasonably convincing.

'You should see the other fella. Right?' He glanced back with concern, lowering his voice to ask, 'Are you all right?'

'It's fine,' she said. 'The door, not so much.'

'Well, it'll help me tell you and your sister apart.' He slowed at the third door along. 'Speaking of doors, this is yours, Miss Chettle. Your sister's across there, nice and close.' He pointed at the door opposite. 'And Lady Althorp's is the one at the end. Bathroom's around that corner.'

He pulled a key from his trouser pocket and slid it into the lock, swinging it open for Violet to enter first. It was a vast improvement over the bottommost bowels of the *Gothic*, containing a large double bed with six pillows, an antique dresser and a shockingly colourful native flower arrangement. Above the bed hung an eighteenth-century portrait of a greying gentleman resplendent in a mauve major general's uniform, a forgotten figment of Australia's colonial past.

'The house manager, Mrs Bruce, is at your service. Round-the-clock chef, domestic help – all here to serve you so you can serve her. And if all else should fail, I'm usually around any time of the day. Your luggage will be delivered shortly.'

Violet nodded.

'Anything else you'd like?' he asked, offering her the room key.

'No. Thank you.' She offered him a weak smile. He smiled back, his eyes examining her face with a hint of concern.

'Plenty of doors around here. Be careful, Violet,' he remarked as he closed the door behind him.

The creaky floorboards outside spoke of Jack's retreat as the painting's eyes silently evaluated her. Violet turned her back to the major general and slouched on the end of the bed, the mattress squeaking under the weight. She took four deep breaths to stave off a rising emotion. The real burden – the combination of anxiety, fear and guilt – was catching up with her. Her throat, like the mattress, rasped under the strain, the way it used to when she'd had asthma as a young girl.

Still fully clothed and splayed under the major general, she was woken two hours later by a polite knock. 'Luggage,' the porter called. The thin boy placed her suitcases in a row beside the dresser. 'And a message for you, ma'am.' He presented her with an envelope, bowed, then retreated as though it were a royal decree.

It was the touring schedule for the next twenty-four hours. Lady Althorp's first official function was only hours away. Not knowing what her sister would be taking responsibility for, Violet rubbed the sleep from her eyes and tamed the wild locks of her hair, dented from sleep, using the water in the pitcher beside the bed to flatten them.

*

'You have a square go, Miss Loo?' asked Bobo.

Violet stood at Lady Althorp's door, poised to knock. 'I'm sorry?'

'A fight! Boxed by a kangaroo already.' She laughed, her voice booming as a convoy of porters carrying trunks followed behind her. The floorboards strained under their heavy footsteps as Bobo led the troops.

'It was an accident. A door.'

'Should've punched him back when ye had the chance,' she said as one of the trunks clipped the plaster. 'Tell me if ye need a door sorted. In the meantime, I might have something to cover that a little better.'

'Careful, they're custom matched umbrellas,' she scolded the page.

Daisie opened her room door and emerged. 'Morning, Mrs MacDonald,' she said sunnily. 'Yes, poor Violet swung the door the wrong way. Does it all the time. I suppose we're upside down here at the bottom of the earth. Most likely that's the confusion.'

Violet bit her lip and avoided eye contact with her sister, who swelled with confidence. Daisie tapped twice on Lady Althorp's door.

'Enter.' Daisie and Violet entered Lady Caroline's room, maintaining a safe distance from each other.

The suite was three times the size of Violet's. It was furnished with a lounge area, a four-poster bed to one side, red carpet, matching drapes and four framed portraits of more eighteenth-century Australians. From the centre of the ornate ceiling work hung a crystal chandelier.

'In the normal course of business, I suspect it's a drawing room,' said Lady Caroline as she sorted documents on her desk. 'There are three doorways in so I'm likely to be ambushed at any moment. Though it's nice to be back on land, no?'

She looked up at them, the twins standing a few feet apart. Lady Caroline leaned in closer towards Violet.

'Oh my. Are you all right?'

'Right as rain. Bruised ego, nothing more.'

'It does look rather sore.' Lady Caroline peered closely at Violet's plasters, then into Violet's eyes as though trying to find the truth.

'She's fine. Brought it on herself,' Daisie added, mimicking a door being opened towards her face.

'Very well. It's a busy couple of days,' Lady Caroline continued. 'We're opening Parliament, visiting a hospital for children and a war memorial, lunching with the local women's auxiliary and attending a State banquet. There are also school children, war widows, the infirm, the racetrack, the beach and a ball – of the tiara variety. And more or less in that order.'

She passed each of them a typed copy of the full itinerary, then parted a sheer curtain to reveal the botanical gardens beyond. 'You would've seen the crowds out there. She's never seen anything like it – well, outside of home. A thousand casualties, apparently. Heat stroke. I'm going to need quite a few outfits at the ready, so you'll need to rattle Bobo's cage. I've noted my wardrobe preferences inside.'

Violet flicked through the document. It was as thick as an Abbey Girls novella.

'Now'—Caroline reclined into the upholstered leather desk chair and evaluated the sisters as though casting for a screen role— 'I'll need one of you to join me to help on the trail.'

Violet's eyes flicked up from the itinerary, her smile creasing hopefully as her eyebrows pricked.

'Daisie, have Bobo find you something to wear. Tell her it needs to be sixty per cent – she'll know what to do.'

Violet's mouth dropped open a little. She closed it quickly, trying not to show her disappointment.

'Yes, Lady Caroline,' said Daisie proudly.

'Violet?'

'Yes, Lady Al— Caroline?'

'Can you find some Glacier Cream for me? Go out and buy it with petty cash from the office girls if you need to. Otherwise I'll return to Britain a cinder.'

'Yes, ma'am,' replied Violet.

'Let the acting master or an equerry know when you leave the property. Would hate to lose you and cause a stir.'

'Yes, of course. Umm . . . what is it?'

'Glacier Cream? For the skin. I need something to spare me from this sunlight. So it begins. Daisie, you stay with me and I'll walk you through some of the basics.'

Violet dropped her chin as Daisie smiled at her condescendingly, then shuffled gradually out of the room while Lady Caroline and Daisie chatted about protocol. Violet closed the door behind her and stood in the hallway for a moment, listening to the mumblings of lost opportunity within.

19

Day 87: *Sydney, New South Wales, Australia*
Population: *1,886,436*
Weather: *79 degrees Fahrenheit, fine with sombre cloudy periods*
Fact: *Between 1788 and 1792, 3546 male and 766 female*
convicts landed at Sydney – many of them 'professional
criminals' with few of the skills required for the establishment
of a colony.

Tourists refused to leave the wrought-iron gates of Government House, chanting, 'We want the Queen,' as though she were a stage act. Violet pressed through the mass of sweaty bodies, the smell and heat unlike anything she'd experienced. Even more oppressive were the accents. 'Potent enough tae remove wallpaper,' Bobo had remarked of them.

Violet clasped her hands over her ears to muffle the sound as she pushed through the throng, sweating in her heavy grey polyester coat in the unforgiving sunlight. She'd put it on so as not to draw attention to her uniform, but it wasn't until she'd passed the police security point that she realised it was like being wrapped in a hot blanket. To double back didn't seem worth the bother, so she ploughed onwards through the mob.

She navigated away from the emerald harbour, following the footpath along the edge of the gardens. The entrance portico of the Treasury building loomed beside her, its carroty sandstone-textured façade rising to an arched roof. Its Classical Revival style reminded her of the Travellers Club on Pall Mall. Her father had spent a week there doing contract work during the bomb damage repairs, as proud of being inside the damaged premises as if he'd been invited for brandy by Dr Livingstone.

Dodging a tram on which sweaty men and women perilously clung to vertical brass bars, Violet turned down a side street. She was shading her eyes from the sunlight that dazzled between the towering buildings when she had to accept she was overheated and hopelessly lost. She turned east – or was it south? – trying to get her bearings as pedestrian traffic flowed around her.

'Excuse me? Can you tell me what street I'm on?' she asked a passing couple. The elderly man wore a broad-brimmed hat, like something a farmer or a cowboy might wear, and the friendly-faced woman clutched a small Union Jack flag.

'Meerkat Street, love,' he replied.

'Pardon?'

'Meerkat Street.'

Violet nodded politely. It seemed a strange name for a street, until she saw a signpost on the side of the block reading 'Market Street'. She plodded on.

In the thirty minutes since she'd left the grounds of Government House, a niggling pain had manifested inside her. She rested her right hand on her abdomen. Perhaps it was her body telling her not to skip breakfast. As she walked deeper into the city, trying to keep to the pockets of shade, the sensation grew from a minor annoyance to a sharp discomfort.

She stopped and bent forward with a gasp, holding herself against a power pole. It felt as though a knitting needle had been plunged into her kidney. Then, like a retreating wave, the pain subsided, but she suspected the tide was coming in. Violet held both hands to her stomach and darted her eyes around the intersection. On the opposite corner a blue store awning caught her attention. *Gray's Pharmacy*. She stepped blindly onto the street. A car skidded to a stop to avoid hitting her, blasting its horn as she stumbled onto the opposite pavement, waving in apology.

'We don't stock Glacier Cream but I'd recommend an aluminium sun protectant called Quik-Tak and perhaps some calamine lotion,' the pharmacist said in a soft voice as he foraged behind the counter. The gentleman was in his late fifties and boasted a finely manicured moustache that pointed outward like the east–west spikes of a compass. He glanced at her bandaged cheek, subtly tilting his head in concern. 'Is there anything else I can help you with, dear?' he asked as she fumbled through a roll of Australian pounds.

Violet frowned. Another wave of pain crashed. She pushed against the edge of the counter with both hands, adjusting her frame to withstand an uncomfortable cramp. 'That's all. Thank you, s-sir,' she said, clenching her teeth.

'Are you certain?' Glancing around the store, which was empty save for an elderly woman fussing over an umbrella display near the front window, he urged her towards a chair at the end of the dispensary.

Violet's face involuntarily creased at his kindness, her tears accumulating faster than she could smear them away with her trembling hands.

'You're with child, yes?' he said softly, standing over her like a concerned school master. 'Your condition . . . it's a choice best made now rather than later.'

She looked up. His words were a seemingly practised routine based on signals Violet had not consciously offered.

'It's all right, dear. Say no more,' he said and reached for a notepad. 'This man will do what you need done.' He spoke softly, because the elderly woman had approached the counter. She noisily dropped a red, white and blue brolly onto the glass top.

Violet clumsily extracted two notes from her roll and pushed them into his hand. He held out the paper bag of lotions with a reassuring look. Under the impatient glare of the elderly woman, Violet snatched the bag and ran to the door.

She walked a block or two back up Market Street in the humid midday air, the atmosphere so thick it made breathing difficult. She paused in the shade of the grand Queen Victoria Building. Violet's mind reeled and her head throbbed as she tried to recall the way back to Government House.

Then she stopped dead. In the centre of the pavement stood a bald, emaciated bird with white plumage and a long down-curved beak. It picked at the pavement for scraps around indifferent pedestrians, as at home in the city as in a marshy wetland, then gathered its pace towards her, determined to snare a banana peel that had stuck to her heel. She walked briskly in panic, lifting her leg every third step to try and knock the rubbish from her shoe. The pedestrians around her barely glanced sideways as the unpleasant bird lunged at the discarded rind. Violet stumbled forward, propelled by panic, as her hand rested against her stomach to ease the tightness.

After two blocks she paused outside a theatre where a matinee crowd had flooded the pavement. As she slowed in the excitable crowd of children and their harried mothers, she reached into her pocket for the slip of paper but instead pulled out an older, crumpled note. It was a shopping list in her mother's well-ordered cursive.

Milk. Eggs. A loaf of bread. Flour. Vanilla essence. Violet remembered the exact day Mum had given it to her. They'd tried to make cupcakes with their rationed eggs but overestimated the level of batter in each cup, so they had overflowed and merged in the pan. That evening they ate cupcake 'chunks', which didn't taste quite the same even though they were essentially no different.

Violet carefully folded the note and placed it in her opposite coat pocket, then took out the other slip. *Hanif. 3 Little Collins Street, Surry Hills* was written in the pharmacist's barely legible handwriting.

Violet flexed her hands, which had locked into fists. She wiped perspiration from her forehead with her sleeve as her mind swam with opposing ideas. How could she make this decision? The polyester coat had started itching as it soaked up her sweat.

'Excuse me,' a mother rudely asserted as she pushed a stroller through the crowd and clipped Violet's left shoe. Violet's agony returned in a new wave, this time with a tinge of claustrophobia. She pushed through the crowd onto the roadway, stumbling along the gutter against the oncoming traffic to circumvent the throng. She hurried down alleyways and laneways, her flat shoes slipping and sliding until her ankles felt raw.

Ten, perhaps twenty minutes had passed before Violet slowed. She caught her breath outside a department store that had been overenthusiastically decorated. Gay bunting and a large, slightly unflattering illustrated portrait of the Queen and Duke hung on the vast façade.

Violet threw her weight against the glass doors to escape the heat. The ceiling fans cooled her sweat as she wilted into a seat by the cosmetics counter and unbuttoned the coat.

'May I help you, miss?' asked a twenty-something makeup girl with a large black freckle on her cheek.

'Can you tell me where I am?'

'Mark Foy's,' the girl said, bemused. Then, after a beat, 'In Sydney. *Australia.*'

'Near Surry Hills?'

'You're pretty much standing in it, dear,' she said with a gentle laugh.

Violet held out the crumpled address. The girl proceeded to draw a crude map on the back of a docket slip.

'Thanks,' Violet mumbled as she stood up from the chair, staring intently at the lines on the paper. The clerk watched Violet collapse against the glass doors in an unsuccessful attempt to leave, before pulling them inwards and disappearing into the white sunlight.

She paused on the street, facing the park across the road that led back to Government House. But the voice inside her was screaming now, wailing for its fate to be known. The dreaded decision that itched her conscience demanded judgement. Either choice was of a consequence too immense for her to grapple. Violet covered her ears, but her mind's cry wouldn't be silenced until she'd confronted the responsibility of bearing an unwanted child.

The voice must be silenced, she decided as she lowered her hands from her ears, balling her sweaty fists tightly beside her. The horrible decision was the sensible one, the end to a nightmare that would linger without decisive action.

She glanced at the map and looked south, where a sloping boulevard of laneways undulated down the hill. Violet walked into the maze of streets lined with uneven rows of small terrace cottages. Most of the dwellings were neglected. It had the feel of a slum, though perhaps this was simply how Australians lived. Most were direct descendants of convicts, after all.

Gradually she began to notice lonely figures lingering in doorways and under awnings, people with no obvious place they needed to be. The bunting and flags that had decorated so many homes along the way had grown scarcer. A woman strode out of a small lane a few steps in front. She wore a plain teal dress with laced shoes and a navy knitted cap, from which strands of her unkempt hair dangled at the edges.

But her profile was their mother's.

Violet hastened her step to creep closer. The resemblance, from what she could see, was remarkable. The woman turned the corner into a narrow laneway and walked faster, perhaps unsettled by the footsteps gaining behind.

Violet ran after her, desperate to know if it was Hazel. 'H-hazel!' she yelled but the woman broke into a run. Violet sprinted, her right heel stumbling on the uneven stones, until she caught up, clasping the woman's arm and spinning her around.

'Don't 'urt me, I'm not 'er!' the terrified woman said breathlessly. And she wasn't. Violet's hope deflated as her lungs filled with the dank laneway air.

'I'm so sorry, I thought you were . . .'

Violet didn't have the words to finish the sentence, and the woman didn't loiter, scuttling away down the alley and glancing over her shoulder as she went, in case the insane woman took chase again.

Violet regained her breath and looked at where she'd ended up – outside a brown sandstone single-level cottage. It had an overgrown

front yard and a rusted corrugated-iron roof. It was the address
she'd been given.

A pale woman with cropped hair exited through the front
door. She was nineteen or twenty, with a glazed stare that hung
over entrenched dark circles below. Behind her was a hallway from
which natural light seemed to withdraw. The woman swung the
waist-high iron gate open then stopped, alerted to Violet's still
presence.

'Hello,' Violet said reactively. The woman cast a look that
seemed to be a warning. Violet took a step towards her.

'Le' me alone,' said the woman as she pulled her handbag closer
and hurried down the hill towards the rail line.

'Well? You comin' in?' a voice barked. A man of Mediterranean
descent, his light blue shirtsleeves rolled up, leaned through the
door, glancing in both directions of the laneway. He stared at Violet,
as though challenging her to enter or be gone.

Violet opened her mouth to respond, but nothing came out.
She ran, shocked out of the possibility, and stumbled back over the
uneven footpaths all the way to Government House without stopping once for breath.

It took ten minutes for her to get through security. She pinned
her bloodshot eyes to the carpet as she crossed the lobby, retreating
to the toilets to avoid any unwanted encounters. She closed the
cubicle door, tore off the heavy coat and dropped it to the floor.

Within moments the main toilet door hinge strained. 'What's
up, missy?' Bobo demanded, her heavy steps pacing. 'What starts
in tears for ye ends up in tears for the rest of us. So best ye get it off
yer chest.'

'It's nothing.' Violet sniffed.

'Don't tell me it's nothin',' Bobo retorted. 'I've been around long enough to know when nothin' is somethin'. Answer me straight or I'll drag you awa by the fringe to Mr Ratcliffe.'

'I'm homesick. I miss England,' she lied, regretting it the moment the words left her mouth. Her coat was splayed on the tiles, curled in a foetal-shaped lump.

'Ye'll be telling people about this trip for the rest of yer life – it's all ye'll be known for. Don't ruin it because you miss *hame*. Ye've got your sister. Toughen up, or *oot*.'

Bobo huffed and left the room, letting the door slam hard behind her. Violet winced as the noise echoed off the tiles. She pulled a few sheets of toilet paper and wiped her nose, feeling wretched, until the corridor had cleared and she could slink back to her quarters unseen.

20

Day 89: Bondi Beach, Sydney, New South Wales
Population: Normally 5678 (estimated to double for the Queen's visit)
Weather: 87 degrees Fahrenheit and absolutely fine
Fact: This half-mile beach is one of the most visited tourist sites in Australia. 'Bondi' is an Aboriginal word meaning 'water breaking over rocks'. In 1936 an untreated sewage outlet was built not far from the north end.

Daisie travelled in the back of a gleaming Daimler alongside Lady Caroline. The little flags mounted above the wheels waved victoriously as the car crawled up Bondi's Beach Road escorted by twin police motorcycles. The Queen and Duke rode in an open-topped vehicle ahead of them. The Queen protected herself from the sun with a lime parasol that she gripped with a gloved hand.

Daisie sported a pastel-blue pleated dress with a white waist-cinch belt, a petticoat and cream shoes with mid-height heels that she'd fallen from twice while getting to the car. 'One shan't be too tall,' Bobo had reminded Daisie as she'd collected the outfit. Lady Caroline had lent her some lipstick and foundation to complete the makeover.

'I barely recognise you,' Lady Caroline flattered Daisie over the noise. The pavements were crowded with cheering flag-wavers so loud that she had to shout to be heard.

A newsreel camera perched on a roof tracked the car as it passed. Daisie imagined how jealous it would make Violet to glimpse her in a newsreel. Bill too. She waved towards the camera as Lady Caroline smirked.

'So, to continue,' said Lady Caroline, as she waved to the revellers passing by, 'if the Queen seems to be ignoring you, she knows where you are. If she stares at you, she needs something done. She never stays longer than required. You'll get to know the body language. You'll also need an antenna for the "awkward squad".'

'Awkward squad?' replied Daisie, with her eyebrows raised.

'Those needing to be calmed before meeting the monarch. Nervous subjects are dangerously time-consuming.'

Up ahead, with a deft wave of his muscular hand, the Duke acknowledged a homemade sign held by a group of teenage girls that proclaimed, '*We love you Prince Philip!*' The shrill cheer that went up in response caused Lady Caroline to pause the conversation while they passed.

'Do you know her? Well, I mean?' Daisie enquired.

'Elizabeth? We grew up together. She was best friends with Margaret, my sister. But she's a private person. A loner. Longs to be in a room with nobody else, except the dogs – or the horses. There must be moments when she simply wants to lock herself in and crawl under a duvet, finish a tumbler of gin and not be gazed at by all around her.'

'She reminds me of a woman I know from school,' Daisie said. 'Nimmy Grosscastle. Promoted within the family printing business but spends her entire time trying to prove her legitimacy for the job.'

Lady Caroline smiled politely. 'She does her job to perfection now but it was agony for her, starting off. Leaving Charles and Anne behind for five months was the toughest decision. Even Bobo isn't there for them. Glad it wasn't my decision. The benefit of not procreating. Meg and her were forever trying to set me up. Meg was on the South Africa tour when Elizabeth learned of her father's death. The tension between them never ended,' she said, nodding to the car in front. 'Despite the tragedy, Margaret and Peter Townsend, and my sister and Jock got together. Commander Carville? Romance always seemed to be in the air for everybody but them. She never missed a footstep though. God and country first – not necessarily in that order.'

'And you?' Daisie asked, emboldened by the carnival atmosphere.

'Me?' Lady Caroline sniffed in an amused manner. 'Inevitably, the prospects are unwrapped mummies or so far in the closet they're practically in Narnia. I look at *them*,' she said, nodding more subtly at the car in front, 'and frankly I don't know how they put up with each other. Or should I say, how she puts up with him. Things are different behind the glittering veil. When it comes down to it, they're just a family like any other. Probably worse.'

Lady Caroline paused as they turned down a side street. The motorcade roared through a suburb of wooden cottages. 'Everything changed after her father died,' she concluded, dismissing the line of conversation. 'So which of you two is more like your mother?'

'I don't know. Probably Violet. She'd probably say I was.'

'Sorry. I forgot.' Lady Caroline offered a pursed smile of encouragement. There wasn't much else to say, the cheering outside the vehicle absorbing the silence. The wide Bondi street was lined with a mix of those who'd dressed for their Queen and some who seemed to have just wandered off the beach.

'It's like she was the best parts of both of us,' Daisie ventured as the Daimler edged around a crowded gutter. 'She'd be so proud, me sitting here with you. The Queen, this car, these clothes. To be honest, I never put much stock in all this. But I think I could get used to it.'

Lady Caroline waved again to the fleeting crowd then gently rested her other hand on top of Daisie's, which lay on the seat between them. Daisie glanced down at Caroline's gloved hand resting atop hers. The simple act seemed deliberate.

Daisie didn't dare move. For the longest moment Caroline's unmoving fingers cupped Daisie's pale skin on the black leather. The car's vibrations gave her touch an exciting but gentle frisson. She blushed brightly, turning her face away so Caroline couldn't see the boldness written there. But the soft contact with Caroline's gloved fingers was electrifying.

After a good ten seconds Caroline lifted her hand to wave at a group of children assembled in a school yard on Daisie's side of the car.

Neither spoke, the noisy jubilation outside masking the suspense.

Daisie's hair fretted in the coastal breeze as her heart percussed inside her chest, thumping like she'd just taken a sprint. She took in a deep breath of the salty sea air. Daisie couldn't bring herself to look into Caroline's eyes for fear that her own would reveal her exhilaration.

Bondi Beach's azure water came into view, the golden sand skirting a promenade of pavilions and storefronts.

'Nothing like a trip to the beach,' Caroline said confidently as she slid on her sunglasses. 'Fifteen minutes, according to the plan.'

The moment had passed.

The motorcade turned onto the beach access road through a police checkpoint. Most of Sydney's population appeared to be crowded onto this single stretch of sand to witness the Queen's historic visit. Local dignitaries, the rotund Mayor, his reedy wife and various overdressed councillors formally welcomed the royal party. Press and locals crowded in a circle around the Queen's vehicle like a human vice that was being prised open by a line of uniformed military police.

Daisie tailed Lady Caroline like a curious pet. She was handed a stream of posies that Lady Caroline or the Queen accepted from the crowd – sixteen in all – returning them to the car when her arms overflowed with flora. The flies were the only things to outnumber the locals, by a factor of ten.

After the short meet and greet, the party was shown to a viewing platform that had been built for the royal visitors to watch a surf carnival being performed in their honour.

'Stay close,' Lady Caroline whispered to Daisie, who edged in beside her as they were shown to the second row behind the Queen and Duke.

Daisie sat under the sweltering sun as the rows filled around her. The Australians wanted to be close to the celebrity visitors. Lady Caroline made small talk with the Mayor's wife while Daisie observed the scene laid before her. The stand had a Roman gladiatorial flavour, like an amphitheatre where feats of strength would be performed for royal amusement.

Daisie's eyes rested on the Queen sitting in the row before her, her makeup slightly heavier – 'to protect her from the sun,' Lady Caroline had explained – her fine neck shrouded by a three-strand pearl necklace. Her frock was the one she had worn when she landed in Suva, a summery sleeveless wild-silk dress in a shade of clear buttercup yellow, with slingback shoes. She attentively observed the hundreds of lifesavers in tiny trunks as they carried flags in unison and rode polished wooden surf boats into crashing surf. The Queen gasped aloud when a longboat overturned in a treacherous wave. Occasionally she flicked a persistent fly away from her mouth with her gloved hand but otherwise seemed genuinely fascinated by the spectacle.

Daisie's gaze wandered to the Duke. He sat diagonally in front of her, barely an arm's length away. His muscular neck was dotted with beads of perspiration below the line of his perfectly tended hair. The occasional fly rested on his skin to drink before being casually batted away.

The Duke glanced back in Daisie's direction as though sensing her.

Daisie feigned innocence and looked elsewhere. But his direct eye contact made her heart beat irregularly, her beguiled glow camouflaged by the scalding effect of the sun.

The crowd roared at the spectacle of brown male bodies in tight shorts running through sand and water. It gripped the royals for a good twenty-five minutes.

'We rarely linger,' remarked Lady Caroline to Daisie as an aside. 'Ratcliffe is having kittens.'

Daisie craned her neck slightly to witness Major Ratcliffe at the end of the Queen's row. He leaned expectantly into the Queen's sightline, hoping to receive the signal for departure. The Queen soon tilted her face towards him and made a sustained but subtle four-second glance, concluded by a single flutter of her eyelids.

'We're off,' whispered Lady Caroline.

*

On the return walk to the motorcade Daisie wrangled four armfuls of bouquets from wellwishers who'd accumulated on the pathway during the surf carnival. In addition to flowers there were roughly two dozen gifts, from toys for the Queen's children to jewellery, cards, stamp albums, jams, cutlery, books, sweets, quilts and framed photographs.

'There's a strict policy that any gift valued at over fifty pounds must be declined, returned or donated to charity,' Lady Caroline explained as their doors were closed.

'The driver could barely fit it all in the boot,' Daisie replied, her blouse stained with orange lily pollen.

The cars roared along the edge of a golf course towards the harbour. More wellwishers were massed along the grassy fenceline to witness the visitors.

'The crowds are much bigger than we expected,' said Lady Caroline from behind her sunglasses.

'Everybody wants to see the show,' replied Daisie as she shielded her eyes from the afternoon glare.

'You handled yourself well.' Caroline held Daisie's gaze.

Daisie accepted with a nod, determined to match her stare.

Caroline smiled mischievously. 'We're going to have some fun on this tour, I can tell.'

Daisie could see her reflection in Caroline's sunglasses. Her lips parted, her squinting eyes vulnerable.

'One last piece of advice. Of the practical sort. Watch out for bees. Last girl got stung on the face. Had hay fever, too. Devastating.'

'The pain?'

'No, losing the job. Nearly lost her mind. Family disowned her.'

'Doesn't sound so bad.'

'Which bit?' Caroline said with a wry smile. 'Still, I'd hate for either of us to get stung.'

Daisie tried to read between her words, uncertain whether she'd charmed Caroline, or whether the banter was merely part of the job and was the cost of advancement.

21

The sun had lowered in the sky until it was directly behind the Harbour Bridge, its rays poking through the shimmering iron struts. The royal party arrived back at Government House to the sounds of ships' horns and sirens jubilantly carrying on as though it were New Year's Eve.

Violet showered and changed, then made her way to the Government House foyer where she joined the other staff, both from the Palace and local, to await the return of the touring party.

Without design the British collected down one side of the foyer and the Australians along the other, each carefully eyeing the other off. The Palace staff stood in a precise line as they had been taught, with their arms by their sides, their hands edged slightly towards the front, hanging not like orangutans but with palms flat and towards the body.

The eyes of the girls on the opposite side flicked across the red carpet, stealing glances at how Violet and the others were poised and subtly adjusting their own positioning to mirror them, until both sides were a perfect match.

The cars eventually pulled up outside, and the doorman and the equerries fanned out to escort the guests to their rooms. Ratcliffe entered the lobby first, ensuring the Queen and Duke behind him were transferred to their quarters without incident.

Lady Caroline was next, her gown flowing like milk over the edges of the carpeted stairs. Violet remained still, waiting until Lady Caroline had passed by to break away and follow her to the suite.

Then Daisie sashayed in. She carried herself into the hall as though she were of blue blood. Her appearance and confidence bestowed an aura that made her almost unrecognisable.

Violet's mouth parted as she passed. It was a transformation.

Daisie wobbled on her right heel. Some of the staff's heads broke formation, their necks tracking her like a returned tennis ball. But she recovered her elegant stride and made her way confidently through the gauntlet.

'She looks different,' uttered Ratcliffe's diminutive assistant, Miss Simmons, to Violet's left. Violet rushed to fall in behind Lady Caroline and Daisie as they turned the corner towards the suite.

She entered as Lady Caroline flung off her silk jacket and picked the pillbox hat from her tangle of hair. 'Thank the Lord for calamine lotion! Thought the sun was going to burn us alive, didn't we, Daisie?'

Daisie slumped into one of the lounge chairs, crossing her legs with a satisfied glower. 'The gifts!' she reminded Lady Caroline.

'Oh yes. Of course,' Caroline said as she busily fussed through the mail on her desk. 'Violet, can you please coordinate the return or destruction of gifts? They're in the car. The equerry will have the key and can probably help, given the amount of them.'

'Yes, Lady Caroline. What do I do with them?'

'Anything out of the ordinary bring to Ratcliffe or me.'

'What is considered out of the ordinary?'

'Threats, dying wishes, messages with a personal connection

of some sort. Or evidence of madness. Sometimes we get the police across it.'

'And what happens to the rest?'

'Flowers are to be sent to hospitals, gifts to the nearest welfare agency and the rest is to be confidentially disposed of. Commander Carville will have the local liaison for that.'

'Disposed of?' Violet asked, unable to mask her incredulity.

'She'd be buried! Very few gifts, if any at all, make their way to the Queen personally.'

Violet's face dropped.

'Don't look so disappointed,' Lady Caroline said, looking back to her desk.

'She sent the Queen a card once,' Daisie teased.

Violet glared back at her sister.

'How sweet,' said Lady Caroline. 'Sorry, Violet, but it's all part of the show, I'm afraid.'

Violet's brow involuntarily pinched a fraction as she turned to leave.

'I'm sure she appreciated the thought, though.' Daisie sniggered.

Lady Caroline looked up to silence her. 'Oh, and Violet,' Lady Caroline said as she kicked off her heeled shoes, 'I have the Lord Mayor's ball tonight. Can you fetch something from Bobo for me? And for Daisie too. I'm going to need an extra pair of hands.'

Violet's eyebrows perched high on her forehead. Daisie bit her lip in pleasure.

'Oh, Violet – make sure you get the tiara.'

Violet gulped.

'That will be all, Violet!' said Daisie smugly as Violet left the room with her shoulders down.

*

For the Lord Mayor's ball that evening Lady Caroline wore a regal embroidered silk gown, a stunning necklace heavily studded with jewels, and a jade sash that gave her the aura of a pageant winner. Daisie wore a flowing cream gown with a light grey silk scarf wrap. Her hair was pinned tightly in an intricate bun and dangling from each lobe were teardrop earrings that dazzled like small chandeliers. Violet tried to repress her jealousy, averting her eyes from Daisie's self-satisfied presence.

'Violet, help me with the tiara,' ordered Lady Caroline. A crease of panic formed around Violet's eyes. She fetched the velvet pouch from the dresser top. There was no time to check if the emerald was still in place, and she wasn't confident that the chewing gum could have held the stone for this long.

She gently lifted the luminous object from the pouch as Lady Caroline flattened her palms against her hair in the mirror. The jewel was there, sparkling brilliantly. She carefully carried the tiara across the carpet and held it over Lady Caroline's head.

'Faster, Violet,' urged Lady Caroline. 'This isn't the Coronation. Though that did go *on* a bit.'

Violet lowered the tiara, fixing it discreetly into place with two hair grips.

'Right,' said Lady Caroline, standing. Her generous hem rustled against the carpet. 'I'll try to bring your sister home in one piece.'

The moment Lady Caroline closed the suite door, Violet released an audible groan. She slumped, exhausted, onto the dresser stool. There, in the mirror, she saw her bandaged reflection, her stomach protruding noticeably as though she'd eaten too many meringues. Violet reactively spun the chair away, unwilling to confront the person she'd become.

22

Day 92: Newcastle, New South Wales
Population: 178,002
Weather: 75 degrees Fahrenheit, heavy rain
Fact: The city of Newcastle is the second-oldest city in Australia and the largest coal-exporting harbour in the world. It features the Bogey Hole, one of the oldest ocean baths in Australia, built in 1820 by convicts for the personal use of Commandant Morisset.

Violet's sickness paid a visit at around four the next morning. Nobody saw her clasping her hand over her mouth as she exploded through the bathroom door.

By five she felt much better. Violet knew she'd need to see a doctor or, worse, tell somebody about her condition. But first she had to visit Newcastle.

Violet had to have Lady Caroline's luggage packed by seven, which meant her own suitcases needed to be ready by five thirty. In between she'd need to service the breakfast order, prepare an outfit and finalise the personal baggage for departure.

'I feel like I just unpacked,' Bobo complained as Violet collected Lady Caroline's garment an hour later. 'And I've got to pack everybody's blooming luggage,' she shouted as two equerries tried to squeeze shut one of many large clothing trunks.

At seven thirty Violet waited in an alcove under the foyer stairs. She quietly observed the equerries herding Lady Caroline, Major Ratcliffe, the Duke's private secretary (the Lieutenant Commander Parker), Commander Carville, an Australian policeman in a suit, and a plain-clothes officer, Detective Reilly, under umbrellas to a line of eight black government cars that encircled the entrance promenade. Reilly was a no-nonsense man who'd arrived from London by air yesterday morning. He had an odd nervous tic whereby he sniffed every few seconds. At first Violet had assumed he'd brought a cold with him from London, but within minutes it became clear there was something involuntary and permanent about it.

Once everybody was bundled into their respective vehicles, the Queen and Duke were ushered to the lead car. Due to the rain it had a closed roof, while discreet British flags were mounted above each headlight. Unlike the grand open-roofed Daimler, it announced that this trip was for business, not show.

'I've got you,' called Jack in his heavy Australian accent, a patina of sunburn over his variegated mass of freckles. Violet hadn't quite had a good look at him yet. His shoulders were broad, stretching the limits of a dark suit he appeared to have been shoehorned into.

'Bag's in the boot,' he chirped, and held the door open for Violet. She climbed into the back seat, her attention taken by the elegance of the vehicle. She brushed her hand across the fine black leather.

Jack swung open the opposite rear passenger door to reveal Daisie standing there, dressed in her service blouse.

'Can I take another car?' she pleaded to Jack, seeing Violet sitting inside.

'Sorry, this has been arranged down to the last step. They'd have my neck.'

She sighed and begrudgingly slid in beside Violet, as Jack pulled on his cap and climbed behind the wheel. 'Chettle party all present and accounted for,' he announced.

'Pardy?' Daisie said. 'What is a "pardy"?'

'Par-ty,' he replied. 'As in "life of the par-ty".'

'Can't understand a word,' Daisie muttered.

Jack winked at Violet in the rear-vision mirror. Violet averted her eyes and crossed her hands in her lap.

The other cars rolled out of the driveway as the rain thickened, dulling the clamour of the patient crowd that had waited since dawn at the gates under umbrellas and spread newspapers.

'Big day ahead,' he continued as they drove through the gates. The crowd peered through the window, hoping to glimpse royalty. 'After Newcastle we fly to Lismore. One of those places the Queen probably wouldn't realise is part of her domain. Better off without it, to be honest. Blue Mountains tomorrow. Then repeat for the next two months, hey? Come April first, you'll have handled about five thousand bouquets of flowers, I reckon,' he teased.

Rain spattered the windshield as the car wended its way through the city traffic.

'Shame about the weather, ladies. Hope it doesn't make you home—'

'Pardon me, but who are you?' Daisie interrupted.

'Jack. I'm a mate of ya sister.'

'A mate?' Violet blurted.

'Why am I not surprised?' Daisie pontificated. 'She does get around. How's your other boyfriend?'

Violet remained silent.

A wry smirk grew on Jack's face. 'Boyfriend, hey, Violet?' he asked.

'My *name* is Miss Chettle. And how dare you ask personal questions. What is your title? Rank?'

'General Dogsbody, equerry-ing, hand-holding, what-noting. Driving, mostly. Speaking of, you must be quite chuffed, Miss Daisie. Riding with the grown-ups yesterday. Ya mum'll be thrilled.'

The comment silenced the sisters. Each turned to stare silently out of her respective window at the rain-swept streets.

'You know, I can tell you two apart,' Jack persisted. 'Violet's hair does that thing over her right ear. Dangles. Like wisteria. Bit fetching, hey,' he said with a swagger of self-convinced charm. Violet blushed at the compliment, a rarity when she was in the presence of her sister. 'And *she*,' he said, referring to Daisie, 'slouches a bit, whereas you don't. And you're Chunder Loo – a legend.'

'Chunder Loo?' asked Violet, scrunching her face like a halved lemon, the buzz of the lingering compliment squashed.

'Are you finished?' Daisie snapped.

The car approached Central station, a sandstone building at the southern end of the city. Its clock tower reached two hundred and fifty feet in the air, each of its four clocks facing a cardinal point. Royal watchers crowded under the arched entrance avoiding the rain, waiting and hoping to glimpse the Queen or Duke entraining. Some spilled onto the pavement clutching umbrellas, stalling the flow of traffic and prompting drivers to sound their horns. The effect was like the staccato tuning of a brass section.

'They tell me twenty thousand people are expected to watch her leave, but I reckon they underestimated yet again,' Jack declared before jumping out into the crowd that enclosed the vehicle.

Daisie and Violet sat in silence.

'Is he coming back?' Violet posed.

Jack suddenly pulled open the door on Daisie's side. As the rain-drops rolled off his broad shoulders, he offered his hand as if to declare, 'Stay close and follow me.'

Jack plunged into the crowd like it was the Amazon jungle, wielding an umbrella like a machete. Crowded beneath, the three of them pushed through the excitable crush towards a wooden bar-ricade manned by a line of Australian police wearing black ties and bandleader-style caps.

Jack flashed his papers and the barricade slid aside. The trio were released from the mass of pressed bodies onto the empty train platform, which had been spruced up for the day with a red carpet and Union Jack bunting.

They strolled briskly alongside the royal train, a six-carriage steam locomotive bearing a custom rear balcony emblazoned with the 'ER' crest. 'It's so they can wave to those they're leaving behind,' Jack explained, as Violet spied Lady Caroline seated in the lounge cabin. Major Ratcliffe sat nearby on a velvet chaise, chatting to a journalist.

'This one, ladies.' Jack held the second carriage door open for them. 'Second compartment along the hall. In with Mrs Bobo.'

The royal dresser was already seated and, by the looks of it, pre-paring for a nap. Violet sat opposite, by the window.

'Is there anywhere there isn't a mob?' Bobo complained as the station master's whistle trilled. 'Ratcliffe's telling the press tae dis-pute false rumours. Two thousand cars blocked a road in the middle of nowhere because word got around she wae seeing some new method for milking cows.'

The train lurched out of the station with a blast of steam and a roar from the crowd. The silt-sullied rear bulwarks of the carriage works gave way to teeming brick terrace houses strung together with clothes lines. British flags hung like hammocks here and there on painted iron-lace railings. Dense stone cottages gradually gave way to fibro houses on quarter-acre suburban grass blocks and houses with red corrugated-iron roofs and silver corrugated-iron tanks. The occasional applauding mob streaked by, popping out from under their umbrellas to wave madly for half a second before the train left them agape in its slipstream.

After around thirty minutes, a loud whoosh of air rattled the windows and the train plunged into a dark tunnel, emerging two minutes later in dense bush as though they'd gone through some black hole into the past. Branches as tough and wiry as frayed bridge cables encroached on the windows, and mossy bush stone and dense foliage darkened the carriage until it opened up to a wide estuary that ran alongside the tracks. Here and there a lattice oyster bed floated above the brackish umber tideway. The Hawkesbury had a prehistoric feel, its weathered stony shoreline and scrubland bordered by jagged grey sandstone cliffs that rose to the sky like perilous sentinels. The occasional fisherman's shack could be spotted perched in isolation between the river and the spiky brush.

Violet nudged her bandaged cheek against the glass, craning towards the sandstone escarpments. With a whistle and a rush of air the train plunged into another tunnel, emerging on flatter earth where wooden boxes with angular tin roofs, painted in shades of pastel green, yellow or blue, dotted the track side on grassy blocks. In the backyards of these suburban residences, wet linen hung from pointed steel structures spun with wires – clothes lines that looked like large umbrellas without canopies.

The driver blew the engine's whistle, announcing the Queen's fleeting presence to the school children lined up under the roof of the station they sped past. The rain was pouring heavily again, the droplets streaking the windows like ant trails. Despite the piercing scream of the whistle, Bobo remained fast asleep.

The train steamed through a hamlet named Gosford at high speed. Locals five deep lined the tracks for miles on either side, hoping to glimpse the Queen. From inside the speeding carriage they were merely a blur of squinting eyes and slack jaws, the sodden throng unlikely to determine how many carriages had sped by, let alone get a glimpse of Her Majesty.

Daisie fidgeted, folding a newspaper in boredom as Bobo's jowls vibrated like a car engine on a winter's morning. Then Daisie's patience snapped. She dropped the newspaper and stood up.

'Where are you going?' asked Violet.

'Lady Caroline,' Daisie said dismissively as the train whipped through a narrow cutting.

'I'm not sure we should go back there,' Violet warned in a whisper, trying not to wake Bobo.

'I don't care what you think!' Daisie stepped defiantly towards the door.

Violet glanced apprehensively at Bobo. Her mouth hung slightly open and her left hand had flopped across the cushioned leather seat. Getting up carefully, Violet tailed Daisie down the corridor. She started as a wet rock escarpment, deeper than the train itself, passed by inches from the window glass.

Daisie stopped at the doorway. Reilly, the Queen's detective, smoked on the other side of the far inter-carriage window as the rain sheeted down in the gap between. He clocked her presence, exhaling a lungful of smoke through the window opening.

'We shouldn't,' Violet urged Daisie as she caught up at the end of the aisle.

'Good – don't then.'

Wet wind and noise flooded in as Daisie pulled open the heavy door. Violet watched nervously as Daisie gripped a single chain and stepped onto the slippery connecting gangway. A fall would plunge her under the train wheels below. Daisie's dress flared up as Reilly pushed open the opposite door and held an arm out to her. She grasped his hand and let him pull her into the royal carriage.

Violet couldn't hear the conversation but Daisie gave Reilly a flirtatious look before he reluctantly took a packet out of his jacket pocket and offered her a cigarette.

Daisie, smirking as she twirled the cigarette in her fingers, glanced at Violet. Violet rolled her eyes.

Unbeknownst to either of them, Prince Philip had appeared further down the narrow corridor, idling towards them with his hand propped in his jacket pocket.

'Oh, thunderation,' Violet cursed under her breath.

Reilly was the first to notice the approaching Prince. He stepped back into an empty travel compartment to allow the Duke to pass.

Daisie stayed her ground in the tight corridor.

Violet swung back out of view. She peered one eye around the cabin doorway to watch the unfolding horror.

Daisie smiled charmingly up at the Duke as he neared. His frame dwarfed her and his charm went straight to her knees, almost causing them to buckle.

Violet gulped air and held it as the Prince and Daisie faced each other in the narrow space, him blushing, her face all innocence and delight. Their clothes made contact, then their bodies brushed against each other in a space designed for one.

The train plunged into a tunnel and everything went to darkness.

The overhead bulbs flickered to life seconds later, Prince Philip's brilliant white naval suit glowing under the weak light as he tactfully negotiated around her, while she twisted and gyrated for intimacy's sake.

As he passed, the Duke appeared to make an offhand comment with a subtle nod. 'The joys of travel,' perhaps, from what Violet could discern from her hiding spot. Daisie made a flirtatious comment in return and exhaled smoke. The Prince acquitted her with another smile before stepping into the safety of Reilly's compartment.

Daisie's face relaxed into a besotted grin as she twirled towards the royal suite, her cigarette still smouldering in her poised right hand.

'What were you doing?' Violet scolded as Daisie re-entered their compartment twenty minutes later. She sported a self-satisfied grin as she plopped down on the seat and fanned the bent newspaper out in front of her like a shield.

Bobo growled and gargled before lolling her head to the other side and resuming her throaty brawl.

'Sleeping beauty over there obviously hasn't been kissed yet,' joked Daisie as she flicked the page.

'You're flirting with him. You shouldn't even be in there!'

'You must be joking,' Daisie scoffed, lowering the paper to make her point. 'Lecturing on morality!'

'This is not about me,' Violet hissed back.

'The moment you slept with *him* you made it about you.'

Violet held her tongue as a roll of thunder crackled outside, declaring its proximity.

Daisie released a deep sigh. 'At least I didn't vomit on him.' She raised the newspaper with a flourish, obstructing her sister's view of her entirely.

23

A twelve-piece brass band competed with the roar of a crowd as the royal train arrived at Newcastle station. The Queen and Duke were welcomed by the local Mayor, his wife and half a million damp wellwishers.

As the formal ceremony got underway, the lower-tier staff alighted to gleaming town cars sporting miniature British and Australian flags above each front wheel brace. Daisie and Violet didn't even pretend to 'coincidentally' depart in separate vehicles, choosing to stand at opposite ends of the transport line to be transferred to an industrial air base fifteen minutes away.

'What's up wae you two?' Bobo enquired as she watched the montage of wooden cottages scroll by outside the car window. 'Wee scunners, ye hate each other.'

'It's complicated,' confessed Violet. 'So much so, to even ponder it gives me a migraine all the way down to my stomach.'

Bobo chuckled as a couple of young boys, aged eleven or twelve, frantically pumped the pedals of their bicycles to try and keep up with the car, the first shouting out with a wide smile in case it carried the Queen.

'We had cousins in Dumfries. They be twins. Spent every Christmas there until we were too old tae care. But I remember the song my auntie used to sing when they started havin' a go at each other.' A few seconds passed, as though Bobo had finished making her point. Then she started quietly singing in a melodic and heartfelt voice, as though from a past that her present wouldn't know.

'I may be a twin, but I am one of a kind. There's two to wash, two to dry; There's two who argue, two who cry; There's two to kiss, two to hug; and best of all, there's two to love.'

The driver couldn't help but smile. By the time Bobo had finished, Violet's eyes had welled. She sniffed, composing herself. 'It used to be that way,' Violet said, her voice creaking.

'You two have to sort ye cac,' Bobo admonished gruffly, 'or you'll be booted.'

The convoy slowed at the Hunter River car ferry as the rain eased. To the south the narrow channel wound out to sea less than half a mile from the crossing. Attendants, obscured by bright yellow oversized raincoats, directed them around a line of waiting cars onto a clanking steel ramp that led to a steam-powered barge. Each car was directed across the wooden deck until they were bumper to bumper. Damp pedestrians lined the railings, gossiping and lingering in the hope of sharing the crossing with Her Majesty. To groans and liberal use of the word 'mate', four policeman herded them towards the aft end, away from the official cars.

As the ferry disengaged from its moorings the driver cut the engine and a quiet resumed to the boat's gentle sway, the breeze punctuated by the clink of rigging and the sporadic squawk of seagulls.

'It wasn't my fault,' Violet whispered, hoping for the driver not to hear.

'Ne'er is,' Bobo replied as a seagull landed on the bonnet and the boat slowed to dock on the opposite side, where a small crowd had gathered. The police waved the cars through, escorting them to an air base two miles further along the coast road, where a briefing room had been temporarily decorated with portraits of Queen Elizabeth and her mother. Leather couches and coffee tables had been placed on hastily purchased rugs to offer the royal staff a 'green room' of sorts. A ceiling fan spun desperately overhead as the staff circled a dull refreshment table like torpid flies.

Violet helped herself to four too many Australian chocolate sponge cakes, or 'lamingtons', as an edgy staff sergeant with acne referred to them. A speaker mounted to the wall relayed the live radio broadcast from the Newcastle ceremony, the heavy Australian commentary effectively rendering it unintelligible.

Across the room, as far from Violet as possible, Daisie scanned the newspapers, flicking through the pictorial displays, probably hoping to see a photo of herself with the Queen at Bondi Beach.

'Can I fetch you anything, Miss Chettle?' a staff sergeant asked Violet.

'Actually, yes, please. Some writing paper. And a pen?'

The waiter returned minutes later with a pen, an envelope and four sheets of letterhead that bore the 'RAAF Base Williamtown' military insignia. Violet frowned with concentration and started writing.

Dear Hazel,

I've started writing this letter four times and can think of no other way to say this but plainly.

Our mother and father, Edith and Edward, passed away last year. Mother died suddenly when hit by a bus, and Father's throat was lost to the fog.

It was a difficult year.

*My sister, Daisie, and I are travelling around Australia on
the royal tour as maids to Lady Althorp. We are currently at an
air base in Newcastle, but this changes by the hour.*

*I must also confess that I have learned I am pregnant.
I will be having the baby. I have kept this a secret from my
sister as it's her boyfriend's baby. Well, he was her boyfriend
until recently. It's somewhat convoluted.*

*Regardless, within weeks, as my stomach becomes further
pronounced, the child will announce itself to her and to the world.*

I have many questions and will try to find you.

*Should this letter find you first, I await your urgent reply,
best sent care of Government House, Melbourne, Victoria,
Australia, where we will be in two weeks.*

Yours expectantly,

Violet

24

Day 95: *Katoomba, New South Wales*
Population: *1205*
Weather: *71 degrees Fahrenheit, petulant rain with some isolated storms*
Fact: *The Greater Blue Mountains Area contains 150 plant species found nowhere else in the world.*

The tour had rolled through Newcastle, Lismore, Casino ('the Duke was quite disappointed it was not an actual casino,' Bobo gossiped to Violet) and Dubbo, where a Western Districts Display (feats of wood chopping and sheep shearing) was performed, before a turbulent flight back to Sydney.

During a morning tea at the Returned Servicemen's Convalescent Camp in Mount Keira on the bumpy road to Wollongong, a bee pricked Violet's right hand while she wrangled a posie of prickly Australian natives. The barb pulsated in her palm like a beating heart. She bit her lip, held her tongue, and flicked the gooey spike out with her left fingernail. Then, with a wrath that surprised even her, Violet crushed the insect under three slams of an ashtray.

The noise raised the attention of Reilly, who charged into the anteroom of the camp hall, alarmed that there might a disturbance.

'Daisie, what the hell are you doing?' he said with a sniff, becoming quite disappointed, almost annoyed, when it transpired there was no real threat.

In her fluster Violet didn't correct Detective Reilly. The bruise had healed and the bandage had come off her cheek that morning. Unfortunately for both sisters, it was the single thing everybody had been relying on to distinguish them. Though soon Violet's pregnancy would distinguish her from everybody.

The art of avoidance had established its own routine. Daisie and Violet woke at six. They took turns bringing Lady Caroline's breakfast along with the British newspapers that arrived via air, courtesy of the Australian Government. They'd take turns collecting Lady Caroline's outfit from Bobo. Any updates to the schedule were slid under their doors each night at around midnight by one of Major Ratcliffe's three secretaries. By eight the next morning, they'd repack Lady Caroline's personal effects, then their own, in time for the 'assembly'. Then the caravan would depart.

The official proceedings typically commenced with a morning function, likely a visit to a school, war memorial or hospital. Then there would be a street 'progress', which consisted of the Queen and Duke driving down a main street, waving at the screaming throng, followed by a formal fifteen-minute civic reception wherein the Queen would read a prepared speech and listen to some local dignitaries speak. If there was no lunch event scheduled with a local community group, they'd dine in private. The Queen and her inner circle, including her lady-in-waiting, would eat together in one room while the support staff dined together in a separate hall.

After lunch the Duke might divert to inspect a mill or a factory, while the Queen would have a scheduled rest break. If there was an evening function, one hour – minimum – was required for the girls to prepare Lady Caroline, organising her outfit, coordinating the loan and return of jewels (if she uttered, 'I'll go vulgar tonight,' it meant ample ornaments), rearranging and overseeing approval and set-up of accommodations and suite, pulling sheets, dusting, servicing food and beverage requests and ensuring the local staff didn't overstep privacy or protocol. Each day ended around 11 p.m. and was repeated the next. There was no respite.

It pained Violet to dispose of the hundreds of personal letters and cards they collected on Her Majesty's behalf. She read them all, and occasionally she'd keep one for herself, hiding them at the bottom of one of her suitcases inside a heavy knitted winter jacket. It felt like the least she could do for the young girls who had reached out to their Queen. She knew it was a sackable offence, but disposing of them felt like the greater sin.

Violet lowered the newspaper. From the train compartment window she could see the motorcade turn into the high street of Katoomba, its pavements and awnings teeming with the usual barrage of excited Australians. 'This town seems a bit more British than the others we've visited. A bit like the Cotswolds, perhaps. Frontier-like, even,' she remarked to Bobo. 'That'—she pointed to the grand Carrington Hotel, which stood at the crest of the hill—'reminds me of that hotel in Brighton.'

'Long way awa from Brighton,' Bobo said, flapping her newspaper.

Violet returned to the Bourke *Western Herald*. Its front-page photograph depicted the Queen and Lady Caroline performing a 'pastoral review' in Dubbo. A row of thirty sheep were being held at the neck by their proud white-coated handlers, rear ends pointed outwards for Her Majesty to inspect. Daisie was visible as a blur in the background.

'It's like a guard of honour of sheep bums. Prize Merino stud stock, thus lot,' Bobo said, mimicking the local brogue in an Australian-by-way-of-Scottish accent. 'Look at this beautiful girl's behind!' she drawled, pronouncing it 'behorned'.

Violet laughed along with her. Even Daisie cracked a smile.

'Lilibet found it right hilarious – I shouldn' be telling ye,' Bobo said, wiping the tears from her ruddy cheeks. 'Nor should I tell ye aboot the constable in Wolloomooloo last week. Said a group of dear mute kiddies lip-read Phil saying to her, "Come on, ducks, a big smile and wave to the children. They're deaf and dumb!"'

Violet read aloud snippets from other regional papers, including a poem written for Her Majesty's benefit in a provincial rag called *The Lockhart Review*.

'Our Queen is here, the Queen beloved. Who hath her regal fitness proved,' Violet regaled in an exaggerated Australian accent. 'Whose loveliness and charm is great, in keeping with her high estate!'

'On the throne she proudly sits,' Bobo improvised, 'but if she's tired and grumpy, she'll have the shits!'

As the half-hour passed and the gifts of the *Nepean Times* ran dry, Bobo drifted back to sleep.

'Can I get you anything?' Jack asked pleasantly, leaning in from the corridor.

'No,' replied Daisie brusquely on behalf of everybody.

'Got the night off in Sydney tonight, if you want to grab a beer?'

'Not interested,' Daisie snapped before Violet could consider it.

'I get it. Hard to get. No worries then.' Undeterred, he smiled and moved on to the next compartment.

25

The roar of the motorcade in the main street of Katoomba was drowned out by the crowds. Spectators spilled over the gutters, with only a stretched-out line of police to restrain them from storming the cars. For Daisie, the relentless adulation was becoming repetitively dull.

'Do you think Violet is putting on weight?' she wondered out loud.

'I'm hoping the Blue Mountains are named for their colour and not their mood,' Lady Caroline said, ignoring the question. She tilted her head towards the window to see down the length of Main Street. 'Looks like they've underestimated again.' The road undulated down a hill teeming with people. The right-hand side of the street was slightly more crowded than the left, it being common knowledge that the Queen always sat on the right-hand side of the royal car. As the car passed, many in the crowd broke away, trying to keep up with the procession, until the pavement became jammed with a breathless mass.

Daisie noticed Lady Caroline's gloved hand start to pick at a single stray thread in the embroidered floral motif that ran around her waist. It wasn't a nervous tic, or annoyance with the stray inch of cotton. She coaxed it between her fingers slowly, massaging it with a relaxed fondness, like she were petting the fur of a placid cat on her lap.

Daisie had the urge to occupy her own fingers, unable to keep them placed in her lap. She rested her left hand on the seat beside her and discreetly traced the tip of her index finger along the fine stitching of the leather seat.

Police motorcycles accelerated from the rear to travel on either side of the motorcade, warding off a crowd that had started to surge inwards. The rider on the Queen's side was chased by a black pup with four brown legs who was determined to bite the rear tyre, until – to a burst of cheers from the audience – its harried owner, chased by a crowd-control official, rushed forth with a lead.

The motorcade arrived at the Echo Point lookout, where a temporary stage had been constructed near the clifftop fence for the welcome. A decked pergola decorated with a mass of gladioli and begonia blooms framed a slightly misshapen crown and 'ER' forged from papier-mâché. The surrounding grassy earth had been covered with a carpet woven with a fleur-de-lis pattern. It had an endearing small-town feel, like a country fete.

The Queen and Duke alighted from their vehicle, prompting a six-piece brass band to play a strident take on 'God Save the Queen', competing with the intense cheering of the crowd.

Her Majesty wore a green Laurel dress with wrist-length cream gloves, matching open-toed shoes and an apricot pansy headdress that was meticulously strewn with glinting crystals. Pinned high on the lapel of her dress was a brooch given to her at the State banquet earlier in the week, depicting sprays of wattle, the national flower, in branchlets of yellow and white diamonds. Bobo had a box devoted to locally presented jewellery. The items were to be worn

once during the itinerary in deference to the host, before being cata-
logued and put into permanent storage.

The Queen and Duke were welcomed by the local mayor, his
aldermen and their attendant wives. One of the women, sweating under a mink stole, presented the Queen with a bound photo
album. Lady Caroline stepped forward to intercept the gift with a
grateful nod.

After the rigour of the greeting line, Queen Elizabeth and Prince
Philip were directed towards the guardrail, encouraged by the
Mayor, who swept his arm like P T Barnum to present the view, as
though he'd created it himself.

Beyond the fence sprawled a vertigo-inducing valley skirted by
sheer sandstone bluffs that descended into impenetrable bush 1500
feet below. In the foreground, rising out of the void, three progres-
sively taller rock pinnacles stood majestically amid a lingering mist.

'That's the Three Sisters, Your Highness,' the Mayor declared,
referring to the strange rock pyres. 'A native legend. After their
father died, three daughters were frozen in stone forever. Trapped,
as it were. That's them.'

The Mayor's words hung in the air as the Queen gazed hypnotised into the void, her controlled demeanour momentarily relaxed.

'Fanciful, of course. But wonderful for tourism,' the Mayor persisted, still to no royal acknowledgement.

'Yes, I imagine so,' offered the Duke, easing the polite tension.

The Queen turned away from the cliff towards the marquee, her
formal visage re-engaged. She stepped up to the microphone and the
crowd of two thousand on the clifftop fell silent.

'My mother has often told me of the rare beauty of these mountains, and today I have been delighted with them myself,' she read
from her speech notes. 'The photographs you have given me will

always serve to remind me of this happy day. I shall certainly show
them to my children, and when they see them, I feel sure that they
will wish to visit you themselves.'

A Boy Scout nervously approached the rise, prodded towards
the Queen by a jumpy Scout leader. He bowed and presented
Her Majesty with a posy of white camellias blended with baby's
breath. Then he stood frozen, terrified. A wetting of the pants was
not out of the question. The Scout leader ran forward, squatting
and grumbling under his breath, to collar the starstruck boy out of
the glare.

Ratcliffe thanked the Mayor and, to warm applause, the tour
party moved towards the transport. The ten-vehicle convoy wound
its way along the clifftop drive, skirting the valley drop before rolling through the hamlet of Leura, whose population had swelled
twenty-fold for the royal progress.

Lady Caroline's gaze rested on the Queen's car ahead. The Duke
waved at a group of secondary school girls, who cheered ravenously,
as they often did.

'What do you make of the Duke?'

'Prince Philip? He's gorgeous,' replied Daisie without hesitation.

'Yes, he has that effect, unfortunately.'

'Unfortunately?'

'It's nothing.' She glanced towards the driver, assessing their
degree of privacy. 'And what do you think of me, then?' Lady
Caroline asked. 'Be honest.'

Daisie considered the question for a moment, careful in her reply.
'You're not like them. You're yourself. There's no . . . pretending.'

'No pretending,' Lady Caroline repeated. She turned her attention to a group of school children singing enthusiastically by the
road, their teacher madly scolding them to 'Pro-ject! Pro-ject!' But

Lady Caroline's eyes had stilled, concealing a rising thought behind them.

She dipped her eyes and revealed them to Daisie as though about to confess a secret. Then she clasped Daisie's hand tightly. Daisie glanced at the rear-vision mirror to ensure the intimate act was out of view.

Lady Caroline then wrapped her fingers into Daisie's and squeezed. Her grip had an urgent physicality. She leaned in and whispered into Daisie's ear. 'Come to my train compartment.'

Daisie gasped a small breath. There was no doubt now. And there was no doubt that the nervous excitement Daisie felt would carry her to Lady Caroline's compartment and away from everybody else's eyes.

In that moment, the car pulled up at Katoomba station. The white noise of the cheering mob flooded the car as the door was enthusiastically pulled open by a waiting equerry. Lady Caroline briskly withdrew her hand and exited gracefully as though nothing had happened.

The gathered crowd started to sing the anthem as the Queen and Duke rose from the Daimler in front. The royal couple waved briefly to the mob before being escorted through the barrier into the station house.

Lady Caroline furtively glanced back at Daisie as she disappeared from view.

Daisie paused in the car, her hand resting on the rumpled leather where Lady Caroline had sat. Despite the risks, the forbidden unknown had claimed her. She'd felt lust many times before, but boys had grown tiresome. And Lady Caroline's beauty and power were uniquely intoxicating.

Daisie's eyes narrowed, lost in the leather as she plotted her game.

'Miss?' asked the equerry patiently holding the door.

A wry smile escaped her lips as she reset her posture. Daisie stepped out of the vehicle with a determined confidence.

'What shall I do with the gifts?' he asked.

'Dispose of them.'

'Where?'

'I don't know, a bin?' she replied curtly, then skipped ahead to catch the royal party's wake.

'Anything happen?' Violet asked breezily as Daisie placed her hat into the overhead rack.

'Mind your own business,' Daisie snapped. 'Oh.' She paused at the door on her way back out. 'We saw some big rocks that were sisters and they are stuck with each other forever. Utter tragedy.'

With a skybound throb of steam and a rousing cheer, the train lurched out of Katoomba station. One excitable chap threw his hat into the air to mark the occasion, the tan stetson landing squarely on the rails just before the train wheels chewed it asunder.

Daisie edged along the hallway of the royal carriage until she arrived at Lady Caroline's open compartment. Lady Caroline was watching the rain that had started to fleck and streak the windows while thick mountain undergrowth rolled by, her feet resting on the opposite seat, her shoes kicked off onto the carpet. An Australian Government information brochure lay open in her hands. Although she hadn't moved, Daisie knew Lady Caroline sensed her standing at the door.

'Apparently the eucalyptus tree emits a chemical that gives the mountains a blue haze,' Lady Caroline announced. 'Used to be called "Carmarthen and Landsdowne Hills". "The Blue Mountains" is better for tourism, I suppose.'

Daisie pulled the door shut and drew the privacy curtain. She sat beside Lady Caroline's stockinged feet.

'I want to ask a favour,' Daisie said.

'Anything,' Lady Caroline replied generously.

'Send my sister home. Back to London.'

Lady Caroline's eyebrows lifted, then her gaze returned to the brochure. 'That's rather excessive.'

'I can't stand to be near her.'

'What has she done?'

'She slept with my boyfriend. More than once, I suspect.' Daisie scowled. 'Before *I* was able to!'

'You had a boyfriend?'

'The sight of her makes me ill.'

A wry curve found the edge of Lady Caroline's lips.

'What's so funny?' asked Daisie.

'To be a twin and nauseous at the sight of yourself. It's Freudian, or something of that ilk.' She chuckled.

'Fire her!'

'I cannot. There are no grounds.'

'Do this for me and you'll earn my devotion.'

'I'd convinced myself I already had it.'

Daisie shifted to sit beside Lady Caroline. She rested her hand on Lady Caroline's in the same way Lady Caroline had earlier done, in the manner of a promise. 'Lady Caroline, I beg you. Anything.'

'I cannot. It's not out of loyalty to your sister. It's just very complicated – and expensive – to send somebody home for no apparent reason. Questions get asked. It would call *my* character into question. Especially given I'd be doing it for unthinkable reasons. Ratcliffe won't tolerate any impropriety. There's *no* tolerance.'

Daisie pulled her hand away in frustration.

'So, Violet,' pondered Lady Caroline. 'Didn't think she had it in her. Lends her some desperately needed intrigue.'

'I could lose my job, being here,' Daisie ventured, as if trying to persuade her.

'Darling, I'm the one with something to lose. You're free to walk away.'

Daisie rested her palm on Lady Caroline's cheek and urged her closer. Their eyes fixed inches apart. Daisie leaned gently towards her, her heart galloping, and Lady Caroline's perfectly painted lips parted.

With a rush of air, the cabin went dark as the train plunged into a tunnel. In the blackness, their lips came together. She closed her eyes as they kissed, tentatively at first. Then, in Lady Caroline's unrestrained affection, her lips engulfed Daisie's, her fingers clasping Daisie's hair with urgency.

The train plunged back into the daylight and Daisie, her eyes now open, glimpsed Lady Caroline's soft cheeks, her skin so pale and flawless. Daisie touched Lady Caroline's slender neck with the palm of her hand. This reality now excited Daisie more than anything she'd previously experienced.

The shrill shock of the steam whistle pierced the air, snapping Daisie out of her trance. Lady Caroline pulled back and gently leaned her forehead against Daisie's cheek, releasing a deep breath. She interlocked her fingers with Daisie's again, staring deeply into her eyes as if a pledge were being made.

'Nobody must know,' Lady Caroline whispered. 'Then it would be me who'd be leaving.'

Daisie smiled awkwardly in reply.

The carriage slowed on its way through a deep hillside cutting. 'Blaxland' read the station sign as the train crawled into a small mountain village. They edged apart as the spectators lining the tracks peered through the windows, waving and awestruck.

Daisie's eyes fell on a small girl standing atop a plain grassy hill above the station. She was eight or nine years old, wearing a knitted blue beret and a short grey dress. A British flag dangled, unwaved, in her left hand, but cradled in the other was a small rabbit with the same snowy white fur as Nicholas. The girl stood still and impassive, like a startled spectre against the brilliant blue sky.

'Have I crossed a line?' Lady Caroline asked as she lit a cigarette.

Daisie, watching the girl slide from view, didn't reply.

'Stay with me, if not tonight, then on the *Gothic*.'

'I'm sorry, I cannot,' Daisie replied. But it was a polite lie, and she had every intention of doing so.

26

Day 100: Sydney, New South Wales
Population: 1,886,451
Weather: 95 degrees Fahrenheit, capricious winds
Fact: The Sydney funnel-web spider is one of the most dangerous spiders on earth, able to kill a human in fifteen minutes. Its fangs are powerful enough to bite through gloves and fingernails.

As the dusk deepened, a swarm of fruit bats congregated in the trees not far from Violet's bedroom window in Government House, Sydney. The silhouettes jostled restlessly in the dark, baying for fruit, though by their screeching it may as well have been blood. Their wailing could've been infighting or exultation – Violet couldn't tell which – but she twice ensured the windows were locked.

'Sounds like an excitable gaggle of Country Women's Association members,' Bobo said as she laid the next day's outfit across an ironing board. The women were a staple of the regional visits and the similarity of the sound was remarkable.

'Is Daisie back from Canberra? I haven't seen her since the Blue Mountains.'

'I havnae either. Sounds fortunate, though. I expect with the fare-well garden party in the morn, the lassie'll be makin' her sartorial demands soon enough. Eight thousand guests and Lilibet's worst nightmare. She'll be glad to board for Tasmania.'

The heat didn't drop below eighty degrees all evening. The air in Violet's room was so thick with humidity that the ceiling fan seemed to struggle to cut through it.

The cicadas started clacking before sunrise, alert to a day of high temperature. The thermometer reached ninety degrees before Violet had delivered Lady Caroline's breakfast, a silver tray on which lay poached eggs, sliced pineapple, her pot of chamomile tea and a slender vase of petunias.

'You must dread returning to the iron lung with your sister,' said Lady Caroline as Violet poured the tea. A few droplets spilled onto the porcelain. 'Perhaps I can see to moving Daisie to another room, so you'll have some privacy?'

'Thank you, Lady Caroline,' she replied. 'That would be most appreciated.'

By ten, the petunias had wilted in the heat. The bats had either moved on or were asleep in the shadows of the leafy canopy. Overdressed locals had started to gather on the lawns, huddled in small groups in the available shade afforded by the trees. Women fanned themselves with their cardboard invitations while men smoked, their suit jackets slung over their shoulders as pockets of sweat grew on their shirts. The tea party didn't commence until midday but they suffered for fear of missing out.

In Lady Caroline's suite the air was stuffy. The oscillation of two ceiling fans produced little more than a droning harmonic resonance. The layer of sweat on Violet's forehead had started to condense into rain-sized droplets. She lowered a peppermint pillbox hat with a matching gauze trim onto Lady Caroline's tightly gathered hair and fixed it with three hairpins.

'Right,' Lady Caroline said, checking herself in the full-length mirror one last time. 'Showtime. When Daisie gets back, tell her to join me in the drawing room for the assembly.'

Violet cleared the dresser then rearranged the petunias so they didn't look quite so ill-fated. As she leaned over the edge of the bed, Violet glimpsed her reflection in the angled dress mirror. She froze. Her abdomen had grown, filling out the loose folds of her uniform so that the buttons were taut. Violet inspected her shape, straightening her spine as though she were trying on a new dress at Bentalls. She sucked in air. Her belly remained disproportionately rotund, even if she held her lungs and tensed her stomach muscles. Violet edged up her blouse, exposing her waist's white skin. She turned to her other profile.

The clunk of the latch and the fix of Daisie's eyes happened too swiftly for Violet to react. Daisie, primped for the garden party, hung motionless like one of the dusty portraits. Her mouth gaped as her hand gripped the door handle. The air in the room changed colour.

Daisie's eyelids cut to a scornful lour while Violet stammered to speak.

Camilla Lackshaft, a squirt of a thing and collector of breakfast trays, rounded Daisie and entered the room.

'Excuse,' she announced perfunctorily, fetching the silver tray, oblivious to the ruin. 'Hot, ain't it?' she said as she loaded the teapot and saucer.

Violet seized the distraction and ran. Daisie chased her down the hall and through the lobby, sidestepping four pages who carried Bobo's *Gothic*-bound trunks.

Daisie pursued Violet outside to the gardens, their pace now an urgent walk. They navigated around tea party guests milling in the shade, who stopped excitedly chatting to watch the unusual display. Violet diverted into the gardens, glancing over her shoulder at Daisie, who followed like a honed predator. The cicadas sang louder, their shrill chorus like the chant of a ritual kill.

Violet ducked under the low hanging branches of a hulking Moreton Bay fig, desperate to find an enclave where she could brave the truth's reckoning. She turned and faced Daisie under the natural canopy of a tree that resembled a head of broccoli. Dozens of bats hung asleep from the sinewy branches.

'Answer me!' Daisie shouted angrily, even though no question had been asked.

Violet's hands quivered as though she were facing her own execution.

Daisie stared with pursed lips and her hands perched on her waist.

'D-Daisie . . .' Violet stammered, not quite knowing which words to use.

'It's his,' Daisie concluded aloud.

Violet's hands hung beside her, fingers trembling as though frostbitten.

For what felt like an age, Daisie didn't speak, exhaling measured breaths to modulate her rage as she stalked back and forth, her jaw clenched like a pent-up boxer's.

'He spoiled me,' Violet confessed, as her eyes dampened. 'I let him. But I despise him. Did from the beginning. I warned you and you did the opposite to spite me. And I'm the one who's paid.'

'You slept with my boyfriend and talk of my spite!'

'I paid your price. For nothing. Ugh, he makes me ill. I wasn't particular as to who I was saving myself for, but it certainly wasn't going to be a repugnant, entitled, moneyed bastard who thinks of us like possessions he can use and discard. I promise—'

'Stop talking! Shut it!'

'Daisie, believe me. I wish I could take it back—'

Daisie raised her right hand threateningly to silence her.

'You're going to strike me down? Kill me like you killed our mother?' Violet exclaimed, her eyes twitching nervously for the retaliation, which came as soon as expected. Daisie swiped Violet's face, sending her tumbling backwards, and paced over her until she regained her breath, holding her clawed right hand like a smoking gun. As Violet sat hopelessly in the dirt, Daisie turned and ducked under the canopy towards the house.

Violet's face throbbed from the scratch of Daisie's fingernails. She dabbed her cheek where a smear of blood told of the damage, but it was her pride that bled most.

A couple dressed formally for the tea party apprehensively lifted a branch and peered under.

'Is everything all right, miss?' the man said.

Violet nodded and slowly eased herself to her feet, brushing the dirt and leaves from her soiled uniform. She stumbled back to her room to tend to the cuts and bruises.

'I was mobbed by a pack of bats while strolling in the gardens' was the excuse she improvised to Lady Caroline, who in turn insisted Violet be examined by a nurse for infection.

Appalled and embarrassed by the incident, the New South Wales government urgently undertook a mass cull of the botanical gardens' fruit bat colony.

'Never seen bats do that, ever,' Jack claimed as Violet, her face patterned with plasters, shuffled up the gangway under a broad-brimmed teal hat she'd borrowed from Bobo. 'Guess they got to

Daisie's right hand too,' he said, as thick crowds jostled and cheered on the dockside below.

An explosion burst overhead. Violet instinctively cowered.

'Hooligans.' Jack laughed as a stray firework fizzed and sputtered in the daylight. A mob of police scuttled into the crowd to howls of delight. Jack turned his concern back to Violet. 'There's something going on with you two. I'm here, if you need me.'

'I'm perfectly fine, nothing to be concerned about whatsoever. Keeping calm carrying—'

She flinched again as the *Gothic*'s horn bellowed for departure.

With a roar from the tens of thousands surrounding the port, the ship retreated gracefully from the pier while Violet was still descending the stairs to her cabin.

A moth swirled hypnotically around the bulb that was still stuck on in the iron lung, casting its dim light into the miserable chamber that Violet knew all too well. As she opened her suitcase and started to unpack, the envelope of photographs slid out of her cardigan onto the bed.

The moth landed on the envelope in a fluster of dust. Violet remained perfectly still as it flapped its young spotted wings and crawled across her mother's handwriting. Violet remained motionless until it lifted off and resumed circling the covered bulb like an untethered satellite.

She placed the envelope on the iron table against the clock, angling it like a portrait. In the boat's grim gutter the whisper of her mother's handwriting offered a small comfort against the diminishing likelihood of ever finding Hazel.

27

Day 101: *Tasman Sea, 34°26´11.9˝S 150°59´48.9˝E*
Population: *0*
Weather: *74 degrees Fahrenheit, obstinate swell with south-westerly winds*
Fact: *The Tasman Sea is informally referred to as 'the ditch'; for example, 'crossing the ditch' means travelling to Australia from New Zealand, or vice versa.*

Sydney had receded to a pronounced ripple on the horizon, twin destroyers trawling either side of the aft as the *Gothic* skirted the coastline south to Tasmania.

Steward Joseph stood at the door to Daisie's new suite as she flopped backwards onto the bed, testing its spring. The luxury cabin was the mirror image of Lady Caroline's – adjacent, no less – with a round porthole window and a puckered bottle-green velvet couch. The curtains lifted in the cool ocean breeze as he checked and rechecked his notes, disappointed there hadn't been a mistake.

'Yes, I suppose you *are* in here now,' he said, frowning. 'I'll double-check with Lady Althorp,' he murmured as he slunk away.

The dusk sun, simmering like a hot coal, dropped below the horizon. Daisie wandered the topside deck with a cigarette clenched in her bruised fingers. She blew smoke into the tailwind as she leaned over the rail, watching the churned froth trail that snaked behind the ship.

'You've found my new hiding spot,' Lady Caroline said, her voice competing with the whoosh and lap of the ocean below. She pressed herself against the railing next to Daisie and breathed in the salty air.

'How's your room?' Lady Caroline asked. Then a look of panic crossed her face. 'You *are* Daisie?'

Daisie laughed. 'Yes. Don't worry. And my room is nicer than our entire house. I don't know how to thank you.'

'Don't get too used to it. We'll be back in dull government buildings soon enough.'

There was a lull in conversation as they watched the flickering specks of coastal towns emerge in the dim light.

'You can trust me,' Daisie implored her, answering a question that had not been asked.

Lady Caroline nodded subtly in reply. 'I used to watch you, back home. The highlight of my day, if you can believe it. I'm so happy you came.'

Daisie raised her eyes to the stars, brilliant against the night's fresh sky. She brushed her hair away from her face.

'What happened?' Lady Caroline asked, referring to Daisie's bruised fingers.

Daisie swept her hand in frustration as if to suggest it wasn't worth even articulating. 'What's the point of him cheating with somebody who looks *exactly* like me? Such a benign adventure,' Daisie confessed.

'Bad decisions are life's tuition. We all make them.' Lady Caroline fixed her gaze on Daisie.

'I want you to sleep in my room tonight,' Daisie declared with determination. 'With me.'

Lady Caroline blushed, beaming like a teenager. 'I was starting to think I had no bad decisions left to make,' she said, flattered.

Daisie turned back to the dark swell. Then she guffawed.

'Why are you laughing?' Lady Caroline asked.

Daisie wrinkled her nose as she grappled with the answer. 'Well, I don't know. The ocean, the stars, this ship – it's a cliché. Like the cover of a pulp novel you'd find on an unmarried auntie's bookshelf while looking for a Trixie Belden adventure.'

Lady Caroline laughed, her hair playing in the breeze as Daisie waited expectantly for the next move. Lady Caroline apprehensively reached out and touched Daisie's cheek with the back of her hand. Daisie reached up and clasped her bruised fingers around Lady Caroline's.

Lady Caroline glanced across the deck to ensure they weren't being watched.

'Trust me,' said Daisie. She led Lady Caroline to her suite and latched the door behind them.

The pre-dawn gloom had coloured the porthole. Lady Caroline lay facedown on Daisie's bed with her eyes closed, even though she was still awake. Daisie lay naked beside her, gently stroking Lady Caroline's hair affectionately. She leaned in and tenderly kissed the back of her head.

'How do you feel?' asked Lady Caroline.

'Powerful.'

Lady Caroline tilted her head towards her curiously. 'Don't let it go to your pretty head,' she said, rolling back onto her side and closing her eyes. 'It's not like we're getting married.'

A shade of disappointment coloured Daisie's face. 'My sister mustn't know.'

'That a shame. I was about to ask if you'd think she'd be interested. I know, it's a cliché, but the idea of you both is positively debauched.'

'*Pardon?*'

'Oh, come on, Daisie. It's one of the reasons I hired you. I'm sure it's not the first time you've been asked. Perhaps by a woman, granted.'

'I thought you were choosing *me*.'

'Well, it's not like you aren't interchangeable. Though to the discerning eye she does have a better behind. Are you jealous of her?'

'Why would I be? She's hopeless!' Daisie scowled in outrage. She raised herself on her elbows, uncertain what to be most offended about – that Lady Caroline saw Violet as more attractive, the disgusting notion of being intimate with her own sister, or that the affair was less meaningful than she'd convinced herself.

'Did you think I was your girlfriend?' asked Lady Caroline, turning her head towards Daisie.

Daisie didn't reply, but her answer was plainly yes.

'I knew this was a mistake. You're a maid, Daisie. Never forget it.'

Lady Caroline dropped her head back to the pillow and turned away from Daisie, signalling the end of the discussion. Daisie pulled the sheets up to her armpits and stared at her reflection in the mirror of the dresser opposite.

'I'm not like you,' Daisie said firmly.

'You can say that again.'

'I mean I don't like being with other women. It's a mistake.'

'Oops,' Lady Caroline joked. 'No turning back now.'

'Well, perhaps I have bigger fish to fry. I'll prove it.'

'Fine. Fry away. I need some rest.'

Daisie brooded for a moment, her mind calculating.

Then she acted, padding to the door to press the call button before waiting on the couch, still naked. She squinted her eyes tightly as though trying to aggressively meditate. A minute later they welled. She sobbed quietly, summoning a performance that was a little theatrical, but effective enough.

'What on earth you doing?' Lady Caroline asked, tilting her head up from the pillow. She turned towards a knock at the door.

'Help!' Daisie squealed.

Steward Joseph entered and froze at the threshold, shocked. Daisie raised her sodden eyes to him, crying in urgent distress as Lady Caroline lay naked in her bed, her face full of confusion.

28

Day 103: *Hobart, Tasmania*
Population: *87,548*
Weather: *67 degrees Fahrenheit, apathetic easterly breeze*
Fact: *Tasmania is an island the size of Ireland and was joined to the mainland of Australia until the end of the last glacial period about 10,000 years ago.*

It was a glorious summer morning when the *Gothic* sailed proudly up the River Derwent. The lush banks, granges and orchards slid leisurely by the bridge observation railings, where the Queen and Duke stood for the purposes of newsreel photography. The conditions showcased Hobart at its loveliest.

The Derwent unfurled into a broad harbour that nestled below Mount Wellington. A small flotilla of watercraft drifted by and followed in the *Gothic*'s wake. Hobart was more a village than a city, seemingly made up exclusively of red and green tin-roofed houses. One could sense the polite, awed restraint of the receiving audience, a blunt contrast to the rapture of the Sydney Harbour crowds.

Violet stood at the stern rail waiting for disembarkation, the draught teasing her hair as she surveyed the passing view.

Her scratches and bruises were slowly healing, though she still sported a patchy arrangement of plasters.

'Watch out! It's Bela Lugosi in *The Mummy*!' Jack had joked the day before as she'd passed by him near the lower staff room. She had not not been amused.

Aside from that incident, the three-day trip down the coast had been far less eventful than she'd anticipated. She had passed Daisie only twice in the hallways during the daily rounds. Lady Caroline had relieved Violet of morning and evening duties, relying exclusively on Daisie during those hours. It had given Violet ample time to sleep and recuperate before the tour recommenced on land.

As the *Gothic* floated towards the port of Hobart, Violet's gaze settled on a young woman standing on the adjacent grassy bank. She was Violet's age, pretty and pale, a baby cradled in her arms. The girl stared down at the tiny child, as fascinated by the minuscule human as she was uninterested in the parade taking place before her. Violet's right hand instinctively rested on her belly as the *Gothic*'s horn boomed.

The touring party disembarked in Hobart to the usual music and revelries. Daisie rode with Lady Caroline in a gleaming grey Daimler while Violet shared a regular town car with Bobo and the Duke's page on the drive to Government House, a glorious Victorian residence with wide verandahs. It was surrounded by elaborate botanical gardens overlooking a wide estuary, and its sandstone and teak interior reminded Violet of Elmbridge End.

She was escorted to a small bedroom towards the upper rear of the house, where desk-shaped indentations in the carpet suggested the room was usually an office. Since she hadn't seen Lady Caroline all day, Violet visited the administration office to check the status of the royal party. The office had been set up in an anteroom adjacent to the French Room, a modest rectangular dining hall with high ceilings. Empire-cushioned antique chaise longues and intricately designed wallpaper in a classical motif set an incongruous backdrop for the bland government-issue filing cabinets, desks and stools temporarily installed for the tour.

'Any messages?' Violet asked one of the secretaries busy unpacking the makeshift office. Three secretaries worked shifts around the clock, and Major Ratcliffe could usually be seen there from around four in the morning making telephone calls to 'BP' ('Buckingham Palace? I feel like I just cracked the Enigma code,' Daisie had said sarcastically the first time she'd heard it).

Violet could see Daisie seated at the far end of the room, her head in her hands, a loose handkerchief clutched in one of them, theatrically weeping in distress. Ratcliffe paced nearby, quizzing her apprehensively. Something had happened.

'No, Daisie!' was the terse reply as the secretary ushered Violet out of the room. Violet didn't bother to correct her.

'Wait a minute,' the girl added, rushing back to snatch an envelope from her desk. 'There's this.' She handed it to Violet. It was the letter she'd written to Hazel, stamped 'RETURNED TO SENDER'.

'Tell your sister you can't just write a name on an envelope "care of Australia" and think it'll get delivered.'

'Of course. How silly of her,' Violet mumbled as she shuffled from the room, turning the unopened envelope over in her hands.

Violet consoled herself by finessing Lady Caroline's room, a stately ground-floor drawing room complete with a mahogany grand piano and a Zenith record player credenza. She moved the screen away from the window – the hosts rarely considered the potential intrusion of press photographers – and unpacked Lady Caroline's dressing table chest. Just after four o'clock, the door swung open and Daisie barged in. She seemed momentarily stunned by Violet's presence.

'Leave,' Daisie ordered, plumping at the dressing table as though it were her throne. She started picking through Lady Caroline's things.

Violet hesitated at the impropriety of her sister's actions, then thought better of it and left the room with her head down and the empty water jug still in her hand. As she approached the corner of the narrow main hallway, she heard female voices. She slowed to a tiptoe and peeked around the corner with one eye.

The Queen and Lady Caroline were having a strident conversation by the doors of the royal suite. The floorboard under Violet's foot creaked as she shifted her weight. They stopped talking and glared at the prying cyclops. Violet involuntarily recoiled like a sprung child. Then she cringed at her clumsiness. There could be no doubt she had been spotted. She gritted her teeth, gripped the jug and took a backwards run-up step to fake an authentic 'arrival', casually sauntering around the corner.

They were both standing there, of course, perfectly still, gazing at the whole facile parade. The Queen frowned, her arms folded, clearly upset. It was the first time Violet had seen her without her controlled public demeanour.

'Can you leave us please, Violet.'

'Yes, Your Majesty.'

Violet ran to her room. She paced like an expectant father, replaying the hallway incident in her mind until the memory had deteriorated into a Jerry Lewis routine.

Finally, she slapped her hand to her forehead. Perhaps Daisie had told Lady Caroline about the baby, and Lady Caroline had just informed the Queen of Violet's shameful behaviour.

She swept a perfectly arranged phalanx of velvet cushions to the floor and slumped facedown onto the bedcovers.

Then a mild nausea returned to her stomach.

Her eyes welled, for as bad as things were, they were likely to get worse.

29

The typist who sat closest to Major Ratcliffe looked like Daisie's primary school teacher Mrs Briers, who hated children and had gone through a very ugly divorce. The relentless *thwack* of typebars hit the ribbon like military shells. The punctuated sound paused as she looked up to interrogate Daisie's presence.

'Mr Ratcliffe sent for me.'

Mrs Briers reluctantly pushed her chair back and walked to the threshold of Ratcliffe's 'office', which was little more than a cramped space under the lean of a stairwell. A sweat had already gathered around the armpits of Ratcliffe's shirt. Daisie eavesdropped as she waited at the desk.

'*Daily Mirror*? Queue to get to the Promised Land, did you say? Wonderful. Eight hundred? Immigration may need to staff up, given what we've got planned.' He turned to admire the full-length portrait of Captain Cook on the wall behind his desk. 'The Queen's speech at the ball the other night seems to have struck a chord there. As intended – wrote it myself. Problem is our research tells us the perception is that Australia's a vast uninhabitable desert. God knows it's ninety-nine per cent that. But we need to show that living "out back" isn't as awful as it probably is. We need the right idea – or person,' he said before glancing up at the intrusion. 'I'll call back your morning, see if there's a teletype in Sydney you can put it to.'

'Miss Chettle is here,' Mrs Briers said.

He nodded.

'Which one are you?' he asked, sighing, as Daisie arrived at the doorway.

'Daisie, sir,' she said, concealing her bruised hand inside the other.

'Good. Right. Just wanted to make sure. Sit,' he said as he moved a pile of papers to the adjacent chair so she could take a seat opposite. His desk was covered with piled paperwork, telegrams, newspapers, invitation lists and a tray of bound Palace correspondence.

An alarm clock began ringing, its bell loud enough to give Daisie a start. Ratcliffe bludgeoned it with the flat of his hand to cease the noise. Outside, Mrs Briers continued firing unremitting rounds.

'One hour from press deadline back home,' he said as he slumped into the reclining leather armchair. He evaluated her for a moment, holding his gaze until it became an awkward silence. She matched his scrutiny unblinkingly.

'Lady Althorp will be returning to London today. She won't be taking part in the remainder of the tour.' He stopped talking to gauge her reaction.

Daisie remained poised, trying to hide her delight.

Ratcliffe withdrew a gold cigarette case from his breast pocket and offered it to her. 'I'm out of Kensitas but the B&H Virginias they have here are perfectly tolerable.'

She extracted a cigarette from the tray.

'Which also presents a problem. If this were reported, even spoken of, it could blemish the Palace's reputation. Not to mention cast a shadow over the smooth running of the tour.'

'I understand that.'

'Good. You'll be signing a document to that effect. Lady Althorp has also signed.'

Daisie straightened her spine. 'I want to be a lady-in-waiting.'

Ratcliffe scoffed. Then he reconsidered her. Her confidence was to be taken seriously.

'Lady Pamela Mountbatten has already agreed to fly from Delhi to assume Caroline's duties for the remainder of the itinerary. She'll join us in Adelaide in just under four weeks – quite a circuitous route from there to here, it would seem.'

Daisie's frame sagged. 'What about the next few weeks?' she replied hopefully. 'Until she arrives?'

'Not backward in coming forward, are you?' He tapped his unlit cigarette on the desk impatiently.

'I have been through a painful ordeal, Major Ratcliffe. The emotional and physical toll I will carry forever. To prey on the vulnerable, so soon after I lost my second parent. There's no telling the extent to which my suffering could manifest itself.'

'You're overestimating your negotiating position,' Ratcliffe said, rubbing his weary eyes. 'It's only a few weeks. The Queen won't want you dressing her. I wouldn't want you anywhere near her, to be honest.'

'It's important to me.'

'What is?'

'All my life I've wanted to be a lady-in-waiting,' she lied, convincingly.

He tapped his finger on the end of his unlit cigarette. 'Will you sign the non-disclosure?'

'Yes.'

He slid his unlit cigarette back into the gold case and shuffled through a pile of papers on his desk. 'Don't get carried away. Attend the events, receive flowers, smile diplomatically, that kind of thing. No interactions. Surely that's within your capability?'

Satisfied, Daisie nodded and held her cigarette out for him to light. He tossed his silver lighter onto the desk. She flicked it open, inhaled the cigarette to life and held the smoke in for a long time.

'And will there be remuneration?' she asked before exhaling.

'Don't push your luck, Miss Chettle. This is a favour, a deal. You get to feel like you're something for a few weeks, and I clean up an annoying mess. And frankly, with Lady Althorp gone and Lady Mountbatten bringing her own entourage, I'm still deciding whether I pack you and your sister off to London the second she arrives.'

'I don't care what you do with my sister.' Daisie's spent smoke twisted in a shaft of morning sunlight.

'Let me be perfectly clear. You keep your trap shut. Sign immediately.'

Daisie flexed her shoulders, unable to conceal the curl of her lips.

'Lady-in-Waiting Daisie Chettle,' she said to herself.

Ratcliffe sighed and pulled a document from his desk drawer. 'There was something of a history, shall we say,' he confessed delicately, as though now off the record. 'Won't be the last time a member of this house slums it, but . . .' He paused, uncertain how to phrase the remainder of the sentence he'd started. '*Assault.* If you can call it that. Two women. Can't keep up with these modern trends.'

He placed a signature page in front of her before his candid words hung in the air for too long and offered her a pen. Daisie could see Lady Caroline's signature beside a blank line that waited for her own. She glanced sideways at the typist, who nervously looked away as she fidgeted to position a sheet of carbon paper.

It was as though she were trying to keep up with transcribing the conversation.

Daisie took the pen and signed.

'We'll tell Bobo to make you presentable. Look impeccable, walk with poise behind her at all times and don't do anything else until Lady Mountbatten gets here. *Nothing* else. I'll be watching, and I will pull you if you mess it up. Miss Pemberton will give you the full schedule. As we say around here, "words spoken are like eggs broken",' Ratcliffe opined with a note of menace. 'Any misspoken words and you will incur the heaviest legal penalties the Crown can inflict.'

30

'Tell me what happened,' Violet insisted.

Lady Caroline, her hands laden with perfume bottles, had the downcast eyes of a berated animal. 'I'm going home,' she replied stoically. 'Pack these two suitcases and arrange for the trunks to follow.' She rifled feverishly through the dresser for her clutch bag, her anger rising as she slammed each drawer open, then shut.

'It's my sister, isn't it?' Violet asked meekly.

Lady Caroline hesitated. Her resolve had broken. She slumped onto the dresser chair and covered her eyes. Violet watched a single tear fall onto Lady Caroline's blouse like the first sign of rain, and quietly resumed packing, uncomfortable with the intimacy. She busied herself filling suitcases with outfits and a makeup bag.

'What she did to you,' Lady Caroline said, glancing at Violet's plaster-laden face, 'I thought was probably called for. Given the circumstances.'

Violet looked down, embarrassed. She snapped the suitcase lock tight.

'But I had no idea what she was capable of. A maid!'

'What about Her Majesty? Can she help?'

'I appealed to her, but she refused to listen. I am banished.'

'Oh,' said Violet, shocked but impressed by the power Daisie now seemed to wield.

Lady Caroline lifted a frame off the desk, a picture of her with Queen Elizabeth and Prince Philip laughing in tennis whites, racquets held high. They all looked much younger and happier. Then she hurled the frame towards the unlit fireplace, the glass splintering on the hearth.

Seconds later, there was a knock at the door. A page nervously peered in.

'I'm here to escort Lady Caroline to her car,' he uttered meekly, as though it were a confession.

Reilly stood behind him, his eyes leaden with the duty. 'Car's waiting, Lady Althorp,' he muttered.

With less fanfare than the delivery of the daily papers, the page gathered the suitcases.

Lady Caroline checked her handbag and glanced around the room one last time. 'Why do you put up with it? Any of it?' she asked Violet with genuine curiosity.

'Daisie – this – it's all I have left.'

Lady Caroline gave a subtle nod of understanding, then was gone.

31

'*Lady* Daisie Chettle,' Daisie whispered to herself. A satisfied smile crept onto her face as she left the meeting with Major Ratcliffe and strode towards the corner of the east-wing hall. She clutched the leather-bound schedule, as thick as a novella, smugly to her chest like a life vest in a squall.

Daisie turned the corner and halted abruptly to avoid a collision with Lady Caroline's giraffe-like frame. She looked up to see Lady Caroline's face, stricken with anger, glaring back at her. Daisie's eyes flicked each way but there was no escape. Reilly and a suitcase-laden page, who walked behind, slowed to maintain a safe distance from the encounter.

Lady Caroline's eyes dropped to the schedule Daisie held tightly to her bosom.

'I see,' Lady Caroline said, referring to the tome, the gravity of the betrayal crystallising. With a fierce strike she slapped Daisie hard across the face.

Thwack.

Then once more for good measure.

The page winced while Daisie's jaw hung slack, her left cheek glowing as the crisp sound of Lady Caroline's strike reverberated through the corridor. Daisie's eyes hardened, fixing on Lady

Caroline like a stung predator evaluating a potential kill. For an eternal moment they locked eyes.

'Speak,' Lady Caroline insisted.

'I'm playing your game,' Daisie said.

'There's no game.'

'You use people and throw them away like sport.'

'Though you accuse me of what you've done. Manipulated by a housemaid. Should've seen you coming, just like the rest. I *deserve* to be stood down.'

Lady Caroline turned to leave and then spun back, inching her nose closer to Daisie's face.

'What is it that damaged you so? What festers deep inside your self-absorbed little gut? Mummy? Daddy? Sister? I lay with you *once*,' she whispered with a hiss, 'but you have to sleep with your venal soul every night for the rest of your wretched existence.'

Daisie's eyes glassed and she dropped her gaze.

'Now I know why that auntie of yours ran all the way here and hid. Your blood is toxic. May she be spared.' Lady Caroline straightened and, stepping around Daisie, marched down the hallway in the direction of the lobby as her two escorts scuttled to keep up.

Daisie stood alone, facing the empty corridor with a flame in her eyes. Then she cocked her chin and marched towards Lady Caroline's old quarters to assume the throne.

32

'What did you do?' Violet demanded. Daisie poked through the dresser drawers in Lady Caroline's suite looking for any remaining evidence of her predecessor.

'I beg your pardon?'

'You did something, I can tell. A r-reprehensible something,' Violet stammered.

'I am now lady-in-waiting to the Queen,' Daisie said, turning to her with a superior grin.

'What?' Violet exclaimed. She stopped pacing.

'Believe me, I earned this. Caroline got what she wanted. And more than she bargained for. Surprising how easy it was, actually.' Daisie removed the tiara pouch from the bottom drawer. She turned the velvet shape over in her hands.

'But you've betrayed her?' Violet's face scrunched as she struggled to comprehend the act.

'A page from your book.'

'Why? To what end?'

'*Why?* The constant adulation of the Empire's constituents? To do little else but be decorous? To no longer be fussing or dressing or serving but to be fussed over, dressed and served? To be closer to the Duke? There are some reasons.'

Violet had no words left, her anger lost in frustration.

There was a knock. An equerry entered carrying Daisie's suitcases. He diligently placed the bags by the wardrobe.

'I'm told I'm quite messy, so I expect my quarters to be clean and presentable at all times. Violet, are you listening?'

Violet realised it was she, rather than the boy, who was being spoken to in a tone normally reserved for the garden staff at Elmbridge End.

'I beg your pardon?' Violet said.

'Beg. Yes, I like that. Perhaps you will. Caroline is gone. I'm now lady-in-waiting to the Queen. You will serve me as you did Caroline.'

'Will that be all, Miss Chettle?' the page asked humbly.

'*Lady* Chettle,' Daisie insisted.

'Oh, for the love of boiled cabbage,' Violet exclaimed. '*Lady Chettle?*'

'That will be all.'

'Miss – Lady – Chettle.' The page scurried towards the exit, unable to escape fast enough.

Daisie called after him, 'And come back and remove those God-awful suitcases once she's finished unpacking!' She turned to Violet. 'Now, start unpacking my things or I will march to Ratcliffe and tell him all about your shameful condition.'

Violet opened a suitcase. Her eyes were open, but her mind was somewhere else as she hastily unpacked her sister's clothes, numbing her to the horror she'd found herself in.

'What is an "investiture"?' Daisie asked as she read aloud from the bound itinerary. 'Sounds dull. Then a school children's display – spare me – a garden party, a civic reception, *follow the Queen around like a well-behaved corgi, bow, polite chat.*'

Daisie slammed the book shut and sighed. 'I expect you to wait outside my door until eleven every evening in the event of any appetite or urge that may arise. Not a good look for a lady to be roaming the hallways in her nightgown. Speaking of which, I've got a craving to celebrate with a glass of Babycham. Must be a bottle somewhere on this outpost isle. Find it within the hour.' She picked up the tiara pouch, extracting the delicate crown to casually test its brittle weight in her hands. 'But first help me try this.'

She tossed the tiara between her hands like a hot potato. Violet gulped, gritting her teeth with each throw as she edged behind her sister. Daisie held the crown out in her flattened hand, enjoying Violet's obvious discomfort.

Violet took the precious item. Its luminous platinum twitched in her nervous hands. With the dread of betrayal written on her face, she trembled as she lowered the gleaming object onto Daisie's scalp.

Her sister's eyes glinted brighter than the diamonds. Daisie basked in the reflection of her sister standing sullenly behind her regal visage. Daisie considered herself then breathed out. She'd enjoyed the moment and was already bored. 'Return it to Bobo. Get me some Babycham, and report back immediately. One failed chore, one word out of place and I will have you fired,' she teased. 'Such fun to be had.'

Bobo's room featured Victorian ceilings and a mauve patterned carpet. Two larger-than-life-size oil portraits hung on either side of the door, one of King George V, the other of Queen Mary. But it was Bobo who reigned over the room with her mess of crates, dummies and spools of thread.

Violet charged into Bobo's workspace out of breath. Bobo lifted her head from behind a dummy draped in a silk gown, with four pins gripped tightly between her lips. Before Violet could speak Bobo rolled her eyes, pre-empting the conversation. She heaved herself up with an impatient groan.

'Tell me what happened with Lady Caroline,' Violet blurted as she handed the pouched tiara to her.

'Aye, worse decisions have been made in the Palace's name.'

'Why was she sent away?'

'Caught with yer sister. Shame. For a so-called lady.'

'Caught doing what?'

'Do I have to spell it all out for yer?' Bobo leaned forward to confide, 'Intimate. That's the gossip. Aye, the mess she's made,' she huffed as she shoved a crate open, pushing the lid off and sending it to the carpet with a dull thud.

'Ridiculous,' Violet muttered dismissively. She slumped into the armchair, an upholstered antique. 'I'm pregnant. To her boyfriend,' she then blurted out. 'And she's on a rampage.'

Bobo was silent. Then a smile broke at the edge of her lips. She chuckled, her laughter growing until it echoed off the salon walls.

'You can't tell a soul! They'd fire me.'

'That is one elaborate revenge strategy, ma girl.' Bobo chuckled again before swallowing her mirth. She leaned in and placed her hand reassuringly on Violet's arm. 'Toughen up, girl. Give it back to her, but do yer job. She'll falter. They always do. Then it might be you in her shoes.'

Violet dabbed her eyes and took a deep, cathartic breath. With another wince Bobo eased herself back behind the sewing machine and threaded the needle. 'Perhaps I'll sabotage Daisie's cleavage line a wee bit,' she said. 'The more rope proffered the better. Even though it might make more trouble for the rest of us.'

33

'What's "Babycham"?' Jack asked, glancing at Violet in the rear-vision mirror of the black Vauxhall.

'Sparkling pear juice. Cheap, alcoholic.'

'Never heard of it.' He steered through Hobart city at a rapid clip, snapping the wheel to the left to avoid an oncoming Holden, blaring his horn as he veered into Elizabeth Street.

Violet couldn't quite pin down Hobart. 'Odd' was the word that kept coming to mind. She'd best describe it as a colonial seaside town, as though Folkestone in Kent had only been established one hundred years ago and had trams running through it. The main street undulated upwards to a grassy hillside on which further development seemed likely. The laced shop awnings and lampposts lining the boulevard had been decorated with blue and red streamers and flower arrangements to celebrate the Queen's arrival. The footpaths buzzed, thick with pedestrians waving the Union Jack and taking in the celebratory atmosphere.

'Next she'll demand a 4 a.m. start, fresh flowers changed three times daily, a foot massage twice a day, and the London papers with breakfast,' said Violet with a sigh.

'Ya bloody galoot!' Jack yelled as a passing car honked its horn. He braked hard. 'A spot!'

He double-parked outside FitzGerald's Department Store. 'One tick – wait here,' Jack announced as he left the car idling. Violet leaned towards the window. The shopfront display proudly boasted a homemade sign welcoming Her Majesty to Hobart, alongside 'the latest fashions from England'.

Five minutes later Jack dashed out of the department store and climbed into the driver's seat with a spring in his step. He shook a brown paper bag in Violet's direction.

'Babycham! Last one. That should shut Princess Daisie up,' he said, revving the engine. Violet could see him beaming proudly in the mirror's reflection.

'Thank you, Jack. I'm safe for the next few hours. That is, until she decides she requires Pontefract cakes at midnight.'

They drove in silence for a few moments until he cleared his throat and spoke. 'You want to see that *Captain Thunderbolt* flick at the State Cinema? Tonight?'

Violet blushed. She'd never been asked on a date and this sounded suspiciously like one. 'I'm exhausted. I'll be lucky to see my own quarters,' she replied, letting him down gently.

'She'll be at the State banquet until eleven, show starts at eight. Come on, she'll never know. When did you last have a day off? It's only a few hours.'

He pulled up at a traffic light as his question hung in the air. Violet's mind reeled while her gaze rested on a woman, perhaps twenty-one years of age, pushing a pram over the crossing.

'Well? What do you reckon?'

'I'm sorry, Jack. I just can't.'

'Bloody chicken. You know what one of the girls in administration called her? "The lady-in-hating". And Paddy, the transport officer? He called her "Weathervane". As in, she's above her station.'

Violet smiled.

'I'm not giving up,' he said in his crude twang.

Violet watched absently as the woman pushing the pram blended in to the pedestrian crowd.

'One bottle of Babycham,' Violet proclaimed as she gently rested the bottle on the dresser top.

Daisie scrunched her face ungratefully, almost disappointed that it had arrived at all. 'I suppose I have no reason to fire you now.'

Daisie continued to admire herself in the mirror, twisting her upper body slightly to test the curves of her close-fitting skirt. She grinned slyly at her reflection. Thanks to Bobo's alterations, her bosom in the pale blue silk dress was generous and destined to garner attention.

Minutes later, Violet leaned her head against the window glass to watch the motorcade prepare to depart. She yawned, her body weary again, as she squinted against the late afternoon sun to observe the fuss below. The simultaneous murmur of car engines signalled the Queen's imminent departure to the banquet. Even from the second floor Violet could discern Daisie's voluminous chest and the glances it provoked from the staff.

The floorboards in the hall creaked. A sealed envelope slid onto the carpet at the foot of the door. Handwritten on the front were the words 'Violet Chettle'.

Violet turned it over curiously in her hands before opening it. Inside was a leftover invitation card from a garden party that had been held the previous day.

The Governor requests the pleasure of the company of
<u>Violet Chettle</u>

At a Garden Party on Tuesday 23rd February, 1954 at ~~4 p.m.~~ NOW!
Her Majesty The Queen
and His Royal Highness The Duke of Edinburgh will be present.
~~*Government House, Hobart*~~ under the willows by the pond.
An answer is requested to the A.D.G. in Waiting.

It was Jack. She smiled to herself. Her sagging posture perked up somewhat as she folded the card between her fingers and considered the invitation.

Cicadas cheered from a row of sagging jacaranda trees as Violet crossed a lawn of manicured grass behind the house. A doorway built into a sandstone wall led to a narrow gravel pathway. It followed a wrought-iron fence to a low ridge that overlooked a private garden enclave beside a brackish pond.

Violet stepped carefully down to water level, where she spied Jack sitting on a blanket in the shade of a wilting willow tree. Its wispy branches swayed in the breeze.

As she edged closer, she could make out the embroidered ER logo on the blanket. It was one of the bedcovers from the house, a duvet with the royal seal in blue stitch. On top he had arranged an assortment of cheese, crackers, grapes and a bottle of Dom Pérignon with two glasses. His suit jacket hung from the branch of a nearby tree.

Jack, unaware of her presence, grappled with the neck of the bottle as though taming a python. His sleeves were rolled up, revealing furry, muscular forearms.

'Is this event officially sanctioned by the Palace?'

He turned and broke into a toothy grin. The cork in the bottle was poked half out, primed to launch. 'I figure at best you have four hours before she returns. If I can just open this bo—'

In that moment the cork launched itself with a loud pop. Champagne surged out of the bottle as the stopper plopped into the pond. Violet tried not to laugh as it showered onto the duvet like precious rain.

'This looks like the royal stock,' Violet said as she picked up the wrapped Stilton cheese that Lady Caroline was so fond of.

'Funny the things you find in cold storage trunks.' Jack poured two flutes and held one out to her.

'Just a nip,' she said, accepting the glass.

He raised his own. 'Cheers.'

'What are we toasting? Your skill at risking our jobs? Stealing the property of Buckingham Palace?'

'Well, not to your bloody sister.'

Violet took a tiny sip. She swirled the thimbleful of champagne around in her mouth, closing her eyes to savour its taste. Jack swigged the entire glass like vodka.

'Who are you, Jack? I don't even know your last name.'

'Smith.'

'That's so *distinctive*. Jack Smith.'

'That's Mr and Mrs Smith for you. Dubbo's finest.'

'Debbo?'

'It's pronounced Dubbo,' he replied with emphasis. 'Dar-bow.'

'Dar-bow,' she tried again, laughing. 'So what's in Dar-bow?'

'Ten million flies. One million sheep. Trained there for my army cadetship in '49. Which led me here – in a roundabout way.'

'All that training to drive me around. Must be spirit-crushing for you.'

'Oh, it is,' he said as he carved a matchbox-sized hunk of cheese.

'Still, brushing with royalty and all. Not bad for a fly farmer.'

'Well, I don't drive Her Majesty's vehicle – that's left to more reputable types. I just drive around the great pretenders. Like your good self.'

'Your parents must be beaming.'

'Dad's a republican. Can't stand her lot, and . . .' He left his sentence unfinished, wafting the rest of it away with his hand like a fly, as though it was a subject he didn't want revisited.

'Yours must be proud,' he continued, changing direction. 'Their girls swanning around with royalty.'

'They're gone. Both of them.' Violet looked down, her voice raspy and soft.

'Oh.' He sighed and raised his eyebrows at his ineptitude. 'Some date I am.'

'It's all right. I haven't talked much about it. Daisie won't. Sometimes I think of it as a bad dream. I'm trying to find my Auntie Hazel – my mother's twin sister. She lives in Australia, somewhere. Hiding away with the family secrets.'

'I think you won.'

'Won what?'

'Most miserable personal backstory.'

She laughed out loud with a genuine hoot. The release of air deep from her lungs and the tingle of the champagne were enjoyable – too enjoyable – for her to allow it. 'Well, Sir Jack of No Repute, this is a very nice function and all, but I have things to attend to before a certain lady returns and makes her unreasonable demands. And I want to keep my job.'

'There's plenty of champagne left,' he tried to tempt her.

'Don't let me interrupt your little garden party. I'm sure you'll work out what to do with the rest of the bottle.'

Violet stood and brushed the creases and jacaranda leaves out of her dress.

'You're quite the dish, you know,' he said with a cheeky smirk as he refilled his glass.

Violet rolled her eyes and turned towards the sandstone staircase. It wasn't difficult for her to decline a man's attention. Just because a man showed interest wasn't a reason to be interested back. But Jack was different. He lifted her mood and made her forget about what had happened with Bill. His attention came at the moment she needed it most, and he seemed funny and kind.

She glanced back as she ascended the stairs. He toasted her with a recharged glass, swallowing the expensive champagne in a single gulp.

34

'It's far from appropriate.' Ratcliffe was fuming. Daisie rubbed her bloodshot eyes as the Daimler drove through the streets of Hobart towards Government House. Even though the air was cool and the public houses had closed at 6 p.m., there were still revellers out – weary families too – roving the streets, thrilled by the Queen being 'within cooee', as Jack might say.

'Just because it's served doesn't obligate you to drink it.'

'I'm fine, Michael.'

'It's Major Ratcliffe! And you're slurring!'

'I'm tired. Been up since five.'

'We all have. It's your damn job. And next time don't dress so . . . aggressively. The Minister for Agriculture's wife didn't know where to look.'

'The Minister did.'

'Yes, and the bloody Duke,' Ratcliffe said, annoyed. He shut his mouth firmly and turned to the window to brood.

Daisie batted aside a dangling forelock that had fallen loose. She sighed, allowing herself a moment to breathe before changing tack. 'Tasmania is the first place in Australia that resembles home, don't you think? As though the settlers tried to recreate their villages here brick for brick. I heard Elizabeth say, "Why, this might be in Kent" when we came around the coast this morning.'

Ratcliffe stayed quiet, silently irate.

'Michael, I've decided I'd like to spend some more time with Elizabeth.'

'Her Majesty!'

'Never was a big fan of the Palace and the pomp, but I'm starting to get used to it. Especially the outfitsh,' she said, slurring.

'This wasn't the deal.'

'Aside from a perfunctory "Good morning" at the start of the day, we've barely spoken. Four times I've tried to initiate conversation. "This heat is insufferable!", "Were the flies this bad in Africa?", "Is there a trick to avoiding tiara friction?", "This heat is insufferable!" Any attempt is met by her *rarefied* air. Understandable, perhaps, given the never-ending vapid small talk she must endure. More than once I've caught myself thinking about what may be served for lunch while an excitable Australian chewed my ear off.'

'Well, stop chewing *her* bloody ear off!' Ratcliffe replied, removing a handkerchief from his lapel pocket to dab the sweat around his neck.

'The Duke joked this morning that my box hat looked like a Terry's chocolate tin and—'

'You will not engage with either of them! Pamela is stuck in Bombay or some bloody place, then you're back in your place. You only have this job so that you'd shut up, so please *do it*.'

Daisie dismissively flapped her hand in the air as if in retreat. She swallowed some indigestion, just.

The car passed through the Government House gates, where even at 11 p.m. civilians waited. A small but vocal group pushed to the front, brandishing placards and chanting at the windows in a most republican manner.

'No genocide! Don't sign the Welfare Ordinance!' A woman of Daisie's age scowled at the window, her beatnik bare midriff and tight Audrey Hepburn trousers a dead giveaway as her spittle stung the window glass.

Among them, a young child of eight or nine nervously held up a hand-painted sign that read 'God Save the Queen'.

'They seem rather ungrateful,' Daisie said as she waved her hand at them in an exaggerated royal manner.

Ratcliffe rubbed his eyes as he replied. 'Ordinance number eight. She signed it in Canberra. Something about welfare and reloca- tion for the natives in the capital. Dreadful bloody timing. Now the Aboriginals aren't happy. Nor this lot.'

'Oh, speaking of doing good, there is one thing I've been mean- ing to ashhk of you, *Major Sir*,' she asked, as a police line wrangled the gates shut behind them. 'I'm trying to find my dear old Auntie Hazel. She moved to Australia years ago and we seem to have lost her.'

'We're a sovereignty, not a missing persons service,' Ratcliffe said, sighing. He flicked the door latch with his fingers in anticipa- tion of getting out of the car.

'It would mean so much to me,' she said as she adjusted the fallen lock of hair.

Ratcliffe sighed more deeply and opened the door himself before the vehicle had slowed to a full stop, desperate to escape.

'I'll – see – something,' he uttered dismissively as he stepped away from the car to the distant sound of protests.

'Thank you, Major Michael Ratcliffe,' Daisie replied to an empty seat. She waited patiently for the equerry to open her door, then wiggled out of the back seat, pulling at her bust line to prevent it slipping any further. Safely on her feet, she found her balance, waved at the horde and, without stumbling, carefully made her way to her suite, where she poured a gin and tonic.

35

Day 108: *Melbourne, Victoria*
Population: *1,524,335*
Weather: *73 degrees Fahrenheit, some morning drizzle, cool south-easterly breeze tending truculent in the afternoon*
Fact: *Before being called Melbourne, the city had a number of names including Bearbrass, Batmania, Dutergalla, and Bareheep.*

It was the Queen's fourth week on Australian soil, and a belligerent hangover pounded Daisie's skull. She glanced in the rear-view mirror. Even heavy makeup couldn't hide her seaweed-green complexion. 'Can you put the window up? These school choirs are stinging my brain,' she complained to the driver on the way to the airport for the flight to Melbourne.

'Yes, Miss – Lady – Violet.'

'It's Lady Chettle!' she retorted, holding her head in her hands. 'And I'm DAISIE!'

Daisie looked down at Essendon as the plane approached the runway. Although bland, it was one degree closer to civilisation after the island of Tasmania. Daisie had been to the toilet at the back of the plane three times during the short flight. She craved a proper hotel with a bathtub and not another government office made up as a suite.

A million people lined the route to Melbourne, the crowd's high-pitched screams like the buzz of a million locusts. By the time they reached Moonee Ponds, Daisie had lost the will to wave. Instead, she just stared blankly out the window at the enchanted crowds like a demented grandmother being transferred to the nursing home.

'My head,' Daisie said as she walked up the carpeted steps of the town hall, though nobody could hear her over the noise. She winced, trying to endure the rabid patriotism, and swatted at a fly which lingered near her mouth.

Her mood was in stark contrast to the Duke's.

'Some city, Melbourne,' he remarked with a smile as they stepped onto the town hall balcony.

In her silk beige coat with a single string of pearls and a black hat, Elizabeth looked immaculate. But it was the Duke who stole Daisie's attention, dashing in his black suit with silver cufflinks that bore his cipher. He looked to the sky and the confetti and cheers that rained down, and she looked to him.

In her suite at Government House it was a familiar scenario: a large drawing room converted into a bedroom, with a great effort made to furnish it tastefully. The room had been appointed with a refreshments tray including spirits and tonic water.

'I have a splitting headache. Find me some Bufferin tablets. And some ice,' Daisie ordered Violet as she flopped onto the bed. She kicked off her high heels, inadvertently knocking a vase of white orchids onto the carpet.

Violet scampered to recover them. 'Ice? For your head? Or your drink?' she said, mopping the water with a serviette.

'For my drink! Tell that cow Bobo I want an outfit similar to what Lilibet was wearing today. And the same set of pearls.'

'You can't call her that,' Violet said accusingly.

'A cow?'

'Lilibet!'

'*You* have no authority!'

Violet held her tongue.

Daisie splayed out on the bed like a crucified tart, disregarding the creases she was making to her gown. 'It's pandemonium out there. And they're to host the Olympics! They'll need the two years to recover.'

Violet slunk away, closing the door behind her. As soon as she heard the latch, Daisie raised her head and padded slowly over to the drinks cart. She snapped open the bottle of gin, poured two measures and winced as each was downed.

36

'I tell Lilibet, "Fondle yer pearls!" That, or put them awa or she'll be gettin a wretched tan mark,' grumbled Bobo.

Violet waited patiently for her to finish steaming Daisie's outfit for the afternoon's garden party. As requested, it was a tailored beige jacket with a black velvet collar and a matching frock to go with a black hat and pearls.

'For yer sister, however,' she said, nodding towards the velvet box on a side table, 'let's hope those pearls leave a noose mark. Maybe we'll be lucky and she catches some of that polio that's knockin' about. The gall, copying the Queen's outfit. She'll notice. I'll make sure of it.'

'She's determined to have me fired, the cow. And she calls her Lilibet,' Violet hissed quietly, as though nervous to even say the name.

'That beast! I've a mind to tell *her*. But girls like that trip. Eventually. So we keep our hands clean, yeah?'

'I can't,' Violet whispered while Jack pleaded. He walked beside her like an obedient dog as Daisie's gown dangled from her raised fingers.

'They go to Essendon airport at ten and return from Warragul at about eight. The opera finishes at six. It's called *The Consul*, or something. Marie Collier? Curlier? I dunno. I've never heard of 'er. Bob gave me the tickets. They're desperate for somebody to turn up.'

'Who's Bob?'

'One of the local drivers. Word of a royal attendance has got the cast excited. Excited about us!'

Violet bit her lip, conflicted. 'Has the mailbag arrived yet?' she asked hopefully.

'Yep, yesterday. You didn't get anything?'

Violet paused a few feet from Daisie's door, her attention drifting from Jack.

'Please,' he begged. 'I don't want to go on my own! I bloody hate opera!'

'I'll come,' she relented. 'But not a word to anybody.'

'Scout's honour!' Jack put three fingers to his forehead in a Boy Scout salute.

Violet nodded and dolefully turned the door handle to the lady-in-waiting's suite as Jack strode back down the hall humming to himself.

The room was empty. Violet breathed a sigh of relief, hung the gown in the wardrobe and slumped on the leather couch. She covered her face with both hands to hide.

'Oh, Violet, what are you doing, you stupid horse?' she said to the room.

The Australian Governor on the wall observed her judgementally.

Violet removed her hands and stared at the ceiling. She rested the back of her hand on her forehead to ease the headache she'd created. Out of the corner of her right eye, she noticed an elaborate flower arrangement resting on the coffee table. A slip of notepaper had been spiked to the tip of a dried flower that looked like a small scythe. On the front was her name.

> *Violet,*
>
> *I have a busy day planned for you tomorrow so don't assume you're getting a day off.*
>
> *I expect all these tasks to be completed by my return.*
>
> *1) Something to repel flies. They're driving me senseless – I nearly swallowed one yesterday!*
>
> *2) Cut your hair short – like Dorothy Dandridge. NO identity confusion!*
>
> *3) Ask what the blue dots on the master calendar are for.*
>
> *4) You are putting on weight ALL OVER. Footman Albert will escort you on a run around Government House at noon. HE WILL REPORT BACK TO ME.*
>
> *5) Replace the artwork in my suite with a portrait of a British monarch (not Edward 8th!) – NO Australian politicians or governors!*
>
> *6) A packet of Spangles.*
>
> *7) DON'T FRATERNISE WITH OTHER STAFF! NO EXCUSES.*

'Is she barking mad?' Violet screamed inside the empty room.

The latch on the door turned and Daisie bounded in.

'No, but she's a little bit drunk,' she announced. She poured herself a gin, one hand on her hip as if to help stay her swaying orientation.

'Jogging?' Violet dropped her voice to a whisper. 'I'm *pregnant*!'

'Look at your thighs. You're unpresentable and need to stave off the fat until *it's* dealt with.'

'Major Ratcliffe won't tolerate this.'

'He'd like nothing more than to *terminate* you. And he won't dare cross me.'

'This is farcical! Swap the painting?' Violet exclaimed.

They simultaneously turned to the intimidating framed portrait hanging above the fireplace. The life-size painting depicted a thin man with fair hair and a pinched nose, identified by the plaque as 'Arthur Phillip'.

'I can't carry that. I won't do any of this.' Violet slumped into an antique chair, its frame creaking as she landed.

'Unless you do what I tell you, you're dumped from the tour. Stranded in one of these fly-ridden, godforsaken towns. You and your bastard.'

Violet's rage erupted. She seized the vase and flung it at Daisie.

Daisie blinked as the expensive-looking antique passed her face and shattered against the wall behind her.

Arthur Phillip calmly observed the fracas from his safe vantage point.

'Retrieve some petty cash from the office girls to complete your tasks,' Daisie said slowly but firmly. 'And replace that vase at your own expense.'

'Where is your mercy? I'm your blood sister,' Violet cursed.

'And I am bloody-minded. You're my maid and you will now do my hair. Perfectly. Or I will add additional items to your little list.'

Daisie sat at the dresser with a huff, waiting for Violet to start crafting her hair into something presentable.

Violet stood frozen, incredulous, until an urgent knock at the door drew her attention.

'Enter,' announced Daisie.

Albert, in his mid-thirties, lean and wiry with a shallow beard and a constable's condescension, leaned in as though summoned. He glanced between them.

'Albert. It's her,' Daisie clarified for him. 'She's getting a haircut tomorrow. It'll make it easier.'

'Yes, Miss Chettle.'

'It's *Lady* Chettle, Albert.'

'But that's a title earned not through the role but—'

'*Lady Chettle!*'

'Yes, *Lady Chettle*,' he uttered with his head bowed, before closing the door behind him.

'Who was he?' Violet asked.

'An enthusiastic local servant of the Empire. Tasked to help during the busier stops of the tour. The government felt we needed extra security given the turnout. I've told him not to be daunted by you, given the association and all. You're to be exercised quite ruthlessly.'

Violet heaved her body upright, the resignation weighing on her. She walked slowly to Daisie's chair. She closed her eyes, swallowed her anger and grasped the ceramic-backed hairbrush. Then slowly, methodically, she worked her sister's hair.

37

'That's a cracker list,' said Jack as he paced Violet's tiny quarters. 'I think she's lost a screw. Why doesn't she just fire you?'

'Because she wants to torture me. Perhaps I *should* give up.'

'And do what?'

'Hide in Australia. Start a new life.'

'Not much of a plan.'

She clutched the crumpled note in her hand, the dull pain of a headache starting to reawaken in her forehead.

Jack grabbed both her arms and leaned in close to her face. 'Stuff her. We can do this. Tick every box, just to annoy her.' He took the list and flattened out the paper. 'Right. Number one, the fly problem. Hmm. A fly swat?'

'That would be quite funny,' she said, almost managing a smile, as a wave of nausea – part fear but also due to her changing body – started to surge.

'Two – haircut. I'd welcome the differentiation.'

'Don't be cheeky.'

'Three – easy, Miss Nicholson will know. She's also the keeper of the petty cash. Four. Now that's just mean. Albert's no pushover. We'll come back to that one. Five. The painting?' He raised his eyebrows and laughed quite loudly, doubling over the foot of the bed.

'You bloody English. That's a big painting. Maybe I can get one of the boys to help switch it with the one in the library. Six. Spangles. What the bloomin' hell is a spangle?'

'It's a boiled sweet. You know, Hopalong Cassidy? "The sweet way to go gay"?'

'Can't say I've sampled it. But we found Babycham. One Spangle, we'll be out of the tangle. Next. No fraternising.' He rolled his eyes in mock disapproval. 'Sorry, that's a deal-breaker. I'm only helping you in return for increased fraternisation.'

Violet forced a smile, which emerged as a grimace.

'Why *are* you helping me, Jack?' she asked.

'I see a damsel in distress, I bloody do something.'

'This isn't an exchange. I won't *owe* you. I just need to be clear.'

'Message received loud and clear,' he said, bowing his head slightly.

'Very well,' said Violet. 'I accept your offer of help.'

'Okey-dokes then, let's focus on one to six,' he said reassuringly. 'The opera starts at three. That gives us a good five hours beforehand. First thing, you head downstairs to Miss Nicholson, get the money and ask about number three. I'm off to plan an artwork heist.'

'The blue dots?'

Miss Nicholson was the one in the administration office with the 'Quasimodo slouch', as Daisie had described her. She peered at Violet over her glasses, pausing midway through counting out a roll of five-pound notes from the lockbox. 'You're *really* asking what the blue dots mean?'

Beside her, Miss Pemberton ceased typing, and a disquiet took the room.

'Yes. Just out of curiosity,' Violet replied innocently. 'Settle a bet,' she volunteered as they looked wearily at each other.

'You best ask Major Ratcliffe. It's highly confidential.' Miss Nicholson leaned in and whispered, 'Though, if you want my advice – and you didn't hear it from me – don't ask.'

Violet signed for the roll of banknotes, stuffed them in her dress pocket and headed towards the door. The office girls stared after her as though a monumental faux pas had been committed.

Before she rounded the doorway into the lobby, she paused to glance at the three-month calendar chart mounted on the wall beside the door. Its detailed entries chronicled every movement of the tour. Scattered here and there, the blue dots stood out.

Violet glanced back at their blank faces, typing hands poised, and nodded calmly before making her way out the door.

'That looks heavy,' Violet said without any optimism. She and Jack stood before a life-size oil portrait of King George V mounted in the library. It was a Silver Jubilee depiction, the austere king in elaborate military garb festooned with an array of medals and a velvet cape. He looked a bit like a monarchist Superman.

In the centre of the room on a coffee table rested a sculpture of an Aboriginal man wielding a spear. Violet read the marking at the base of the statue: 'Bennelong'. An adjacent antique sideboard was decorated with an array of native Australian flowers. To Violet's eye they were alien and slightly frightening. 'It wouldn't surprise me if one of the bulbous flowers sprayed us with an acidic venom when our backs were turned.'

Jack tried to pry the baroque frame away from the wall, testing it for weight and stability. Violet kept glancing towards the hallway door, nervous that a staff member, especially Albert might barge through at any moment.

'It's not *that* heavy,' he grunted bravely as he held his breath and lifted one corner, his arms bulging under his short sleeves. With a heave he sent the entire portrait sliding on its hanging wire until it dangled at an alarming angle. Violet grappled the opposite corner and they slowly pulled the bulky painting off its mount until it rested on the carpet. They breathed out and shared a relieved glance.

'Phase two,' he announced.

'What if somebody appears in the hallway?' she whispered.

'She'll be jake. They'll either think we're wags, or we tell them the truth – that the lady-in-warlock is a mullock.'

'What language is that?' she said, half serious.

'On the count of three,' he said. They took a synchronised deep breath and with a 'one, two, three' lifted the painting off the floor. Like amateur removalists, they carried the king across the room.

As they moved into the hall, the ornate frame bumped the top of the doorway with a heavy thud.

'I can't see any damage,' hissed Violet from her position at the rear. They gently eased it under and into the wide hall.

'It's deserted – for now,' whispered Jack. Their steps trudged along the carpeted hallway towards Daisie's door, about fifty feet down the corridor.

A house attendant, a young girl of nineteen or twenty in a black service uniform, exited one of the rooms only two doors along. They paused, standing still as though playing a parlour game. Violet struggled with the weight of the frame, her face filling as they held their breath. The king swayed, the painting tipping like a caber in their sweaty grips.

The maid locked the door and turned away down the hall and into the stairwell, oblivious to the heist occurring behind her.

With a shared sigh of relief, Violet and Jack lumbered onwards to Daisie's room.

Jack rested the corner of the frame on his knees as he fumbled the door open with his spare hand. They entered the room, the King smacking the upper door frame once again.

Once inside, they closed the door and heaved Arthur Phillip off the wall before placing the new picture on the hooks. Violet had to lean on her knees to regain her breath.

'These *are* bloody heavy. You all right?' Jack asked. He jumped to the floor from the top of the mantel like a circus performer.

'Just out of shape,' Violet replied, holding her side.

Jack took a step back to admire their work. The king looked perfectly regal above the fireplace in place of Admiral Phillip. Jack adjusted the tilt of the frame against the marble mantelpiece, the scuff marks on the upper corners from the door altercations only barely noticeable. They leaned Arthur Phillip against the closed door, where he waited to be escorted to his new place of residence down the hall.

A gentle *tap-tap* sounded. Jack froze. Arthur and George stared like unwitting accomplices.

There was another knock at the door.

'Who is it?' Violet called.

'Flowers, ma'am?' a young male voice enquired.

'Please come back in half an hour.'

'Yes, ma'am,' he said, before the hall floorboards creaked with his departure.

Jack smiled to himself, enjoying this far more than he should.

'Right, let's get this fella out of here.'

They waited until the hallway was clear again before lifting the painting of Arthur Phillip and making their way back towards the library. Violet grimaced, her hands starting to slip on the smooth frame. As they passed an open doorway Violet noticed a young man replacing flowers in one of the bedrooms. He faced away from them, unaware of the charade.

'Hurry,' she whispered as they shuffled closer, her teeth gritted as the frame cut into her fingers.

Thud!

'Bloody hell,' said Jack loudly, looking at the dent in the upper door frame.

They regained their poise and quickly lowered the frame in order to enter the library. Safely inside, they set it on the floor to lean against the back of the sofa. Violet massaged her fingers while Jack closed the door, jamming a chair under the handle.

'He's changing all the flowers on this level. He'll be here shortly,' Violet said.

'Righto, let's do this,' said Jack as they eased the painting onto a hook.

'It's skewed slightly to the left,' urged Violet.

Jack lowered the right corner. She gave a thumbs up as there was another knock.

'Who is it?' she called again.

'Flowers, ma'am.'

Jack shrugged, then pulled the chair away from the door and swung it back into position near the coffee table.

'Come in,' Violet replied nonchalantly.

The flower boy entered, pushing a cart that bustled with native blossoms. He nodded and made his way to the triffid arrangement.

Jack caught Violet's eye and nodded at the exit. They slunk

out the door together and walked briskly to Daisie's suite. As they escaped down the hall, they giggled like school mates who'd eluded a caning.

Just as Violet touched the door handle of Daisie's room, as though she'd triggered it, an enormous crashing sound came from the end of the hallway. The floor shook and the glassware rattled as the almighty noise echoed throughout the house.

They looked at each other with dread. Voices were raised throughout the hallways. Two breathless footmen and a police-man appeared from the stairwell. Staff emerged dazed from behind doors as though the Blitz had returned. The police pointed and ran towards the library door.

Jack and Violet stood still, uncertain whether to hide or fall in with the growing crowd. They slowly walked back down the hall, their guilt palpable as they tried to blend in with the dozen or so gathering.

The portrait of Arthur Phillip had fallen forward, the extracted wall hook dangling from the mounting wire. The canvas, splin-tered from its frame, was bent over the coffee table, punctured in the middle by Bennelong's spear.

The staff and security stood solemnly around the torn artwork as though it were the aftermath of an assassination.

Jack and Violet quietly backtracked from the scene as others stormed in.

38

While the house was distracted, Jack took one of the cars to find some Spangles. Meanwhile, Violet trudged to Bobo's workroom with flies on her mind. The fuss around the painting seemed to have subsided, with most assuming it was a random coincidence. Nobody had realised the portraits had been switched.

'D'ye hear the ungodly noise upstairs? Shook my foundations,' said Bobo as Violet entered her disorganised war room. 'Ye want somethin', don't ye? Ask or leave, I've got nae assistant and fourteen occasions – unless you're offerin' tae help?'

'What do you know about flies?'

'Blowflies?'

'Daisie doesn't like them. Wants me to find a cure for them. Today.'

Bobo laughed as she slammed a trunk lid down. 'I dinnae ken. If I had something to *draw* them, I'd be stitchin' it into her hem.'

Violet turned to leave.

'Wait a minute. Wait one minute. Yer not the first to ask. They're driving her batty.'

'Daisie?'

'Lilibet! Wee thing can't open her gob without a cloud of flies thinking it's a moist hole to live in. Phil's complaining about pains in his right arm from relentlessly flapping,' she said with a cheeky smirk, wildly waving her rotund arm to scare imaginary flies. 'Lieutenant Commander Parker made some enquiries after the Duke swallowed one of them in Sydney and coughed it oot in front of an audience of blind nuns! Pay the Commander a visit. I heard they sent him a solution but naebody had the nerve to try it.'

Lieutenant Commander Parker sat in his small first-floor office smoking a thin cigar. Violet found it difficult not to stare at the fly that sat on the top of his bald head. His jacket, adorned with an array of medals, hung on a brass hat stand by the door beside a slightly off-centre map of Australia.

He stubbed out his cigar in the glass ashtray, the smoke wending its way out through the open window into the hot sunlight, and reached for the drawer behind the desk. The fly remained in place, content. 'A few weeks back, we put in a request to the government. Damn things have been driving everybody mad,' he said as he produced a black aerosol can with a plain label. 'Flies, that is.'

He thumped the can on the desk and unfolded an accompanying letter.

'Re: flies and per the Governor-General's request, please find enclosed a sample of modified diethyltoluamide. Apply to the exposed skin for no more than two to three seconds three times daily. Do not under any circumstances ingest or inhale. This should resolve Her Majesty's Diptera issues. Kind regards, Professor Waterhouse, Scientific Research Organisation, Australia.'

'Is it safe?' Violet asked, hesitant to touch the cylindrical object.

'Who knows? I guess so. Though after we read this,' Lieutenant

Commander Parker said, fanning his face with the letter, 'we decided it inappropriate to *experiment* on Her Majesty. Or the Duke, for that matter. Made sense to try it out on a guinea pig. Nobody put up their hand, so it ended up here. One of you then, perhaps?'

'We'd be delighted. *She'd* be delighted.'

'Very well. Report your findings back to me. Whatever the consequences.'

At noon on the dot, there was a knock at Violet's door.

'Are ya there, Miss Chettle?' Albert asked in a stout Australian accent.

Violet dragged herself off the bed and opened the door. 'Albert. I'm feeling under the weather. Can we postpone—'

'Sorry, Miss Chettle, but *Lady* Chettle has given me strict instructions.' He straightened his back. 'So please come with me and we can start.'

'This is ridiculous,' she replied hopelessly.

'That's for others to judge, Miss Chettle. If the Palace instructed me to bring the head of an Aborigine, I'd do it.'

'Oh my God, that's horrible,' Violet said as she pulled on flat shoes. 'She's mad, you know. Lost her mind.'

Albert frogmarched Violet towards the lobby.

'I'm in no state for this. I could collapse and you'd have to call an ambulance. A member of the royal household hospitalised on your watch – wouldn't look good. Might even make the newspapers.'

'You'll need to take that up with Lady Chettle.'

They stepped out onto the front lawn of Government House and headed towards the perimeter path. The murmur of the crowd could be heard beyond the gate, a row of heads pricking to attention like zoo animals bobbing along the fenceline.

Albert led Violet to a fold-up chair placed under a tree, from which he had an overview of the entire grounds. He removed a stopwatch from his pocket.

'Lady Chettle said I am to see you to do ten laps of the fence path. I reckon the perimeter is around fifteen hundred yards. With no dawdling, you should be able to complete a lap in five and a half minutes. Ten laps. One hour total. Your time commences now.'

'One hour? That's impossible!'

Without warning, he clicked the stopwatch button. 'Clock's ticking, mate,' he said. 'Wasting time.'

She sighed. To the relentless *tick-tick* of the stopwatch, she reluctantly lurched off down the path, jogging awkwardly alongside the perimeter fence.

'You'll need to pick up the pace, lass,' Albert yelled.

Violet started to find a rhythm of sorts, her breathing heavy as she shuffled at a medium stride along the gravel path. Pebbles crunched underfoot as she left the garden area and crossed the main driveway. Roughly forty observers clung to the gate bars with flowers for the Queen. Violet tried not to acknowledge their stares as she stumbled past, sweat starting to trickle down her back.

About halfway through the first lap, she felt a stitch prick her stomach. Her mouth hung open for air as she flailed across the grassy square. She paused to catch her breath while Albert's view was obscured by the main building, then pushed on through a small paved rose garden, traversing a series of steps that led back to the perimeter pathway.

'Faster. Or you'll need to start again,' Albert shouted as she passed.

'Onya, luv,' a broad Australian accent yelled from the crowd, followed by a small group cheer.

Overwhelmed by exhaustion, Violet's body started to resist. She pushed herself forward until she ran behind the house again. She faltered to a stop, her breathing wretched as she doubled over. After a few breaths she drove on, her frail legs barely able to maintain a straight line.

'Still falling behind, lassie. Pick it up,' Albert yelled from his chair.

Violet pushed into the third lap as perspiration seeped through the front of her blouse. She wiped her eyes, stinging from the sweat, as she jogged by the main gate once more.

The entire group stood and cheered as she passed. Then her legs weakened as a sharp stitch struck her stomach. Violet stumbled then fell to the ground.

The audience gasped.

'You all right, luv?' the ringleader yelled.

'Get an ambulance!' somebody else yelled.

Then everything went black.

39

'Are you all right?'

Jack was kneeling over her, looking concerned, as her eyes fluttered open. He touched her forehead, checking her temperature, and helped her sit up.

'Very disappointing. Lady Chettle will not be happy,' Albert said. He stood a few metres away with his fold-up chair under his arm.

'Leave her alone,' a female voice yelled from the fenceline.

'Albert, you're a real dickhead,' Jack said, scowling. 'You need your bloody block knocked off.'

'Is that a threat?' Albert asked as he took a step closer to Jack.

'Settle down,' Jack said dismissively. He placed his arm under Violet's elbow to assist her to her feet.

'Lady Chettle will hear about it the moment she gets back,' Albert spat as he stormed towards the lobby.

'Forget about it,' Violet said with a raspy throat before Jack helped her inside.

An hour later, Violet awoke in her clothes. Someone was knocking on the door. She instinctively reached for her stomach, her hand feeling under her blouse as she tested it for sensitivity.

'It's Jack,' he said outside her door.

'What time is it?' she asked as she let him in. Jack was dressed in a formal black suit with a white shirt, black tie and a white carnation nestled in his lapel.

'Time to get ready to go to the opera. Read this,' he said as he twisted a sheet of notepaper between his fingers.

Violet took the slip and read out loud.

'Dear Lady Chettle. This is to confirm that Violet Chettle completed the exercise task as required. Regards, Footman Albert.'

'How?'

'I ran into your friend Mrs MacDonald. She had a chat to our Albert. Said she'd speak to the Queen personally about promoting him to head footman for the rest of the tour.'

'I can't believe it.'

'Spangles, however, remain elusive in these parts. If we get your hair cut and pass off some Pez, then case closed, I reckon.'

'My head hurts,' she said, frowning.

'No time for complaining, we've got forty minutes to get dressed and get to the theatre.'

'I don't care any more. I should never have taken her on.'

'Don't let her break you – we're this close to winning!'

'Daisie and I, we've already lost.'

Jack flopped onto the sofa, deflated. 'So if it's all over, let's go to the opera anyway. A final send-off.'

She looked deep into his pleading eyes, his fringe falling across his face.

'Besides, you owe me. I ran the length of Collins Street looking for British sweets.'

*

Jack had arranged for another driver to take them to the Princess Theatre. They scrambled into the lobby just as the session bell rang.

'It's a pleasure to have you here, we're honoured,' the theatre manager gushed as he escorted them to their seats. Their private box was by the stage, so close they could reach out and touch the curtains.

The crowd chattered in anticipation as an unseen string section could be heard tuning their instruments. Vendors roamed the aisles selling drinks and eyeglasses from neck-mounted concession trays.

'And to think, only two hours ago you were fainting in public in front of the royal residence,' said Jack. 'Now, best seats in the house.'

'My sister is a lady-in-waiting, you know. I'm very well connected,' Violet said sarcastically. She reclined into her velvet seat as a wave of relief spread across her face.

Jack reached over the armrest and placed his hand on Violet's. He gently slid his fingers in between hers, clasping their hands together. 'I'm falling a little bit for you, you know,' he said matter-of-factly.

Violet couldn't help but smile as her heart surged. She stared back into his eager brown eyes.

He leaned close to her ear and whispered, 'I've got something to confess. I don't even like the monarchy. I'm a bloody republican.' Then he kissed her.

Violet closed her eyes and lost herself to his slow lips. She savoured the moment as long as he let it last.

'Champagne? Sweets?' a female voice called from behind them. They swiftly separated as though discovered by a parent in the back row of the Odeon cinema.

Jack turned towards the interruption. 'No, thanks,' he said, then froze, with his gaze fixed above her right shoulder. Violet sheepishly glanced back. On the girl's tray, beside the filled champagne glasses, boxed mints and sets of brass binoculars, were four packets of Spangles.

Around 4.30 p.m. the audience filled the lobby, cooling down in their Sunday best before the second half. After the intermission bell, Violet and Jack slipped away from the theatre.

The Continental Salon commanded the corner of Lonsdale Street. The display windows boasted five busts that depicted the current styles.

'You sure you want to go through with this?' Jack asked. He clutched her hand. Violet nodded confidently and they entered.

The proprietor, an elderly woman with reading glasses and a tightly curled mop of lavender hair, looked up from the counter.

'Like Dorothy Dandridge,' Jack told her.

Within forty-five minutes Violet's hair had been washed, cut, crimped and styled. Her spit curls hugged her ears and neck.

'I love it!' Jack boasted as Violet admired her bold cropped look in the mirror. 'It's modern. Do you like it?'

'You can see a lot of ear,' she replied. She turned her head this way and that to see how it held. Then she smiled, pleased with the radically new look.

On the dusk walk back, they detoured through the Queen Victoria Gardens and King's Domain. The manicured grounds bordered the northern end of the parklands adjoining Government House.

Violet sighed. 'Such a horrible day, with more horror to come. But it's also been one of the best days, Jack.'

Jack stopped beside a monument to King George V. He took a

step closer to her until their faces were only a foot apart. The thrill of near contact gave her a visible charge; her lips parted in anticipation of kissing him. He had worked his way into her affections and she was close to surrendering.

'Guess we failed the "no fraternising" rule,' Jack said. She turned her back on him, teasing, and continued towards the gates of Government House. 'But did you work out what the blue dots are?'

'Not for the life of me. We'd better get back.'

Just before they neared the gates, Jack stopped under a jacaranda tree and pulled her gently to him again. They kissed for a long time under the twisted overhanging branches.

Violet didn't want it to end. 'I have to prepare for her return,' she lamented. Packs of rainbow lorikeets shrieked for their last meal of the day as the sun dropped to the horizon.

'I'll slip through the rear gate,' Jack said, peeking through the wrought-iron fence. 'Avoid wagging any tongues.'

'I couldn't have done it without you. Any of it.'

He mock saluted and padded towards the rear gate as Violet brushed a curl from her cheek, breathed in deeply and walked towards the main gate.

40

Day 114: Yallourn, Victoria
Population: 5580
Weather: 84.5 degrees Fahrenheit, low-dwelling cloud, claggy humidity
Fact: Yallourn is unique in Australia as the only model town planned and built by a public authority. Its name is thought to derive from Aboriginal words meaning 'brown fire', referring to the substantial brown coal reserves buried beneath it.

'Ma'am?' a male voice asked meekly as Daisie jerked awake in the back seat of the car. She clutched her splitting head as the driver held the door open to the cheering crowds at Essendon airport. She wiped dribble from the corner of her mouth and propped herself up, adjusting the sleeves of her spotted swing dress, which had bunched up around her armpits as she'd slid down the leather seat over the course of the journey.

The nervous chap – Australian, by his sunburnt appearance – offered his hand as she steadied herself against the door arch.

Queen Elizabeth and the Duke paused momentarily to greet wellwishers before they were escorted through the airport onto the tarmac, where two Trans Australia Airlines Convair planes sat waiting.

After the royals had boarded, Daisie carefully scaled the stairs onto the first plane and took her seat. The interior had been converted for the tour, the front section boasting reclining lounge chairs and pale blue carpet.

'Two minutes to departure,' the captain alerted over the intercom. Daisie made her way to the lavatory at the rear of the cabin. The toilet was in use but the adjacent corridor provided discretion, so she took out her perfume bottle and sprayed a few bursts into her mouth.

'That's a novel way to fix bad breath,' the Duke quipped as he exited the lavatory.

Daisie's painted lips transitioned from agape to puckered to smirking. 'It's gin. Can I offer you a taste?'

The Duke paused and chuckled to himself, unused to such game chatter. 'You're an audacious one, aren't you?' he said.

'Please prepare for take-off,' the captain announced over the PA system.

'Are you drunk?' the Duke asked with a smile, leaning in so as not to be heard by others. 'Perfectly fine if you are, need all the help one can get to push through all this.'

'Maybe. But if I admit that to you, it will need to be our secret.' Daisie dropped the atomiser into her handbag.

The Duke put his finger to his lips, pretending to lock them before he returned to the front of the cabin.

Daisie lingered to savour the moment, her face flushed from the frisson of perfume-tinged alcohol and forbidden flirtation.

Twenty minutes later, the plane touched down at a rural airstrip in the township of Sale in country Victoria, and within forty minutes the entourage had transferred to a train headed for the regional industrial town of Yallourn. Yallourn was an odd mishmash of new suburbia, blue-collar industry and government housing, as though the entire town had been designed by committee. The motorcade left Yallourn station, passing beneath a sign strung between two mini electricity towers that proclaimed, 'Welcome to Your Gracious Majesty'. Men in suits, miners by day most likely, lined the roads with their wives and children on flatbed trucks holding signs that read 'Loyalty to our Queen' and 'Yallourn Chamber of Commerce'.

After the official welcome by the Mayor, a long-winded soliloquy by the Minister for Fuel and Power, and the obligatory awkward curtsy from a posy-bearing child, the tour departed again for the Yallourn mine, an open-cut brown coal excavation a mile square and three hundred feet deep.

'It's cooled by a complex network of water fountains,' the proud Minister explained breathlessly to the seemingly interested Prince Philip.

Daisie stole the occasional glance at him, but his attentiveness to Queen Elizabeth and the hosts prevailed. 'Seems more enamoured with a dirt hole than me,' Daisie thought to herself before she snuck a squirt of gin.

The overbearing sunshine started to produce a veil of sweat on her brow, pulling in the flies in thicker abundance.

Ratcliffe took the Queen's signal and a respectful departure was engineered. 'Further delay will make us late for a government function in Melbourne later this evening,' he confessed to the Mayor.

At 4.05 p.m., after precisely one hour in Yallourn, the motorcade departed for Warragul through vast stretches of thick bushland and hilly green countryside. Occasionally a small dead animal could be seen lying prone at the side of the road. Daisie counted two dead kangaroos and one small round animal that resembled an oversized hamster. Alone in the third car, aside from the driver, she refreshed herself with some 'fragrance' to bolster her energy. 'Does that radio work?' she asked.

'I believe so, miss,' the driver replied.

'It's Lady Chettle.'

'I believe so, Lady Chettle,' he repeated after an indignant pause.

'Well, turn it up!'

There was a perceptible sigh as he leaned forward and twisted the dial. The speaker crackled to life with the tinny sound of a jingle, which segued into Eartha Kitt singing '*C'est si bon*'.

Daisie recognised the song from her first visit to Bill's house. 'Turn it up,' she ordered the driver. 'Louder!'

The motorcade drove over the crest of a low hill and descended onto a plateau of green pastures broken up by the occasional shrugging gum tree. The surrounding fields were dotted with cattle baking in the hot sun.

Daisie craned her neck towards the window. Her car was in third position, with the Queen and Duke's Daimler in front and Ratcliffe riding in the lead. She could see the profile of the Duke looking through the side window. He observed the scenery, seeming not to be engaged in much conversation with his wife.

'Accelerate,' she told the driver.

'Pardon?'

'Accelerate up beside the Duke.'

'I'm sorry, ma'am, it's too dangerous.'

'It's an open road. There're no cars. We're in the middle of nowhere,' Daisie exclaimed as she reached into her bag for more perfume.

'My instructions are to maintain a three-car distance at all times.'

'And *my* strict instructions'—she paused to squirt some gin into her mouth—'are for you to drive beside the Duke's vehicle so I can say hello. I'm a member of the royal household, you know. A lady! I could have you sacked.'

The driver made a beleaguered exhalation.

'Well?' Daisie persisted, her voice raised.

The driver frowned and turned on the indicator. It clicked relentlessly as he glanced nervously into the rear-vision mirror and steered carefully into the oncoming lane.

The car crawled alongside the Daimler. The driver of the Queen and Duke looked nervously across, confusion on his face as he tried to understand why Daisie's car was running alongside. The Duke turned towards them with a confused look on his face.

Daisie put on her sunglasses. Her window crept beside the Duke's until they were an arm's length apart. He smirked, shaking his head.

The Queen leaned forward with a look of concern on her face.

Daisie offered a small wave with her cupped hand. The Duke couldn't help laughing. The Queen was not amused.

'I have to pull back, Miss Chettle, it's too dangerous,' said the driver fretfully.

'Very well—'

With a frightful *BROONK* an emu smashed into the bumper bar and rolled off the bonnet, its odd flailing form thrown as the driver desperately yanked the steering wheel sideways. The piercing screech of rubber on tar came as the car braked sharply, hurling Daisie forward in her seat.

The car pulled to a dramatic stop in the dirt beside the road. The engine coughed and stalled. As a dust cloud cleared, the driver stared straight ahead in dumbfounded shock.

The radio continued without missing a beat, Eartha Kitt singing in French a contrast to the shock of the accident.

The driver pushed the door open and paced beside the car. His face was white with fear. Daisie squirted some more gin to calm her mildly stirred nerves as the driver bent over and vomited onto the dirt.

The other vehicles rounded beside the car, the occupants running urgently to assist. The Queen and Duke's Daimler sat by the side of the road a hundred feet away, with the detective alert by the rear doors. Daisie watched the bemused monarchs peer through the rear window. One of the other drivers stood on the road and held his hands up to the trailing cars, some of which were press and local joyriders.

Ratcliffe's driver, a man in a navy suit and hat, strode over and leaned through the passenger window. He reached in and snapped the radio off. 'You all right, miss?'

'I'm fine. I think.'

'What the bloody hell were you doin'?' he said, turning on the driver, who had by then turned a shade of eucalyptus green.

'She ordered me to!' the driver replied desperately. He dropped his hat and bent over again in preparation to vomit. The flies gathered.

'Preposterous,' Daisie quietly confided to the man in the navy hat. He wandered over to the carcass of the animal lying prone in the dirt, the emu a mess of legs and feathers.

Ratcliffe, out of breath, poked his head through the driver's window. He weighed Daisie up with his pinched eyes, as though he was trying to work out what mood he should be in.

With a guttural, prehistoric cry, the emu maniacally resurrected like an avian Frankenstein. Its broken leg failed as it attempted to traverse the paddock fence. The beast crashed into a pile, more feathers dropping as it bounded behind the car and crossed the road, limping into the thin bushes on the opposite side.

The Duke walked urgently towards Daisie, trailed by a detective. The Duke was taking charge authoritatively, his jacket unbuttoned and his hat in his right hand as she hurriedly checked her lipstick in the rear-vision mirror.

'Are you all right?' he asked through the window, his voice rich with genuine concern.

She smiled and dipped her eyelids. 'Fully unscathed, I think,' she said, her voice rising as though it were a question and perhaps he'd investigate further. 'Shame about that large chicken.'

Philip glanced towards her driver and frowned. He was still bent over, off to the side of the road.

'Apologies, sir,' the driver uttered as he wiped his mouth.

'He seems a bit under the weather,' the Duke said. 'Why don't you join us?' He opened her door and held out his hand. 'I insist.'

Daisie snatched it, unable to grasp his muscular hand quickly enough. They walked across the broken dirt by the roadway, Daisie doing her best to navigate the uneven ground in fine heels. She held her head with pride, her handbag slung over her arm as the pair walked slowly towards the Daimler. 'I seem to make men do irrational things,' she said with her best feigned innocence, flicking a fly away with her hand.

'No doubt. No damage done, fortunately.'

'Are you sure *she* won't mind me sharing her car?' Daisie asked, looking ahead to the Daimler.

'It's *our* car. We can't be that far from the next place. The next place I can't even pronounce.'

She smirked at his jest as the Duke opened the rear door for her. The Queen sat poised like an ornament, elegantly still in sunglasses with her eyes fixed straight ahead.

'Darling, poor Daisie is a bit shaken so she's going to ride with us to the next stop.'

Queen Elizabeth made no acknowledgement, so he motioned for Daisie to climb onto the leather seat. She slid into the centre beside Her Majesty, pleased as punch, pulling her dress in tight to clear space for Philip.

The Queen, hands resting on her lap, stared coolly out the window at nothing in particular, as though her mind willed her to be anywhere else. The Duke pulled the door closed and ran his fingers through his perfectly clipped and oiled hair.

The car smelled good. Rarefied. Such that Daisie became conscious of her own air – that of perfume mixed with Gordon's. She discreetly covered her mouth with her hand.

The detective got into the passenger seat and turned a suspicious glare upon Daisie. She met his stern gaze for as long as he held it, his thin moustache lending him a Dickensian archness. Eventually he turned back to the front and quietly asked the driver to proceed.

'Cosy,' Philip said, gamely trying to ease the mood. 'How much further?' he asked the driver.

'Approximately twenty minutes, Your Royal Highness.'

'Twenty minutes,' he repeated. 'I'm sure we can manage that.' Prince Philip smiled.

Daisie could feel the warmth of the Duke's leg against her stockings, his Savile Row tailored suit silky against her lower calf. After an extended silence, and the diffusing of the gin into her bloodstream, she felt an obligation to fill the conversational void. 'That's a beautiful ensemble, Your Majesty. Bobo has excelled.' The Queen wore a light spotted dress, white gloves and matching heels and a pillbox hat. 'Simple and stylish, perfect for the conditions.'

Her Majesty didn't flinch.

'Everything all right, ducks?' Philip asked.

The Queen perceptibly stiffened on the word 'ducks'. His gaze didn't leave the passing countryside. The detective shifted a little in his seat. The tension now wound, nobody else dared utter a word.

For Daisie the overwrought mood soon became so overbearing, so ridiculous, it shifted into the realm of absurdity. A burst of laughter escaped from her lungs. And like Violet's vomit on the *Gothic*, once it started, it wouldn't stop. She covered her mouth but the restrained giggle escaped. She closed her eyes, concentrating on grim subjects to deter it. *The Piltdown Man! The Korean War! The causes thereof!* But to no avail.

She took two deep breaths, one a choking half laugh, and opened her eyes.

Nobody else had moved.

She wiped the teary corner of her left eye with her finger and tried to regain some manner of composure.

'I don't see what's quite so funny,' said the Queen in a pinched tone.

The detective turned back, glowering. The driver glanced nervously in the rear-view mirror.

And then Daisie's laughter broke again, tickled by the silliness of it all. It snowballed out of control. Inside, she prayed for another emu.

The Duke started chuckling, the disregard for propriety seemingly infectious. 'We need you at some of these dreary ceremonies to liven things up,' he said.

'Philip,' the Queen fired across Daisie. It was terse and insistent and silenced them both.

The remainder of the trip was spent in silence. When the car arrived at the welcoming party in Warragul, the Queen alighted, leaving the Duke and Daisie momentarily alone together in the back seat. A military serviceman waited patiently with the door open.

'Thanks for the ride,' she whispered before exiting. He smiled at her.

Sixty minutes later, after a dedication ceremony and a lap of the trotting track, the tour party assembled on the tarmac to board the Convair back to Melbourne.

Ratcliffe took Daisie aside with a grip on her forearm to ensure she was seated as far away from the royal couple as possible.

41

Violet admired her hair in the dresser mirror of Daisie's suite. She'd turned down the bed and laid out her sister's nightgown.

The door was flung open and Daisie stumbled in: wilted, reddened and in need of a scrub. 'Here I come, ready or not,' she announced, uncharacteristically upbeat and seemingly drunk. Violet remained silent, standing to attention by the dresser.

'I suppose it suits you,' Daisie said in an annoyed tone, casting an eye over Violet's hair before turning to the painting.

'Spangles in the top drawer,' Violet said, pointing to the desk.

Daisie slowly removed her left earring, the smell of alcohol heavy on her breath. She paused before removing the right one. 'But you didn't complete the exercise, of course.'

'Footman Albert's letter of confirmation is on your desk.'

Daisie walked to the desk and unfolded the slip of paper. 'The flies?'

'I have a fly formula, which was intended for Her Majesty. She'd be delighted if you try it first.'

'Really? Resourceful, aren't you? I'm genuinely impreshed,' Daisie slurred. She flopped onto the bed. 'And genuinely tired. I think my monthly visitor has finally arrived so that's enough for today. Begone.'

Violet's eyes widened with a sudden realisation.

'Sorry if I've been a dragon,' Daisie continued, kicking both shoes across the carpet. 'But you did destroy my life, so can you please hop along and run a shallow bath for me?'

Violet turned to the door as Daisie began to disrobe, pulling her elegant clothes from her body and flinging them across the room like an amateur burlesque act.

'Ah yes, I forgot,' Daisie said as she tried to pull a tight slip sideways over her head without stumbling over. 'The blue dots – what *are* they?'

'Her Majesty's monthly friend,' Violet replied confidently. 'Dare we speak of it.'

Even Daisie blushed. 'Quite,' she said agreeably. 'Of course, I knew it meant that. Just wanted to embarrass you,' she added flippantly, though her flushed face suggested otherwise.

'Then you received your wish,' Violet surrendered, indulging her.

'Shall we try this?' Daisie had noticed the aerosol canister resting on the dressing table beside Albert's note. She grasped it in her right hand and turned it over curiously, shaking it to get a reaction. 'It will fix the fly problem? Thank God. Damn things near carried me off in Yallourn.' Down to her black bra and knickers, she turned to face her sister, one hand on her hip and the spray in the other. Violet lingered at the door, her immediate escape foiled. 'Perhaps I've been too hard on you. Then again, you haven't gone easy on me by any measure. Still, we are sisters. Must say, your hair does look rather good.' She held the aerosol can out to Violet. 'Does it work?'

Violet tentatively took it as though it were a bomb, sniffing the nozzle before raising it to eye level. 'Close your eyes and hold your breath,' Violet said uncertainly.

'Hurry up!' Daisie insisted with her eyelids squeezed tight.

Violet pressed the nozzle. With a hiss, a clear spray atomised over Daisie's face. It smelled like a mix of menthol and gasoline.

'It feels rather hot,' Daisie said, her eyes clasped tight.

'Keep your mouth shut,' Violet urged her.

'It's stinging me!'

'Maybe that's what kills the flies?'

'Get me water! A towel!'

Violet snatched a bath towel from the dresser as Daisie clutched her eyes.

'It's burning!' Daisie rubbed her face furiously, dashing to the mirror in a panic. She dropped the towel. Her face was blemished as though it had been afflicted by a rare disease. 'I'm disfigured!' she screamed, and desperately rubbed lotion onto her pockmarked skin as Violet watched on.

'Well, they can certainly differentiate us now,' Violet offered unhelpfully.

The next day the professor sent an official apology. Apparently the formula worked, but that particular canister had been left to ferment and the expiry date stamped on the base had been overlooked.

An Australian doctor, the best the State of Victoria could provide, tended to Daisie's face, swathing it carefully in creams and bandages. Violet dared not make light of her sister's appearance. Everybody became less vocal about the flies.

'I'll handle the rest of your duties. At least until the burns clear,' Ratcliffe informed her. 'Lady Mountbatten arrives in a week, so rest and recover.'

The week passed in a blur of towns, villages, airports and train stations, each crowded by a sea of faces no less excited than those that had first greeted them in Sydney. The royal caravan moved over two hundred and fifty miles by train, car and plane to traverse the state. Jack was so busy with transportation that Violet barely saw him.

Some of the visits were cursory: fifteen minutes in Rochester, twenty minutes in Echuca (where the royal couple stepped off the train, received a bouquet, then literally stepped back on board to depart) and barely any longer in Shepparton and Ballarat. Yet the crowds in the smaller towns seemed to grow with each visit. Entire rural populations deserted their farming obligations to glimpse the growing spectacle of the royal tour. Every civic centre on the route was dressed with flowers and bunting, each town competing with the last, as civilians dressed in their Sunday best revelled in these briefest of stopovers by their Queen.

'Polio has been reported in some districts,' read an official communiqué, slipped under every door in the middle of the night, 'so the Victorian government has determined that we are not to stop in the towns of Maryborough and Castlemaine due to the slim risk of infection. The train will slow at the platform and speeches of welcome will be passed through the window by the Private Secretary.'

Some of the press thought it a conspiracy, but most of the staff whispered that they were just happy to avoid a few civic presentations in a schedule dense with them.

'Mailbag!' the page called as he moved from door to door, the staff lingering around him like moths to a bulb.

Daisie hid, her face and eyes swollen red from the reaction or the gin, or both.

42

Day 120: Brisbane, Queensland
Population: 468,988
Weather: 88 degrees Fahrenheit, humidity at 47 per cent
Fact: The world's first cultivated macadamia tree lives in the City Botanic Gardens. Planted in 1858 by Sir Walter Hill, the tree still produces nuts every year.

The heat rose from the tarmac at Eagle Farm Airport as the royal Convairs taxied towards the terminal. Palm trees lined the airstrip like a tropical regiment, gently waving in the breeze.

When the royal party exited the plane, the humidity hit them like a downpour. The Queen and Duke were whisked out of the sun to a welcome ceremony with the Premier and the Mayor. The rest were transferred in regular cars to Government House in Brisbane. The two-storey Italianate Victorian building boasted a balustraded roof parapet, segmented arches under bracketed eaves and a white stucco finish. It overlooked the city to the south-east and the khaki sinews of sprawling Mount Coot-tha to the west. The city was dense with vegetation and the cries of birdlife, as though the prehistoric era was determined not to relent.

'Full-time job keepin' the sweat and flies awa,' Bobo, drenched with perspiration, complained later that day. Violet dallied, leaning against one of the unloaded trunks in Bobo's airless basement room. 'Shouldn't ye be busy, lass?'

'Not much to do since she's been stood down.'

'Ye did us all a favour. She'll be lucky. Ratcliffe almost ate the boss of Queensland. Premier insisted on presenting Lilibet to two hundred and sixty people in the course of forty-one minutes. A new record! She thought Ratcliffe was going to punch him.'

'Her bandages are off. Burns are almost healed,' Violet said, a tinge of disappointment in her voice. 'I'm not sure what's worse – the reddish blotches that give her the pall of an alcoholic, or the dressings that make her look like Doctor Dan the Bandage Man.' She'd read the book to Amanda, the four-year-old daughter of widow Mrs Martin from six doors down.

Bobo laughed as she lifted a heavy sewing machine out of a trunk with a grunt.

'I should get back, make sure she doesn't want anything.' Violet smiled glumly as she turned towards the hall.

'I want my hair plaited,' Daisie tersely instructed Violet the second she returned. 'A single tight braid. French. Tied with that brooch I wore in Mount Gambier.'

Violet started working on her sister's hair, coarsely brushing it flat. She then gathered it into a ponytail and brushed it in her fist. Each stroke gently yanked Daisie's head.

'You haven't been communicating with that Australian driver, Jack, have you? It's a poor choice if you have.'

Violet pursed her lips tightly. 'I tolerate him.'

Daisie took a sip of tea, her head bobbing as Violet brushed a knot out. 'My spy saw you two chatting last night in the staff room. Does he know you're pregnant? With somebody else's child? I'm assuming not.'

Violet pulled Daisie's hair tight, causing her to spill some tea on her lap.

'That's steaming hot!' she shrieked. Violet yanked a handful of her hair under the guise of grooming. Daisie turned and glared. Violet persisted, yanking her hair again – harder this time – before folding it into a plait. Daisie spun and slapped her hand away.

'That hurt!' Violet winced.

'Good! You're doing it to me on purpose.'

Violet pulled the plait yet again, tightly enough for it to trigger her sister's rage. Daisie pivoted. She slapped her hand across Violet's face, her eyes burning with anger, her scarred face flaring a shade of pink.

Violet's mouth hung agape. The gravity of the confrontation took a second to land.

They froze as somebody knocked on the door. Daisie straightened her back and walked to the door.

Miss Pemberton, rarely seen outside her natural office environment, balanced awkwardly behind the door. 'Major Ratcliffe has asked to see both of you in exactly forty-five minutes,' she said. Her right eyebrow cocked slightly as though intuiting the altercation.

'Both of us?' asked Daisie calmly as she smoothed her hair with both hands.

'Yes. Not a minute late,' she said, before she trailed off down the hallway.

Daisie closed the door and leaned back against it to regain her breath. The sisters glanced at each other in a wordless truce.

Forty minutes later they walked the ground-floor corridor of the labyrinthine Brisbane Government House, avoiding workmen who were dismantling a rainforest display and removing armfuls of gladioli and palm ferns that had been mounted for the prior evening's civic ball.

'Bloody live koalas,' a workman complained as he collected the pungent droppings off the floorboards. 'Still, he seemed quite fond of the things.'

Miss Pemberton rose as Violet and Daisie entered the administration rooms. 'You can go in now,' she said, gesturing towards the corridor that led to the ballroom.

They stood shoulder to shoulder at the double doors. Violet glanced back at Miss Pemberton to ensure they were in the right place. Daisie swung the double doors apart to reveal the cavernous main ballroom. The room had two arched windows on the east side that overlooked the grounds. A portrait of Queen Elizabeth hung above the fireplace at one end, a grand piano sat in the adjacent corner and a row of antique chairs ran along the west wall. Navy blue patterned carpet framed a central rectangular teak dance floor.

In the centre of the wooden floor sat a lengthy banquet table, around which a dozen suited men were gathered. They simultaneously turned towards the intrusion.

Violet and Daisie paused. They were the only women at what looked like a board meeting for a soon-to-be-bankrupt firm. At the head of the table sat Ratcliffe. Lieutenant Commander Parker was seated to his immediate right.

'The Chettle sisters,' Ratcliffe announced ominously. 'Take a seat.' The men watched with a heavy gaze as Violet and Daisie tentatively walked towards the table. Violet lagged behind, nervously fussing with the buttons on her dress. 'Not sure which is which,'

Ratcliffe said disdainfully to the men as the twins apprehensively took two spare seats at the far end.

The anonymous men wore bland suits, conservative haircuts and badges on their lapels, and they all possessed bound document folders. One or two had a military patina: shaved hair and tightly buttoned clothes. They were Australian government.

'Right,' said Ratcliffe, resuming his seat. 'These are her nieces,' as though they were exhibits rather than the actual people being referred to. 'Her brother-in-law, Edward, is their father.'

'May I ask you,' one of the faceless men asked, 'have you had any contact with your Aunt Hazel?'

'Auntie Hazel?' Violet's voice echoed in the emptiness of the ballroom. 'She moved here when we were very young.'

The men made positive murmurs, nodding to each other with approval.

'Are her relations with your family on good ground?' another suit asked. 'No ill feeling?'

'Nobody ever really talks about her,' Violet said. Her curiosity relaxed her guard. 'We're not sure if she's alive.'

The men chuckled to themselves.

The sisters shared a confused glance. 'Is everything all right? Has she . . . passed?' Violet asked, her voice straining.

The men laughed a little louder. Ratcliffe silenced the table by speaking over the laughter. 'She's perfectly fine. Mr Harrison, can you explain what it is the government intends?'

Mr Harrison, with tight Brylcreemed hair and a nose one-third bigger than the average, shuffled a set of papers nervously as he stood to speak.

'Mr Harrison is the Australian Minister in Charge of the Royal Tour,' Ratcliffe said as an aside.

'Yes, Major Ratcliffe, that's right,' Harrison said in a nervous Australian accent. 'On March 18th we'd planned for Her Majesty to make a radio call from the Royal Flying Doctor Service base to a remote family, to reach out to those living in central Australia. The Palace loves the idea but we were struggling to find an appropriate family, an appropriate representative, to speak to Her Majesty. The broadcast will be relayed around the world, so there is some inherent risk should we choose the wrong person. There'll also be a film crew filming for a documentary about the tour. For cinemas. It'll all be scripted, of course, but still, being live, we want it to go as smoothly as possible. And given the inevitable press interest, we want the family to be – how should I put this – as *presentable* as possible.'

He paused, as though waiting for the twins' acknowledgement.

'I'm sorry, but I don't understand,' Violet confessed.

'When Major Ratcliffe's office contacted us about tracing your auntie, we found her. And she fits the criteria perfectly. Lake Eyre is one of the most remote places in Australia. Our South Australian field office paid her a visit, and she's presentable for radio *and* news-reels. She's an expatriate who's forged a life for herself in Australia. Runs a cattle station. And with her connection to the Palace, via you both, it's a good news story about the family ties between Australia and Mother Britain. The British Minister for Immigration can't contain himself.'

The men laughed to themselves again.

'So you've met her? Auntie Hazel?' asked Violet, breaking her silence.

'Why, yes,' replied Harrison, fussing with one of his folders. 'In fact, I have a recent photo.'

A black-and-white photograph was pushed down the table through four sets of white hands and slid in front of the sisters.

The image depicted a woman, roughly forty years of age, wearing a simple house dress and standing in front of a weather-beaten homestead with a baby boy perched on her hip. Beside her stood a muscular, sun-stained man dressed in farming attire.

Hazel's face was warm and familiar, her pinched nose like her sister's.

'Hazel Lawson. Took her companion's name a few years back. They live on Ti-ra-rey Station.'

'It's pronounced Tirari Station, sir,' an aide interrupted.

'Right, Tear-are-ray. Three hundred miles from Broken Hill. Gibber country. Needless to say, a bloody long way from anywhere.'

'The station has a powerful transmitter capable of overcoming any adverse weather conditions,' continued the aide. 'She has a young child too. Harry is his name. Hazel's other half is a dinky-di Australian stockman. Plus the repressive isolation. It's ideal!'

'Hazel will represent remote Australia,' added another bureaucrat. 'And she has already agreed to take part. Our people are there now, running checks and making sure the radio signal is boosted. So thank you for bringing her to our attention.'

'The other candidates we'd narrowed it down to,' said Ratcliffe, rubbing his eyes, 'were worrying at best. Could hardly understand a damn word most were saying. One kept swearing every time he botched the script.'

The men laughed but Violet was speechless. Her mind had drifted off to another place, or time.

'We understand this must be an emotional moment for you,' Harrison added once their laughter subsided.

'Would've thought a stay of execution might've cheered you up,' offered a blasé Ratcliffe. 'Anyway, keep your heads down until Broken Hill. No more distractions. We won't require your services in waiting. Lady Mountbatten will arrive within the week.' He lowered his voice and turned to Harrison. 'I'm not certain about putting them in front of the press.'

'It is a unique twist, twins. The Palace connection and all,' Harrison replied quietly.

'The problem is that any time these two get involved in anything, it tends to go arse-up,' Ratcliffe said.

'We are sitting right here!' Daisie blurted out, frustrated.

'Well, you shouldn't be. Dismissed.'

43

The heavy murmur of the motorcade and the hoots of the assembled crowds signalled the Queen and Duke's departure to Toowoomba.

Daisie was more than happy not to be part of the daytrip. It would be yet another monotonous progress swarming with flies. She rolled over on the four-poster bed, lit a cigarette and flicked through the *Australian Women's Weekly*.

'*The Bridesmaid Who Forgot! The tale of a tempted secretary who trapped a professional man into marriage!*'

Daisie pushed the magazine away and downed the rest of a tumbler of gin. 'Violet?' she called. Her voice suffocated in the empty room's thick silence. She let the glass drop to the carpet beside the bed, where it landed with a dull thud. She knew Violet would pick it up, along with the clothes that were strewn across the floor.

Daisie sighed, bored beyond belief. *Brisbane*. There was one more day of it to endure before the entire caravan departed for Broken Hill. She lifted the stopper and tilted the bottle sideways. The decanter was bone-dry.

On a visit to the lavatory, she'd noticed a drinks cart in the drawing room down the hall. Daisie opened the door, peered both ways and then padded in her socks along the empty corridor until she reached the open doorway. The room was ornate but in a modern way – it was less than a hundred years old, after all. Through arched corner windows, leafy branches swayed in a slow dance. Between two of the windows rested the silver bar cart. She smiled, then froze for a moment as her footsteps caused the teak floorboards to rasp. When she heard no reaction, she bounded across them and checked the gin decanter. Unfortunately it had not yet been refilled.

Dawdling back to her suite, Daisie glanced down the east hallway towards the Queen and Duke's wing. The policeman guarding the entrance to their suite was absent, his vacant chair beside the door like that of a ghostly sentinel. Fortified by gin, she edged down the hall towards the door, glancing over her shoulder before gently pressing her ear against it.

Silence.

She tested the brass door handle. With a click it dropped and the doors parted, the dry hinge squeaking its misgiving. Daisie slipped into the room and turned the latch to lock it behind her.

The royal living quarters had been smartly outfitted inside a large dining room. Its ceiling, two storeys high and framed with elaborate cornices, crowned a living area defined by a bedroom-sized Persian rug. Against the west wall the British and Australian flags stood to attention, mounted on either side of a marble fireplace stacked with dry wood. The centre of the room was commanded by a circular dining table set with silver around a jade vase of red and golden Australian natives. A small mahogany desk sat against the opposite wall beside a wide antique bookcase stocked with dull volumes.

Daisie glanced up at the chandelier hanging above the dining table, its multiple tiers of crystal casting pinpricks of light onto the silver and glassware below. She wandered over to the desk. A copper reading lamp leaned over two neatly arranged piles of documents. One was emblazoned with the ER symbol and was marked 'FYEO: Cabinet Documents March 1954'. The other, a leather-bound folder, appeared to be forthcoming tour schedules and speeches.

A black and gold-trimmed Conway Stewart fountain pen rested on the papers. Daisie picked it up, removed the cap and turned the pen over in her delicate fingers. With the fine tip she drew a small dot on her palm. It had a handsome heft, and for a moment she considered sliding it into her pocket, but she replaced the cap and returned it to the pile.

A low rumble beyond the windows broke the quiet. The noise lasted just a few seconds, as though a small explosion had occurred in the distance. She thought the floor was vibrating but it was just her heart racing faster. Daisie parted the sheer curtains. Across the treetops, to the tips of Brisbane city to the north, loomed murky clouds that filled the horizon. A lightning spark's violent illumination confirmed a thunderstorm was headed her way.

Daisie's eyes dropped to a fly that railed against the window, caught between the curtains and the glass in a haste of perpetual panic. She released the curtain, leaving the insect to its fate.

Away in the rear corner of the room, alongside the bookcase, stood an unassuming doorway. Daisie paused at the threshold, peeking in uncertainly.

The royal bedchamber.

Dominating the space was a regal four-poster bed covered with a gold velvet spread and a soft matching valance. Antique nightstands on both sides carried the royal couple's diligently arranged personal effects. A marble fireplace corresponded perfectly to the bed; beside it stood a full-length mirror and a silver drinks cart fully stocked with all manner of crystal flasks.

Incongruously, a cleaning bucket, a soiled rag and a mop leaned against a cream Victorian four-door wardrobe.

Daisie tiptoed to the Queen's bedside to examine the nightstand, holding her breath lest she disrupt the tiniest thing. Three framed photos stood proudly by her bedside next to a jar of Elizabeth Arden's Eight Hour Cream and a silver-plated hairbrush. A recent portrait of Her Majesty's young children, Charles, five, and Anne, three, playing with some corgis on a grassy lawn; a candid photo of her father, Albert, in his ceremonial military uniform carrying Elizabeth as a young child; and a photograph of Queen Elizabeth and Prince Philip on their wedding day. The last image had an unstaged feel. They seemed to be sharing a private joke, her smile the broadest Daisie had seen, toothy and full of genuine happiness. Unlike their carefully controlled public image, they appeared like any normal couple celebrating their big day.

Daisie carefully picked up the silver frame, feeling its weight in her hand. She brought it close to her eye and inspected Philip's handsome image, obscuring the Queen's face with the flat of her thumb. She'd always found herself attracted to him, and now she had something to prove to her sister and to herself.

On the Duke's side table rested a glass water jug, a tumbler, an open velvet case displaying his cufflinks and a small grey teddy bear. She held it to her face and inhaled, her heart now beating faster still. It smelled loved, its fur worn from years of affection.

The dressing table opposite the foot of the bed displayed a French Empire bronze antique clock and a velvet placemat on which some of the Queen's jewellery had been laid out – a pair of earrings, two sets of pearls, a small brooch and a tiara. On closer inspection Daisie recognised it as the tiara Caroline had worn on occasion.

Daisie instinctively froze as the door latch in the sitting room clicked. She crouched to the floor on the Duke's side of the bed as light footsteps navigated through the adjacent living room. The floorboards creaked as the steps grew closer. She lay flat with her face pressed to the carpet beside a pair of slippers parked underneath the bed.

The mop clanged against the bucket seconds before a stout fifty-something cleaning lady walked by Daisie's feet without noticing her lying prostrate beside the royal bed. Daisie held her breath. Oblivious, the cleaner rattled the mop against the tin bucket as she paced into the main room.

With a clunk, the sitting room door was latched again.

Daisie breathed out. She tiptoed, staying crouched, into the living room and waited a few moments before the hall was clear, then turned the handle to make her exit. The lever resisted.

The cleaner had locked it from the outside.

'Bloody sod!' Daisie hissed under her breath. She urgently fossicked through the desk drawers but found nothing resembling a key. The window ledge offered no escape, leading only to a forty-foot drop on either side.

Bonnng!

Daisie startled as the clock chimed eleven, then slumped into one of the dining room chairs, helpless. 'I'm done for,' she said out loud.

The bar cart by the wall stole her attention. She walked over and lifted a bottle of Gordon's gin from the selection. She uncapped the bottle and inhaled the familiar smell.

After the second double shot she was able to relax a little more. As she poured a third, curiosity got the better of her. She started opening the dresser drawers, pawing through the forbidden contents as the antique clock facing her ticked like a time bomb. The

Duke's apparel – mostly tweed, wool knit and fine cotton – smelled masculine with a hint of musky cologne. The second drawer down was wholly devoted to socks and handkerchiefs, the latter monogrammed with a silver 'EP' above a Crown symbol. Daisie caressed the heavily starched, pressed fabric between her fingers and slid one into her waist pocket.

She poured a fourth glass of gin and flung open the cupboard doors, rifling through the dozen or so dangling formal gowns with one hand, her drink poised in the other. One in particular demanded Daisie's attention: a dazzling silk ball gown made of champagne chiffon printed in gold with a bold blue sash slung over the neck.

Its luminescence mesmerised her. She spontaneously slid out of her own dress, unhooked the heavy gown from its hanger and pulled it over her head. After yet another drink, she located two long white gloves in the drawer and pulled them on before perusing the Queen's collection of earrings and pearls.

Daisie stood before the mirror. The fine clasps on the back were out of reach, so the gown hung loosely off her shoulders, but the dress and jewellery radiated like a full moon, and so did she. She paraded into the living room, testing the outfit for its regality, before seating herself at the desk with the voluminous fabric bunched around her legs. She uncapped the pen, held it poised over the Palace stationery then drew a small rabbit with accentuated whiskers. Violet had taught her how to draw them when they was six and it had stuck.

Daisie lolled about in the dress, splaying on the bed, the ruffles of the gown spread out like a throw rug. She pushed her face into the princely pillow, inhaled deeply, closed her eyes and imagined waking up to Philip.

*

'You're lucky I didn't mistake you for my wife,' said the confident, deep voice.

The light stung Daisie's eyes as she squinted into the pillow. She prised her right eye open. Prince Philip stood casually by the bedside table with a smirk fixed to his face. She rubbed her sockets to ensure it wasn't the gin, which had once again left her tongue dry and her head split open. He wore a single-breasted suit, a pin-striped navy tie and his hair was, as always, immaculate.

'Made yourself at home, I see? If you could call this a home.'

As Daisie eased herself up, the shoulder of the gown fell slack on the left side, revealing her bare shoulder. 'I'm so sorry,' she confessed, glancing nervously towards the sitting room. The sky outside had turned dark.

'She's at some Country Women's Association fundraiser. Giving the farm girls a cheer. So you're safe.'

The room rotated as Daisie steadied herself against the rising tide of the mattress. Philip sat on the opposite side and crossed his legs, still bearing his Cheshire Cat smile. Daisie felt like the caught mouse that he hadn't quite decided how to kill. 'Can I fetch you a drink? Gin? The heat in Toowoomba could've melted steel.' At her nod, he strolled into the sitting room, his physique towering so his head almost touched the tip of the doorframe.

Daisie pulled the tiara from her sinewy hair and lifted herself to her feet. The enjoyable effects of the gin were gone and only the horrid ones remained.

'Lime?' he shouted from the other room.

'Yes, please,' Daisie replied. Every word she spoke felt like a knitting needle being thrust deeper into her brain. She cringed at her reflection in the mirror. The gown was as badly crushed as her pride.

Before she could do anything about it, the Duke returned, brandishing two tall glasses. 'Bottoms up,' he said, taking a measured sip and considering the dress. 'You wear it well. Don't know if she'd agree though.'

'I'm so sorry. I got locked in and helped myself to the Gordon's.'

'There was barely any left to make these two. You must feel rather phalanxed.'

'I should change,' Daisie said, reaching for her clothes. 'I'm sorry.'

'Yes. Before we're both in trouble. Go right ahead,' he said, leaning against the bedpost with a broad smile on his face.

Daisie imagined him slowly walking over and kissing her square on the mouth. The thought alone sent a surge of blood through her heart and head. His hands, heavy and confident, would find her hips and she would—

With an ungainly fumble, Daisie's left leg collapsed from under her as though kicked by a ghost. She dropped to the floor in a splayed heap. Daisie didn't remember putting on a pair of the Queen's heeled shoes but there they now were, dangling off her ankles.

He knelt and took her elbow, assisting her onto the bed. Daisie steadied herself, her eyes widening as she tried to distil the scope of her indignity.

Fireworks started to explode outside, each burst casting flashes of coloured light into the room. The Duke peered through the curtains. 'Best you leave soon. Would hate for somebody to find you here and get the right idea.'

'Of course,' Daisie replied.

'I'll wait out here, where it's safe.' He closed the bedroom door behind him and she quickly slid back into her clothes, crawling on hands and knees around the bed to locate her own shoes. She tiptoed into the sitting room where Philip turned to face her.

'I'll make sure you're on for the furlough in Victoria. Three days' break from the battle for hearts and minds. We could both use it, by the looks. Won't know myself without a thousand children screaming in my ears.' He walked her to the door and held it open. 'Until then.'

'Until then.' She nodded and walked into the hallway, tripping slightly on the edge of the carpet. Minutes later, Daisie locked the door of her suite and slumped onto her bed. She winced as she replayed the encounter, but soon a sly smile grew on her face.

'Until then,' he'd said, and she could barely wait.

<h1 style="text-align:center">44</h1>

Day 123: *Bundaberg, Queensland*
Population: *19,951*
Weather: *86 degrees Fahrenheit, early scattered showers, fewer thereafter*
Fact: *Situated on the coast 239 miles north of Brisbane, the city is best known for its namesake export, Bundaberg Rum.*

'I want to stay in bed,' Daisie complained, her bloodshot eyes the colour of a Bloody Mary.

Violet parted the bedroom curtains like swift justice. 'Hungover or not, forward we go,' she asserted cheerily. She'd found renewed spirit since handing her letter for Hazel back to the office for posting.

> TO: *Hazel Lawson*
> *Tirari Station*
> *Lake Eyre, Australia*

Writing the full address on the envelope filled her with hope.

As she boarded the royal aircraft, a Trans Australia DC-4, later that morning, Violet spied Jack across the tarmac. She waved, but he was too busy corralling those who were already late for departure.

The staff took their seats at the back of the aircraft cabin. Daisie sat alone by the window, sunglasses her last line of defence keeping the world from seeing the remaining flecks of discolouration on her skin. A flurry of activity in the front cabin signalled the boarding of the Queen, the Duke and Ratcliffe, and within minutes the plane taxied for take-off.

Violet gripped the armrests as the aircraft lifted off the ground. The fuselage creaked as the plane yawed, then levelled north, travelling parallel to the aqua Queensland coastline over cane fields and the variegated colours of the tropical north.

On the tarmac of Hinkler aerodrome, the touring party were welcomed by the Bundaberg Mayor and his over-tanned, bosomy wife. The Queen, the Duke and Ratcliffe were escorted to an opentopped Humber for their civic progress.

The staff were directed to a waiting area in the hangar, which had been set up with chairs and refreshments. Cool shade and sandwiches lovingly cut into the shape of Queensland welcomed the thirty or so touring members who were to patiently wait the two hours it would take for the Queen to perform her royal duties.

Jack edged up beside Violet as she poured a glass of orange juice. 'Want to get out of here?' he asked secretively, as though he were Colonel March of Scotland Yard.

Violet glanced across the room to where Daisie sat on a lounge sipping lemonade and reading a *Women's Weekly*. 'We don't have time,' she replied. 'Plane departs in less than two hours.'

'I've got the keys to a spare car. Nobody will know – or care. Your memory of Bundy can't be the inside of a hangar. And technically, I'm your superior so I can order you to accompany me.'

'You are not my superior!'

'You're in my country, which makes me your host. And as a responsible host it's my duty to show you a real slice of Australia before you go back to your cold, miserable homeland.' He flicked his eyes towards the exit. 'See those glass doors over there? In five minutes, pretend you're looking for the ladies' room. I'll be waiting outside in a black Holden coupé.' He sidled through the glass double doors.

Violet glanced towards Daisie, who was still flipping through the magazine, her eyes dark and drowsy. After the requisite five minutes, she feigned looking for the toilets and casually wandered through the doors into an empty corridor. An engine revved behind her. At the far end, through an open exit door, Jack waited in a black town car that bore the official 'ER' markings. She smiled and ran to the passenger door, sliding into the seat with an excited shriek.

Waved through by the guard at the gate, Jack accelerated away from the hangar. 'Royal car, we can do whatever we want,' he said excitedly. 'Could probably hit a group of school children and they'd worry if we were all right.'

'Only for an hour!' Violet insisted.

'One hour and a bit,' Jack countered.

'All right, one hour and a little bit.'

'Deal.'

'So what are we going to do?' she asked as the car turned onto an unsealed road that crossed dank mangroves in still, sallow water.

'What all Australians do when they aren't working – we're going to the pub.'

On the approach to Bundaberg the streets buzzed with citizens wearing their best, many jogging towards the civic reception, which was underway. Sugar-cane arches adorned every paved street and British flags hung in the windows of fibro dwellings and storefronts.

Groups of children walked alongside the Burnett River, a wide, pale blue estuary bordered by deep green mangroves that ran adjacent to the main thoroughfare.

Jack pulled up outside the Custom House Hotel, a corner establishment with a corrugated-iron roof and wide Federation verandahs. Its bronzed male clientele spilled lazily onto the street, their wives nowhere to be seen.

'Right! A beer and a Bundaberg Rum,' Jack said as he pulled up the handbrake.

'I can't go in there!' Violet exclaimed.

'Why not?'

'I'm a woman. I'm underage. And I'm with the Queen!'

'C'mon, Miss Chettle. You're no lady-in-waiting, so stop waiting and start doing!'

Violet reluctantly got out, the sunlight piercing her skin as Jack took her hand, leading her through wiry, sunburnt patrons, sweaty under jackets and ties, to find the public bar entrance. Inside, the bar was thick with perspiration and male chatter. Coarse twang punctuated the cigarette smoke as bloodshot eyes followed them through the crowd.

'Front lounge, luv – Sophie's Bar. That's the ladies' lounge,' the publican behind the bar shouted over the din.

'Just one round and we'll be on our way,' Jack shouted, undeterred.

'Sorry, mate, no ladies! Sophie's is empty.'

'All the sheilas are out chasing royalty!' a flyblown local called out.

Violet became the centre of attention. 'Jack, let's go,' she urged.

'Do you know who this is, mate?' Jack shouted back at the publican, loud enough for some of the bar flies to notice. 'She's from Buckingham Palace. She's the Queen's bloody maid! Miss Chettle, this is. And the Queen asked her to try the local rum and report back to her.'

The publican and a handful of drinkers within earshot shifted their gaze from Jack to Violet.

'Really?' asked the publican. Violet smiled innocently. 'Well, strewth, what the bloody hell do you know. We've got royalty in here. Come over here, luv.'

As she took a tentative step closer to the bar through the crush, some of the men started to assemble around her. 'Hey Smithy, we've got the Queen's bloody maid over here! She wants to have a rum at the Customs. Her Majesty's orders!'

Word rippled the length of the bar and a round of applause started to break out. Violet flushed as Jack loosened his tie and leaned against the bar with a broad smirk, pleased with the inordinate amount of attention he'd brought on her.

A small cast-iron ship's bell hung at the far end of the bar was enthusiastically rung by the bartender. A further horde of sweaty male bodies, all with schooners of beer poised at their chests, crowded in from the pavement. Gradually, like trying to start a distemperate lawnmower, a slurry choir staggered into voice.

'*God save our gracious Queen!*' they sang, laughing and cajoling, as a glass of beer was pushed into Violet's hands. She shyly nodded along, trying to stand as 'regally' as possible on the sticky carpet. Jack sang louder than any of them, building the anthem to a crescendo until it climaxed in an enormous cheer.

'Here you go, a shot of Bundy's finest. On the house,' the publican said as he poured two shot glasses. Jack handed one to Violet.

'On Her Majesty's service, Miss Chettle will now try the rum,' the publican announced. The circle of men fell quiet, waiting for Violet to sample their pride.

She held a beer glass in one hand, a shot glass in the other, and the burden of a child growing in between. But their eyes craved validation.

'Bottoms up,' Violet said and sipped a tiny sliver of the brown liquid. At first there was a burning sensation, lightly searing her tongue before it became warm and sweet. She gave the thumbs up.

The men cheered and slapped her on the back. 'Finish it!' they started chanting.

Jack sensed the apprehension in her eyes. 'Just a taste, gents! This is nothing, though – she actually vomited on the Queen once.'

An endless stream of questions came from the men, all eager to get a story to tell their wives.

'What's *she* like?'

'What's *she* think of Australia?'

'Does *she* drink beer? What about Phil the Greek?'

After half an hour, Jack prised Violet out of the pub to the sound of playful boos. He put on a big show of opening the rear door of the car for the benefit of the drinkers on the pavement. She played along and the overflow crowd gave a rousing send-off cheer.

Jack pulled the car onto the main street and turned right at the river. The road led all the way to the shore. 'We've got thirty minutes. There's one more thing I need to show you.'

'We should really go back, Jack, in case they finish up early.'

'They *never* finish early. One last thing. Trust me.' He pulled up at the edge of the yellow sand and opened her door.

'Pretending to be a perfect gentlemen again?'

'Perfect, a low tide,' he said, ignoring her, as he started removing his shoes and socks.

'We're not swimming!' Violet was horrified. The ocean looked inviting but it was bad enough they were playing truant, without going for a swim.

'Of course not. We're catching pipis.'

'Pee-pees?' she replied incredulously. 'What is a pee-pee? Aside from *that*.'

'Shellfish. Delicious. If we're lucky enough to catch the buggers.'

She laughed spontaneously at this choice of words. 'I don't know if that means what you think it means.'

'C'mon, it's just sand. Take off your shoes.'

Violet glanced at her watch then reluctantly removed her shoes, shaking her head as she rolled her hem and held it up with both hands.

They stepped onto the hot beach, tiptoeing briskly to the wet sand. Azure waves rhythmically roared and smashed the shore under a heavy blue sky, such that they could barely hear each other speak.

Violet smiled as the water cooled her feet. She wriggled her toes in the soothing wet grit. 'I haven't taken my shoes off outdoors since last summer,' she yelled over the crashing waves.

'I live for the ocean!' Jack said. 'Right, look for small air bubbles when the waves roll back. They leave a "v" in the run-off. There – there's some,' he said excitedly, pointing at the wet sand. 'If you step on the sand with the ball of your heel after a wave has gone back, it will dry in a circle around you. If you see two little holes appear, they're caused by the pipis feeding. So dig there.'

He swivelled his feet back and forth as though badly dancing until he was buried up to his ankles. 'There's bubbles there, there!' he shouted as she started shuffling in the wash. 'Feel for shells rubbing against your feet.'

'Do these things bite?'

'Wait! Wait!' Jack reached carefully into the sand beside his foot, felt around and, with a slop of wet sand, pulled out a shilling-sized white shell. He washed it clean in the water and held the triangular clamshell up to the sky. 'One pipi!'

Violet shrieked with laughter, dodging the spray as she swivelled her waist to withstand the push and pull of the waves. Despite her initial hesitation, her face was full of joy.

He took the small shell carefully between his thumb and fore-finger. Its polished white surface gleamed like a pearl. 'So you can eat—'

Violet screamed as a wave dumped her and she tumbled backwards into the churning water. Even though it was only a few feet deep, for a moment she flailed, lost as she tumbled in the underwater vacuum, before the tide stilled and she righted herself, clawing at the sandy floor. She opened her eyes and saw Jack's hand grasping down. There was a desperate beauty to the image, as his strong hand clasped hers through the rolling sand and weed. She pulled on it, finding her feet against the roar of the receding wave. Her clothes were drenched and heavy, as Jack, still standing and wet from only the waist down, laughed boisterously.

She wanted to be furious, but the cool water and his boyish laughter diffused her anger and she burst into giggles. Another wave lurched towards them and knocked them both over as they stumbled and wrestled through the thick froth and then headed back to the car.

Violet crouched beside the open door, removing her dress over her bra and bloomers. Jack stood sheepishly in boxer shorts on the opposite side of the car, trying to look anywhere but Violet's semi-naked body on the other side. He slung his trousers and shirt on the roof like pancakes slapped onto a griddle. She glanced towards the road before spreading her wet dress on the roof of the car, the evaporating water steaming off the hot metal.

'So hot on there I'm nervous they'll ignite,' he joked, prodding his trousers like they were bacon.

Violet remembered her rotund stomach, cradling her arms around her tummy as she crouched lower.

'Promise I won't look,' said Jack. From where she sat she could see across the front seat to where Jack stood. He couldn't see her, but she glimpsed his taut, muscular legs and abdomen, the spear of stomach hair running from his chest glistening with ocean droplets.

'That's one side cooked,' he announced barely a minute later. 'Car!' He crouched and caught her looking at him. She held his gaze, too exhilarated to turn away, as the car passed.

Within ten minutes they'd dressed and were driving back to the airstrip. Violet wrung out her hair with her fingers in the rear-vision mirror as a group of pavement drinkers walking past in the other direction recognised the car and cheered.

'That went pretty well,' said Jack as he rubbed his ear to expunge salty water. 'Probably a good time to tell you I'm sweet on you, hey?' he quipped nonchalantly.

Violet stopped fixing her hair. His words ignited the air like a lit fuse. He focused on steering, chewing his lower lip as he waited for her response.

The silence was finally broken by a passing lorry honking its horn in revelry.

'I'm pregnant. Four months,' Violet confessed.

Jack chuckled, perhaps hoping it was a joke. Her reaction confirmed it wasn't.

'Whose is it?' Jack asked uncertainly.

'Daisie's boyfriend.'

'Her boyfriend?' he repeated, shocked. His body seemed to slump forward a little as the impact of the truth stung and seemed to paralyse him.

'I've been lying by not telling you,' she said, her voice heavy with sadness.

'That's quite a . . . situation,' he replied. His shoulders visibly sagged. 'Here I am thinking I'm showing a nice British girl the wild side. Not that you aren't a nice girl,' he backtracked. 'You know what I mean.' There was a sting of disappointment in Jack's voice, an acerbity Violet hadn't heard from him before.

She watched the passing fibro houses emblazoned with her home flag as the painful silence resumed.

'Do you love him? The father?'

'No. I despise him.'

'No wonder your sister's been such a bitch.'

'It's not something I planned,' she pleaded.

'Still, must be tough for her.'

'That doesn't excuse her behaviour,' Violet protested. 'She's a drunk. She used Lady Caroline. And now she's got her eye on Prince Philip.'

'Bloody hell.'

'Bill wasn't a good man,' Violet confessed. 'I saved her from a disaster.'

Jack stewed and bit his lip again. 'Let's just forget about it, hey?' he said dejectedly.

As the car sped towards the airstrip gate, Violet gently leaned her head out the passenger window into the rushing air. The wind in her ears offered a temporary respite from the conversation.

A crowd had built at the airport to witness the royal departure. Ahead, the royal motorcade was being tailed by a police escort with flashing lights. Jack accelerated angrily, slipstreaming into the end of the line where the police escort noted the official badge and waved them through.

There were no more words to say. Jack pulled up with a skid and they paced through the glass doors back to the waiting room, which had emptied. Outside on the tarmac she could see a cluster of local dignitaries standing in line to farewell the Queen and Duke. Jack and Violet crept up the plane stairway behind the ceremony and sneaked onto the aircraft.

Daisie clocked Violet's arrival on the plane. Violet chose a seat towards the back and as far from her sister's sightline as possible. Jack settled into a seat on the opposite side, alone. As he strapped himself in, he glanced over at Violet. His eyes were sullen.

Violet shifted uncomfortably. Not only was her heart heavy but her undergarments were peppered with beach grit. She turned towards the window and watched the ground drift by for the entire flight back to Brisbane.

45

Day 129: Broken Hill, New South Wales
Population: 28,400
Weather: 87 degrees Fahrenheit with a minimum of 54 overnight,
fresh to robust northerly winds
Fact: Broken Hill, an inland mining city in the far west of outback
New South Wales, is only a few minutes from the desert no matter
which direction you travel.

It was March 18, one hundred and twenty-nine days since they'd
boarded at Southampton, and even with loose-fitting clothes Violet's
bump was showing.

She sat in the narrow airplane seat on the flight back from
Bundaberg in her damp clothes, nursing the pronouncement in her
abdomen. Inside the tiny toilet cubicle on board the Trans Australia
DC-4 flying to Broken Hill, she examined her profile in the mirror.
The protrusion was beyond what one could pass off as too many
visits to the dessert table. 'Point of no return,' she whispered to herself under the hum of the plane engine. Her nerves prickled with
fear. Violet was going to have a baby.

Below, the lush green of Queensland gave way to the endless
flat ochre plains of central Australia. The Barrier Range rose from

the rocky desert like a lunar surface. Barren, vast but undeniably breathtaking, the South Australian outback also begged the question of why their Auntie Hazel would persist living out there.

The plane touched down on the dusty Broken Hill airstrip, where flocks of admirers surrounded the gates. The aircraft skidded to a stop at the far end of the uneven strip and looped back to the welcome point.

'The fair weather in Scotland would never be as cruel,' Bobo said of the repressive heat as they waited for the equerry to coordinate their transport. The flies flourished in the blanket of choking dust that lingered over Broken Hill like a dry fug.

The main motorcade departed for the Royal Flying Doctor Service, the site of the official welcome and the radio broadcast. Violet spied Daisie watching it leave with a dejected dullness in her eyes. They were allowed to attend the ceremony on the condition that they stood towards the back and didn't 'interact with anybody or each other'.

A polished black Holden driven by a uniformed Australian police officer pulled up. Daisie stood and waited for the door to be opened for her.

'All aboard!' said the policeman cheerily from his seat.

Daisie waited for a moment, sighed, then pulled the door open disapprovingly. She slumped onto the rear seat as Violet awkwardly slid in beside her.

'Just drive,' Daisie said, sliding on her sunglasses.

'We're going to the Royal Flying Doctor Service,' Violet told the driver in an attempt to defrost the mood.

'Oh yes, we're very excited about the radio broadcast. They tell me it'll be heard around the world!'

'Is Lake Eyre near here?' Violet asked.

''Fraid not. Bloody long way. Takes days – two or three at least. And when you got there you'd probably wonder what you were thinkin'. Don't know how farmers work that land, unless you're herding dust. Lake's due for a fill, though. Sure they could use rain up that way.'

The motorcade pushed along the dusty road, passing under an arched steel sign that proclaimed, 'Welcome to Broken Hill,' and was shrouded in British flags that flexed and billowed in the gritty wind. Along the dusty road the daytime sun blazed down like a scorching rain. Bundaberg felt glamorous by comparison.

'So this is "Broken" Hill. Appropriate,' Daisie said wryly.

'You've been drinking, haven't you?' Violet whispered. 'You're drinking too much, it's making you mean, and I fear you're becoming an alcoholic. Like Father.'

The mention of Father stilled Daisie for a moment.

'Not really any of your business,' she eventually replied. 'So keep your opinion to yourself.'

'I can smell it. You're repelling flies with your breath!'

'Preferable to face acid. How's your boyfriend, Jack? Does he know you're pregnant yet? Or does he need to be told?'

The policeman's eyes remained determinedly fixed on the road ahead.

The car turned into the driveway of the Royal Flying Doctor Service behind the rest of the convoy. The large corrugated-iron aircraft hangar housed three light passenger planes and an adjacent small fibro hospital. Beyond the surrounding wire fence was nothing but flat red earth pocked with razor-sharp pebbles and thorny shrubs. The interior shell of the hangar was incongruously decorated with colourful bunting, under which a large crowd had assembled to witness the Queen's visit and broadcast.

The Queen and Duke were already on a red carpet going through the motions.

'I'm aware a "sorry" won't cut it any more. So I won't insult you with one,' Violet said. 'In a few days Lady Mountbatten will be here and we'll both be assigned to the scrap heap anyway.'

'*I'll* be more than fine. What happens to you is not my problem. Though I'd welcome you making every attempt to stay as far away from me as possible.'

The driver dared not breathe as loaded seconds passed.

Violet started speaking faster, knowing the window for her speech was closing. 'I'm terrified about having his baby—'

'Don't talk about the baby,' Daisie interrupted, releasing pent-up frustration. 'At least Mother was spared your duplicity!'

'Well . . .' Violet stammered, trying to find words to express her outrage. 'Mum only carries the burden of *death*, thanks to you! *You* tore us apart – you alone are to blame for everything that has gone wrong. Yet somehow you're still alive, making those who remain suffer.'

Daisie's mouth fell open an inch, her jaw slack like a loose shoe sole as a fly hovered. She closed her eyes for a moment, as though controlling her temper.

'That is a horrible thing to say. Even for you.'

'You're going to do something stupid to prove a point, I can feel it.'

'Philip and I are friends. He's invited me to spend the weekend in Victoria. So know your place,' she said authoritatively.

The policeman coughed and rubbed his forehead. The pride and joy of driving royal guests around was long gone.

Violet pushed the door open in disgust. A small pack of flies swarmed the car and flocked to her face. She swatted them away, stepping into the gathered throng inside the hangar as Daisie held her head high and alighted on the opposite side.

'Miss Chettle? Doug Stanhope, ABC Mildura. Can I ask you a few questions?'

Violet froze as a microphone was pushed into her face by a rotund man with a sweat-stained shirt and a ruddy complexion who had a recording deck slung over his meaty shoulder. Its reels rotated slowly and deliberately, listening like a vindictive jury.

'You're one of Hazel Lawson's nieces, aren't you? The twins?'

Violet's tongue had swelled in fear and blocked her wind passage.

'How does it feel to be reconnecting with your long-lost auntie? Will you speak with her today?'

'I . . . I don't know if I'm allowed to,' Violet stammered between breaths.

'And your mother? She must be proud of you and your sister?'

'My mother?'

'Yeah, good old Mum back home. You want to say hi to her? This'll go all round the world, luv.'

'I'm a maid. I don't think we're allowed to speak to—'

'Don't worry about that. What do you think of Broken Hill?'

Violet held her hand to her throat. Her complexion started to resemble Doug's.

'What do you think of Australia? We just love Her Majesty and all things royal out here.'

Violet's lips mimed desperate words, but the reels could claim nothing.

'So tell us, have you met any nice fellas during the tour?' he persisted.

Violet's lip quivered as her eyes started to flicker and glaze over.

'Any fellas at all?'

Out of nowhere Daisie's hand reached across and pulled the microphone.

'I have,' she announced, dismissing a fly with a mortal flail of her hand. 'I'm Lady Daisie Chettle.'

'Tell us all about the lucky fella, Lady Daisie Chettle.' The reporter smiled, relieved.

'He's powerfully tall, tremendously wealthy, devastatingly handsome with a strong backside, and he's perhaps the most charming man you will ever meet.'

The reporter seemed momentarily stunned by her enthusiasm, before he returned the microphone to his mouth. 'What's your new bloke's name then?'

'Philip Mountbatten. And I love him!'

The reporter's eyes doubled. Violet's pharynx expanded in shock, causing an abrupt intake of air that made her choke.

Daisie nodded conclusively and walked into the hangar with her head held high. Violet slunk behind her in a mild daze, her lungs replenishing with each tentative breath.

On the west side of the hangar, a wide doorway opened into a smaller annexe where film cameras and orderly rows of chairs waited. A glassed-in vestibule at the front housed radio apparatus and a suited operator wearing headphones listened intently as he tweaked an instrument panel of twitching needles.

Daisie found the seat closest to where the Duke would be welcomed and claimed it.

Violet hid near the back, standing close to a draped Australian flag so that its loose folds obscured her from view.

In time the room filled, and then the Queen and Duke arrived. The press and local dignitaries swelled to silence, leaving the gentle clicking whir of a film camera at the side. Her Majesty was shown to the booth by the Mayor, and the Duke was directed to a front-row seat near Daisie. The operator nervously tapped his pen against his right headphone cup, his eyes restless in the presence of the Queen.

Ratcliffe glanced regularly at his watch as the Mayor reverentially showed the Queen to a seat in front of a microphone. Ratcliffe placed the Queen's speech on the table before her.

'Two minutes to broadcast,' the operator announced. A silence rippled across the seventy or so attendees. Press, local ministers, facility staff and government VIPs sat to attention. Harrison, whom Violet remembered from the Brisbane ballroom, fidgeted with a leather document folder by the hangar door.

A ping and a flurry of static burst from the wall-mounted speaker above the booth window. Ratcliffe closed the door as though some sort of experiment, or perhaps an execution, were about to take place.

Violet could see Her Majesty sitting in the chamber, her small white handbag slung over her forearm as her gloved hands held the sheet of paper. The radio operator, seated at the console behind, twisted a dial that activated a red light. The speaker emitted a low crackling sound.

'ABC controller Adelaide, this is RFDS VJC3 Broken Hill. Her Majesty is awaiting your cue. Eight HX Tirari – Mrs Lawson, are you still on standby?' said the operator, his voice amplified in the viewing room.

Violet saw the Queen glance sideways through the window at the Duke. She observed him remaining perfectly still with his jaw relaxed. Then he slowly craned his neck to the right, his eyes scanning the seats around him. The dignitaries smiled as his gaze passed over them.

Surely Daisie was telling another of her lies. Though in her unhinged state she was capable of anything.

Violet watched as Philip's eyes found Daisie. She watched Daisie smile back at him brazenly. Philip returned his gaze to the glass window where the Queen reviewed her speech with a tiny frown of concentration.

The tinny sound of cathedral bells sounded over the radio speaker then segued into the BBC radio fanfare. 'This is the BBC World Service,' spoke a high-pitched British accent.

'This is London via the Australian Broadcasting Service and the Royal Flying Doctor Service in Broken Hill. Mrs Hazel Lawson, of Tirari Station in South Australia, speaks to Her Majesty on behalf of those living in the remote outback of Australia.'

There was a pause of five seconds, more, as the operator urgently tweaked a dial on the console. As empty static filled the room, Ratcliffe exhaled impatiently.

And then a female voice with a broad Australian accent crackled forth. 'Eight HX Tirari to VJC and VJC3 Broken Hill. Your Majesty, Your Royal Highness.'

The voice was soft, uncultured. Any British accent Hazel may have had was long gone. From the poor quality of the signal, Hazel may as well have been further than London.

'We people of Australia's great outback acknowledge our humble allegiance to you as our sovereign. We know you have had first-hand knowledge of the difficulties as well as the joys of the lives of the men and the mothers and families who live in these distant parts of your realm. I am speaking from a wireless transceiver three hundred miles from Your Majesty at Broken Hill. My family is very isolated, our nearest settlement being thirty-five miles away.'

Daisie sat upright, clinging to every word and ignoring an errant fly that barraged her face like a boxer working a bag.

'We have one child. We would like you to know that the Royal Flying Doctor Service has proved to be one of the greatest benefits of our lives. Without this great mantle of safety, we mothers would not dare to bring up our families so far from medical help.'

Behind the flag, Violet's eyes moistened. She was enraptured by the sound of Hazel's voice. Without thinking she dabbed them with the cloth of the flag, leaving a dull spot amid the Southern Cross.

A green light lit up on the desk beside the Queen. The operator made a subtle hand signal indicating that the microphone was live. 'And now it is our esteemed privilege and honour to present Her Majesty the Queen,' said the BBC compere.

The Queen began to speak, her voice inside the room audible a second or so before it was relayed back through the speaker in the viewing gallery.

'My husband and I send to you who are listening, and indeed to all who live and work in the great outback of Australia, our sincere thanks for the kind words that have just been spoken on your behalf. Many Australians I have met in the United Kingdom and in Australia since I have been here have spoken to me with unstinted admiration of you men, women and children who have made your homes in the bush. They have told me of your fortitude, your courage, your humour and your friendliness. And of the magnificent way in which you have overcome the problems of living in this region of vast distances and great loneliness. Now that I have met some of you and seen from the air something of the immense and challenging country in which you live, I know that they were right. My only regret is that my husband and I cannot visit some of you in your stations and in your homesteads. I am especially glad to be able to speak to you from the Flying Doctor's base, as I have heard so much of the Royal Flying Doctor Service, and of the security and comfort it brings to every part of the outback. I express my admiration to all those, past and present, who have contributed to its splendid work. I send you all my best wishes for your health and happiness.'

Ratcliffe sat nervously upright, clinging to every word and checking his watch every ten seconds.

The green light went dark and the radio operator indicated the microphone was clear. The Queen took a slight breath and gently placed the speech on the desk. Ratcliffe guided her out of the radio room to the annexe gathering, where she was met with the usual spontaneous applause.

Daisie and Violet remained standing in the radio room in silent contemplation as the royal party was shepherded towards the waiting motorcade. The gallery had emptied, the radio operator departed, but Hazel's presence lingered.

Violet watched as Daisie walked slowly towards the radio room, hypnotised and drawn to the microphone like one of the unopened bottles of Gordon's gin Violet knew Daisie was stealing from the drinks cupboards.

'Daisie!' Violet hissed as she edged towards the door.

Daisie sat on the chair left vacant by the Queen and stared at the ball of the microphone. Violet lingered in the doorway and glanced nervously behind her shoulder.

A burst of muted static emitted from the operator's headset. A tinny voice followed. It was barely audible but it sounded female. It sounded like Hazel.

'Is it her?' Violet asked as she slunk closer.

'Shhh! Quiet!' Daisie pulled the headset closer to her ear.

'She's still there.' Violet impulsively pushed the 'talk' button at the base of the microphone. 'Auntie Hazel!' she called into the meshed ball. 'Auntie Hazel, it's me!'

They listened with their heads suspended in reluctant proximity as spits of white noise hissed from the earpiece between them.

'I think she's gone,' Violet whispered softly.

'We need to find her.'

Although Hazel was gone and their questions remained unanswered, the moment had brought them to a brief truce. There was nothing else they could say to each other, so they dawdled quietly back outside into the heat and the crowd and the flies.

46

Day 130: *Adelaide, South Australia*
Population: *495,246*
Weather: *67 degrees Fahrenheit, with cool, tender breezes*
Fact: *Eighteen days prior to this date, Adelaide was shaken by the most destructive earthquake in recorded Australian history. The total cost of the damage was estimated at around £17 million.*

'All the way from the Bombay Gymkhana Club, the lady-in-waiting we've all been waiting for,' Ratcliffe gushed as he swept his arm towards the newcomer.

'I've arrived preconditioned to the heat,' Lady Pamela Mountbatten joked in her cultured accent, holding out her hand theatrically for him to kiss. Violet couldn't stop staring, even though she knew she shouldn't.

Lady Mountbatten was all of about twenty-five years of age and silver-screen beautiful, with a strong jaw and intelligent eyes below kinked eyebrows that cast a wicked humour over her every glance. She dressed with a modernity that the Queen wouldn't dare risk, arriving in a knee-length floral-patterned dress with a bold match-ing headband and flame-red heels the same brilliant colour as her lipstick. The ceremonial spectacle had become somewhat routine to Violet, but Lady Mountbatten's presence brought a renewed excitement to the party.

Violet saw a squint of jealousy in Daisie's eyes as the twins lined up with the other staff in the Adelaide Government House lobby. The company had been instructed to assemble for Lady Mountbatten's arrival, the same as had been done for the Queen and Duke in Jamaica.

Lady Mountbatten walked the line, effusively charming staff members regardless of their status. She winked at Violet, then paused a few places along at Daisie moments later. Lady Mountbatten glanced back to Violet, then to Daisie.

'Am I seeing double?' she quipped. 'I've been sober for hours.'

Daisie smiled and opened her mouth to speak.

'Pay no mind,' Ratcliffe interrupted, stepping forward to urge her along. 'The less you know of those two, the better.'

Violet swallowed the dismissal; it wasn't as though it hadn't been earned. She glanced sideways towards her sister, whose mouth still hung open, no doubt harbouring a dry retort that would never be heard.

Three days later, Lady Mountbatten had injected much-needed verve into the eight-day Adelaide stop. A lifelong aristocrat and cousin to Prince Philip, with her energy and freewheeling wit – and unlimited enthusiasm for fine champagne – she filled Lady Caroline's shoes with ease. Even Queen Elizabeth seemed to gain a subtle spring in her step, and Daisie starting swallowing her vowels, trying to emulate Lady Mountbatten's aristocratic accent.

'I'm sorry, Daisie – can't understand a word you're saying,' the page carped when Daisie asked him for some tonic using her newfound inflection.

'It's Lady Chettle!' she insisted, but the joke was increasingly on her, and both she and Violet became more or less ignored. Beyond her own preoccupations Violet had very little work to do, as Lady Mountbatten had arrived with her own entourage.

Desperate to be the chosen one again, Daisie tried to make conversation with Lady Mountbatten as the touring party gathered to depart for the Morphettville races.

'Sorry, ma'am, not behind this point,' ordered an enthusiastic Citizen Military Force guard, cutting her off with his arm like a boom gate.

'Don't you know who I am?' Daisie insisted in her freshly clipped accent, her vowels dripping like honey.

'Yeah, yer a maid,' the guard retorted. The dressing-down was made worse by his guttural Australian accent.

Locking herself inside her tiny downgraded room, Daisie paced like a wild animal in a constricted pen. It was the claustrophobic sensation she'd felt back home, when the walls would lean in and start to suffocate her. She'd been heavily reprimanded after her comments to the reporter about the Duke. But she'd brought such attention to herself that dumping her from the tour would've raised rumours about her and Prince Philip. 'Enemies close,' Ratcliffe had muttered, although she could tell he was close to throttling her – woman or not – and that the staff were avoiding her under instruction, at least more than usual. Even a new *Women's Weekly* couldn't ease her ill temper.

Daisie leaned her forehead against the wall. She rapped it against the plaster.

Again.

The sound of her mother's death had returned like a taunt, the deathly thud rattling in her inner ear like a chant. The pain of her forehead convened an odd relief, like the two somehow annulled each other.

Her eyes closed, she imagined what Hazel would make of it all. Maybe Hazel was like her, stuck in purgatory and paying for her sins.

Or perhaps, like the others, Hazel was gone too, and it was just her and Violet now. And they were stuck with each other like ghosts who carried inside them the memory of those who'd already passed, destined to end up the same way.

She made her hands into fists and pushed them against the sockets of her eyes until her knuckles stung. The cycle had to be broken. By self-destruction, if needed. The noise in her head had to be muzzled.

47

Violet occupied her time by walking the perimeter of Adelaide, lazily navigating the rectangular geography and its skirting parklands. The 'city' seemed comprised of little more than churches, public houses and flies, which appeared languid from the oppressive summer temperatures.

'The Yarra Ranges?' Violet asked Bobo, examining the new schedule. 'Daisie and I have been assigned.' Bobo's lair had been fashioned inside the ballroom of the 1840 building, its creaking floorboards pockmarked by countless stiletto heels.

'Short straw. Everybody else wants three days off,' replied Bobo as she pulled the steam press onto some trousers, then moved over to a sewing machine. 'The private secretary, a housekeeper and a detective will be there to keep an eye on ye. Can't trust that Daisie of yours. Did ye hear the radio interview? That be the drink talkin'. Where is she now?'

'Who knows. Drinking and reading magazines, most likely.'

'Duke's at a rocket launch facility in the desert. Safer there than near yer sister.' Bobo ran the machine, its *thunk-thunk-thunk* like a machine gun as she closed a seam. Violet, unable to be heard, waved and left.

'Which one are you?' a cultured British female voice asked Violet from the carpeted stairway leading to the second level. Violet looked up to see an attractive girl of nineteen or twenty dressed in a polka-dot swing dress, a black belt and a red scarf. Her poodle hairstyle framed a pale face and her lips were empowered by fire-engine-red lipstick. Two department store shopping bags were slung over each forearm.

'Pardon?' Violet asked.

'The vomiter or the other one? Caroline's maids?'

Violet blushed. Her impulse was to turn and run but she'd been ensnared by the assertive waif.

'You must feel like an orphan with her gone now. Can't help herself. That's Caroline for you, though – the Spinster of Surrey.' She gave a high-pitched laugh, a bit like a hyena. 'Sorry, introductions are in order. My name's Fiona Bramford. I'm with Lady Pamela.'

Violet glanced at the shopping bags, one of them from Birks department store.

Fiona noticed her looking. 'Oh, these? Rundle Street isn't exactly Regent Street, but I did find a pink halter I had to have. Your name?'

'I'm Violet.'

'Violet,' Fiona repeated, then turned to continue on her way before spinning back to point a finger directly at her.

'Wait – it's you, isn't it?' she exclaimed. '*You're* the spewer! Chunder Loo! My God, I've never heard of something so ridiculously goopy. They were even talking about it at Kippers in Delhi. I can't believe you're still on the tour. Bully for you. Us girls should stick together – don't want to set expectations too high for Lady Pamela, or I'll end up with a duster in my hand instead of a Bellini.'

Violet's lips warbled silent confusion.

'It's a drink. Most parts prosecco. Anyway, ta-ta. See you in the soup.' Fiona flicked her hand as she sashayed upstairs.

Violet escaped beyond the grounds to clear her mind. She followed the tramline along North Terrace, which led to yet another park. She wandered across the dry brown grass, taking in plots of shade cast by a line of slouching gum trees, their leaves withered in the hot breeze that blew in from the desert to the north. Her circular path lead back to the city and Hindley Street, which was lined with department stores. She stopped outside West's Olympia theatre, its façade reminiscent of the Odeon with 'Noose for a Lady' emblazoned on the marquee. A small crowd had gathered at the corner of Hindley and Charles streets outside the John Martin & Co. department store. In the circular corner display window, two store clerks were putting the finishing touches to a stunning black silk gown on display. It was a bulging Balenciaga dress with an elbow-length bolero. The sign proclaimed the outfit was 'Direct from Paris!' Office girls and harried mothers with prams gossiped in awe at the precious garment, safe behind smudged glass.

A stout lady with a broad-brimmed hat stood before her, a baby girl slung over her shoulder like a sack of oranges. The infant eyed Violet with the same fascination as the crowd gazed at the couture. Her cherubic face was rendered imperfect only by a smear of baby food on her chin.

Violet was transfixed. The baby's fine downy tufts of hair swayed in the hot breeze like dandelion fluff. Violet shyly looked away, but her gaze returned to the curious child, who reached out, her rotund digits flailing inches from Violet's nose. Then she started to smile, emitting not quite a laugh but an open-mouthed gurgle, her plump cheeks swollen as though concealing marbles.

Violet smiled back, lost in the baby's joy. Her fingertip lifted towards the tiny outreached fingers. Then the woman strode away, oblivious to the moment she was breaking. Violet watched as the tiny face disappeared deeper into the crowd until she could no longer make her out in the lunchtime masses. Her hand hung in the air. She dropped it to rest on the bump of her stomach as pedestrians made their way around her.

Violet paced up King William Street purposefully, eyes on the pavement. She pushed through the layers of onlookers around the Government House gate, showing her identification papers and striding across the front lawn, past a small golden elm sapling in freshly turned soil that the Duke had planted that morning under the obsessive gaze of the local press.

She quickstepped up the stairs and into the main entrance hall, stalking the corridor towards the staff waiting room behind the kitchens, where the drivers tended to loiter when not in service. As she approached she could hear Jack's drawl. Violet couldn't help smiling to herself.

And then followed another voice. British, feminine and self-assured.

Violet peeked around the doorframe. Jack leaned back in a chair, chatting to Fiona Bramford. They were alone.

'Here, you'd be known as a "bludger",' Jack said to Fiona's appreciative titter.

'And what was the other thing you said, about the heat?' she asked.

'Hotter than a shearer's armpit. Desert wind'd blow the bloody milk out of your tea,' he said to her overloaded hysterics.

'I *get* it, you're *Australian*,' said Fiona, playfully touching his arm.

The muscles in Violet's neck clenched.

'Well, Miss Fiona, I've gotta love you and leave you, get the horses round front.' Jack's chair scraped against the floor as he stood.

Panicked, Violet spun to hide.

'May I help you?' Detective Reilly stood behind her, his thinly trimmed moustache hovering at eye level. 'No lurking in the corridors without valid reason, Miss Chettle,' he intoned.

Jack paused in the doorway to see the detective standing over Violet. Fiona appeared behind him, eager to intrude.

'So sorry. I was lost,' Violet confessed, starting to creep backwards down the hall, trying to physically remove herself from the centre of attention.

Jack's face had turned a noticeable shade of guilty.

Fiona craned her neck around him to enjoy Violet's retreat. 'Violet? Or is it Daisie?' she asked, then, lowering her voice to Jack, 'How do people tell?'

Violet hastily retreated to her room. Safe behind the closed door she cringed and smashed her palm against a chest of drawers in frustration. 'Fiona bloody Bramford!'

48

Fiona Bramford had a habit of turning up everywhere. On the final day in Adelaide, Violet spent much of her time 'accidentally' trying to run into Jack, but inevitably it would be Fiona she'd cross paths with instead.

She waited up until around midnight, inched her door open and snuck into the hall. Adelaide's Government House took on the eerie atmosphere of a haunted house after dark. Its long dim corridors, creaking woodwork and unsettling colonial portraits made it decidedly unnerving to explore at night. A housemaid had told Bobo of a mischievous ghost who supposedly inhabited the second floor. The rumour told of Harriet Joyce, the Governor's six-year-old daughter, who in 1874 had fallen into a scalding bath while the nanny had been called away. Doctors were able to do little to salve her extensive burns, and the child had lingered in agony for days until she succumbed to her injuries.

Violet padded along the shadowy second-floor hallway, her eyes flicking nervously in the darkness as she made her way to Jack's door on the far west corner. A sheer curtain seemed to wave for help in the breeze of an open window at the end of the corridor.

'Jack!' Violet whispered through the keyhole. His room was

deathly quiet. No snoring, breathing – nothing. She sighed and turned to go back. Halfway up the flight of stairs to the second floor she hesitated. Plodding but urgent footsteps could be heard approaching, thumping heavily along the second-floor carpet. She peeked through the gap in the railing but could see nobody.

Then a flustered Bobo rushed by in her nightgown. 'What a disaster,' she muttered to herself before waddling out of sight.

Violet snuck back to her bedroom unseen.

Within minutes, a clamour of footsteps could be heard coming up the stairs. Violet cracked the door open an inch. Major Ratcliffe, looking most annoyed in his dressing gown and slippers, followed by two harried equerries, Detective Reilly and an Australian police officer charged by. Bobo followed at a short distance, stopping to catch her breath not far from Violet's door.

'Is everything all right?' Violet whispered through the gap.

Bobo shook her head as she tried to regain her breath. 'The emerald is stolen.'

'What emerald?'

'The peak of the tiara!'

Violet felt her gut drop. Bobo would've heard the beating of her heart were she not so close to a cardiac attack of her own.

'Back to bed, missy. Or ye'll end up being grilled as well.'

The motorcade left Government House for Parafield Airport at eight o'clock the following morning. Violet hadn't been questioned but she was terrified by the prospect of it. She knew she wouldn't respond well to interrogation – her nature was to wear guilt on her sleeve even when there was nothing to feel guilty about.

'Most certainly foul play,' gossiped one of the pages. 'Worth more than fifty thousand pounds. Dectective Reilly said the thief had tried to replace the rock with chewing gum!'

Violet put her head down as she boarded the DC-4.

'This seat taken?' chirped Fiona as she gestured towards the spare seat beside Violet where she had left a magazine, holding it in case Jack boarded.

'N-no,' Violet stammered.

'What a perfectly pleasant place to be leaving,' Fiona quipped as she unpacked her black quilted Chanel handbag onto the shared armrest. 'Pammy is so looking forward to having the weekend off. Melbourne is far better for shopping, I hear. Apparently it has the most wonderful milliners. Ludlows? Dame Melba used to give them custom, apparently,' she said, continuing to talk as she applied lipstick. 'I'd say join us, but I hear you and your sister have been roped into house duty for Lilibet and Philip for the weekend, you poor things. Maybe they'll go easy on you out of sympathy. Do them good to be left alone for a spell. Six weeks in this heat would do anybody in.'

Violet spied Jack making his way down the aisle towards her, his leather overnight bag hoisted over his shoulder as he scanned for a spare seat. They locked eyes momentarily before he glanced at Fiona and lowered his gaze. He took a seat three rows behind, not once looking back at Violet.

'He's quite yummy, that one,' uttered Fiona. She peered flirtatiously in Jack's direction and leaned to whisper into Violet's ear. 'Makes me hot and bothered indeed.'

The words shook Violet, but her reaction was lost on Fiona, whose eyes were locked on Jack with a rapacious spark.

'Can barely understand a word he says, but with arms like that, who cares.' She turned back to Violet. 'What happens on tour stays on tour!' She tittered, salting Violet's wounds.

'Please prepare for departure,' the captain announced over the speaker. Fiona closed her eyes for a nap while Violet pretended to read a magazine, but the words had left her restless and raw.

Below, the relentless burnt-orange landscape drifted by as the plane navigated towards Melbourne. Eventually the coarse, barren desert gave way to dense bushland.

'I can't imagine why anybody would choose to live here,' Fiona observed, having woken from her doze. 'Though, to be fair, many of them came against their will. It boggles the mind how women who stole a loaf of bread in London to support their families coped with being dropped into this inhospitable place.'

The propeller hum dropped an octave as the aircraft shifted earthwards. Gliding low over a patchwork of suburban blocks, each with a brick dwelling, a grass backyard and a red tiled roof, the plane touched the runway with a jolt and a skid before taxiing to the hangar.

'Can Miss Daisie Chettle, Miss Violet Chettle, Detective Reilly and Mr Carville please alight first,' the steward announced.

'Oh, lucky you,' Fiona said, pouting.

The Queen and Duke were escorted to a Daimler. At the base of the exit stairs a handful of ministers greeted them but without the usual fanfare.

Reilly, Carville, Violet and Daisie followed a groundsman to another car. With a police escort in front and at the rear, the vehicles drove through the empty hangar and off the airbase into the suburbs of Melbourne.

Violet chewed her fingernails. Jack hadn't even looked up from his seat when she stepped off the plane, and the thought of spending the weekend with Daisie in the intimate presence of the Queen and Duke filled her with a burning dread.

49

Day 133: *Warburton, Yarra Ranges, Victoria*
Population: *248*
Weather: *73 degrees Fahrenheit, early inclemency, then*
clement
Fact: *Warburton is an old goldmining town 45 miles east of*
Melbourne city, on the land of the Wurundjeri Aboriginal people.

The sun had disappeared behind the Dandenong mountain ranges
to the west by the time the train arrived at Warburton station, the
end of the line. The simple wood and iron terminal was cloistered
within thick forest, buttressed from nature's unforgiving advance by
stone sidings built into the hillside.

Normally the Queen and Duke would spend a few minutes
making small talk and receiving bouquets, but tonight they moved
straight to the cars. After three months on tour, it seemed their first
weekend off couldn't start soon enough.

Inside the last car Violet and Daisie sat apart on the back seat.
The township itself was a 'blink and you'll miss it' affair, the only
building of note being a small Presbyterian church that resembled a
doll's house with a green roof, a white picket fence, an oval window
and a bright yellow door.

The ten-mile transfer to O'Shannassy Chalet led through bushland so dense that dusk's faint gloom could barely be glimpsed
between the monstrous grey tree stumps lining the narrow dirt road
through the Yarra Ranges.

'Have you been briefed?' Violet asked, breaking the testy silence.
'I suppose we're to do what we used to do for Lady Caroline. Until
you did her in.'

'Don't know why *you're* here,' Daisie replied with a sigh. 'Ruins
a perfectly good holiday.'

'It's *their* holiday, not yours!' Violet snapped. 'You aren't going
to embarrass us again, are you? With him? I'd quite like to make it
through this without you getting us discharged three weeks before
we leave for home.'

'I will do whatever he expects of me. And willingly,' Daisie said
suggestively, projecting her voice so the driver could hear. His eyes
stayed fixed on the shadowy winding road.

Violet sat in disgusted silence as the car started to climb. The
headlights illuminated the impenetrable bushland either side of the
valley road until the car turned through a gate and lit an unpreten-
tious timber homestead. The 'chalet' had a red galvanised-iron roof
and wide verandahs.

'This passes for a chalet? I was expecting basic, but not *camping*,'
Daisie complained as she squinted through the window at the
accommodation.

The four cars circled and parked out the front on the round.
A figure emerged through the front screen door and hurried around
the Queen's vehicle to escort her inside. Daisie watched Prince Philip
climb from the car and stare into the curtain of darkness around
the house, batting the cavity of his hat on his fist as he tried to get
a sense of the landscape beyond the short throw of the headlights.

There wasn't much to discern twenty feet beyond the verandah's edge, the porch lights too weak to penetrate the gloom that harboured an unnerving chorus of bugs, birds and God-knows-what. The cicada hum stopped and started as though signalling in Morse code, their rattle silenced every now and then by the screech of some unseen animal lurking beyond the perimeter.

'Luggage, girls,' Carville ordered. Daisie ignored him and followed the entourage inside the chalet while Violet struggled with the luggage, accidentally dropping one of the Duke's cases as she tried to balance them.

The interior was modest compared with the accommodation they'd grown accustomed to. To the right of the entry foyer was a large living room with four leather couches and a stone fireplace. The decor could be termed 'colonial', with oil paintings of Australian outback scenes, vases of native flowers and a heavy looking wagon-wheel chandelier that hung over a rustic wooden coffee table. To the left of the lobby was a large kitchen and an adjoining dining table, which had been set for dinner.

The cook and housekeeper, Mrs Holding, a plump, mousy woman of around sixty, toiled in the kitchen preparing the evening meal with a quiet diligence. She nodded at the newcomers, avoiding eye contact.

A wide hallway extended north, from which six doors led presumably to the bedrooms. A second smaller house, a freestanding bedroom with its own bathroom, extended from a rear courtyard.

'This is where Her Majesty and the Duke will reside,' Carville advised. 'Do not go in there unless asked to.'

'There and there for you two,' Carville said, pointing to two doors halfway down the short central hallway as Violet stumbled behind with the suitcases. Thank goodness they didn't have to share.

Daisie opened the door of the first room and turned on the light. It revealed a neat bedroom with a four-poster double bed, lilac and grey carpet, glazed chintz curtains in chartreuse, and a teak dresser with a ceramic washbasin. 'Bags it,' she said.

Violet just shrugged and lumbered down the hall to the next door.

The low rumble of car engines could be heard departing and the house fell quiet to the intimidating noises of the Australian bush. Even the creak of floorboards stilled. It seemed to Violet that everybody was most likely in their rooms trying to avoid one another. Seemed like the best idea.

Daisie eventually came out of her room to explore and see what the Duke was up to. She turned the corner of the dining room, where she confronted the Queen and Duke seated for dinner at opposite ends of the table, eating soup in silence while Mrs Holding fussed quietly over the next course. Violet had made herself busy in the kitchen beside her, rummaging through cupboards for no apparent purpose and diligently cleaning pots the second Mrs Holding put them down.

Philip glanced fleetingly in Daisie's direction. The Queen raised her eyes, aware of the third presence in the room. She gently placed her soup spoon on her plate and stared into the middle distance, waiting for Daisie to depart.

Daisie paused in the doorway for a second or two longer than was needed. She smirked at the Duke, raised her chin and walked calmly back towards her bedroom.

50

Violet rose with the sun at around six o'clock, making herself 'available' in the common areas in case the Queen and Duke required anything when they emerged. Mrs Holding toiled under the range hood preparing breakfast as Violet kept herself busy polishing the silver cutlery.

'Why don't you take a morning walk?' Mrs Holding suggested, eager to expel Violet's nervous energy from her kitchen.

Violet wandered outside through the kitchen door. The morning sun rose over the eastern peak as the branches of the surrounding gums churned in the hot breeze. The occasional native bird call interrupted the familiar chirrup of waking cicadas.

She followed a concrete path behind the house and up the grassy hillside. From the top, near where the paddock met the bush, she looked back towards the chalet. Its L-shaped frame fronted a semicircular lawn dotted with trees that sloped away to the valley below. On the eastern side of the chalet was a neatly maintained tennis court and putting green, and further behind was a poultry shed and vegetable garden, where a dozen or so chickens clucked and scratched in the dirt.

She continued walking towards the edge of the bush. The path was lined with tended shrubberies exhibiting petunias, phlox, marigolds, dahlias, zinnias, pansies, portulaca and sweet peas ablaze with colour. The cloak of thick gum trees and ferns closed in around her as she wandered into the shady woodland. A newly painted sign indicated it was a four-mile walk to the O'Shannassy dam, suggested to the royal couple as a place they could catch trout 'should the inclination arise'.

Violet ambled lazily through the scrubland, maintaining a keen eye on the treetops for the koalas that had been strategically lodged there for Her Majesty's benefit. Warm winds buffeted the branches, and the occasional creak of a warped tree trunk, like the aching hull of a wooden ship, lent a strange fractured percussion to the white noise of cicadas and breeze. The effect was mildly hypnotic, and her thoughts meandered. She imagined Fiona Bramford pestering Jack to light her cigarette, or insisting he escort her on some entrapment masquerading as a shopping escapade. Or perhaps insisting she come to his room for a whisky. The dirt track narrowed as Violet rounded a mossy boulder.

Then she saw something.

Initially it looked like a ghostly apparition, its white human form contrasting with the deep greens and browns of the bush about fifty feet ahead of her. Violet stood still, observing the thing as its head tilted towards the sky. She edged silently behind the boulder, careful not to snap twigs underfoot as she watched the figure walk slowly against the gentle sway of knee-length ferns.

As its profile turned she recognised it to be Queen Elizabeth. She was dressed impeccably in a white jacket, coordinating checked dress and pale gloves that stood out proudly against the muted bushland. Her handbag hung from her forearm as though she were attending a reception. She stared into the treetops far above, searching for something. Then her eyes dropped slowly as though captured by a trenchant thought. She hadn't noticed Violet yet.

Violet remained still, realising that if she continued they'd be forced to acknowledge each other on the pathway. She crouched down and tiptoed over damp leaves and dirt to hide further behind the stone bluff.

The Queen idled along the path towards her. Should she have glanced sideways, she'd have seen Violet crouching in the bushes as though urinating merely ten feet away.

Violet held her breath and waited.

The Queen's shoulders were relaxed: she was lost in what could've been the first moment of solitude she'd had in months. She paused along the trail to observe the flora, her eyes scanning the leafy branches for signs of movement.

She froze. Violet followed her sightline to find the object of her attention: a lumpy shape at the crest of a branch about thirty feet above. It was a koala resting in the shade. It had the appearance of a baby polar bear crossed with an old man, with a dark pebble nose and tufted ears. Chewing on gum leaves like a cow with its cud, it lazily evaluated Queen Elizabeth.

A wondrous smile formed on her lips as she steadied herself against the trunk of a grey gum tree to gain a better view. The koala chewed and stared back at her, blinking sleepily. After a minute the Queen took a deep breath and, with a sigh of resignation, made her way into the direct sunlight of the paddock.

Violet stood slowly, watched by the curious koala. She walked back, ensuring a safe distance between herself and the Queen. Ten minutes later, as she stepped into the valley clearing, she could see Her Majesty entering the house by the kitchen doors.

Mrs Holding had laid out an elaborate breakfast on the outside courtyard table. The sun, higher in the sky now, had cast the house in its warmth. Further down the valley, where the driveway met the fence, Violet spotted three or four men in dark hats and coats loitering at the boundary. They were most likely British press hoping to get a candid photo of the Queen and Duke relaxing in the Australian bush.

The occasional displaced grasshopper flung itself out of her path as Violet ambled down the gentle incline of the grassy hillside. Reilly loitered in the rose garden beside the house, finishing a cigarette. He nodded in acknowledgement as she passed, stubbing the butt out in the dirt as Violet stepped into the chalet.

'Morning walk?' he asked as they entered the lobby together.

Violet was about to reply when the sound of breaking glass exploded in the kitchen. 'Don't "Cabbage" me!' came the Queen's voice, angry and commanding, and in a controlled pitch that Violet had never heard before.

Reilly froze. Mrs Holding, face flushed, ran briskly out of the kitchen through the archway with her head down as though released from a hostage situation. She waved her hands at Violet – stay away – before continuing down the hallway to her room.

Reilly and Violet swapped a bemused stare. Each remained rooted to the spot in the hallway entrance, just out of sight of the kitchen.

'Lilibet . . .' Prince Philip could be heard appealing to her in a conciliatory tone, though they couldn't make out the words. Their footsteps scuffled on the kitchen floorboards.

Violet's bedroom door was twenty feet away. She carefully slipped out of her shoes then crouched slowly to pick them up.

The Queen curtly interrupted the Duke's attempts. 'That's not true!' she cried angrily. The power of Her Majesty's voice, its restrained intensity, could've started a war.

Violet's face flushed in horror. Reilly edged backwards towards the front door.

Just as Violet started tiptoeing down the hallway, shoes in hand, a tennis ball hurled through the kitchen arch and bounced off the opposite wall, rolling down the hallway carpet until it came to a stop at Violet's bare feet.

Reilly, terrified, fixed his eyes on the ground and sheepishly slid outside.

Violet backed slowly up against the hallway wall. She held her breath. The slap and scuff of physical contact came from the kitchen. An altercation?

'It's nothing like Pat,' argued Prince Philip defensively, louder now.

'Again under *my* roof,' shouted the Queen in a voice that absorbed all the breathable oxygen in the room.

'It's all in her damn head. She's infatuated!'

Daisie! Violet gnashed her teeth angrily.

'What are you doing about it – apart from encouraging it?' the Queen responded.

'Fine! I'll have Ratcliffe sack them. I can't stop people throwing themselves at me!' He paused. 'Frankly, it's good to know *somebody's* still interested.' Prince Philip, dressed in tennis whites, ran into the hallway to avoid a thrown tennis shoe that struck him hard on the back.

He lunged for the front door just as the Queen appeared in the archway and lobbed a tennis racquet forcefully after him. She picked up the tennis ball from the floor and threw it again with a grunt of frustration then ran outside in livid pursuit.

They had no idea Violet was even there. She stayed still as if she were a wall relief, breath held and face turning red.

A distant outbreak of commotion could be heard, other raised voices and the click and whir of cameras. With the door still wide open, Violet spun on her heels to make an escape.

Prince Philip stormed back into the house, his eyes pinched in a deep frown. He paced right past Violet again without seeing her, charging through the living room towards the royal quarters.

A moment later the Queen returned. Her contained anger palpable, she closed the front door behind her. Then she saw the Chettle pressed against the wall.

Violet gasped for breath – she'd forgotten she was holding it.

The Queen balled her fists. She commanded Violet's gaze for eternal seconds, staring into her with fury. The Queen took one determined step forward and raised her hand.

Violet clenched her eyes shut in anticipation of her punishment. Seconds passed. Then footsteps marched hurriedly away. Violet peeked through one eye. The Queen was on her way to find her husband.

Carville burst in through the kitchen doors.

'What on earth's happening?'

Violet shook her head, unable to speak and on the verge of tears. Carville charged outside towards the press gang. Violet turned angrily towards Daisie's room and flung open the door.

Daisie was lying in bed reading the *Women's Weekly*. Her face was a smear of self-satisfaction.

Violet started pacing beside the bed in a nervous anger. 'What did you *do*? The Queen was going to hit me!'

Daisie tossed the magazine aside and leaped out of bed in her nightdress. 'Bully for her! I need a cigarette,' she muttered as she sashayed to the wardrobe to pull on a dressing gown.

'You did something to him, didn't you?'

'I checked on him,' Daisie replied, pulling on a chiffon robe. 'That's all. Just doing my job.'

'In your pyjamas?'

'We have a rapport. It was an opportunity to get to know him better.'

'And she walked in on you *getting to know him better*?'

'Nothing happened. I was just chatting.' She smirked again. 'On the bed.'

'He's done nothing. He has *no* interest in you, Daisie! You're a *maid*. And now we're dead – both of us!' Violet twisted and pulled aggressively at her apron, her frustration channelled so ferociously that a tearing sound indicated she'd pulled the stitching apart.

'I can't help it if he likes the look of me,' Daisie countered with a raised voice.

'You're imagining it! He has *no* interest in you. "Likes the look" of you? You *look* like me!'

'Well, I think their marriage is a sham. For show. And he's sad and needs somebody like me.'

Violet was speechless.

'Best a bandaid ripped off anyway,' Daisie added, fossicking for a cigarette in her suitcase.

'The Queen is *not* a bandaid!' Violet rubbed her temples as a headache started to form. 'I am not going to let you do to him what you did to Lady Althorp.'

Daisie found a cigarette and twirled it in her fingers as she opened the door. Standing in the hallway on the other side were Carville and Reilly, grim expressions fixed on their faces.

Reilly sat in the front beside the driver. Carville was uncomfortably wedged in between Violet and Daisie in the back seat of the car. His aftershave smelled of musk.

Nobody spoke a word as they drove off the property through the small clutch of press by the driveway. A camera was thrust against the glass of the window, the flash firing twice as the driver turned onto the dirt roadway. Daisie smiled endearingly for the cameras.

They drove in silence for about fifteen minutes until Reilly gestured to the driver to pull over on a deserted stretch of road beside a pasture. The car pulled over to the grassy roadside, its engine idling.

'Are you dumping our bodies here?' Daisie asked, trying to break the tension.

Reilly passed two sets of handcuffs to Carville. 'Excuse me, ladies. Necessary measure, I'm afraid,' he said as Carville placed Violet's arm into one of the cuffs and the other end on his own wrist with some satisfaction.

'Easy, Jock,' Reilly whispered. Violet had suspected Carville held a grudge ever since Caroline's termination.

Violet looked as though she was about to cry.

'You must be joking,' Daisie complained. 'What are we charged with?'

'Can't risk losing you two until we know exactly what Mr Ratcliffe *wants* to charge you with.'

'I've done nothing wrong,' Violet protested as her eyes welled.

'It's true,' said Daisie. 'It's me. Daisie.'

'Still can't tell you two apart,' he murmured as he clasped the heavy steel cuff onto her wrist. Carville now had a twin chained to each arm.

'I demand to speak to the Duke,' Daisie said confidently. 'You'll be lucky not to be fired on the spot.'

Reilly laughed as though she'd told the punchline to a joke.

'Well, at least let me put on some gloves so these things don't chafe as much,' Daisie insisted.

'About bloody time,' Carville sneered as the driver revved the engine.

'Relax. We have a long drive to Melbourne,' said Reilly as Violet sniffled.

'I wish Mum was here,' Violet said as the heavy handcuffs rubbed her skin and the car rolled back onto the road.

51

Day 134: Port Melbourne, Victoria
Population: 13,104
Weather: 75 degrees Fahrenheit, understated winds
Fact: Port Melbourne, an inner suburb of Melbourne, came to
prominence during Victoria's gold rush of the 1850s, and for
many years was a focus of Melbourne's criminal underworld,
which operated smuggling syndicates on the docks.

The iron lung hadn't changed, though it felt smaller since they'd
become accustomed to having normal-sized bedrooms for the past
few weeks. Its permanently-on bulkhead light and clammy smell
had an infuriating familiarity. Returning felt like visiting an annoying relative purely out of obligation.

The dead cockroach Violet had kicked under the bed on
their very first day was still there, its six legs extending heaven-
wards out of its dried shell. But there was a new occupant. Every
now and then the chirp of a sole cricket broke the silence. For
the life of her, she couldn't figure out how the insect had found
itself in this part of the ship, nor could she find the damn thing, its
random rattle reverberating through the chamber every time she
was near sleep.

'Where is it?' Violet growled, pulling her suitcase apart trying to locate it.

Steward Joseph was stationed outside the door. Soup and bread had been brought. But nobody was telling them anything.

Violet buried her face in the pillow. She verged on tears at the thought of the shame to come her way. She tried to think of happier times, like Bundaberg's warm air and Jack changing his clothes behind the car at the beach. But the dread always returned.

'There aren't as many rats as before. Perhaps they've all migrated,' Daisie said, breaking the silence. Despite everything, she was in a fine mood. 'Philip will spare me. Perhaps you too. I pity them both in some ways. The awful thing for him is that she'll have this job till she dies in twenty years or so. He's trapped forever.'

The clank of steel echoed through the walls. It had been hours since anyone had talked to them. Daisie sat up expectantly. Violet rose to her elbows, resigned and exhausted.

It was Reilly, his eyes grave. 'Come with me, please,' he said, with all the optimism of an executioner.

'Where are we going?' asked Daisie.

'You'll know soon enough,' he intoned as the cricket cheered.

They followed him upstairs to the A deck, where Ratcliffe's office door was already open. He paced inside reading a sheet of paper.

'Bring them in,' Ratcliffe commanded. 'Then leave us.'

He took his seat as the girls stood before him. 'This has all become far more serious than you can appreciate. The time for discipline has passed.'

Daisie sighed and seated herself on the couch, unintimidated.

'Why don't you join your sister?' He gestured to Violet.

She sat beside Daisie, the leather creaking under her weight.

She nervously twisted one of the buttons on her blouse, which hung by a single thread.

'Are you going to keep us locked up here, Michael? *Can* you keep us locked up?' Daisie asked boldly.

He barely blinked at her casual mode of address, grinning with delight at the hole she continued digging for herself. 'Well, technically the *Gothic* is Her Majesty's jurisdiction. The option is available to me. I wouldn't waste your time trying to make some question of the legalities. So why don't you sit there while I tell you how bad this is for you.' He paused, inviting Daisie to retort.

She breathed out impatiently but held her tongue.

'Very well,' he continued. 'Her Majesty is refusing to appear. A shame, as there are already two thousand people sleeping on the street outside the Exhibition Building to see her farewell Melbourne tomorrow. But I don't really care about that. The Queen can always be taken ill, excuses can be made. We can shape any message we need to. However, the business of governing must carry on. Her Majesty has parliamentary amendments to sign and trade agreements to sight on behalf of the Privy Council. All "rubberstamping", in practice – she doesn't get too involved in the minutiae of things. But a delay of a day isn't good for the home economy. And this time zone doesn't help. A short-lived constitutional crisis is still a crisis. What you did,' he said, turning to Daisie, 'has upset her. You're not the first to try to *comfort* the Duke, shall we say? Far from it. She'll front up in a day or two, as professional as ever. And she's *very* professional. However, Her Majesty has specifically asked that you be *dealt* with. Her word. So that's where I need to decide what the "dealt with" part should be. The *Gothic* departs this weekend for Fremantle, so one option is to just lock you up here for two months until we get home. Though, frankly, I would be much more relieved to not have you in our midst. Seems things tend to *happen* when either of you are around.'

'What does Philip say?' Daisie asked.

'Says nothing happened. Claims one of the staff tried to take advantage.'

'Well, for your information, Michael, he flirted with me.'

'Do you think your word counts for anything? The word of a housemaid?' Ratcliffe sat back in his chair and reached for a cigar from the box on his desk. He turned the tan cylinder over in his fingers as if it were a bullet.

'Perhaps one of the many members of the press outside might be interested?' Daisie said.

'Miss Chettle, what particular genre of press are you referring to? They wouldn't dare run a story like that. We'd have been in deep trouble long before today if they did. I was willing to trade with you when it came to Lady Althorp, but this hand you can't play. The press will *never* trade in royal gossip.'

Daisie folded her arms across her chest as though withholding an outburst.

'Did you know a film crew recorded their entire argument at the chalet?' Ratcliffe continued. 'Commander Carville merely had to approach them and they relinquished the footage on the spot. That's how it works. So you can forget that tack.'

'Philip will be furious,' Daisie replied tersely. 'He'll be apprised by me of your disrespect.'

Ratcliffe scoffed, placed the cigar case on the desk and started reading a draft telegram resting on his desk. 'You can provoke if you like but know what the response will be. The legal system serves the Crown so I urge you not to be stupid, think things through and go quietly. You should also give up any hope that the Duke will

ride in on his horse and rescue you. It's quite remarkable you'd
think anybody would choose *either* of you over Her Majesty. Shows
a certain arrogance, really, if not a basic lack of understanding of
society. Should've thrown you both overboard after the vomit.'

He stood as Daisie and Violet sat in silence. 'You'll be released,
effective immediately. You'll have a driver at your disposal to drop
you off at the destination of your choice. Then you can both find your
own way home. Don't presume the British taxpayer is paying for it.
Wouldn't look good.'

'I'm so sorry, Major Ratcliffe,' Violet said, her chin buried in her
chest.

'Believe it or not, I take no satisfaction in any of this. It's all a
pain in the backside, to be honest,' he remarked as he opened the
door, where Reilly waited. 'Gather their things, arrange a driver,
and then ensure they don't come anywhere near us again.'

52

Charcoal-coloured steam billowed into the otherwise flawless azure sky, inking it like a stain. Over four thousand Australians crowded the port barricades to see the *SS Gothic*'s departure from Melbourne for Western Australia.

Violet heard the crowd's excited hum grow once she reached the second deck below on the slow, demeaning march from the cabin to expulsion. Her shoulders arched with the weight of her battered resilience and her suitcase, as she walked behind Daisie, chin high, her ego undamaged to the end.

Joseph glanced back occasionally to ensure they were still following. He pushed the door outwards onto the main landing deck. The girls squinted as they stepped into the brilliant sunlight.

Violet bowed her head and shuffled past Daisie to walk just behind Joseph.

'Joseph? Um, could you please give Bobo a message?' she asked nervously.

'I'm not meant to talk to you,' he replied.

Violet nodded courteously and fell silent.

A cheer sparked from the crowd. The royal motorcade had turned onto the dock road parallel to the *Gothic*, causing the audience to roar with delight. Hundreds of tiny Union Jack flags fluttered in the air as the cars slowed to a stop beside a red carpet at the bottom of the gangway.

Violet glanced up. About twenty feet away, Ratcliffe leaned against the railing. Bearing witness to their removal, he shook his head and cast his cigarette into the water before turning away.

'Follow me and stay close,' Joseph ordered as he stepped onto the sloping gangway.

Violet kept her head down as they passed behind the Victorian dignitaries lining the carpet, pleased to wait for their moment with the Queen and Duke.

Daisie slowed her step as they crossed behind the dignitaries away from the ship. The car doors were ceremoniously opened, and the Queen and Duke stepped out to an ebullient cheer.

'Oh criminy,' uttered Violet under her breath. Lady Mountbatten and Fiona Bramford had stepped out of the second car. Fiona, fully styled in a cream silk dress with heels as tall as the ship's smokestacks, lingered in her entitled way in the thick of the pomp.

'Who on earth does she think she is? She's a lowly maid,' Daisie muttered, failing to see the humour of this coming from her, of all people.

'And a terrible one at that.'

As Joseph motioned for them to keep walking, Daisie twisted her neck to maintain her view of the Duke amid the fuss. Violet was familiar with that fixated look in Daisie's eyes. When it appeared, history had taught her to get out of the way.

'Keep walking, Daisie,' Violet intoned quietly.

Steward Joseph was still weaving them through the thinning crowd, assuming the two girls were immediately behind him, as Daisie again stopped walking, this time putting her suitcases on the cement. She turned back towards the ceremony. The Duke was about forty feet away, shaking a line of eager hands with his usual grace.

'Philip!' she cried, her voice desperate.

'Daisie!' Violet hissed, using the suitcases in her arms in an effort to block Daisie's magnetic pull.

'Philip! Over here!' Daisie screeched louder, her protestations barely able to cut through the clamour as she pushed past Violet to get closer.

Fiona's eyes found Violet's. From her position beside Lady Mountbatten, she tilted her head in confusion before a bemused smirk proved she'd deciphered the unfolding dramatic scene.

Joseph lunged and looped his arms around Daisie's waist, pulling her away from the carpet.

'Philip! They arrested me!' she hollered as Fiona shook her head in delight.

Violet's face surged with shame. She scuttled behind Joseph as Daisie was corralled like a known suspect being taken in. They rounded a small tower of unmarked wooden crates where a black town car idled on the port road.

'Jack!' Violet exclaimed with relief.

He stepped out of the driver's side of the car, pinching the rheum from his eyes and stretching his jaw as though he'd been taking a nap. His eyes rested on her stomach. 'You're showing. The baby. Suits you, to be honest.'

In that moment his eyes were only for her, unconcerned with Joseph bundling a recalcitrant Daisie into the back seat. Violet's shame melted.

Jack's eyes held the promise of hope. With a whole-hearted smile he reached over to take the suitcases that dangled like weights from her sore arms. 'Last day on the job today, so I got the assignment nobody else wanted.'

'Spare me,' Daisie muttered from inside the car.

'Where to then?' he asked Joseph.

'Anywhere but here,' Joseph pleaded as he forced the suitcases into the boot and tried to slam the lid shut.

Violet lingered in front of Jack, biting her bottom lip and still buzzing from his proximity.

'Lake Eyre,' Daisie announced from the cabin. 'You will take us to our auntie in Lake Eyre.'

Jack looked to Joseph, who leaned against the car. Violet climbed into the back seat and sat beside her sister in a gesture of unity.

'Fine, whatever it be. Go,' urged Joseph.

'That's two days' drive,' Jack replied. 'At least.'

The *Gothic*'s horn boomed, triggering the crowd to give another roar.

Joseph nervously checked his watch, then shoved his hands in his pockets, eager to return to the ship.

'Major Ratcliffe's orders were to get them as far away as possible,' Joseph said impatiently.

'That's bloody far,' Jack said. But his incredulous tone did nothing to dissuade any of them.

Violet's eyes pleaded what she couldn't say; Daisie's threatened to make life difficult.

'Well, I guess we better get going then,' Jack relented, raising his eyebrows as he climbed into the front seat and pulled the door shut.

'Excellent, fine, good luck, so long,' Joseph chanted as he edged backwards towards the *Gothic*. Jack turned the key in the ignition and revved the engine.

The car circled back towards the boom gate and police waved them through, blowing their whistles to part the crowd so it could pass the ceremony. The pedestrian congestion slowed them to a stop beside the Daimlers as the Queen and Duke stepped onto the *Gothic*'s walkway.

Daisie pushed both hands against the window glass, desperate for Philip's attention, but he was distracted by the crew at the foot of the bridge, who saluted dutifully as he nodded and disarmed them. Just ahead of him, Queen Elizabeth paused and turned her head slightly back towards the crowd, her gloved hand offering one last gentle farewell.

For a fleeting moment, Violet saw her cool gaze alight on Daisie in the car. The Queen's eyes held on to hers like a firm grip. Daisie's eyes tightened into a glare, holding in reply. The moment felt eternal; the stare sustained just long enough to sting.

The Queen broke the stand-off, releasing her eyes to the crowd as she continued further along the walkway. Then something stepped into the foreground, a mincing flurry of cream silk and breasts.

'Are you taking out the rubbish, darling?'

Fiona Bramford appeared by Jack's window, dangling her sunglasses like a medieval flail with a possessive smirk that stretched across her chin.

'What?' Jack asked tentatively.

'Be careful of this cargo, they're tricky. Perhaps I'll stay a day longer, make sure you survived them.'

Jack went to reply but the words didn't quite escape.

Uninvited, Fiona leaned aggressively through the window and passionately kissed Jack. Before she detached from him, her eyes found Violet, who could only watch in stunned revulsion at the proprietorial display.

Fiona took a sultry slow-step back from the window, weap-onising her posture to offer Jack a level view of her bosom. She seductively slid her pinky finger along the gutter of her lower lip as she turned to saunter between the Daimler bumpers and back to Lady Mountbatten's side.

Daisie's left eyebrow peaked, angled so sharp it could've trimmed her fringe. She pivoted from Jack, with his jaw limp in embarrassment, to her withering sister, whose face appeared debilitated by stroke.

'Very well,' Daisie declared. With a resolute determination she quickly rolled her window down like she was priming a jack-in-the-box. She then cupped both hands around her mouth to project her voice and leaned into the gap.

'Bramford!' she yelled loud enough to defeat the crowd noise.

Fiona spun her head back towards the outburst, her satisfied smirk still cooling.

'Yer a *slapper*!' Daisie shouted it in a coarse Australian accent, the shrill inflexion almost as shocking as the word itself.

Violet looked up from her stupor, her mouth dangling as she turned in time to see Fiona's face demolish. The dignitaries on the carpet pivoted in unison to Fiona, then to Daisie. After that they didn't know where to park their attention, eyes darting to deny the word's existence.

With dowager poise and her chin perched high, Daisie proudly rolled up the window. 'Better watch out, Sir Jack Smith,' she declared. 'Bramford'll eat you up and spit you out. Wouldn't happen with a Chettle. We're the real deal.'

'She terrifies me,' he confessed. 'I feel a bit – what's the word? – desecrated.'

Violet choked on a sob that escaped awkwardly, like a cat's furball.

'What is it now?' Daisie sighed impatiently.

'That's the nicest thing you've ever done for me!'

Violet's words unscrambled something in Daisie's demeanour. The creases of angry determination in her face relaxed and her eyes opened – just a fraction – to reveal an empathy Violet had assumed was long gone.

The shift struck Violet like the recollection of a fond memory.

Violet watched Daisie chew the inside of her mouth, uncomfortable with the sentimentality of the moment. But something in Daisie had changed. 'Take us as far away as possible,' Daisie ordered Jack.

'That's Lake Eyre, all right.'

Jack planted his hand on the chrome button in the centre of the steering wheel. The horn dispersed the crowd and he accelerated off the dockside apron onto The Boulevard, leaving the billowing smokestack plumes of the *Gothic* behind.

53

Day 136: Flinders Ranges, South Australia
Population: 23
Weather: 85 degrees Fahrenheit, clear skies, perilous heat
Fact: The first humans to inhabit the Flinders Ranges were the Adnyamathanha people (meaning 'hill people' or 'rock people'), whose descendants still reside in the area.

It was now dark, so Violet watched the scenery transition in the light cast by the car headlights. Deserted suburban streets gave way to flat, fertile farming country then to arid, dusty desert. The distance between lampposts grew until there were none. The occasional town sign passed in the glare: Burra, Orroroo, Ulooloo, Barndioota.

After a toilet and refuelling stop at the Yanyarrie general store, Jack continued driving through the dark into the arid crags of the Flinders Ranges and up the desolate red nothingness of the Outback Highway. The uneven stretch of isolated road carved a straight line into the heart of Australia. Somewhere along the way Violet leaned against Daisie, who'd fallen asleep, placing her head on Daisie's bony shoulder until she drifted off.

*

Violet's eyes prickled at the morning sun's sting. About the same time Jack stirred in the front seat, the sprung leather squeaking with his subtle movements. She mashed her hand against her ear to dissuade an erratic fly. Through the sliver of window she could see an eagle in the sky, drifting in concentric circles in wait for a kill.

She shielded her eyes and eased onto her left elbow. Jack righted himself and rubbed his eyes with a groan, glancing in the rear-vision mirror, where he intercepted Violet's tired eyes. He smiled to himself at the preposterousness of it all.

'Singing toorali-oorali-addity
Singing toorali-oorali-ay
Singing toorali-oorali-addity
We're bound for Botany Bay.'

Violet peered out the window. Crouched by the roadside and singing quietly to herself was Daisie, her dress hoisted over her knees with a trickle of urine puddled between her feet.

Grimacing to push the opposite door open, Violet extended her feet onto a patchy dirt road that stretched to infinity in each direction. She swatted another fly, then hesitated at the vastness of the landscape. It was a moonscape of ochre dust pocked by sharp rocks and scattered prickly scrub that had survived despite the otherworldly conditions.

The sun hovered just above the horizon, its mass so fiery and brilliant that it left a ghost on her retina as she turned away. Violet breathed in deeply and held the arid air in her lungs. As she exhaled she felt the tightness inside her skull ease.

'How much further?' Daisie asked as she adjusted her garments on the opposite side of the car.

'Four, five hours tops? I've got no idea, to be honest.' Jack faced away from the car, standing behind a four-foot-tall shrub to relieve himself into the dust.

Two hours had passed, and the road was so straight that Jack propped up the wheel with his knee and hung his arm out the window. The occasional wild kangaroo, eagle or emu broke the monotony. Some ran out of the way, and some lay dead by the roadside as the result of an earlier ill-timed crossing.

Around lunchtime the dirt road became a track. Their vehicle bumped over potholes and hat-sized stones, sending a thin dust cloud into the sky in its wake.

'Kangaroos!' Violet pointed to a group bouncing parallel to the car across the dirt, each kick of their muscular legs leaving a small explosion in the dust. The animals were taller than the car roof and bounded with a powerful grace, pivoting in subtle direction changes with each stride.

Jack pointed out the window as he drove. 'That roo's got a joey, that second one.'

'Where? I can't see,' exclaimed Daisie as she leaned across her sister. 'Oh, is that the—'

A horrifying thud sounded on the glass windscreen.

Jack braked hard, causing the car to slide sideways across the dirt through a hedge of wiry scrub. The twins slammed against the seat back as Jack yanked the wheel left then right to correct the fishtailing vehicle. He fought until the car ground to a halt, the engine stalled and the dust cloud caught up. A thick fog of red sand momentarily enclosed the vehicle.

The engine ticked down to a stop. After the shock and noise, silence.

Violet opened her eyes again. She'd been thrown to the floor and was tangled in a heap on top of Daisie. Her delayed nerves caught up, her head now throbbing where she'd struck it against the ashtray on the seat back. Violet's right hand was pinned under her chest. She stretched her fingers and touched her nose. It radiated pain and left a smear of blood on her fingertips.

'Violet!' Jack exclaimed as he pulled at his seatbelt to get to her. 'Violet! You all right?' he asked desperately. He reached over and grasped her blouse, pulling her off Daisie.

Violet slid back onto the seat, her hands cradling her stomach. She'd taken the impact with her nose, fortunately. 'I think I'm all right,' she replied. 'Daisie?'

Jack kicked open his door and circled the car to open theirs as Daisie gripped the door handle and righted herself on the bench seat.

Violet tested her nose with the back of her hand. More blood, a trickle but not a stream. The flies convened, swirling around her like mosquitoes.

Daisie's eyes moved with a dazed lethargy, grasping for orientation as she processed the shock of it all.

'What the hell?' Jack exclaimed angrily. 'Are they blind?' He looked back along the track. Twenty feet behind, a lump of fur and legs quivered in the dirt. 'A bloody roo.' He dusted the fine layer of sand off his clothes as he approached the kangaroo. It was a big one, as tall as a man when righted but now breathing in rapid rhythmic jolts, clinging to life as its body spasmed.

Violet watched Daisie step unsteadily out of the car and walk slowly towards the animal, hypnotised. Fifty feet away a mob of kangaroos, the ones they'd been trailing, stood together in a pack watching the scene.

Daisie's shadow cast across the agitated kangaroo. Violet stood behind her, watching as Daisie fixated on the animal, its body too broken to flee. A deep cut down its side made it look like it had been gutted by a butcher.

Its disoriented eye found Daisie. Then, as though jolted with a battery, its legs kicked out in an attempt to jump. The kangaroo's breathing slowed to an irregular few beats before it ceased and stilled. The tiny paw of a joey protruding from the pouch hung limp like a stick.

Daisie knelt beside the body. She tentatively rested her hand on the blood-flecked fur of its neck, letting the spiky coat bristle against her palm.

'Daisie?' asked Jack, confused. Violet stepped closer.

Daisie tightened her lips as her eyelids clasped and her walled fingers clutched over her ears in a strange panic, as though a painful memory had returned with a force greater than the kangaroo's impact with the car. A single tear streamed down her face, cleansing a path through the coat of dust on her cheek.

Violet rested her hand awkwardly on Daisie's shoulder.

Daisie opened her damp eyes, squinting against the sun as her hand reached out and rested gently on Violet's bulging stomach.

Violet stood still for as long as it took and Daisie had breathed through whatever sadness had erupted inside her.

Ten minutes later the bull ants made a move on the carcass, and the three returned to the car without saying a word.

To be safe, Jack drove the rest of the way at only twenty miles per hour.

54

Day 136: *Marree, South Australia*
Population: *23*
Weather: *86 degrees Fahrenheit, sporadic cloud, ruthless sunshine*
Fact: *Teamsters, cameleers, stockmen, hawkers, railway workers and explorers passed through Marree to travel the Overland Telegraph Line, the Oodnadatta and Birdsville tracks and the Ghan railway.*

The engine made a *tock-tock-tock* sound, not unlike a sewing machine, which sped up when Jack accelerated. By the time they neared Marree, close to Tirari Station, the sun had lowered towards the western horizon and was casting a blood-red glow across the fractured desert plain.

They'd been driving for two hours since the accident, and the track had become a road again. Daisie hadn't yet spoken, still in a sullen state of shock. Jack put up a brave front but his voice was quieter, shaken by what could've been. He'd given Violet the map so he could focus on the road.

'What is the point of it all?' The timbre of Violet's voice strayed between confused and annoyed as she interrogated her own belief.

'That's a big question, Violet. Would you like to narrow it down?' Jack glanced over at her.

'Elizabeth. She's just some girl, like us. She didn't choose her parents, had no choice over what her duties were. He wouldn't have even married her were she not in line to the throne.'

'Uneasy lies the head that wears a crown,' Jack quoted as he shifted the engine up a gear. 'You know, since you picked her up in Jamaica, the United States has tested H-bombs in the Pacific, Crimea has transferred from Russia to the Ukraine, and Marilyn Monroe married Joe DiMaggio,' said Jack. 'But all you'll read about on the front pages is the Queen wore *this*, and the Duke said *that*. Are you still a believer, then? In the monarchy?'

His words seemed to be directed at Violet.

'I don't know,' Violet mumbled. 'I just don't know.'

'And you, Daisie?'

'Never was,' Daisie replied sombrely, breaking her silence. 'Never will be.'

Through the dusty, cracked windshield a rigid shape loomed in the distance – a house, perhaps. A bullet-riddled sign by the side of the dirt road announced 'Marree'.

'Civilisation,' Jack said with an ominous inflection.

The Great Northern Hotel was a two-storey sandstone Victorian building with a green corrugated-iron gabled roof, through which four chimneys touched the sky. On the second-storey balcony a few grimy men in trampled wide-brimmed hats leaned against the verandah posts and stared down at the unlikely arrivals as Jack slowed the car. The mood was less than inviting.

'Toilet stop?' Jack asked.

'No,' the sisters replied in unison.

With a billow of dust and another *tock-tock-tock*, the car accelerated away from the hotel towards a T-intersection a hundred yards down the road. A small wooden sign read 'Tirari Station – 30 Miles'.

Jack turned off the main dirt road onto a track that wended through scrub and stone bluffs, as though leading to nowhere.

The car dawdled past what seemed to be a deserted sandstone dwelling from the last century. As the sun touched the evening horizon, long shadows were cast by the lowest scrub and soon the grey dusk made it difficult to tell the road from the desert.

From the passenger seat, Violet watched Jack squint through the cracked windscreen. The headlights occasionally spotted an emu or kangaroo bounding out of the way. A speck on the horizon became the ghostly shape of a large house shadowed against the residual light.

The road stopped at a timber gate, with a hand-painted sign that read 'Tirari Station. No transients.'

Jack raised his eyebrows and got out of the car to push the gate open.

Violet looked out the window, trying to discern something in the remaining light. 'Jack!'

About eight or nine people were ambling slowly through the scrub twenty feet from the car, in the direction of the house. Their bodies were lanky and their posture weary, as they carried tools and fence posts on their shoulders. The group sidled to the edge of the road to let the car pass, pausing to stare before sauntering on.

'Aboriginals,' Jack whispered as he climbed back in and drove through the gate.

The car lumbered slowly across the uneven ground, approaching what appeared to be a large weatherboard homestead with an enclosed verandah. It looked like a fortress, with the electric light inside illuminating the windows that wrapped the rectangular building on all sides. A tall steel antenna, around thirty feet in height, was mounted to the corrugated-iron roof. They could just make it out in the twilight, but nothing else bar gravel and earth could be seen beyond the short reach of the headlights.

'This is it, then,' said Jack, pulling up twenty feet from the house and turning off the ignition. The electric buzz of cicadas filled the air as the engine silenced. 'Family reunion.'

'What am I going to say? What are we going to say?' Violet asked with a rising panic.

'You're asking now? It's a long way to come just to sit in the car.' Jack laughed as the engine croaked and cooled.

'I'm going to speak to her,' Daisie said confidently. Before she could act, the front door of the house burst open, revealing the shape of a stocky woman with a baby on her hip. In her other hand hung a long object – a walking stick or a horse whip, perhaps. Her face was obscured in shadow.

They stared at the woman through the windscreen. She stared back at them. The baby let out a small impatient whine of boredom or hunger.

Daisie forthrightly pulled the handle down, pushed the door open and stepped out of the car.

Violet turned at a noise behind them. Through the rear window she could see the Aboriginal workers they'd passed moseying up the road, the cloud of dirt slowing as they approached the car.

'Who's it?' asked the woman tersely.

Violet stepped from the car and stood beside her sister as Jack waited inside.

'Hazel Lawson?' asked Daisie uncertainly.

'Auntie Hazel?' Violet followed with a delicate hope in her voice.

Hazel stepped directly into the glow of the porchlight under a knot of spiralling moths. The walking stick was in fact a rifle, which hung casually from her trigger finger and thumb. But Violet only had eyes for the ghost in the flesh before her. It was as if their mother had been reincarnated.

On either side of the familiar pinched nose, Hazel had short curly brown hair and ruddy cheeks, as though her English rose skin was still resisting the punitive climate. And her face and legs looked stouter and stronger than their mother's.

But it was as good as her.

The baby boy, cherubic with a tussock of fine hair, perched unhappily on Hazel's hip. He yawned and clutched desperately at the sleeve of Hazel's floral house dress as a fly tried to get at the dribble leaking from his mouth.

'It's all right, boys,' she shouted over their heads. The workers shuffled onwards behind the house with their eyes fixed on the visitors. Although her accent was a broad Australian one, with a twang like taut wire, a subtle British inflection remained.

Hazel lifted the barrel of the gun, resting the stock against her waist so it was aimed at them.

Violet covered her stomach with one hand and glanced back at Jack, who remained in the car. He raised his fingers off the wheel, indicating she should stay calm.

'Frank!' Hazel yelled into the house. A fit man in his mid-thirties with a firm jaw and a farmer's weariness appeared behind her. His sleeves were rolled up and his hair was thick with the day's sweat and dust.

'Come closer,' Hazel ordered. 'Into the light.'

Daisie took a step forward.

'You too. Both of ya.'

Violet crept up beside her sister. She was close enough now to see the wrinkles patterned on Hazel's face. They replicated her mother's like a matching fingerprint, her forehead lines running in parallel above her eyes with the same measure and dip.

Daisie hesitantly opened her mouth to speak. 'I'm Daisie. This is Violet. Edith's our mother.'

'I hope you don't mind us'—Violet searched for the words—'dropping in?'

'What do ya want?' There was an aggression in her voice that was still present and raw. Her finger remained on the trigger.

'I want to know what happened,' Daisie replied.

'What'd she tell ya?'

'Nothing. And now she's dead. Because of me.' Daisie spoke bravely, her voice calm and honest with atonement. Hazel's face wilted slightly, though she didn't otherwise flinch. Violet glanced nervously to Jack, then back to Hazel. She'd seen *Shane* and knew how these stand-offs usually ended. Not well.

Nobody moved as the pitch of the cicadas vacillated.

Frank rested his hand against Hazel's arm to calm her. The nose of the rifle lowered an inch, though a shot would still hit them.

'Past always finds you, hey, Frank?' she muttered sarcastically. Then she guffawed, the boisterous laugh growing until she relaxed the gun. A rotund cattle dog waddled up beside Hazel, stretching its legs as though still waking up, and sniffed the air towards them.

'Gracie's pregnant too. No idea how, though. No mutts around here. Immaculate conception, maybe. Thinking of changing her name to Mary. Who's the valiant gentleman?'

Jack hesitantly swung the door open and stood by the car.

'Who are you, then?'

'I'm Jack. Just the driver.'

'Well, Just Jack, I guess you and your two bodyguards may as well come in so we can get it bloody over with. And to think I was gonna have an early night and curl up with a book.'

55

'You still got problems if ya think the answer to everything is here,' Hazel huffed as she put the good plates out and Frank heated a pot of soup on the stove. Gracie, splayed across the floorboards under the table, occasionally got up to lick Violet's knees. The dog's tongue felt like steel wool, and she persisted no matter how much Violet pushed her away.

Since they'd arrived, Violet had found it difficult to take her eyes off Hazel. The resemblance was near-perfect, if sullied by the years living in a different world.

Before dinner Hazel had given them a short tour as Frank toiled in the kitchen. Her home was comfortable and unexpectedly well decorated. A wide central hallway led to four large bedrooms and a bathroom. Jack sized up the lounge as Daisie and Violet were shown to one of the bedrooms. The room smelled of fresh lavender and housed a double bed, a well-worn timber dresser and a window. An amateur watercolour painting that depicted a dry desert lake pan hung on the wall above the bed.

'I dabble. Not much else to bloody do,' Hazel said half apologetically before they were led to a dark back verandah sealed from the elements by flyscreens as thick as wire.

'This is it,' she announced and flicked on a light switch. It revealed a radio transceiver unit and a microphone resting on a jade formica table. The equipment was decorated with an array of tiny Union Jack and Australian flags. Red, white and blue bunting hung from the roof and a framed portrait of Queen Elizabeth rested beside a crown fashioned from cardboard.

'Was all over in a flash, but I read what they gave me and got told I sounded pretty good. Most excitement we've ever had around here. Since the rains anyway. Speakin' of which, rain forecast this week. Only fills every ten years or so. Hope you two aren't a bad omen. Could use those rains.'

Violet, Jack and Daisie sat at a long wooden dining table off the kitchen. The furniture was simple, and here and there were small items that spoke of home: a stoneware ginger-beer jug from Wells & Sons, and an oak Westminster chime clock like Auntie Maisel used to have in her kitchen.

Hazel finished setting the table as Frank carried over bowls of thick vegetable soup one at a time, then slices of bread cut thicker than the breadboard and piled like pallets beside a messy dollop of butter.

'First things first,' Hazel said as she parked herself at the head of the table. She closed her eyes and bowed her head. Frank watched with a smirk as Violet, Daisie and Jack uncertainly closed their eyes to pray. 'Lord. Thanks for the soup that Frank cooked. Even if the carrot chunks aren't soft right through again. And no thanks for our visitors, who travelled all this way to ruin my evening with Patricia Highsmith. Now they're gonna want to talk about all the horrible things and I may have to shoot them.'

Violet's eyes flew open. Hazel's face was dead serious in solemn communion. Confused, Daisie scrunched her nose. Jack's mouth dropped open a little.

'And sorry for never saying grace before dinner, except when calling the dog. This is the first time I've talked to you since I lived in Surbiton and asked you to let me spend the night at Margie Lyell's house. But Mum still didn't let me go. So here we are again then, hey. Amen.'

Hazel sprung her eyes open and guffawed, revealing the joke and laughing until Violet felt she had to join in. Frank grinned and spooned soup into his mouth like he was in on the yarn. Jack tilted his head in an unsettled gesture as he spread the napkin on his lap.

'Right, so when'd she die?' asked Hazel as she took her spoon.

'Just over a year ago,' Violet said with a choked rasp as Daisie lowered her eyes.

'Better open that wine, Frank.'

He pushed his chair back and walked to the kitchen to get the drink.

'Was an accident,' Daisie said quietly, shamed.

'Guess you did me a favour,' Hazel said cruelly.

Violet glanced at Daisie, then back to Hazel. 'Did you get my letter?' Violet asked. 'I wrote to you.'

'Letter? You see a letter, Frank?'

Frank perfunctorily shook his head as he distributed a bottle of red wine into five water glasses.

'Mail arrives once a month and takes twice that long to get out here,' Hazel said with a yawn.

Gracie's rough tongue revisited Violet's knee. She shook her legs to deter the persistent beast. 'Dad's gone too. About a year back.'

Daisie took a mouthful of red wine, almost finishing the tiny cup in a single gulp.

Hazel stirred her spoon slowly in the bowl, but her eyes were lost in a memory, the lack of response suggesting the news had cut through her bravado.

'It's just us now. And Auntie Maisel,' Violet continued.

Frank's spoon clinked against the ceramic as he rested it and glanced to Hazel with a frown of concern.

Hazel continued stirring in a trance as Violet's words hung in the air. 'Maisel,' she uttered under her breath, sunk in a returning memory.

'Excuse me one moment.' Violet stood and draped her napkin on the chair. She walked down the hall to the bedroom where the suitcases stood in a line, and lifted one onto the mattress, rummaging inside to find the lime cardigan.

She returned to the table with her mother's envelope in her hand. Hazel continued to stir her soup in silence, still lost in thought.

'We found this after Mum died. She never got around to sending it.' Violet slid the envelope across the table to Hazel.

She ignored it. 'You're with child.'

'I am, yes.'

'Is it his?' Hazel retorted, glancing at Jack, who enthusiastically shook his head with a full mouth.

'It's nobody's,' Violet replied.

'Nobody, hey? You been lying down with dogs, like Grace?' She screamed with laughter, slamming the table with the palm of her hand. 'The Immaculate Mistake! 'Bout the biggest ya can make.'

'It was a big mistake,' Violet confessed, trying to calm her down.

Hazel turned her gaze on Daisie, who blanched and stared down at the table, avoiding scrutiny. Hazel's eyebrows lifted with glee at the sensitivity of the subject.

'Don't tell me,' she said, leaning back in her chair with a sly grin. 'You did it with *her* boyfriend.' She nodded towards Daisie.

The look of shock on Violet's face confirmed it.

Hazel shrieked again, delighted at the drama, and finished her glass. Grace lifted her head languidly, then eased it back to the floor.

'Yes, it's his,' Violet blurted with embarrassment.

'Technically!'

'Yes! It's his. Mine. I mean, it's mine. *Now* it's mine. I didn't even want it! That horrible, horrible man.'

Her words seemed to sink into Jack. Violet's reddened eyes found him. The shame was written on his face; he couldn't hold her brief glance.

Hazel roared again as Frank tipped his bowl of soup to corner the last drop.

'Sorry for making you share a room with her,' Hazel cackled, taking too much delight in the discomfort she'd created. 'So what horror will this be, then?' she continued, turning her attention to the envelope which bore her name. She sketched her finger across Edith's handwriting before tearing the flap open.

Hazel flicked through the photos with a perfunctory air. 'Bugger me, then,' she said. She was gripped but was trying not to show it. Her hand started to tremble, causing the photo to quiver.

'Mum and Dad never told us anything,' Violet explained, anxious of Hazel's outbursts. 'We didn't even know you existed until Auntie Maisel'—a knowing smile broke on Hazel's lips—'said you disappeared. And then she never heard from you again. I found the photos but that was all there was.'

Something screeched outside. Grace rose with a low growl, ready to defend them against the nocturnal assailant. As Hazel stood to pour another glass, a solitary cricket started clicking in the scrub beyond the window.

'Probably no point keeping secrets now,' Hazel said.

She was tense, her fists gripped tightly on the olive tablecloth.

'Your mum walked in on your father and me. Right into the bedroom, no knock. Feet pointing everywhere. No lie could cover it, so I ran. On that day, and ever since. Stupid, really – should've faced up to the dread. But in that moment I knew I needed to be forgotten, for everybody's sake. Couldn't accidentally bump into Mrs Bulvers or whom-bloody-ever was in the lane, havin' to small-talk around the thing everybody was talkin' 'bout. This country is great for hiding. First I was in Melbourne, got my feet. Then I was pregnant. So I had to hide. Again. And here I am. Queen of the desert.'

She glanced at Violet as she wrapped both hands around the glass, her rough fingers massaging themselves nervously.

'Daisie's stood by you. Everything would've been different if I hadn't run. Maybe she'd be here giving me the shits.'

'The baby?' Violet asked sadly.

Hazel shook her head dismissively and sipped from her glass.

'Did you tell Dad?' Daisie asked, determined to know.

'"The shame it'd bring,"' she said, imitating Edward. 'All it took.'

Hazel's eyes tightened as her mind touched the past. 'Bit sad, really, how you can see things after it's all too late.'

She sniffed, clearing her nostrils. Then she brought the glass to her lips, but rather than sip from it, she let her lips rest on the rim as she stared at the table.

Violet picked up the photo, turning it over. 'And Rosie and Poppy?' she asked.

Hazel chuckled but said nothing more. A brooding rumble in the distance hinted at a storm. 'Hear that? Rain's comin'. Ants've been running crazy.' She emptied the glass in one swallow, taking the garnet liquid quickly as though for its numbing quality rather than its palate. 'I've had too much. You two remind me of too much. Shall I pour another?'

Frank stood, walked to Hazel then knelt beside her.

She looked up to him with a resigned stare. Then she dropped her chin and seemed to retreat into herself, like her awareness had subsided. 'I've had enough,' she said with vacant eyes.

Frank patiently led her out of the room by her elbow. Grace got up with a groan and lumbered behind them.

Violet heard Hazel mutter, 'Goodnight, Rosie, goodnight, Poppy,' as she followed Frank down the hall.

56

As Violet made her way out of the bathroom, wet from a cold shower in grey water, she caught a glimpse through Hazel's bedroom door, which stood slightly ajar. Frank was by Hazel's bedside, leaning over her in bed and placing something into her cupped hand. He held a glass of water in the other. The floorboard creaked, so Violet kept moving to avoid being caught.

Jack cornered her in the hallway just before she reached her door. He carried an armful of pillows and blankets. Grace seemed to have taken a liking to him and dwelled at his knees as though he might drop food. 'I've got to make a start at first light,' he whispered. 'Get the car back before they think I've stolen it. Not that this isn't all highly entertaining.'

'Give us a hand with this couch, will ya, Jack?' Frank interrupted as he walked out of Hazel's bedroom into the living room.

Jack held Violet's desperate gaze for a precious few seconds. Both hoped the other would say the words. But he turned towards the living room before Violet could open her mouth.

She closed the bedroom door behind her and crawled onto the creaky mattress under the fly netting beside Daisie. 'Something's not right,' Violet whispered.

'None of it is *right*! Not any of it. I thought knowing might make things better, but now I don't know. It's all too much.'

'She seems odd.'

'It's like seeing Mum. But it's not.'

'Not just that. It's like she's—' But Violet couldn't articulate what it was.

'Off her rocker.' Daisie concluded.

'Generator's switchin' off!'

It was Frank, shouting with the regularity of a well-worn routine from somewhere within the house. Seconds later, with the *thunk* of a heavy switch, the room plunged into darkness, the sort where you can't see your hand move in front of your face and your eyes start to conjure shapes.

'Jack's going. In the morning,' Violet whispered in the dark.

'He's leaving us here?' Daisie exclaimed, raising her voice.

'Shh! We can't just run.'

'*She* did!'

'Well, there's not much to go back to.'

'Precious little here,' Daisie said as she turned and tried to sleep.

'Are we Rosie and Poppy?' asked Violet.

'Don't care.'

'And Dad?' Violet dared to ask with a hushed voice.

Daisie said nothing and a profound quiet settled in.

Violet was restless. Jack's presence in the living room pricked at her. He lay so near, merely twenty feet away down the hall, but he may as well have been in Melbourne.

Thirty minutes later Daisie was snoring like a hoarse camel.

Violet gave in, the pain of future regret too acute. She fumbled out of bed, feeling her way across the room like a blind woman.

Gently turning the doorknob, she edged one vigilant step after another along the hallway with her arms extended like a zombie. Her eyes searched for some sliver of light, some shade of grey, but the pitch-black was total.

As she neared the living area, she could hear the sound of Jack breathing, his rhythmic exhalations those of a deep sleep. She pushed a hand forward to feel for the couch, sliding it across the fabric until she touched the blanket he slept under.

Violet's hand hovered in the air above his legs, the tips of her fingers gently touching his form as she explored until she was within inches of his face. The expelled air of his breath struck her forehead as he respired deeply.

She stayed there for desperate minutes, breathing his stale air. She wanted Jack to wake and take charge. She edged carefully closer, bringing her lips parallel to his, or where she thought his might be, her nerve afforded by the cloak of night and bolstered by the finality of his imminent departure.

Jack stirred as though unconsciously sensing her proximity.

She let her top lip find his skin – his nose – and kissed it lightly.

His breathing steadied and quietened, no longer in a deep unconsciousness. Violet brought her lips closer until hers felt the warm air that escaped his lungs. She knew he knew she was there.

Jack moved his hands, conscious of her presence. Violet's heart swelled with nervous fear and exhilaration. Their faces were an inch apart, close enough to negate words. He shifted under the blanket, his arm finding its way closer to her in the dark.

Violet remained poised over him, her knee aching from propping herself up awkwardly like a flamingo. She gave up trying to perceive light and surrendered to the dark. She closed her eyes. It made everything more dreamlike, emboldening her to move onto him until her breath brushed his chin.

Jack pulled Violet closer, his hand clasping her head and his lips enveloping hers with the power of a desire long contemplated. Each overt movement yielded a sound, a creak of floorboard or squeak of couch spring, that disclosed them to the household.

'Are you sure?' Jack whispered.

Violet hesitated before responding. 'Be brave,' she thought to herself, before responding with a whispered 'Yes.'

So they persisted cautiously, exploring each other in slow motion, the pleasure of each caress heightened by the necessity for quiet.

Violet sensed the discordant breathing of a third presence. Grace had wandered into the room, her hot, pungent snout finding their sweaty union. They froze, knowing they couldn't laugh aloud, and could only wait until the dog lost interest. Soon enough she did, parking herself a few feet away for a scratch on the rug before going to sleep.

Close to dawn, Violet reluctantly left Jack's arms and replaced her nightgown. She returned to her room and slid back into bed, where she slept as deeply as she ever had.

By the time Violet emerged, Hazel was busy feeding Harry. He was perched in a highchair with a mass of scrambled eggs spread on both the floor and his chin.

Violet peered through the front door. The car was gone. Clouds had gathered, casting a gloom.

'Jack?'

'Long gone,' Hazel said.

'What time is it?'

'Ten thirty, thereabouts. Could use somebody like Just Jack around here, need an extra pair of hands. Think he quite liked the idea. He likes you.'

'What did he say?'

The baby gazed at Violet curiously before breaking into a giddy smile. His grin revealed two tiny teeth fighting through his gums.

'Nothing, can just tell. I'm perceptive that way. Might be a bit crazy, but the less I'm around people the more I can read the few I come across.'

'Where's Daisie?'

'She went with Frank to Leigh Creek.' Hazel cleaned egg off the floor with a tired cloth.

'What's Leigh Creek?'

'A general store and a pub. A thriving metropolis by Lake Eyre standards.'

'Can I walk there?'

Hazel laughed out loud. The baby giggled, joining in.

'It's a four-hour drive each way, luv. It takes almost an hour just to get to the edge of the station. Fifteen thousand square miles. Been here fifteen years and only seen about a fraction of it.'

Violet knelt beside Hazel to help with the mess.

'Sorry 'bout last night,' Hazel said sheepishly. 'I say stupid things sometimes. Most I don't even remember.'

Violet didn't know how to respond, so she let Harry's gurgled chatter fill the air.

'You've got your work cut out,' Hazel continued as another blob of egg landed on the floor. 'Nobody tells ya how tough it is raising kids. Did it on my own, at first, until Frank moved in.'

'So Frank isn't the—' Violet didn't finish the question, not wanting to inadvertently trap herself in an awkward conversation.

'Frank? I'm not his type, if ya get my drift. Good man, though.'

Hazel leaned on her knee with a groan and cleaned the eggy dishcloth in the basin. 'What are your plans, then?'

'Today?'

'Today, tomorrow. Next week. Baby's comin', whether ya like it or not.'

'Home. Somehow. Though even if I went, I don't know what I'd be going back for.'

Hazel wrung out the cloth, twisting it in her hands under the flow of grey water like she was interrogating a thought. 'I spent all night thinkin',' she confessed. 'Things I could've done different. Head's hurting from it all. Seeing that photo, I knew I'd made a mistake. We all make 'em. But I shoulda fixed it. Your mum's gone now, so the joke's on me.' She turned the tap off and stayed leaning over the sink. 'It's never too late, Violet. Until it is.'

No longer hypnotised by his mother's confession, Harry started striking his spoon on the highchair's tray. Violet looked out the window towards the lake bed as Hazel busied herself.

'Stay as long as you like, dear. Both of you. That baby needs a home. This is a home.' She hoisted Harry out of his chair, plumped him on her waist. 'I smell poo, Harry,' she half-sung, carrying him to the nursery.

Violet walked to the front door, looking out through the screen at where Jack's car had been parked. She stepped onto the verandah and stood in the spot where Hazel had threatened them the night before.

From the elevated vantage point of the house, in the full light of day, the dusty uneven desert stretched all the way to vast ranges in the distant east. To the north-west was the flat dry pan of Lake Eyre, its salty bed a vast featureless plain. A blurry heat haze simmered where its horizon met the sky.

The sun hid behind cloud cover but it still prickled Violet's skin with its intensity. She wandered down the incline away from the house, concentrating on each step to avoid skating on the loose razor-sharp pebbles.

The lake bed was all dry clay and erosion. She took a hesitant step onto the surface to test its foundation. Then another. With each step the pan started to develop a white sandy texture. Violet leaned down to touch the surface with the tips of her fingers, pushing into a light dusting of crystallised salt residue that resembled dry snow.

Violet turned to face Tirari Station, now a milk-crate-sized dwelling on the distant rise. Its antenna stood high above everything, like a beacon. The paddocks around the homestead were dotted with livestock standing sullenly in the heat.

She felt a subtle movement in her stomach. It wasn't her appetite, though that was there too. It was a strange sensation, like the gentle working of organs, but like nothing she'd ever sensed.

Her hand rested on her stomach and she felt it again.

A smile grew on her lips. It was the gentle tap of the baby, *her* baby. She took a deep breath and rubbed her stomach lovingly, hoping the calm movements would reassure it. The surge of love Violet experienced was like adrenaline, leaving her as happy as when her mother was alive. Despite the salt pan's strange otherworldliness, she could imagine making a home here, or some strange version of it.

PART 3

57

Day 142: Lake Eyre, South Australia
Population: 32
Weather: 89 degrees Fahrenheit, clear skies, pitiless sunshine
Fact: Lake Eyre is the largest lake in Australia, covering 3668 square miles.

It had been six days since they'd arrived at Tirari Station and Daisie was beyond bored. The isolation and dust were taking their toll; she'd swallowed four blowflies since arriving and she'd had enough. She was a city girl, not a country bumpkin.

Violet had taken to Harry and was quite fond of walking at dusk. It seemed like the serenity of the isolation had started to settle into her.

Hazel's outbursts had become less abrasive, usually driven by a fit of paranoia or red wine. At worst they were mildly insulting, and at best amusing. She'd apologise after for any offence, but by day five even that started to feel unnecessary. Often she was simply stating the blunt truth.

'*She* knows,' Hazel had ranted, pointing her fork at Daisie. 'No joy being the chosen one, no joy at all,' she lectured over a meal of barbecued kangaroo meat and vinegared tomatoes that Frank had cooked on the second evening. 'Ted had it coming. He's the one at peace, so don't feel nothin' for him. Put your energy into each other. Even the maggots would've finished with him.'

Daisie smarted at the callous remarks but there was a catharsis in them, and she started to enjoy Hazel's eccentric company.

The clouds had gathered but still hadn't yielded rain, despite the tease of thunder and the odd crack of lightning in the distance. The bull ants had slowed and even Frank, in a rare moment of speech, started to doubt whether the rain would bless them at all.

'Girls!' Hazel yelled from the closed verandah late in the morning on the seventh day. 'Queen's farewell broadcast.' Daisie, Frank and Violet crowded around the radio as Hazel tweaked the tuning dial. The noise of cheering crowds was reduced to a thin hiss on the tinny short-wave speaker as Harry roamed the closed-in space. Grace appeared at the door to see what the fuss was, then returned to her cool spot under the dining table.

The speaker crackled with interference and then the announcer's voice tuned into focus, the strange radio whirs and whines weaving throughout his breathless narration. 'For two months our royal visitors have moved among us and met us in our millions.'

Hazel held her hand up for silence as Daisie pulled up a chair and sat beside her, close to the speaker.

'And now the time for leave-taking has come,' the commentator continued. 'And then, we can hardly believe it, but the *Gothic* is in Fremantle waiting to bear the Queen away.'

'I want to express my gratitude to all those who have been concerned with this tour,' the Queen's voice announced. 'Our thanks go to you all for your welcome, your hospitality and your loyalty.'

The master's whistle sounded, then they heard the *Gothic*'s horn over rabid cheers as a surge of static washed the signal.

'Feels like months ago,' Violet said as Daisie shushed her.

'The Queen, elegant and proud, is waving from the deck,' the announcer continued. 'The Duke, charming as ever, delighting every woman he meets—'

The signal dropped in a crackling array of interference.

'Not *every* woman he meets,' Daisie commented sarcastically as Hazel tuned the dial.

'Signal's dropped,' Hazel said as she flicked the volume down. 'Clouds down south probably.'

'Good riddance, I say,' Daisie remarked, before she headed outside to walk to the lake bed. The dull routine had forced her to reflect on all that had passed. In her isolation she saw things with greater clarity. And despite what Hazel had told them on the first night, she questioned whether being with her sister was the best thing for both of them.

'You shouldn't disparage the monarchy in front of her,' Violet whispered as they climbed into bed that evening. Violet groaned slightly as she tried to get comfortable; her back had become increasingly sore with her lopsided weight and she complained frequently.

'Are you serious?' Daisie replied. 'After everything that's happened? After what they did to me? To you? It's all about *keeping up appearances*. Well, I'm sick of bloody appearances.'

Violet didn't reply, pulling the sheet over her ears to ward off the odd mosquito that whined during the night.

'Generator's switchin' off!' yelled Frank as usual, then the room plunged into blackness.

'I want to go home,' said Daisie.

*

Daisie woke, rubbed her eyes and sighed. Another day of dust.

Hazel was nowhere to be seen, so Daisie made some toast, covering the thick bread with a heavy dose of Frank's thick strawberry jam.

Daisie stepped off the front porch. In the time it had taken her to eat breakfast, the sky had gone from overcast to ominous, the clouds a chorus of charcoal grey hanging like malevolent angels amid wispy white curls. An occasional flash of lightning in the distance was followed by the simmering murmur of thunder.

Grace dawdled behind her, belly swinging heavy with each step, until she gave up about thirty feet from the house and turned back, her legs too weary to bother.

A minuscule droplet landed on Daisie's forehead. At her feet another struck the baked salt like a small meteor. Then another. As the rain gathered, she extended her arms as if to catch the drops, letting them cool her skin like a salve. It reminded her of home.

By the time Daisie reached the lake edge, the rain was falling heavily. Her clothes were drenched but she stood with her eyes closed and let the rain take her.

'Daisie?' Violet shouted from the verandah as raindrops pecked the corrugated-iron roof like an army of chickens. Standing at the edge of the bowl, Daisie raised her arms as though she'd summoned the rainfall herself.

The rain was falling harder by the time Violet reached her sister, skidding haphazardly here and there across the dust that had turned slippery in the wet.

'I'm drenched,' Violet shouted over the clatter, holding a newspaper over her head as she came up behind Daisie.

Daisie's eyes were still closed in a meditative joy as the thunder grumbled and the squawk of enlivened parrots filled the damp sky, but she opened them as her sister touched her shoulder. The salt-crusted veneer of Lake Eyre began to turn glassy in the distance as the lake filled. 'I miss this,' she said.

'What?'

'The rain. It reminds me of home.'

Violet's hair was getting wetter as the newspaper became a sagging rag.

'I want to go home,' Daisie persisted.

'Hazel asked us to stay. I think I want to.'

'She's mad, you know,' said Daisie, blinking, the rain stinging her eyes as the wind flung it against them. She watched Violet turn back to look at the house. The water had started to collect in the gutters, cascading at each corner in a small torrent that splashed into the mud. The antenna tip pinged and swung, lashed by the wind.

'You may not believe me, but I never set out to hurt you,' Violet said. 'I guess I just wanted to see what it was like to be you, for once. To live without thought for the consequences.'

'Well, you've seen how well that's been working out for me,' Daisie said with a sly grin.

They were both quiet for a moment as the wind howled around them.

'Why don't things ever work out? Between us?' asked Daisie.

'Because,' Violet replied, 'everybody thinks we're the same. They don't know the half of it. We *aren't*!'

Daisie's lips curled at the edges in recognition of the tiny shared truth.

'Don't even know who *I* am yet.'

'What would she think?'

'Mum?'

Violet nodded.

'She'd think, "It's raining chair legs, stop talking codswallop and get inside, you two."'

Violet smiled and started making her way up the slope, clumsily skidding here and there on the orange clay. Halfway to the house, she heard Daisie's voice still by the lake edge, singing 'Blood Red Roses' over the white noise of the rain.

The rain was still falling as they dressed for bed that evening. The occasional rip of lightning filled the room, the thunder's boom, as always, calling its warning late.

'How will you get home?' asked Violet as she pulled the bedsheet under her chin. 'The money I've saved wouldn't pay for the petrol to Melbourne.'

Daisie didn't reply. She stood and closed the door, then pulled one of the empty suitcases onto the bed and snapped the lid open. She reached under a fold in the lining, easing her fingers deep into the gap.

Violet sat up, watching curiously as Daisie carefully extracted a fabric pouch with the initials 'EP' and the symbol of the Crown.

'Is that . . .?' Violet trailed off breathlessly.

'One of his.' With gentle caution, Daisie flattened the handkerchief onto the bedsheet, opening its folds to reveal the sparkling tiara emerald. It glittered brilliantly on the starched white fabric.

A residue of grey chewing-gum mould was visible on one perfect edge.

'*You* stole it!' Violet hissed under her breath.

'It fell into my possession.' Daisie smirked.

'It *fell* into your hand. You could go to jail.'

Daisie cupped her hand over Violet's mouth. 'Never to be spoken of again.'

Against her better instincts, Violet nodded in complicity.

'Coober Pedy is the place, according to one of the workers,' Daisie whispered. 'Mining town a few hours from here. I'll ask Frank to drive me. Sell it for cash, buy a flight home. First class.'

Violet carefully prodded the emerald with her tip of her little finger, marvelling at the brilliant refractions that it spun on the handkerchief like a kaleidoscope.

'I'm the one who broke it,' Violet blurted. 'On the ship.'

In the same instant they burst out laughing, their eyes wide in hysterical childish rapture. They pressed their faces into the mattress to smother the noise, rolling on the bed giggling until they were exhausted.

Frank loaded Daisie's battered suitcases into the boot of an equally battered lemon Holden. The rains had ceased but the ground was still moist. Here and there, tiny green weed shoots poked hopefully through the clay.

Hazel and Violet stood at the top of the steps. Daisie lingered on the bottom step swatting a fly from her lips. None of them quite knew how to say goodbye, so they quietly stood and watched Frank pack the luggage, as Grace's hind leg obsessively scratched her right ear.

'Well,' surrendered Daisie. 'This is it, I suppose.'

'Come here, girl,' Hazel pleaded. Her eyes bulged as she pulled Daisie in towards her, hugging her tightly with both arms. Daisie's cheek mushed into Hazel's generous left breast, an affectionate embrace that smelled of sweat and talcum powder. For a moment Daisie closed her eyes and pretended it was her mother, and she was back home before everything had broken.

Hazel released her grip on Daisie to wipe her watery eyes. She took a step back so the twins could have their emotional farewell.

Daisie glanced uncertainly at Hazel. The expectation of an intimate exchange weighed heavily in Hazel's bloodshot eyes. Grace looked up in anticipation, her rear leg poised in the air.

Daisie could read Violet's awkwardness, so she pulled Violet towards her for a stiff hug. They held each other, both with their eyes wide open. Daisie could feel Violet's heart gently tapping away under her thin cotton dress. As they moved apart she realised it was her own.

'Last chance to run for it,' Daisie whispered into Violet's ear.

Daisie felt Violet squeeze more tightly. Daisie surrendered to it as the immensity of their separation dawned on her.

Hazel blew her nose into a ratty handkerchief she'd clawed from her apron pocket.

Daisie climbed into the passenger seat and slammed the door. Frank turned the ignition and the engine roared to life with a thick burst of exhaust.

'Wait!' Hazel called. As she bounded down the hallway into the house, Daisie wound down her window.

Hazel returned holding two dolls and the photo on which her mother had scrawled *Rosie & Poppy* on the back. She walked to the window of the car and handed one of the dolls to Daisie.

The knitted dolls were handmade of wool and about seven inches tall. Each had a mass of black wiry hair, square stitched eyes, a slim single stitch for a nose and a red dress with a black collar and two buttons. In a strange way they looked a little like Hazel. They were worn and aged, with some wild broken threads and faded patches.

'Mum made them. We never went anywhere without them. Rosie was Edith's. I stole it when I left. To spite her.'

Daisie turned it over in her hands. Stitched on the doll's foot was the word *Rosie*.

Hazel gave her the photo, then, clutching Poppy tightly like a small child might hold a beloved teddy bear, she stepped back from the car to allow them to leave.

Daisie gave a small wave, and glanced at her sister one last time.

Violet nodded at her. Daisie blinked her eyes slowly back at her in acknowledgement, then looked away, tapping Frank on the shoulder to signal she was ready to go. The car pulled away.

Violet watched the Holden gently pitch and yaw as it negotiated the uneven road around the verge. And then they were gone.

Hazel shuffled back inside to tend to Harry, who'd woken and was crying for attention. Violet turned towards Lake Eyre, its mirror surface gleaming with renewal, the basin full of the promise of life. A flock of pelicans with black-tipped wings and heavy beaks glided overhead like a phalanx of B-17 bombers, their formation reflected in the glassy surface below.

A slight breeze touched Violet's skin like a whisper. She filled her lungs with warm air. For the first time in years, she felt at ease, with a sense of belonging and assurance that had long eluded her. It was the last place she'd imagined could feel like a home.

But it did.

58

Pathé Newsreel
May 15, 1954

THE QUEEN COMES HOME

The Royal Yacht Britannia *escorts Her Royal Majesty the Queen and the Duke of Edinburgh back into home waters following visits to thirteen countries or territories including Australia, the Cocos Islands and Ceylon.*

London – the day of the royal homecoming. A chill dawn, but from first light, the city has made ready to greet Her Majesty. Crowds line the royal route as the Gothic – a brave and sterling sight – moves up the Thames. The massive bascules of Tower Bridge are swung upwards as the ship comes near. Standing with the royal family is Sir Winston Churchill, who boarded the ship yesterday. Now Londoners will see again, for the first time in nearly six months, the Queen who has charmed and captivated all who saw her in the most distant lands of her Commonwealth.

The Gothic passes through Tower Bridge, gateway to the capital, and this moment above all means that the Queen has

come home. Now follows the climax of Her Majesty's
return. The royal journey that took her and Prince Philip
fifty thousand miles around the world ends under the shadow
of Big Ben as Her Majesty sets foot on English soil again.

It had taken four weeks for Daisie's complexion to revert to an 'anaemic glow', as Sally Potts had coined it. She'd befriended Miss Potts at her new job as a legal clerk at Sacker & Partners. Daisie had landed the first job she'd applied for. It was a perk of her association with Buckingham Palace.

Daisie thought Sally was a hoot and a lark. On Daisie's first day, Sally took her for an after-work drink at the Viaduct Tavern near St Paul's station to extract gossip about the royal family. They'd returned every day since, ostensibly to flirt with lawyers but usually ending up flirting with each other, laughing between themselves so loudly that the game, drunk ones would be scared off.

The mild spring sunlight felt toothless after what Daisie had experienced in Australia. On the last day before summer the temperature in Kingston barely reached seventy degrees, yet men were stripping down to their undershirts in Bushy Park.

'This heatwave! It'll be the death of us,' Mrs Bulvers complained from her first-floor window as Daisie stumbled in from after-work drinks.

'Heatwave! Nothing but a light sweat Down Under,' Daisie retorted. Mrs Bulvers didn't know the colloquialism and mistook Daisie's meaning. 'Imagine the flies I've had to deal with!' Daisie teased her, revelling in her misplaced outrage.

*

By the fourth month since she'd returned from Lake Eyre, Daisie found herself checking for mail more often than usual. Violet hadn't written once and the baby was due.

In Violet's absence the house had descended into a permanent mess. Not only had the buckthorn weeds overtaken the courtyard but their leafy tentacles had started creeping through the gap under the kitchen door.

Daisie prodded a lifeless wither of celery with her fork. She'd forgotten to do the shopping again. Violet's bland Lancashire hotpot, with its limpid potatoes and raw onion chunks, had never seemed more appetising.

One Saturday afternoon in the summer, Daisie waited in line at the Odeon cinema to purchase a ticket to *Hobson's Choice* starring Charles Laughton. 'A widower with a weakness for the pub opposite tries forcefully to run the lives of his unruly daughters,' read the lobby card. Daisie was sold.

As she paid for her single ticket, a familiar male voice pontificated condescendingly in the line behind her. She turned to lock eyes with Bill Dunclark. The ear he was chewing was that of a woman, barely more than a girl, decorated with generous rouge and a tight-knit sweater styled for entrapment.

Bill's eyes skated wildly as Daisie stared with a threatening intent. He urgently whispered into the woman's ear and steered her by the elbow across the foyer towards the exit.

'But I want to see *Hudson's Voice*,' his date complained with a cockney twang.

'Just go, go,' he urged as he tried to drag his date to safety.

Daisie strode over and blocked their retreat.

'Why hello, Violet, fancy seeing you here,' Bill said, resorting to charm.

'Who's this then, William?' the girl asked suspiciously.

Daisie briskly smacked his face with her open palm, striking with the ferocity of a death adder. 'That's for Violet,' she hissed before she clenched her right hand into a ball.

'And this is for me.' Daisie thrust her fist into his stomach, mimicking the handsome 'One Punch' Billy Ellaway from the newsreel she'd seen the Saturday before.

Bill wheezed as he doubled over, his nostrils flaring like the bell of a trumpet. Heaving, he clutched his stomach in agony. The surrounding patrons retreated to a safe perimeter.

'Enjoy the main feature,' Daisie uttered to the dumbfounded lass as Bill choked for air. She shook her fist open and strolled out onto Claremont Road.

Daisie's lips parted as her smile grew until she grinned from ear to ear. Passers-by glanced back at her as though she might be insane. She slowed at the pedestrian crossing on Wood Street. Her fist stung, but something new itched her. Her smile relaxed into a frown and she stared into space as a thought fomented in her mind, her satisfaction displaced by a solemn determination.

Daisie powered along the long gravel driveway to Elmbridge End. She'd walked this stretch of road many times, but this was the first time she'd done it with purpose. The Daimler was parked in its usual place on the round, its chrome gleaming in the sun. Nothing else had changed except the purple flowers that bloomed along the boulevards of elms.

Daisie paused at the stone steps that graduated to the wide porch like an altar. She took a deep breath and pressed the doorbell button.

The double doors parted to reveal Mrs Turner. 'Oh. It's you,' she said, radiating disdain.

'Is Caroline in?' Daisie feigned assurance, arching her back to match Mrs Turner's imposing height. Only the subtle quiver of her lower lip betrayed her.

'Wait here,' Mrs Turner said gruffly before slamming the doors shut.

Daisie crossed her arms and anxiously paced.

Minutes later Mrs Turner opened the door with a smug arrogance. 'Lady Althorp does not wish to see you.'

'Just two minutes, Mrs Turner.'

'Lady Althorp's mind is made up. Leave.'

'If I can just speak with her—'

'Listen, missy,' she interrupted, poking her chubby finger into Daisie's face. 'Go! We've suffered the Chettles enough.'

'Please,' Daisie pleaded. 'I'm not a bad person.'

'You are, Miss Chettle. You're bad. Born or raised, I don't know. I don't care. Leave or I'll call Surrey police.' Mrs Turner slammed the doors in Daisie's face.

Daisie stepped off the porch onto the lawn, then turned and looked back towards the upper west-corner window of the second storey. Caroline's corner salon.

There Caroline stood, framed by the arch, passively watching her.

For the longest moment they stared at each other. There was no longing or forgiveness in Caroline's eyes, only sadness. They bore a dark puffiness, her skin a dull pallor. Caroline turned away from the window and retreated out of view into the salon.

Daisie kept staring up at the arch. She imagined the clock by the unlit fireplace *tock-tock*ing as though no time had passed since she'd first met Caroline, even though everything had changed.

*

Daisie slumped onto the kitchen chair, twisting her cup of tea in its saucer. In the quiet of the house the squeak of the ceramic sounded like a suffocated cry. The silence was welcome, uninhabited by the horrible sound of her mother's demise that had plagued her.

The stillness was broken by the clack of the letter slot. Daisie padded to the hallway. Five or six letters were scattered on the floor beside the front door. The envelopes all bore the familiar markings of creditors, except one. It was large, as big as a magazine, and had a blue and red Par Avion airmail stamp and a circular postmark that read 'Adelaide, South Australia'. The postage stamp featured an image of the Queen and Philip commemorating their Australian visit. The couple stared out of the little perforated square. Their smiles held a certain ambivalence, the meaning of which would be lost on anybody who hadn't been on the tour.

Daisie turned the envelope over. In Violet's handwriting were the words *Sender: Violet Chettle, Tirari Station.* Daisie smiled as her breath quickened, tearing at the edge of the envelope then cautiously sliding her finger across the flap.

Two photographs and a *Women's Weekly* slid into her palm.

The first was of Violet and Jack perched on a horse by the edge of the lake pan. Both were smiling as though it were a fairground ride, with Jack gripping the reins and Violet gripping Jack around his waist.

Daisie gasped at the second photo. It was an image of two tiny newborn twins. Each face was creased in a confounded grimace, their miniature bodies dressed in matching white smocks, propped up on a white knit blanket. Their fingers, thin as matchsticks, clutched at the air. But their pinched noses were unmistakably of Chettle blood.

Daisie laughed out loud, unable to take her eyes off them. On the back, in Violet's handwriting, was written, 'Lily and Flora, Tirari Station – August 1954.'

Daisie looked inside the envelope. There was a letter, folded in half and dense with handwriting. She set herself on the couch and read.

My dear sister,

It has been many months since you left, and by the time you get this it will have been a couple more. There is too much to tell you, and so much to say, but this letter will be short as Frank is waiting to leave for Leigh Creek with it.

Meet Lily and Flora.

Frankly, the specifics of the birth are distasteful and best forgotten. A medieval ordeal. The nurse visits the station once a week and assists with feeding. Lily hasn't been taking enough in and is reliant on powdered milk – but she will be fine. For its apparent simplicity, breastfeeding is nothing but frustration. By the time I've mastered it, men will have landed on the moon.

Jack and I are in love. He thinks of the girls as his own. He hitchhiked all the way from Melbourne, and while Hazel doesn't pay much, there's nowhere to spend it so we're saving money for our own house. With the money you left us we should ensure we have our own home by Christmas. When Frank gave me the parcel I assumed it would be a forgotten cardigan, or a souvenir of Coober Pedy. Your generosity near brought me to tears, damn you. I told Jack it was an inheritance. He sends his kind regards.

Hazel has improved from when you were here. Occasionally her temper flares for no apparent reason, but with less frequency since the girls arrived. She loves them as much as her own and the support has been a blessing.

This land has grown on me too, despite curious snakes, dust storms, flies and bone-melting heat. I even have gossip. Frank prefers the same sex. He confirmed it to me himself, albeit in somewhat coded language. I had my suspicions given he never shared a room with Hazel. She assumed I knew all along, and laughed herself proper when I queried why he spent so much time with Bag Paddock Bob, the Aboriginal post digger.

I've had a lot of time to think about why we hurt each other so much. Why did I betray you? Is it because no matter how badly we treat each other, we know we're stuck with each other?

It's strange how the ravelling of things goes. What a student psychiatrist would make of us I'd prefer not to know. I still seek your approval, I don't know why. I always have.

Please write to me with all the gossip, no matter how insignificant, and send a Times.

Always alongside you.

Violet

P.S. They're still fawning over the royal visit. I don't know how this country will ever live up to it.

It was unlike Daisie to cry but a tear puddled in her eye. She felt surprisingly better for it. Daisie positioned the photos proudly on the mantelpiece beside the image of Edith and Hazel. The doll, Rosie, rested in between them with legs splayed and knitted dot eyes staring out blankly.

She took a step back and admired the tableau. Somehow the symmetry of the three objects made the room not quite so empty any more.

Author's Note

In the year following her succession to the throne, Queen Elizabeth II and her husband, Prince Philip, embarked on a six-month grand tour of the Commonwealth. It was the first time a reigning British monarch had visited Australia. During their fifty-eight days Down Under, the Queen and the Duke of Edinburgh visited fifty-seven cities and towns across most states and territories. An estimated seventy-five per cent of the population turned out to catch a glimpse of their beloved monarch. In Sydney, more than half of the city's population of 1,863,161 lined the streets and the harbour to welcome Her Majesty. In all, the Queen and the Duke travelled 50,000 miles by air, road and train. It remains the biggest single event ever planned in Australia. The Queen returned in 1963, 1970, 1973, 1974, 1977, 1980, 1981, 1982, 1986, 1988, 1992, 2000, 2002, 2006 and 2011.

On 6 March 1954 a camera crew captured the Queen and Duke having an altercation at the O'Shannassy Chalet in the Yarra Ranges. The footage depicted the front door flying open and Prince Philip charging out, followed by a pair of tennis shoes and a racquet. The Queen then appeared, screaming at him to return. After she dragged him back inside, Commander Sir Richard Colville approached the crew. They volunteered the footage, exposing it to the daylight to ruin the film stock. The Queen later apologised to the crew and allowed them to film her candidly in the grounds.

It was this short reel of exposed film that sparked the idea for *The Tour*. I was inspired by the fun that could be had by dropping feuding twin sisters into this delicious incident. Gradually a new story extrapolated itself from this glorious scenario and into every untrue word of the book you're holding.

Needless to say, creative licence reigned. Certain historical facts have been tweaked here and there, and the timeline and itinerary of the Queen's actual tour has been varied to suit the trajectory of the invented Chettle drama. Dates, places, events and almost everything have been changed to serve the higher purpose of telling Daisie and Violet's story. It's worth noting that there are so few accounts of life 'on tour' that comic inspiration became not only far more interesting, but necessary. However, I've no doubt that the royal family's lowliest staff would never be made to reside in an airless bunker deep in the hull of the *Gothic*. But from a storytelling perspective, the temptation to make it so was too great.

While Hazel Lawson is a fictitious character, Hazel Mitchell, the wife of a cattle station owner living in remote Australia, was specially chosen to speak to the Queen via radio on behalf of thousands of outback Australians. The descendants of Hazel Mitchell still operate their family cattle station to this day.

The Queen's main staff as depicted in *The Tour* are an invention, a composite based on archetypes from film and television depictions of the royal household. In actuality, Edward John 'Johnnie' Spencer, Eighth Earl Spencer, or Viscount Althorp until June 1975, was the Queen's equerry on the 1954 tour of the Commonwealth. He was also the father of Diana, Princess of Wales, who was born seven years after the tour.

There is one exception. Margaret 'Bobo' MacDonald was a nanny, dresser and confidante of the Queen for sixty-seven years. She passed away at age eighty-nine at her home in Buckingham Palace in 1993. Her nickname, Bobo, is thought to have been the first word the Queen uttered.

Between 1938 and 1961, Doug Waterhouse carried out pioneering studies on the blowfly, developing a personal insecticide on behalf of the Commonwealth Scientific and Industrial Research Organisation (CSIRO). Although the Queen was meant to be sprayed with the repellent at a garden party at Government House in Canberra during the 1963 tour, the aide responsible lost his nerve at the last minute. The next day the staff made sure the Queen was liberally sprayed before heading off for a game of golf. Journalists following the Queen noted the absence of flies around the official party, and word about CSIRO's new fly-repellent spread. (To be clear, no harm resulted from this formula.) A few days later Mortein called Doug Waterhouse for his formula, which he passed on freely, as was CSIRO's policy at the time. Aerogard went on to become an iconic Australian consumer product. The temptation to bring this wonderful detail into the 1954 tour was irresistible. Daisie was the perfect guinea pig for a chemical formula that was perhaps a few too many years away from being perfected.

Lady Caroline was inspired in part by Pamela Mountbatten but mostly by Lady Alice Egerton, the youngest child of the fourth Earl of Ellesmere and his wife, Violet. In 1949, Lady Egerton replaced her sister, Lady Margaret Colville, as a lady-in-waiting to the then Princess Elizabeth. Lady Egerton never married and held a continuous time of service with the Palace for twenty-four years. In 1977, aged fifty-two, she was found dead in her home near Flodden Field in Northumberland. The suicide was claimed by some to have resulted from being dismissed from the royal household, allegedly for warning the Queen about Prince Philip's infidelity, although Lady Alice's family firmly attributed her death to a history of depression.

Acknowledgements

Amy, Ted and Grace Mackie, Ali Watts, Catherine Drayton, Amanda Martin, Kathryn Heyman, Nikki Lusk, Penelope Goodes, Jane Connors for her book *Royal Visits to Australia*, Richard Payten, George and Patricia Mackie, the Hewitts, Alexandra Mills for the early encouragement and Jillian Heggie, Joyce Heggie and Rosemary MacLean for yer invaluable Scottish influence.

Discover a
new favourite

Visit **penguin.com.au/readmore**